HAVOC KILLED HER ALPHA

THE POISONVERSE

MARIE MACKAY

ISBN: 978-1-998801-06-0

Copyright © 2023 by Marie Mackay

Edition 5.0

All rights reserved.

Edited by Caity Hides

Cover design by Marie Mackay

To Renée and Amy, who devoured this by the chapter as I wrote it and gave me the fuel to get it out and into the world

CONTENT

HOLD UP! Is there anything I should be aware of as a reader?

Yes! Actually, let me get you a list so you know what you're getting into!

There's cursing, violence + spice

Got it, for adult readers only, right?

Yes! And our FMC, Havoc has a history of sexual + physical abuse, explored in 1st POV flashbacks with non-explicit detail.

So like mentioned, but not lingered on?

Yes. The emotional journey is the focus + history explored, (Please note that!) but there is also no detailed accounts of the active experience of SA.

And lastly, this is enemies to lovers romance. There is discourse between FMC and her (psycho) love interests for portions of the novel via intimidation + threat (But they never threaten sexual violence) It's also has sweet sweet group scenes and mild MM!

Oh, also! I write in British English (Realize/realise) I was born in England and now live in Canada. Sometimes my language and dialogue has some funky flavour (I've given up fighting it)

Cheerio, let's have a cuppa, eh bud?

...

Thanks for giving this book a shot, and enjoy the ride!

PROLOGUE

Angel

She was found beside his body, gun in hand.

The establishment was high end, the room furnished with couches, a bar table and a large bed. Right now, it was swarming with cops.

I'd known the moment Logan died. We all had. The severed bond still crackled in my chest; a frayed live wire, making it impossible to focus.

My phone was blowing up—my pack brothers texting. I'd come alone. Half because I was nearest, half because the others didn't need to see this.

When I entered, three scents slammed into me.

Blood hit first, then the twisting, fading scent of Logan in death—marred whisky and bitter chocolate.

Then her. Unmistakably, incongruously irresistible. And I knew, in a moment of horror, that she was ours.

Our omega.

The mate we'd been waiting for.

Her scent was calming; rainfall and firewood, though right now it had an edge of terror.

"...If we try to take her from the body, she starts screaming..." A cop was speaking to me. Even he seemed off-balanced by the whole situation.

Logan lay upon the bed, but all I could stand to look at was the blood soaking into the sheets. She was kneeling on the floor at the bedside, hugging herself. Staring at him. Blood smeared her olive skin and matted brown waves.

"...*Sir!*"

I looked back to the cop, trying to focus.

"She's an omega—under jurisdiction of the Alpha-Omega Institute. We're waiting on your decision."

"Now?" I tried to shake the fog from my brain.

"She killed your pack lead; you get first priority. You take her or we do."

...*She killed your pack lead...* The words choked up every thought.

"...Once in police custody, you lose rights..."

I stared at the trembling omega and hatred warred with hopelessness. I couldn't be the one to make this decision.

"We... We'll take her."

We could go back on it later—return her to the cops, but my brothers had to be the ones to choose. I was the one who needed her most.

What was broken in me, only a scent matched omega could heal.

ONE

Havoc

They came for me in the end.

I heard the knock on the door first, which was a little insane, but it gave me time to get to the bathroom and lock myself in. I heard voices outside. Was the whole pack out there?

My mates...

I had to stifle an incongruous thrill, as if I could return to being the innocent little girl who romanticised a pack who would sweep her off her feet.

A loud bang on the door made me jump and a low voice sounded. "We need to talk."

Talk?

I wrung my fingers. Things were a bit beyond talking. It wasn't inconceivable that if I opened that door right now, they might not just kill me. After what I'd done, they wouldn't even get into trouble for it.

"You're gold pack, Havoc. The laws don't protect you like they do everyone else..."

I was the omega who'd killed their pack brother.

I was the omega who killed her own alpha.

That thought made me quake, but there was a bang on the door again. "Open it, or I'll break it down." That was Angel's voice.

I wrapped my arms around my stomach, steeling myself and staring at the broad white door for a long time before edging over to it and undoing the lock with a click. I backed up, hugging myself at the same time as I tried to keep my head high. No matter what I thought of them, I couldn't afford to let them see my fear.

The door creaked open. Angel looked over at me. He was the one who'd been there at the club. The one who'd found me next to Logan's body. His eyes were dark as they held mine, then he waved me over.

"Come." He was just as beautiful as the picture I owned. Before, when he'd been there, I had been too far in the throes of shock to notice. His skin was a rich mid-brown, his dark hair was buzzed short, and there were heavy bags under his dark green eyes. I took a breath, relieved at least that he didn't have a weapon, which I was half expecting at this point.

Before, he'd been in shock, but now he'd had time to process everything. That the mate he had never known was trapped in his own house, and that I'd killed his pack brother.

Slowly I stepped up to the door, trying to clear my expression of all terror. I wasn't just afraid of meeting them because of what I'd done; I was afraid of meeting them because of the possibility that they were everything I'd ever dreamed of. Because now, I was too late.

Now they hated me.

Angel took me by the arm and tugged me across the room as if expecting I'd make a break for it. The others in the pack were there. Two were on the cove of couches; I noticed Kai first by his white hair and mismatched eyes—one white and one crimson.

My gaze slid to the one I recognised as Caspian. He leaned

6

against the wall beside the door, pale jaw set, looking as though he wished to be anywhere but here. He was tall, with long dark hair that was tied back, and tattoos that tangled up his neck to his jaw. I shoved down the flutter in my chest at seeing him for the first time.

I was met with cold eyes and hatred from them all, aside from Bane. He was the largest of them, with dark hair that was neatly buzzed at the sides and pale skin. He watched me from his seat on the couch with an expression I couldn't read.

Angel tugged me to the sofa and then waited for me to sit down. He took a seat much further away. I didn't know if he was trying to give me space for my sake, or if he just didn't want to be anywhere near me.

"You're Havoc?" he asked.

I blinked at my name on his tongue. *Angel knew my name?*

I felt an ache in my chest. Something to remind me I was in a room with four men I'd dreamed of every night for months. My mates. My white knights. The ones who had never come.

I didn't reply, glancing between them, trying to gauge the situation.

Were they going to kill me...? That thought made me much too numb.

"Right now, we just want answers." Angel seemed to be reading my mind. An impossible ask. One truth from my tongue might damn me. They were alphas, just like Logan.

"The little omega who needs her mates to save her. Get on your knees and beg one more time and you never know... I just might."

"We want the truth." Angel's voice obliterated the taunt in my head. "You owe us that."

"Owe you?" My sanity cracked around that whisper as it slipped from my mouth. My eyes darted between them as mania, choked down by hours of shock, finally clawed its way out of my soul.

7

"Did you mean to kill him?" Angel pushed.

What a question.

Did their omega mean to kill their alpha?

Logan had been the pack brother of everyone in this room. A thick laugh came from my throat.

I wanted them to hurt, *needed* to witness their pain, because they'd never come, even when I'd pleaded with the universe every night.

"I put a gun to his head and pulled the trigger." My voice was a rasp as I glanced around. Caspian, the one at the door, tensed, dark eyes glacial. "I meant it with every ounce of my blackened soul."

"Why?" Angel was still the only one who had spoken. The rich brown of his skin had turned ashen. But the answer to that was one they couldn't have. Not because I didn't want to scream it at them, but because I could never be so vulnerable again.

Looking around at their dumbstruck faces, my mania slipped into rage. Rage at them, for never saving me. At Logan, who still had his grip on me from the grave I'd just sent him to. At myself, more than anything, because all of this was my fault.

Angel stood before me with such a perfect look of concern, so gentle even confronted by the woman who'd killed his pack brother. As if he believed there might be hope for me. He was dangerously close to being everything I imagined. So, I had to see him break—had to see him become worse than every picture I'd spun of him.

"Did you see the body?" I asked. "There was so much blood, I didn't think..." I shook my head, another smile twisting my lips. That part—the vindication I felt every time Logan's pale, bloodied face crept into my mind—was real. "I was dreaming small," I whispered. "Now I've met you..." I glanced between them, lifting my hand in a fake gun to point at Angel. There was a sneer on my expression as I levelled it at his head.

And there it was: the thing I needed to see. He was warring with himself, completely still, his eyes burning. The power of his aura tried to pin me in place. As an omega—as his omega—it was almost impossible to fight. I should be unable to move, but I was broken, so that power slipped through all the cracks and fractures of my soul as if I were a brittle, hollow tree.

Instead, I bit the tip of my tongue through my smile, cocked my head, shut one eye and shot a fake bullet from my fake gun right into the centre of his face.

What I wasn't expecting was the way that motion split my ears again, and for a flash, I was back in that room. My prison. My nightmare. The metal was real. The bullet was real. The crack of gunfire shattered the last of what made me an omega. A defiance of nature itself, for it should have been impossible. But he broke me, and then he found out what that meant.

When I blinked, I was in this lush penthouse room. Before me, I watched that promised golden heart of Angel fracture. His pupils blew, the last of his humanity draining away for the alpha beneath. He stepped forward, a low growl rumbling in his chest.

I staggered away, clumsily darting around the couch, not taking my eyes from him. I backed up one more step but hit a solid wall of muscle behind me. A hand clamped over my mouth, dragging me against a broad chest.

Pain erupted from where his skin pressed against mine, and the shock of it got a whimper from me.

No.

No.

Tears burned my eyes. This couldn't be happening. I'd killed for freedom, but it hadn't broken my curse. The pain was still here.

My breathing was ragged as I realised the truth.

I wasn't free at all.

"Can we kill her now?" Caspian asked from behind me. Angel

had drawn himself up, a war in his expression as his fists clenched and unclenched.

"It's... wrong," Angel said.

"She killed him," Caspian snarled. "How long have we been searching for our omega?"

Kai, the one with the mismatched eyes, placed a hand on Angel's shoulder. "We *need* her if we want to fix Angel."

"We wanted her so we could be whole!" Caspian—the one behind me, spat. "And she made absolutely fucking sure that was impossible."

I struggled against his grip. The pain elevated, but that wasn't the worst that would happen if he continued holding me... My pain peaked and I shut my eyes tight, desperate for him not to notice.

Next thing, he let go of me like he was burned, shoving me away. I sagged to my knees, blinked tears away and got my bearings. I spun, hands coming out in case—but he was staring at me with shock and... something else.

"Fuck." His growl was strained. He took a step closer to me and then forced himself to stop.

I scrambled away, all my instincts lighting in terror as my stomach twisted in discomfort. The pain was fading now that he was no longer touching me. I never took my eyes from him, ready to fight to the death if that was what it took.

I was broken. I thought if I killed Logan, I'd be free of that curse. Instead, it had been handed over to them... I shut my eyes. My nightmare wasn't over.

Any touch from my mates was torture for me, but for them, it was ecstasy.

TWO

Caspian

One touch and she was scarred into my mind. I'd held her against me, the world red, fury tinging my vision at what she'd said. She'd threatened to kill Angel. Kai. Bane.

But then something changed. Heat flooded my body from where my skin met hers. It was like a drug hit my system. Every movement she'd made was torture. She fought against me, her body pressed against mine, a whine escaping her chest.

Fuck...

I was heady with desire, drowning in a new reality. My rage collided with need, leaving behind chaos. I had just enough control to shove her away—and had I waited another few seconds, I knew I wouldn't have been able to.

She stumbled, crashing to the floor and spinning, her hands coming out. Her scent rose in the room like the first birdsong at dawn. Rainfall and firewood.

The world shifted.

Her golden eyes held mine, the slight part to her plush red lips as she panted, her chest rising and falling rapidly. It wasn't just fear, though, her own desire flooded the bond like a drug. The bond was too faint, just the slightest connection between mates. I could fix that. I could bite her.

My eyes traced her neck, but she was wearing a black hoodie that obscured my vision of it. A growl rose in my chest. *Why would she want to hide that from me?*

She scrambled away at the sound, eyes wide. She had a slight form with an eye-catching curve to her thighs and hips. She'd fit against me perfectly, even if she only reached my shoulders.

But... No. That was fear on her face. Definitely fear. Lust lost to something much stronger. She was mine. I was an alpha; protecting her—that was in my blood, and right now she was afraid of something—afraid of... of me?

How?

When she'd just been so much larger than life, challenging Angel as if she hadn't a fear in the world. That memory almost dragged me back, but I focused again. Her eyes were still wide with terror.

I took a step away, despite every desire to reach out, to draw her into my arms and offer her anything in the world—anything to make her feel safe. I took another step, the faintest bell in my head sounding its warning. Another, and I reached the door and then staggered into the hallway and slammed the door.

Cut off from the blanket of her scent, my thoughts steadied, flooding back to me. Disgust ripped through my veins. I had almost lost myself completely.

To the woman who'd killed my pack brother.

Havoc

There was a scar burned into my mind.

I clutched the bathroom counter, trying to break the memories that wouldn't leave me in peace.

After Caspian shoved me away and left, the others had followed. Angel had been last, giving me a dark look. But it was the disgust in Caspian's eyes I couldn't rid myself of. The disgust he'd had after he touched me.

The worn piece of paper lay on the countertop beside me, and I was trying and failing not to look at it.

In the photo, Caspian had a sullen look and was shooting the camera a middle finger. Bane had a half smile on his face, a drink part way to his lips. Kai was closest to the camera, his mismatched eyes bright with joy as he snapped the shot. Angel was nearest to him, his hand clutching Kai's. Angel wasn't looking at the camera, instead his eyes were on Kai, and there was a softness in them. It was so different from the hardened look he had for me.

My eyes skipped over the black scribble in the middle of the photo, returning instead to Caspian, lingering on the little heart drawn next to him.

Tears threatened, but I shoved them away. After everything today, I wouldn't cry over something so stupid. I wouldn't weep because Caspian didn't want me.

Why had I brought out the stupid photo? To torture myself?

They were no longer mine to claim. With an ear-splitting bang, my nightmare had shattered along with my dreams.

There had been a moment before Logan collapsed on me, when his face had gone slack, like something out of a horror movie. The split second between when he had been there, body, mind and soul, and then he was gone and there was nothing left but empty flesh and bone and a rush of hot blood soaking me.

But I knew now Logan's death hadn't meant my freedom. I had just passed from one captor to the next.

"What will I do if you leave and never come back?" I'd asked my father once upon a time.

"Havoc. That's never going to happen."

"In the movies, they all have dreams."

"You don't need dreams. The world will never have you. I will always protect you."

It had been a lie.

I clutched the counter, not ready for the wave of panic that overcame me. My father had trained me to accept such simple promises—and then he'd left me to the mercy of wolves.

I spent my life sheltered by him, yet my own father considered me nothing more than property—sheltered for the sake of his pride. He spun me frightening tales to convince me to stay hidden away from the world.

Within a year of perfuming for the first time, omegas were required to register with the Alpha-Omega Institute. If they didn't, then that damning golden ring would appear, and they would be marked for life.

A gold pack omega.

Since my father didn't believe in such systems—a violation of nature, he'd always said—I was never enrolled.

So now, as I stared at my reflection in the mirror, my eyes shone a liquid gold.

The problem, however, was that my father, as dispassionate as he was, had been right. And the protection he offered died the day he had. The day he'd been killed for his hatred of the system.

Three months ago, at the age of twenty-two, I was taken in the wake of his murder. I had been claimed like a trophy. The daughter of the greatest gold pack sympathiser in the city. And as a gold pack omega, I was lower than any beta.

I didn't know the city, or its cruelty, not until I was purchased by Gavin's Treasures. A club for alphas.

I waited tables and told daily to earn my keep. I was told over and over I had to be one of the only untrained omegas in the world. Instead of having taken dance lessons, fashion or cooking to seduce high society, I'd been bundled away in my father's cluttered pad as he tried to keep me hidden.

So that had been my life. Serving alphas in a high-end club, owned by a business, frightened of what might happen when my next heat came. My father wasn't here to medicate me and put me under until it was over. This was my destiny, to exist as a service to alphas, undesirable as a bonded mate.

Everything changed the day I met Logan.

The moment he stepped into the grand hosting room, I remember goosebumps erupted across my entire body. He was as fixated on me as I was on him. He was across the room in an instant, present company forgotten.

"Who are you?" he'd asked. I felt his touch on the small of my back. The scent of whiskey and chocolate rose in the air, so sweet it wiped all rational thought from my mind.

I'd frozen, but he'd nudged my chin up so I was looking right at him. When his rich blue eyes met mine, instead of the resentment I was so used to, he looked... curious.

There was static between us, and my stomach did a flip, heat seeping through my veins at the touch.

"Havoc Saint." I heard the voice of my superior, who was behind the bar. "Not our best sir, I—"

"Saint?" Logan had asked, his eyebrows rising.

I'd gone stiff with fear. My father's name was notorious. I knew that. My superior nodded quickly, shrinking beneath the intensity of this man's aura.

"Get us a room." Logan clicked his fingers. "Make sure we aren't interrupted."

Next thing I knew, I was being led through to one of the private rooms.

"Don't worry, sweet Havoc," he murmured in my ear.

I remembered his touch. I remembered how, in all my life with my own father, I'd never felt safer than I did with his arm around me.

That day had been a dream. Right up until the end.

My knuckles were white as I tried to ground myself. I hadn't known at the time what a fool I was. Even as I dressed this morning, I'd been ignorant. Not just at what the world was capable of doing, but of my own nature.

Something was caught in my throat as I stared at myself. Because even when I'd won, I'd lost.

I was never enough, not for him, and not to escape my own torture.

"I could give you the world, little omega. All you have to do is accept my bite." Logan had been so beautiful, so sweet and loving. With more affection in his arms than my father had ever offered.

Slowly, I stripped myself of my red-crusted top and jeans. I could still smell him on me. My alpha's scent. Whiskey and dark chocolate.

The dark makeup around my eyes was enough to hide how haunted I looked now. Everything on my body was exactly as I'd placed it this morning. The tiny braids of hair still circled my right ear. I wore tight black leggings and black combat boots. My black shirt was low cut.

I peeled it off to reveal what was beneath. Beautiful black lace, ready to tease, to beg for attention. It was everything Logan liked, designed to entice, to be so irresistible that he wouldn't be able to deny me.

"I'll be whatever you need."

I squeezed my eyes shut.

There was a massive tub in the bathroom—more of a hot tub than an actual bath, but I opted for the shower. I ran the water ice cold. As the water scalded goosebumps across my skin, I clung to the discomfort of it, knowing that with every drop I was washing his scent from my skin. I stared at the red that circled the drain, watching the last trace of him seep away.

When I climbed out, I grabbed the large white dressing gown and wrapped it around myself. That was good enough for now because I wouldn't be putting my old clothing back on.

I checked the huge walk-in closet attached to the bathroom. To my surprise, there were clothes in the room. Lots, in fact, in a variety of sizes. I slipped on a pair of leggings and a baggy long-sleeved t-shirt, hugging myself still from the cold shower as I looked around.

It hit me at last.

I was in their house.

The pack's house.

The men I'd dreamed of every night for months, praying that they'd save me. The men that never came. Not until I'd saved myself and given them a reason to hate me.

I had to figure out what I was going to do.

One of them at least wanted me dead, but the others... Well, if the others did, then wouldn't I be dead already?

So why was I still here?

The thought came unbidden, the obvious answer I tried to reject. Could they possibly... still want to bite me in?

I sank down onto the couch cushions, contemplating that. Hating the ever so distant thrill that lit my blood. Denial claimed its moment, wishing me back to a better time...

No.

Of the three kinds of bond an omega could host, there was only one they would want of me. A dark bond. That bond wouldn't be freedom. It would be chains.

I remembered the shock on their faces as I said what I had to Angel, about killing them. That's what I had to do. I had to make it impossible for them to keep me around.

I would take the police over this torture.

But Omegas don't go to prison... A little voice whispered. *Too much of a waste.*

I swallowed. No. Omegas were far too rare not to be put to use. I'd be claimed by the Alpha-Omega Institute. I'd been told that my experience at Gavin's was mild compared to what some gold pack omegas had to do to escape unwanted bonds.

So those were my choices. Try to convince my mates to keep me or live my life as an unbonded gold pack criminal.

I knew what I'd choose. I'd made the choice once already.

I'd take a life of suffering over leaving my fate to them. Better to live a life of pain than ever again risk what had happened to me.

I searched the room until I found a drawer of jewellery. There were some delicate black bracelets that I strung together until I'd fashioned a thick necklace of black cords and jewels and clipped it around my neck to hide what was beneath.

It was evidence of my past, of my own mistake. One I never intended to make again. And no one else in the world deserved to see it. They couldn't learn what had happened, not the truth of it, or I might find myself in the same place I just escaped.

I sat for a long time until I felt the faintest uncomfortable twist in my stomach. I ignored it, looking over at the huge bed in the room. It was so much bigger than the beds at Gavin's. Was this... a nest? A room designed for an omega. Was that where they had put me? I shoved that thought down, not wanting to consider it.

The covers were fresh, the pillows and duvet a cream white. It was empty of scents. Unfamiliar and clinical.

I didn't need anyone but myself.

The only thing I had to my name was a small handbag that had been brought with me. It didn't have much in it at all. In my bedside table, I tucked the picture of the pack—face down—and beside it, I placed my little blue prayer angel.

I didn't need anyone but myself.

I could survive this. I had changed.

Once I'd have given anything to consolidate a bond with this pack of alphas. Now I'd rather suffer my whole life than be trapped with men with the power to hurt me like they could.

The tightening of my chest and another twinge in my stomach warned me that I was running out of time.

I had to get them to send me away soon.

My heat wasn't far off.

THREE

Angel

Havoc was everything we ever dreamed of, and she was pure destruction. Yet, even now, with what she'd done, we needed her. *I* needed her, or I would lose my brothers.

There was one thing I couldn't shake, and that was the fear in her eyes when she'd scrambled away from Caspian. My blood had roared in my ears, drowning everything else out—my hatred, my anger, my shock at what she'd just said to me. Every instinct had screamed at me to go to her, to protect her. She would be my undoing. All of us, if we weren't careful.

I hadn't seen Caspian like this before. We'd all grown alongside one another for years, but right now, in one day without Logan, we were unravelling. We were turning back into the broken men he'd found and dragged together.

Caspian was stock still, hands balled into fists as he stood at the kitchen island. He was usually a closed book, and it was absolutely impossible to tell how he was feeling without the pack bond. But right now, even with the dark tattoos decorating his neck, I could see the strain in his muscles. His dark eyes were fixed down the hall where Havoc was right now.

The main living room was huge, with a tall ceiling that easily accommodated the second-floor balcony that led to mine and Kai's quarters. It was an open concept kitchen with a large island, and the rest of the room was taken up by a huge ebony dining table that seconded as a workstation, and a large crescent moon of couches facing the TV. There was enough space to host the huge parties that Logan had enjoyed.

Bane was silent. Kai was the only one who was behaving normally—though I knew him well enough to know he was off balance. He had plucked a packet of chips from the cupboard and dropped onto the couch, turning on the TV as if it were a regular evening. He rubbed his chin, eyes darting to his own belt. Nervous tick. He needed reassurance, and that came in three forms for Kai: the pack, me, or the knife he carried at his belt. It was a remnant from his youth on the streets, since we didn't allow him to carry in the house.

It was Caspian who spoke first. "She has to die before she ruins us."

"We need her." Kai barely glanced away from the TV, where a true crime documentary was playing.

"We don't need her." Caspian was resolute.

I met Bane's eyes, and he looked as caught off guard by this interaction as I was.

"It's simple," Kai grunted. "We keep her. We keep Angel."

My stomach dropped as he brought me into this.

"It's not worth—" Caspian began, but Kai stood in a flash, the chips forgotten on the couch. His blazing gaze was levelled on Caspian. Kai was a seer, which meant he had one pure white eye and one with a red pupil. Right now, the red of his pupil glowed.

Caspian and Kai never fought. Not ever, unless... I swallowed, staring at the burning fire in Kai's eyes. Not unless I was involved. I hated that I could get between them like this. They had grown up on the streets together, brothers in everything but blood. And then Kai had met me, and it had been love at first sight, but I never wanted to step between the bond he had with Caspian.

"We'll find another way to fix Angel," Caspian snarled. His fists were balled, a muscle ticking in his pale jaw.

I had aura sickness, which meant my alpha aura was fading. It had been for months now. Eventually, it would vanish completely, leaving me bondless.

A scent matched omega—bitten in. It would heal me without a doubt.

Havoc could heal me.

"There is no other way." Kai's voice was low. "She's our mate. She's the answer."

"She... killed Logan." My voice was hoarse.

Yet... without healing, I would slip from the pack and my mind would be alone and silent. "What if...?" I clenched my jaw. "We let my aura die."

I could still be bitten in like a beta. It wouldn't be the same, but... Havoc would break us. I knew it already.

A crash sent my thoughts scattering, but I was numb as I watched Kai throw the remote control at the broad glass window of the deck.

The pieces splintered but hadn't hit the floor before he'd grabbed a glass from the marble coffee table.

I should stop him before he got too wound up, but I couldn't move. Neither, it seemed, could Caspian, who knew the consequences of Kai's meltdowns the same as me.

We both just watched as he picked up the next glass and sent it shattering against the broad deck window.

Kai could never find words to speak about his pain, even when we felt echoes of it through the bond we shared. He was shattered long before I met him, used so much for the powers his eyes offered that every normal response, feeling, and reaction had been scorched away.

Right now, his pain was clear.

Kai didn't love often. He hadn't even loved Logan, not like the rest of us had, but when he did, it was a bonfire on a moonless night.

And Kai loved me. With the open, bleeding wound of Logan's severed bond still so raw, he was afraid. We all were.

So instead, I watched as he picked up object after object and shattered them against the deck wall. It was Bane in the end, who placed a hand on Kai's shoulder to stop him. Bane had said nothing until now, instead running his fingers over and over through his short black hair. His skin was paler than usual, and his piercing grey eyes were as empty as I felt.

"We aren't going to kill her," Bane said quietly.

"Like fuck we aren't," Caspian began, but he cut off as Bane's cold silver eyes snapped to him. The low hum of the obscene aura he could wield when he chose, smothered the bond that tied us together.

"We're going to find out why she did it," Bane said coldly. He dropped the full weight of his alpha aura into his voice, which was enough to get Kai to relax.

"It doesn't make any sense," I said.

Havoc had killed Logan, something we still didn't know the details of. Could it have been an accident even if she wanted to deny it? She clearly didn't want any of us, like our fated omega should.

She wasn't just an omega, or even just our mate. She was a gold pack omega, a cursed omega that was destined for a bondless life being passed from pack to pack. Getting a scent match—finding her mates—as a gold pack omega was the best chance she would ever get for a good life.

It wasn't a matter of pride. The fact was, our pack was desirable. We had some of the most elite alpha blood, and we were considered one of the best in the city.

Yet, she didn't want us.

She killed Logan, which made her insane. She shouldn't have been able to, but gold pack omegas found ways to break the laws that bound most omegas and alphas. It was exactly why they were considered a threat to society—both gold pack omegas and any alpha children they bore could shatter the laws that kept alphas in line. That kept society protected from the feral, wild side that surfaced without those restraints.

Still, something nagged at me. It hadn't just been mania in her eyes when she'd taunted me. There had been something else underneath it all. It was something I'd seen before, when Kai was still prone to his outbursts. It happened when his trauma surfaced, convincing him he wasn't enough, that he had to shove everyone away.

Was she broken, just like Kai had been?

I steeled myself.

It didn't matter.

Kai had never destroyed us, not like she had.

FOUR

Havoc

It was the middle of the night, and I was hungry.

Slowly, I opened my door, checking for creaks. The hallway outside was dark and silent, so I slipped out. I hurried down the hallway toward the low light of the broad room ahead. I was aiming for the kitchen, hoping to find a snack.

When I reached the end of the hallway I paused. The room was huge, with massive ceilings and a staircase spiralling up to a balcony above. Through the railings, there were more rooms.

The couches circling the TV area were curved; a clean grey, given personality by the chaotic array of different cushions and blankets scattered across them. The kitchen was behind a large island, and I made for it, drawing up only as my eyes snagged on the front door.

My heart fluttered in my chest as I stared at it. It had a keypad on it—*on the inside?* Had they got that just for me? I was tempted to reach over and try to open it anyway.

My eyes slid back to the room. Most of the wall on the opposite side was a huge window, and the way the lights shone from beyond the sheer curtains made me wonder how high up this apartment was.

I crossed the room quietly, brushing aside the curtains and peering out. Outside was a balcony, and beyond that—my breath caught.

The city stretched out for miles, far far below, a million golden lights in the dark, bright enough that the clouds above glowed faintly orange.

I'd seen snapshots of cityscapes in the movies I'd watched. I'd been out to the neighbourhood my father lived in, but it hadn't been in the city. Instead, it was far out where buildings sprawled after each other, not on top of one another.

With the wonder came a sense of panic. If I escaped, what would I do? In my head, I'd flee back to the police, to let the system deal with me, but I was realising how foolish that plan was. The city was huge. How could I know where to get to the police station, when it could be anywhere? I was an omega, my scent—as my father always reminded me—marked me even to betas.

What if I was taken by someone else? My father had been distant with me my whole life, constantly keeping me at arm's length and denying me opportunities to get close to him. But his warnings of the world had all been right.

There was a certain safety in the system, as foreboding as my fate might be. Now though, even that fate might be unattainable. I took a step back, my reflection in the glass shifting, the dull golden glow to my eyes visible even here.

I swallowed, turning and making for the kitchen, ignoring the keypad on the door. I scanned the marble countertops and sleek white cabinets. One at the end was half-open, and I saw something colourful beyond. I made for it, but the shelf was too high, so I hauled myself up onto the counter. An unfamiliar smile tugged at my lips as I saw what was within.

A variety pack of chips. A treat my dad only brought home on occasion.

Jackpot.

I dug into the box, pulling out a few bags at a time, trying to find at least one of each of the flavours.

I froze as Angel's voice floated into the kitchen. "Already told Bane you'd gone through all the crackers, getting more next—" He cut off as he caught sight of me, frozen as he rubbed his eye blearily.

His expression contorted with hatred as he took me in. I was balanced precariously on the edge of the counter, bundles of chips clutched in my arms.

I swallowed. I couldn't let that hatred hurt me. He was as beautiful as he was devastating, a temptation from the first time I'd heard of him.

Logan led me into one of the VIP rooms. Inside, it was large, with a bar-height booth lined with velvet and an oval table. A grand bed was hidden from sight behind huge wine-red curtains. There was a set of low couches in a circle, topped with plush pillows and blankets —the visitors' nests, as the others called them.

These rooms were only available for the top guests.

"Havoc?" Logan asked, as if testing my name out.

I nodded, eyes darting between him and the dark-haired alpha who seated himself in the booth. I didn't feel the same pull toward the other alpha.

"Fitting," he breathed. I was captured again by how stunning Logan was. He wasn't holding me anymore, but I didn't want to create any more space between us. Quite the opposite.

He held out his hand as he joined his friend in the booth and swept me into the seat next to him, his attention not leaving me for a second. "My little gold pack mate..." He almost sang the words, as if something about them amused him.

Mate?

The word collided with a wall in my brain. What? But then everything fit into place. The way I'd felt the moment he'd entered, the static between us, the way I was drowned with the desire to never leave his piercing gaze.

His white-blond hair was tied loosely in a bun, strands fluttering around the strong cut of his jaw. He was the most beautiful man I'd ever seen; I was sure of that at that moment. He had bright blue eyes and thick lashes, a heavy brow, and a strong, straight nose.

"You are going to devastate the pack."

Pack?

"There are more of you?" The stupid question fled my lips before I could catch it.

Logan laughed. A hand cupping my cheek, his thumb trailing to my lips where his eyes lingered. The scent of whisky and chocolate was smothering, and with his touch came little jolts of pleasure.

"There are and they will be falling over themselves for your attention."

For a long, long moment, we just looked at one another.

Angel still hadn't moved. His jaw was clenched as he stared at me. He had piercing forest green eyes, rich brown skin, dark eyebrows, two golden stud earrings, and dark hair that was buzzed short. His scent—something cinnamon and something sweet—hit me. My body was having a fit, broken as it was. My stomach was tightening, and blood was getting hotter in my veins the longer I drank him in.

I needed to get out of here. My room was safer. They'd not get any of my scent, and I'd not get any of theirs.

I slipped down slowly from the counter, my heart beating in

my chest. I shoved the chips back down on the counter but paused, my eyes snagging on them longingly. I shoved them further away and then edged toward Angel, who was taking up only half the entrance to the kitchen. His eyes were locked on me as I slipped by him, pressing myself as close to the counter and as far away from him as possible.

I almost fled when I made it to the hallway, but I had enough dignity to stop myself from breaking into a sprint.

It wasn't that I was scared of them—not in the way I should be. If they decided they wanted to kill me for what I'd done, I might just be more heartbroken than afraid. It would make the world make sense in a way I never wanted it to.

"We've all been waiting to find you," Logan told me.

Waiting...? I wondered. "Can I meet them?"

"Yes." His smile was dazzling. "Later. But allow me to be selfish first. I want to get to know you."

There were butterflies in my stomach.

He... wanted to get to know me?

I'd spent so many nights thinking about them in the last few months. My nights had been wracked by pain, leaving me desperate for saviours that would never come.

So, if they killed me? No love lost. They'd just be proving me right.

By the time I got to my room, my throat was tight. I needed to get a grip.

I could give them nothing but coldness. He didn't deserve my love. My saviours were figments of my imagination.

I needed to let them go.

FIVE

Angel

I stared at the discarded packets of chips for much too long, the image of Havoc's startled expression burned into my brain. Since I'd touched her for the first time, it was impossible to look at her and not dream of... I grimaced. No. Mate or not, I'd not fantasise about the woman who killed my brother.

Fuck alpha and omega bonds.

I picked the chips up and tucked them in their cupboard, then pulled down a bag of pasta. I sliced up chicken, as penne and veggies boiled. Logan's face haunted me again with each cut. *There was a hole in his head and a frozen smile on his deathly pale face...*

I didn't know why I was doing this.

Not when I'd been with Logan in this room just this afternoon. *What had we been talking about?*

A little flutter of panic rose in my chest as I scrambled to recall. Something about which restaurant he wanted to visit this weekend...

"Get Kai to change his vote. I can't stand another burger from that damned place."

He'd been more irritable than usual, but I'd blown it off. Told him to suck it up.

Now, he was gone. He wouldn't join us at any restaurant ever again.

It felt as though there was a stone in my chest as I fried up the chicken with some garlic and veggies. I was more empty than ever as I tossed the contents in the pan, my mind wandering back to Havoc.

She was covered in blood, trembling as she hugged herself. They'd told me she'd not left his body. They'd taken the gun from her, and she'd screamed when they'd tried to pull her away. She hadn't taken her eyes from Logan until I arrived.

Why had she killed him? Could it be as simple as it looked? Was she just insane? When she'd seen me, she'd broken down, her eyes manic. For one strange moment she'd reached for me as if she knew me, as if I was a place of comfort. Then she withdrew, her ragged rasps indiscernible from breathless laughter as tears flooded her face.

Only... it didn't look like insanity. It looked like grief.

That was a memory I tried not to return to, but it haunted me.

I added a splash of red wine vinegar as I fried the meal together and then dished out some of the pasta into a bowl. I made my way down the dark hall with the food.

I had the doorknob in my grip before I thought twice.

We were all feeling the effects of Logan's death. It was up to me to step up, now. For a long time, I'd used Logan as a shield to avoid having to take responsibility the way my parents would have wanted.

He was gone, just like they were. It was up to me to protect what I had left.

I knocked gently, then waited. I heard nothing from within, so I tried again. Again, there was no response. Had she not returned to her room?

Slowly, I cracked the door and peered in. Her scent hit me instantly. Rainfall and firewood. It was intoxicating. I needed to give her the food and get the fuck out.

I should just leave it at her door, but a traitorous part of me didn't want to.

My eyes scanned the huge bed and collection of couches. I couldn't see her. Then the door to the bathroom cracked and she was stepping out, twisting wet hair in her fingers, a towel wrapped around her body.

Shit.

I got way too hot at the sight of it. Her gaze found me instantly and her eyes went wide.

I cleared my throat and lifted the bowl awkwardly. She swallowed and even from where I was standing, I could see the movement down her throat. She took a quick step back into the bathroom and I heard her rummaging around in the drawers. When she stepped back out, she was tying a bow on a black silken dressing gown as she peered around the bathroom door. Around her neck, I noticed, she had placed a black choker—just a little added fuck you. Neck coverings between alphas and omegas were statements.

I hadn't moved.

"You're..." I cleared my throat again. "Hungry."

Obviously.

She said nothing.

I could just set the damn food down and leave. But of course, I didn't.

Instead, I stepped in. The room was filling with hot steam, which was lifting her scent into the air, but I *could* control myself.

I crossed the room to the circle of couches and set the bowl down, then took a seat in the farthest chair. She hadn't moved from where she peered around the bathroom door.

"Sit." I almost winced at how weak the command was. My dying alpha aura wasn't what I wanted to think about right now.

She listened though, holding her head high as she grabbed the bowl and sat down. She was a small thing, and her smooth tanned legs that peeked through the silken black dressing gown set my heart pounding. She had large gold eyes and plush lips, and her wet hair stuck in strands to her pink cheeks.

I didn't think I'd ever seen a more beautiful woman. I couldn't help the flash of imaginings. Of how those cute brows might pinch and those large gold eyes might cross if I had her pinned between Kai and me—*fuck*.

I grimaced. It didn't help that she was staring at me with a similar horrified expression, her cheeks suddenly much more flushed.

"What do you want?" she asked, grabbing the fork and spearing pieces of penne aggressively.

"Why did you do it?"

She regarded me for a moment. "I didn't like him, so I killed him."

Even her voice was sweet. Light, with a slight husk to it. Some of her inflections almost sounded like a purr. "Why didn't you like him?" I pressed.

"He was a prick."

"He was a good person." My teeth were gritted. What the fuck did she know about Logan? The owner of the establishment had told me they'd met for the first time that evening.

Havoc sighed. "Okay... That's not why I did it."

"Then why?"

"It was an accident." Her voice lowered, her expression shifting to something much more nervous. "I didn't know it was loaded. We were just playing around."

I stared at her, my mouth working. "An... accident?"

"Yeah."

"Why didn't you say that at the start? It changes everything—"

"Hold up," she lifted the spoon. "I forgot, actually. Truth was, Logan wanted to kill himself, but he was way too scared to do it himself. He asked me since he didn't want you guys—"

I was on my feet in a second. "How dare you—"

She lifted a hand in mock defeat. "Joking. The real truth? We were playing Russian roulette. Could have been me or him— neither of us knew. Call it a real fucked up kink."

Rage boiled in my chest. The way she was just sitting there, legs crossed like she owned the room, poking at the food I'd brought her while she made fun of my brother's death... "You're sick."

"Which one sounded best?" She looked up at me from beneath thick lashes. "You like the accident one?"

"Fuck you."

"Your aura's dying."

I went completely still.

"That's why you're here, right? To try to find a reason not to hate me so I can save you from losing them?"

I knew there was a sour expression twisting my face as she popped the last bite of pasta into her mouth and then set the bowl down.

I couldn't move. My chest was heaving. It truly was taking every ounce of strength not to leap for her.

When she spoke next, her voice was lower and much more serious. "Angel, with a heart of gold." There was a bitter expression on her face. "You weren't going to believe anything I said unless it's what you wanted to hear."

I blinked, taking that in. I opened my mouth then shut it again.

"I'm just the undesirable gold pack omega you want to fit into a box so you can get me to be what you need."

An incredulous laugh slipped out before I caught it.

Undesirable?

She was a snake.

She'd killed my brother in the last twenty-four hours and I couldn't look at her without imagining what was underneath that silken black gown...

She knew exactly the kind of effect she was having on me—on the others too. Maybe it had been a mistake bringing her here. But it was too late. The others knew she was their only chance of curing my aura sickness. They'd never let her go now, even if she destroyed us.

She leaned forward. "But I'd rather die than fit into your stupid box, and if you want me to fix that pathetic aura, you'll have to make me."

I realised much too late that the best option was to abandon her in that room for the police to claim.

How could I have known exactly how manipulative she was, though?

Better than any omega I'd ever come across. She was as stunning as she was a wild card. Most omegas had silver tongues, which was what they were trained for, but Havoc?

She was fucking frightening because I had no idea what to expect next. We needed to get a lock on her door. And apparently, I was completely capable of being concerned she might slit Caspian or Kai, or Bane's throat, while dreaming of knotting her in the next second.

I had to leave.

Havoc

Angel snatched the bowl from the table as he passed, leaving without another word.

As soon as the door shut, I sagged, hugging myself, my mind running a million miles an hour. He'd brought food...

Right. Because he wants answers. He's playing nice guy.

But... The way he'd looked when I'd said killing Logan was an accident, like he was so primed to believe... No. I couldn't go there.

If Angel wished it was an accident, it was because it would make it simpler for him and his aura problem. I really needed to be careful about what I said.

"You'll have to make me?" Had I really said that? I shouldn't be daring them to bond me. The only bond they would offer was a dark bond. A bond of servitude.

When it had come out of my mouth I hadn't thought through the ramifications. It had always been a possibility that they would try to dark bond me, but until I saw the flash in Angel's eyes when I'd made that dare, I hadn't considered it. Mainly because I couldn't imagine a world in which they wanted me at all.

I may disgust them, but I couldn't underestimate their desire to fix Angel and repair their pack. Even so, they couldn't wish for a bond like that. They would be cursed with it for the rest of their lives, too.

Right now, it was impossible not to compare the Angel I'd imagined with the one who'd just slammed my door. The one who'd just now considered bonding me like that, even if it would be nothing more than a prison.

Logan leaned close. "Please tell me. If the night goes well, is there the slightest chance you'd want to come home with me?" Logan asked. "You don't have to decide tonight—I know you must be well taken care of here—"

"I would." I had to work to fight back the desperate tears that

suddenly burned my eyes. He'd said tonight like it was a possibility?
"I'd like that... I mean." I sounded so desperate to my own ears.

But he was my mate.

It was every dream I'd ever had. He was my mate, and he hadn't flinched away from my golden eyes.

Living here was hell. I hadn't hit my heat, hadn't had an alpha calling after me yet, but it was only a matter of time. And the longer no alpha was interested, the worse the establishment treated me.

This man was so sweet and interested. More than that—he offered a thing I'd never truly had.

A home.

A family.

SIX

Kai

I opened the front door to see an alpha on the doorstep with a bundle of bags in his arms.

"Boris," I grunted. One of Angel's rich friends.

"Thought I'd stop by." Boris said with his usual obscene cheer. He was tall and slender with short blonde hair, wearing one of his usual business suits. He always looked like a pretentious twit. Most of Angel's friends did, but Boris was alright, really.

He began unpacking a few dishes on the marble top island that split the kitchen from the lounge. A baked casserole, a lasagne, and a pot of mac and cheese that I eyed with interest. Bane cooked for us most days, but it was always so damn healthy.

"Blame Lacy," Boris said. "Said you shouldn't have to think about cooking."

"Thanks," Angel muttered. He'd made his way to the island and clapped Boris on the shoulder. I sank back down onto the bar stool, fixed on their point of contact out of the corner of my eye.

I was a seer, which meant I could visualise auras when I wanted, but it also meant I didn't see the rest of the world in colour. Not until Havoc. Or unless it was—as the therapist Angel forced me to see that one tragic time had called them—intrusive thoughts.

A vision flashed into my head, colours blossoming to life as I pictured pulling the knife from my belt and digging it right between the tendons on the back of Boris's hand.

I let it play out once—twice—three times and there was a smile on my face. Boris was giving me a shifty look which meant my smile was all wrong. I adjusted, searching for one of my 'dinner table' expressions, but blood seeped down Boris's wrist, over his Rolex and beneath the cuff of his buttoned grey sleeve... Boris removed his hand and the intruder vanished. My smile shifted easily.

It wasn't that Boris was a bad guy. But the thoughts were much more about gratification than karma. And they were *really* protective over Angel.

Plus, the vision was off. Blood had been smeared across Havoc's cheek when I'd seen her yesterday. It was the first time I'd ever seen blood in colour, and I'd been imagining red all wrong—this whole time.

"How...?" Boris looked uncomfortable as he glanced between us all. "How are you holding up?"

There was a long silence.

Was it tense?

I perked up. I wasn't great at noticing these sorts of things, but I did like to see how others responded to them. Especially my pack. It helped me understand them better—in ways that actually mattered. Caspian broke it—because of course he did, which was as disappointing as it was predictable. I already knew Caspian better than I knew myself.

"Our pack lead was killed by our omega, and now she's holed up in our nest. How do you think we're doing?" Caspian asked.

"She's here?" Boris froze, staring at Caspian in shock.

"What were we supposed to do?" Angel asked as my mind

drifted to Havoc. I could feel her, a restless ball of energy in my mind, telling me where she was. What was she getting up to right now?

I'd slipped into her room last night in a moment of weakness while she was sleeping. I hated the idea that someone I didn't know had something I wanted, but her draw was too much. What she offered in colours I'd never seen, it was... soothing.

"Police would have taken her," Angel was saying. "There wouldn't have been a trial, and she'd have been shipped to the—"

"Wait—no trial...?" Boris asked. "She's gold pack?"

Angel nodded, his jaw clenched. He looked tired, there was no more brightness in his eyes these days. He loved Logan. Now there was a gaping hole where our pack brother had been, and it hurt him. I hadn't loved Logan, but I hated that.

Angel was the most beautiful person on the planet, and I wanted to destroy anything that stole away his light.

Havoc... she was beautiful too... I'd watched her curled up, clutching her blankets as nightmares stole her sleep. I was entranced by the bright brown of her tangled hair, the flush of her olive skin, the red of her lips. I'd been disappointed to find she'd showered the red of Logan's blood away.

And the whole time I'd not heard the slightest stirring of violent thoughts.

I didn't need them, I supposed, when she offered me the colour they gave. Was that why I wanted to go back tonight? I *really* hated when someone I didn't know had something I wanted, but those visions? They had me in a vice more than anything. They took and took *and took*—

"Damn..." Boris muttered, and the sound ripped me from my thoughts.

I stared at him intently, cocking my head as I remembered something about him. "Lacy's gold pack?" I asked. His omega was just like Havoc.

"Yeah."

"What kind of bond do you have?" When I asked, I watched the others straighten. Bane's eyes flickered up from the book he was reading on the armchair.

"Normal bite. Kor wanted to offer her the princess bond, but pressure from above—" Boris rolled his eyes. "None of the grand-parents-to-be wanted us to risk her walking."

There were three types of bonds an omega could get. A fated mate could be offered the princess bond—a choice to take the pack or ditch. If they chose to ditch, then the omega would be free of all duties and rank like a regular civilian. But if she took it, the bond with her pack would be the strongest it could be.

Omegas were so rare, however, it wasn't common to see princess bonds. The risk was too high. Its technical name was a prosperity bond, but everyone I knew called it a princess bond because that's basically what you were offering. A place like royalty.

That... that would be best for Havoc—if we wanted the strongest way to save Angel's aura. But even I wasn't blind enough to know she wouldn't just take it and run.

Then there were the regular bonds that most omegas had with their packs—or genesis bonds. Those could be offered to any omega, fated or not, and packs could have multiple omegas with regular bonds. It took a bite and mutual consent. It stabilised alpha energy, but didn't always offer a cure to aura sickness—the cure we *needed* to stop Angel from leaving me.

"What are you going to do?" Boris asked. "You uh, thinking of dark bonding her?" He threw that out like it was just any old topic, but his face went a bit pale.

A dark bond was the last bond an omega could host. Illegal to any but gold pack omegas. It was a bond of control and subservience.

My daydreams ran away with me.

Dark bonds meant weaker ties between omega and alpha, but we could take it without consent. And with a gold pack omega it *would* offer healing to Angel's aura sickness. Packs couldn't have more than one bond if they had a dark bonded omega—but that didn't matter to me.

For a moment I pictured heading down the hallway right now, pinning her down and sinking my teeth into her neck. The faintest low growl stirred in my chest at the thought of it, blood rushing... places. The thought of what her flushed skin would feel like beneath my bite... I quickly covered the sound with a cough, so I didn't have to explain myself to Angel.

But... If I did... that would be it. Everything would be fixed.

"Only if we have to." Angel's voice was quiet. It drew me up, and I scowled. Could he drop the nobility for five fucking seconds to save our connection?

Still. The rule with Angel was that I absolutely respected his wishes at all costs.

Unless his wishes were dumb as fuck.

If Angel decided he'd rather lose his bond with the pack than dark bond Havoc, I'd rule his wishes 'dumb as fuck' with ease. I'd bite her and he could be pissed for as long as he liked—and I'd be able to feel every single juicy moment of his resentment, since the bond would be intact.

And... I'd be able to keep her forever.

I realised there was an unexpected frown on my face. I shook it off. There was no reason at all to flinch at the idea of dark bonding Havoc, yet what stirred alongside what *should* be perfectly good daydreams, was unsettled and foreign.

The image of her curled up in her bed clutching a pillow, tense and frightened in the face of her nightmares, flashed in my mind. Would I become one of those nightmares?

Usually, I found comfort in the idea of becoming someone's nightmare. It made me feel less alone. If *I* had to deal with my nightmares, I'd rather more of the world understood what that felt like.

But... the idea of being Havoc's...? Unsettling was a mild word for how that felt. A distressed part of my mind that didn't understand, seized the whole trailing thought and shoved it somewhere deep and dark. I'd deal with that later.

And *later* had a wonderful wonderful habit of turning into never.

"We're not making any decisions on bonding her until we know the full truth," Angel said.

I perked up at that. I knew the others were intent on Havoc's history, even if none of it really bothered me—but *that* was all they needed to make a decision on her bond?

Bond Havoc, save Angel.

If they needed her to talk, I could make that happen. Easy peasy. I opened my mouth, fully ready to derail this conversation when I caught myself. The others didn't like my methods at all. I clenched my jaw.

As soon as Boris left, I'd go and sort it out. They could complain about my choice while I was handing them the information they needed.

Then we'd bite Havoc, and everything would be right.

"She's in my head all the time. The bond is fucking me up," Caspian said quietly.

"You can *feel* the bond?" Boris seemed surprised.

"You couldn't?" Caspian's eyes were narrowed.

"Not until after biting her in. I mean..." Boris looked thoughtful. "I knew she was my mate. Most beautiful woman I'd ever seen. But the connection... Actually, even after the bite it wasn't tangible. Not until we'd been together a while."

"Great. So... Havoc's breaking all the rules?" Caspian asked.

Boris raised his eyebrows.

"What?" I asked.

"Good name." Boris shrugged.

It was actually, a great name. Matched her perfectly. She was a flaming ball of destruction, and all threats aside, I'd be a fool not to admit all of that was just... damn hot. I almost detached from the conversation again, my mind spinning plans of how to get Havoc to talk in record time without breaking her completely—or Angel would be pissed. But then Caspian was speaking, and his words caught me off guard.

"It's not just..." Caspian wrinkled his nose. "The obvious stuff. It's unnatural. All I can think of is finding her and fixing shit. Like I've done something wrong, and owe her."

I straightened. I knew what he meant by that. Dreams of biting her aside, it would be a lie to suggest a part of me didn't ache to seek her out right now, just to make sure she was okay.

"The way you're feeling the bond, it's like I was with Lacy after she'd developed a connection with the pack—and it didn't always have to be me, mind. Once Lacy and Kor got into a tiff and she wandered off in the park alone. She almost got grabbed by an alpha near the river. I remember the next time I saw her, feeling like I'd failed, like I never wanted her to hurt again—I wasn't even in the same state when it happened. It's pack bonds, not just individual."

"Right. So, she kills Logan, and somehow that forged a bond that makes us feel like *we've* failed *her*?" Angel asked.

I glanced at the others. Caspian had a dark look, but Bane was fixated on Boris, his piercing silver eyes narrowed. One of his ankles rested on his other knee, the true crime book he was reading, propped on it. His fingers were frozen in the air, pinching the page he was halfway through turning. For a moment it was like I could see the thoughts racing through his mind.

Boris scratched his chin with a sigh, tugging my attention back to him. "There's something I've learned about gold pack omegas. They run the show, even with a normal bond. If Lacy feels betrayed, we all feel it. Even when she might be..." Boris paused, a slight smile on his face. "A little... unreasonable. It doesn't matter. If she believes it, we all feel it."

"What are you saying?" Bane asked. Both Caspian and Angel glanced at him in surprise. The image of Bane's hulking frame taking up most of the armchair with a book in his lap was so familiar it always risked fading into the background. Bane was so quiet it might be easy to forget he was there at all.

I never did. Bane was a man of few words and rigid routine. Even now he was dressed in his button-up shirt and dark jeans he wore for work—even if we'd all taken the week off. I depended on routine, yet struggled to make it happen, so I'd attached myself to Bane's habits. His silent presence was an anchor.

"Does Havoc believe you've failed her?" Boris asked.

"How could she?" Caspian cut in with a snarl. "When we didn't even meet her until she put a bullet in Logan's fucking skull."

Bane's eyes darted between Caspian and Boris, absolutely intent. I wondered what he was thinking.

Boris just winced, raising his hands defensively. "I'm just saying it's the only answer I have. Figure out if there's *any* possible way Havoc might believe you failed her."

SEVEN

Angel

"We have to make a decision about her," I said quietly.

It was late. Boris had left after an hour or two. I was happy for his company, needing the change.

Kai had been shifty today; I could feel his energy across the room. Bane was more on edge than usual, and Caspian was still seething every time I saw him.

"There is no decision," Caspian muttered. He was standing behind one of the armchairs, fists curled over its back. "I don't give a shit what Boris suggests."

Kai was slouched on the arm of the couch, glancing between us. Bane was seated in his armchair. He set his mug on his coffee table, glancing up. He'd remained there for the duration of Boris's visit, eyes on his book, but the pages never seemed to turn.

"I hate it as much as you do, but there it is." I slumped down on the couch beside Kai. I needed to be near him more than usual these days, the looming threat of losing my aura setting me on edge.

But right now—especially after that damned conversation with Boris—we had to talk. The problem was, we'd not talked pack lead. Logan had remained unreplaced, and it was unsettling us all.

Dealing with this, it was on me. It wasn't that I didn't trust the others, but I'd done this before. It wasn't the first time I'd stepped in and taken responsibility after a loss. Last time, though, there hadn't been a choice. When my parents had died, it was sink or swim, my family's estate under threat of being snatched by vultures—even if I'd just been a teenager. Even if I had been almost destroyed by paranoia.

No. This time, with Logan, it *was* my choice. The others, they could take their time to grieve, they deserved that.

I took a breath. "I say we vote on her. If we choose a pack lead, we re-evaluate, then."

None of us wanted to talk about who was going to be Logan's replacement. Some pack leads had that discussion before they died, but Logan hadn't been the type to plan for his own death. He was the kind of guy who believed he'd live forever.

"You know my vote," Caspian said without hesitation.

"You would really kill her?" The thought sent a chill through my veins.

"She killed Logan. How is it complicated?" Caspian demanded. I could see the streets in him at that moment. His skin was ghostly pale—more than usual with the stress of the last few days. The tattoos that crawled up to his sharp jawline were starker with the deadly look in his beetle black eyes. "You lot are soft because she's got her claws in you," he said.

Kai's expression shifted, something resentful in the way he looked at Caspian. Caspian met that gaze unapologetically.

"We all know there's more to it than that," I murmured.

"What's your vote, then?" Caspian asked.

I regarded him carefully. I'd asked for this, but now challenged by Caspian's dark gaze, it was hard to say.

I realised it wasn't only hard to say because it damned me, my aura would die and I'd be bitten in like a beta, my connection with my pack a ghost of what it once was. It was hard to say because something closed around my throat at the idea of losing her so quickly after we'd found her.

It wasn't pity or sympathy, or even lust. It was born of the curiosity of years spent waiting to find our match.

My own aura wasn't the only reason I'd wanted an omega—in fact, my aura had only started to fade months ago. Her room—the nest—had been put together long before that. Then we'd known we wouldn't just bite anyone in.

We wanted our mate.

She was supposed to be the final piece.

Still. Now it was too late.

"I vote to take her back to the police," I said. "Let the system deal with her."

Kai stiffened, and I heard the faintest rumble in his chest as he fixed his blazing eyes on me. I couldn't meet that gaze because I might crack beneath it. I loved him—more than anything else in the world. That was why I was choosing this.

"Kai?" Caspian asked.

"We bond her." Kai didn't even hesitate. I knew it was coming, but I still shut my eyes briefly.

Caspian scowled.

I forced myself to look at Bane. "What do you think?" I always felt he responded so much better if he was invited in. I didn't know why after years of being with us, he wasn't comfortable opening up.

He was it. The deciding factor. Whoever he sided with; they got what they wanted.

There was a strange silence in the room as the truth settled on us. Bane himself looked startled.

I realised I'd been so caught up in Kai, in my own grief, even trying to get through to Caspian, that I'd not thought of Bane. I had no idea how he felt, how he was coping or what he would choose. There'd been very little through the bond from him, but that wasn't unusual.

The uncomfortable look on Caspian's face told me he might be thinking the same thing. Even Kai didn't seem sure what to expect.

Had none of us checked in on Bane in the last few days?

Bane didn't move as his eyes slid to each of us. There wasn't an ounce of resentment on his face, not like perhaps there should be.

"She stays," he said finally.

A guilty rush of relief hit me. It came from the small part of me that wanted my aura saved. The part that wanted more time with Havoc.

"Why?" Caspian asked, clearly pissed. "You'd let her destroy the pack?"

"Hey—" I began.

"No." Bane's reply was firm. Caspian didn't look ready to accept it, but Bane hadn't finished. "She's the pack's only salvation."

I blinked, and Caspian paused, neither of us having expected the declaration from Bane. I'd believed he might just be lukewarm on the topic until now, perhaps even lukewarm on the fate of the pack.

"This is fucked up," Caspian snapped, glaring at me. He waved a hand at Bane. "He doesn't—there are no stakes for him."

I hadn't ever quite tuned into this particular discomfort regarding Bane before, but now that I was, my stomach twisted. Caspian had just spoken about him like he wasn't there. No one else was flinching—Bane didn't even seem deterred.

Was it normal—and I'd just never noticed before? Did I do it?

"If we're talking stakes—Angel wins," Kai growled.

"That's not how voting works," I said through gritted teeth. "Bane's vote is worth the same. Not up for debate."

Bane's gaze found me and there was something appreciative in it—which was even worse. Like... like he hadn't expected it from me.

Logan was lead before. How had he handled this? Had he never noticed how we pushed Bane out?

"You know what you're saying you want, if you want to keep her here?"

"Yeah..." I said, my attention snapping back to the issue at hand.

I knew. We all did. We'd be tied to her for life. The woman who'd killed one of our own.

"Boris said it. Why haven't we talked about a dark bond?" Kai asked.

"Okay. Alright. The vote is that we keep her. But can we at least get a bit more information before deciding on a bond?" I did not want to discuss the possibility of a dark bond right now.

We could never undo it. The world would know why, and we had more reason than most, but it carried with it a weight. Everyone who ever met her would know what we'd done.

Kai nodded, and Bane shrugged.

"Right. Then, we all agree. She stays—"

"No. I don't fucking well agree," Caspian snarled, getting to his feet. "You're spitting on his name—not a week after he's dead."

I knew how Caspian felt about Logan—it was more than love; I had loved Logan. But Logan had claimed Caspian's loyalty a long time ago. What Logan had done for Caspian; it wasn't something he could ever repay. Even now, with Logan dead, I could see the simmering panic in Caspian's eyes, as if somehow, if he turned on his brother now, he might lose what Logan had saved.

"Cass—" Kai began.

"Don't," Caspian snarled. "I won't... I won't stand by while you all turn on him."

The room fell silent, and I knew we were all thinking the same thing. A pack lead could make final decisions on any bond we made with an omega. If one of us took lead, they could choose without a vote.

Caspian was still, and for a moment I felt him lose it. For the briefest flicker, his eyes flashed, and his aura hit the room in a burst of energy.

Every one of us tensed.

"Drag hormones into this, Cass, go on." Bane's voice was low.

I stiffened, not having expected that. Every gaze snapped to Bane in shock, then I glanced at Kai as we both shared the same look of surprise.

It'd already begun.

Just another thing Havoc was screwing up.

A pack lead could be chosen, or the position could be seized. We hadn't talked about it, but until now it had gone unsaid that we'd just have a rational discussion and make a decision. But Havoc's presence tossed all rational discussions out the window.

Claiming lead involved a fight, but not just in visible strength.

In a pack lead fight, we went feral, and our aura offered aid, making us stronger, faster, more alert.

Bane could ground any one of us, no aura needed—but with his behemoth of an essence he quietly walked around with? It wasn't a debate.

But he hadn't—and even if he was quiet, reclusive, and I was less connected with him than I was than any of my brothers, I knew he didn't want it.

Would Bane claim that very position he didn't want, in order to protect Havoc?

Caspian could push the matter and call Bane's bluff, but there was a beauty to Bane's challenge. Beautiful in its karma. I realised as I watched the doubt in Caspian's eyes that neither of us knew Bane well enough to know if he was serious.

Kai leaned forward slightly, eyes twinkling as he glanced between them both, that part of him that loved to watch chaos unfold, uncontained.

Right.

This was going to shit. Fast.

"Enough," I snapped at Caspian. "You don't want her destroying us, but you're willing to start a pack fight over her?"

"It's not *over* her."

"Get a grip," I said. "We all need to take some time. We took a vote, she's staying, that's the end of it. Doesn't mean we can't change our mind later."

Caspian's chest was heaving as he glared around at us, and then he stormed down the hallway to his bedroom. I couldn't help following his figure until it was well past Havoc's room.

"So..." Bane looked around at us. "Can I tell her?"

Kai shrugged, and I raised my eyebrows. "Uh... Yeah. I guess." To be honest, having another one-on-one conversation with Havoc wasn't on the top of my to do list. She had a way of sinking claws into my brain and not letting go.

If Bane wanted to do it, let him.

EIGHT

Havoc

"Let us surprise them, then," Logan said.

"How?" I asked.

"I would like to offer you something."

I nodded, unsure as I clasped my hands together.

"A bond. I'm pack lead. I could offer it to you," Logan said.

"A bond?" I asked. What kind? If it were being offered, then it wasn't a dark bond. That was all I'd ever learned to expect.

"If I offered you the princess bond, what would you do?"

My mouth dropped open as I stared at him. The smile he flashed was breath-taking.

"Why... would you do that?" I couldn't help the question. I was gold pack. I wasn't destined for a princess bond—any bond, really. It could only be offered to an omega with a scent match, but it also meant they would never be able to bite in another omega.

Given that any alpha children I had would be at risk of hosting the gold pack gene—a danger to society—I wasn't allowed any. At Gavin's I'd been injected with birth control to ensure it never happened.

No pack in their right mind should want a princess bond with a gold pack omega—not unless they wanted to have children outside of pack bonds...

"You're lovely, Havoc." Logan's words ripped me from my panic. "Beautiful, clever, the most powerful omega I've ever met, you're everything my brothers and I ever dreamed of. If you took the princess bond, we could go back to them tonight—with the strongest bond possible. They would be..." He let out a breath. "They would be blown away and I... I care for them so much. I'd love to be able to offer them that." He looked nervous. "Maybe... I'm a little prideful, but to be able to say I secured it for them, well that does have a ring to it."

I smiled, my heart in my throat. "I would take it."

"You would?" Logan's eyes lit up.

"A million times yes."

He was staring at me reverently, his touch drawing me closer. "Havoc..." He swallowed.

"Yes?"

"Can I kiss you?"

I barely hesitated, all of my instincts reacting.

I took his face in my hands and pulled him into a kiss. His touch wound around me as he held me closer, a breath of his laugh passing between our lips at my enthusiasm.

He was whisky and coco and every vein in my body lit at his touch.

I woke with a start at the sound of my door opening.

For a moment I was back in Gavin's and the door was banging open. It was Logan. He was back again with Eli. This time it was late—I'd had no warning. I sat up blearily, trying to pull myself together. I was in my nightdress. That wasn't... I couldn't change anything in a *nightdress*. I blinked.

Where was he?

I swear he'd been unsteadied in how he made his way over to the bar. He didn't arrive drunk, not usually...

The room around me focused, and I froze at an unfamiliar figure in the door. But then reality slammed in, and I realised it was Bane.

I wasn't at Gavin's anymore. Logan was gone. He wouldn't offer me fear ever again. But he wouldn't offer me hope either. I'd destroyed both at the same time.

Bane was holding a tray in his hands.

Angel had taken to leaving my meals outside the door, clearly not wanting a repeat of the last time he'd spoken to me. This evening I'd checked three times for food, my stomach rumbling. I'd heard unfamiliar voices from the living room. Had they had a guest?

I glanced to the TV. It was midnight.

Bane stepped into my room, not waiting for an invitation.

I wasn't in a nightdress, instead I'd tugged on a comfortable baggy pyjama top to sleep in—mainly for this exact possibility. Beneath were comfy silken leggings.

At Gavin's I'd not had the options for almost any covering clothing. Here there were hoodies and t-shirts some many sizes up and I was taking advantage.

Bane was the tallest of the pack and built like a fighter, his eyes were cool silver as they held mine. His black hair was messy at the top and buzzed short on the sides. He wore dark jeans and a fitted, long sleeved grey shirt that hovered somewhere between casual and formal. He looked like hired muscle, well dressed, and more put together than the others. The only thing that stood out was the thick chain of silver around his throat. It almost looked like a collar. Somehow it shifted his look from business to something a little more sinister.

I was wary of him. Not just because he had a huge physical presence, but I had no information on him. Not like the others.

"Tell me about Bane?" I'd asked one day.

"Not much to tell." Logan said. *"He hates the world. Has a dark streak. Love is off the table, but he's one hell of a fighter. If you're one of the pack, he'd die for you."*

Bane sat on the couch, throwing an arm around the back and looking over to me. "Come here."

The words were low and struck me to the core. I was crossing the room before I'd realised it and only caught myself a few paces away.

Holy fucking shit.

I measured my expression so I wasn't gaping at him. It wasn't like any alpha command I'd ever heard. It hadn't been loud or demanding, it had just smoothly carried all the weight of Bane's aura. He was... he was ridiculously strong. Stronger than Logan had been—by a long shot.

He was smirking. "You're my omega. Normal, isn't it? To want to do as I ask..."

"I'm not yours."

"Ours. Mine. Whatever." He shrugged. "Anyway. Came to tell you the news."

"What news?" I asked, edging back a step.

"We're keeping you."

I froze. Uh... That couldn't be right. "You don't want me."

"Strange, because we just had a vote."

He dropped his arm from the couch, leaning forward, eyes fixed on me. I couldn't help taking another step away.

"Skittish," he noted.

I wrinkled my nose. There was no way I could convince them that they didn't want me around like this. If they thought I was afraid, they certainly wouldn't be worried I'd kill another of them.

With difficulty I strode over and sat down on the couch right beside him. I was slammed with his scent. Leather and applewood. I blinked, trying to compose myself and not choke on it. It was intoxicating, more than any of the other's had been.

I reached out and grabbed the packet of cheesy chips from the tray, ripping it open and digging in like I hadn't a care in the world.

He reached out, knuckle bent to touch my cheek, but I spun on him, catching his sleeve, careful not to touch his skin.

"Don't touch me."

"You're ours little Havoc. I can do what I want." His voice was a low, soothing rumble. Even with the threatening words I couldn't help how it unwound something in my chest, loosening my breath, lowering my guard.

I clenched my jaw. "You *don't* want me."

"You'd rather we turn you in?"

I glanced at him, trying not to let the hope show on my face. I nodded curtly, as if it didn't mean that much to me. "Better that way."

He grinned. "Better for you."

"Better for all of you. Can't promise staying here won't end in another Logan."

To my surprise, Bane barked a laugh.

"You think I'm bluffing?" I asked, irritation pricking my voice.

"If you're not, you prove it to me now."

I set the packet of chips down as he shifted. Then my heart dropped as he pulled a gun from his waist and pressed it into my hands.

I tensed as the weighted piece pressed against my thighs, my pulse suddenly roaring in my ears.

"Go on," he said.

I hadn't moved, my throat dry. "It's not loaded."

"It is."

But I was already reaching for it, my instincts taking over. My finger slid across the chamber indicator the way my father had taught me. A strip of crimson stared back at me.

Loaded.

My eyes flicked to Bane in shock.

"An omega who knows how to use a gun," Bane murmured. "That *is* hot."

I couldn't focus on his words though, living a Deja Vu. I had been here before. The memory of the ear-splitting bang shattered my thoughts.

I had to get myself together. I was shaking.

"So?" Bane asked.

I couldn't move.

"I can help you." Bane's voice dragged me back to the present. He pressed my palms to the gun and then dragged it up toward him.

My breathing hitched, and I tried to pull away, but he wasn't letting go.

He was insane.

"Where did you hold it for him?" Bane asked, shifting the gun from beneath his chin and resting it so it pointed right between his eyes. "Here?"

For a moment I was staring into Logan's eyes again.

I didn't have any other choice. I thought... I thought this was my dream, but I was wrong.

"Go on, little Havoc. Kill me like you killed him," Bane breathed, pressing my grip harder against the gun.

A breath of terror broke from me, my chest heaving as I tried to pull away.

I *couldn't* do this again.

"There's the real truth of it." He released my hand. Relief shocked my system as he took the gun from my grip.

One hand still holding my hoodie so I couldn't get away, he flicked the safety and tossed the gun onto the coffee table. Then, against protests, he dragged me closer. I tried to shove away, but he was much stronger and next thing I knew I was on his lap, facing him.

I hissed, trying to get free, but his grip on my hips was vice-like. He was twice my size, had to be. He chuckled as I squirmed which drew me to a halt.

"You aren't going to kill any of us, are you?"

"I would—"

"You're *not* a killer..."

"I did kill him," I snarled.

"Did he give you a choice?"

My fingers, which were clutching his arms through the sleeves of his long sleeve shirt, dug in. I couldn't meet his gaze.

He regarded me with those silver eyes, and something about them was mesmerising, as if he was looking straight through me.

"I can imagine, when he met you, he wanted to keep you all to himself..." Bane went on. My blood ran hot. "You are lovely."

My nerves were worn too thin. I'd suffered too long—all for my own foolishness.

"How do we do a princess bond?" I asked Logan.

Hope was blossoming in my mind like a flower in spring after a cold winter. It drowned any other thoughts.

Beautiful. Powerful. Everything we dreamed of... He'd used all those words to describe me? I couldn't understand it, but I wanted it. Wanted it so badly it hurt.

"It's simple," Logan said. "I offer it, and if you say yes, then you take my bite. We're pack for life."

"What happens if I say no?"

"Nothing. You walk. And you'll be protected from dark bonds by law."

. . .

I'd known the right choice. The smart one. A gift no gold pack omega would even dream of seeing...

And I'd been the fool.

Never. Again.

Instead of walking away with true freedom, I'd given myself to an alpha. The way my father had always warned against.

But Bane was right here, his grip on my hips unrelenting as he offered me sweet words like he could melt my heart... "The most beautiful woman I've ever seen," he murmured.

Before I caught myself my hand crashed into Bane's cheek. I was jolted by the flash of pain at the contact.

He moved like lightning, shoving me back and in the next moment I was pressed against the bed of the couch, and he was on top of me, caging me in, his fists around my wrists. The hoodie offered a blessed layer of fabric between his skin and mine. His eyes were dark and for a moment I could see the monster Logan had described. I stopped struggling, instinct freezing me in place.

Bane blinked, the depravity draining away as he stared at me. "I've been slapped for a lot of things, Havoc. But calling a woman beautiful is a first for me."

"I'm not playing your game," I hissed. I'd heard this all before.

He leaned close. "You're not playing *my* game, or you're not playing *Logan's* game?" His breath was hot in my ear.

Every thought crashed out of my mind. "I d-don't... know what you're talking about."

"How long did you know him?" Bane asked. "The others think you killed him on your first meeting, but I don't believe it."

"W-why?"

"Because Logan's a saint to all at first. He only makes you wish he was dead after he gets you hooked."

My fists balled but I couldn't find an answer, my eyes darting between his.

"How did he get you hooked, little omega? It must have been good if he dropped his mask. What did he have on you?"

His words were too close to the truth. What was this? How did he know? Panic spiked my veins. Was he the same?

"Were you one of his experiments?" Bane didn't speak the words, he sung them in a low taunt.

Only I'd heard taunts like that over and over.

It was Logan. The sound of his delight the moment he knew he'd won. Memories crashed into me.

The way Logan had sung to me the first time I met him—only that time I hadn't known it was a taunt.

"My little gold pack mate..."

My throat was closing up, my chest heaving in panic.

Bane was taunting me just like Logan had. But then, all the triumph drained from Bane's face as he watched my reaction. "You were." His words were low and full of fury, and there was no satisfaction in them at all.

"How long did he hide you from us?" Bane asked, his voice lower. It felt as though he'd just reached into my soul and seized something precious.

"I *didn't* know him." I sounded much too aggressive, and I knew that Bane could hear the desperation in my voice. He would know the truth: that the lie was just as much for me as it was for him.

"He loved the broken ones so he could use it against them, keep them around under his rules," he said. "Is that what you are, Havoc. One of the broken ones?"

"Shut *up!*" I threw my weight against him, rage burning every survival instinct away.

Bane let out a snort. "The others so desperately wanted to find our omega so we could fix the pack. I never believed you would be capable of it—not really. Our problems were so much deeper than what an omega could fix. But I can admit when I was wrong. I suppose I never imagined an omega would come with a bullet and a gun."

I stopped fighting at those words, searching his face for a lie.

I found none.

He pressed in closer. I knew I shouldn't want him to, but I couldn't get any words up my throat as he gazed at me with those captivating silver irises.

"You saved us, Havoc. The others just don't know it yet."

I couldn't breathe all of a sudden.

Whatever I'd been expecting when he'd come in, this wasn't it. I'd been prepping for violence and anger, not whatever was glittering in the depths of Bane's eyes. He released me, reaching as if he wanted to touch my cheek once more, something softer in his expression. Once more, I caught his wrist.

"I accept," I whispered. I felt something tighten around my soul, connecting me to the perfect man before my eyes.

"Show me your neck," Logan breathed in my ear. I tugged my hair out of the way, desperate and giddy. He let out a groan and the way his eyes held me, I'd never been looked at like that. Attention I'd received from other alphas in the club had been cruel and debasing. Logan was looking at me like I was the centre of the universe. Like he'd never seen something so precious.

The bite didn't hurt in the way I expected. It wasn't sharp, instead a prickle of pain along my skin like static. He came alight in my mind, and I wouldn't have thought it possible to find him more stunning than before, except he was. It was intoxicating, looking into the glittering blue of his eyes. His alpha scent filled the room, making me feel warm and cosy and safe.

"I need you." I'd never whined like that before and a blush hit my cheeks.

But there was something off about him... The light in his eyes had died as he looked at me, his brows furrowed.

"Is... is there something wrong?"

"Don't *touch* me," I spat. Bane stopped, his skin only an inch from my face. I could practically feel the static between us, that touch promising pain... and something much much worse.

"Is he still in your head?" Bane asked.

"Fuck you."

"I'll tell you a secret." Bane leaned closer and whispered in my ear. "He's still in mine."

I stopped struggling all at once.

"What?"

"Even the others don't know what was under that mask of his. But I do," Bane murmured. "You saved us." He repeated the words, but they were no less a shock to my system. In that second, I couldn't have moved if I wanted to. His scent, leather and apple-wood, was everywhere all at once.

Why did my crazy omega brain feel... safe right now?

One of my hands reached up, fingers curling around his shirt without me realising it, a tiny sound escaping my chest, just more than a breath, before I shoved it down.

"You're perfect, Havoc," Bane breathed. "I'm going to find a way to convince them of that."

"I'm n-not." I released him, knowing how desperate I sounded.

One compliment and I was melting?

It was disgusting.

"It's not what I expected," Logan murmured.

"What do you mean?" I asked.

"I thought, after I bit you, you'd be irresistible." The words were like a blow to the gut.

"I'm..." I swallowed. *"Not?"*

He *was*—I was heady with need; I'd just assumed it was the same for him.

He released me, straightening, brows drawn together. "I barely feel a thing, Havoc."

I couldn't help darting a glance to the other alpha in the room. I didn't know why, perhaps to see if he was reacting to any of the tension. He wasn't my mate, but my perfume was drowning the space.

"Maybe... if we go to the others?" I asked.

Logan raised his eyebrows. "I can't bring an omega like you home."

"I don't... understand..." My fingers trailed to the bite fresh on my skin. He couldn't undo it. We were pack bound now.

"They deserve only the best," Logan stood, leaving me stunned in the seat beside him. "Until I can ensure you are worth a thing, you don't exist."

"How much did he screw with that pretty little head of yours?" Bane asked, his eyes darting between mine as he sat up, putting blessed distance between me and his dizzying scent.

He stood, still not taking his gaze from me. "Do I have to convince you, too?"

Bane

It still hadn't hit me. Not until today. Not until I'd felt her against me.

Logan was dead. Logan was dead, and I had been right about her.

She could have pulled that trigger on me, but she hadn't. I drew out the gun and placed it in the box on my desk.

She could have killed me, she'd known it and so had I. I hadn't been scared. If I was wrong about her, being dead was the better option.

She was the last hope for us, and my brothers were the only thing I had left.

And then there was what had happened after I'd told her she'd saved us. The way her fingers had curled around my shirt. I leaned back in my desk chair, trying to cool my blood.

Damn.

I'd pinned her down. She had slapped me, and it had been pure reaction, but still. I was twice her size.

Would she hate me?

Yet, the way she'd reached up and held on—it was *after* I'd done that. That little noise she made deep in her chest—the one that yearned to trust me, to give in and let me protect her? That was after I had her pressed against the couch.

No. She wasn't nearly as fragile as she looked.

And... Did she want me? The lowest of the pack? The one chained to subservience... But *she* didn't know that. What I might be to her, it was of my own making. Without Logan. And maybe... maybe she would be drawn to it, even if I gave her all the ugly pieces of it...

You're perfect, Havoc. I'm going to find a way to convince them of that.

Was I making promises I couldn't keep?

I imagined going to my brothers right now and telling them everything I believed. It was almost laughable. I knew the bonds Logan forged, the way he'd made himself irreplaceable. And the more irreplaceable he became, the more invisible he needed me.

No, if I did that I would be rejected, and Havoc's chances would shrink to almost nothing. Even now, the ghost of Logan was closer to the rest of my pack than I was.

Logan had been the one to make sure of that.

The best way was Havoc. Give her hope and let her shift the others even if just a little.

I could feel the tangles loosen, Logan's grip slipping away. All the walls he'd placed, keeping me from everything I cared about, it was gone.

I wasn't ready for it, my mind unable to grasp that sort of freedom. So instead, it was one thing at a time.

The first was this necklace.

I reached up, fingers biting down on the clasp of the metal ringed choker that had been around my neck for years. Only... I couldn't remove it.

I shut my eyes, slumping in the chair, hands dropping to my sides. *Why* couldn't I release it?

It had come with a note, one that was tucked in the bottom drawer beside my bed.

"Let slip one more secret and I'll make you wear the leash, too."

I couldn't take it off, because I wasn't free of him.

Not yet.

She was still wearing black around her neck. Hiding from us in fear. Because of Logan—I knew it, no matter what she denied.

No. His chains weren't gone.

Not yet.

I wouldn't take this off until there was nothing between Havoc and the rest of the pack. And maybe—just maybe if she broke down that wall, I could let my brothers see me, too.

NINE

Havoc

I had made and unmade the bed a dozen times.

It had nothing to do with making a nest, or the faint twists of my stomach. I just... didn't like the way the blankets were. And it was hard to sort out a bed just right.

The TV said it was 01:00am.

Five times I'd gone to the couch and grabbed the green cushion Bane had leaned against. Then rushed to my bed, tucking it amongst the other pillows, guilty in my enjoyment of the scent.

Then I panicked and returned it.

Now it had been there enough times that the nest—*bed*—still had the faintest aroma of leather and applewood.

Get a grip, Havoc.

He could be lying.

All of it could be a trap. Too good to be true, like Logan's promises.

How did I know I could trust Bane?

I had crossed the room before I realised it and Bane's emerald green pillow was clutched in my arms before I caught myself.

Shit.

I needed to change my environment. The others would be in bed, right?

I peered down the hallway, thinking of heading into the kitchen again for more snacks. It was late, and my confidence was bolstered by the interaction with Bane.

I was aware of how insane that was, since he'd almost made me shoot him in the face and then pinned me against the couch.

But Logan... He thought Logan was a threat too.

My eyes caught on the door at the far end of the hall, the opposite direction of the kitchen.

I'd stared at it before. I knew Caspian's door was on the opposite side of the hallway and Bane's was next to mine. Kai and Angel were upstairs past the kitchen.

That left one room unclaimed.

Before, I'd been terrified of that door, but now... now the world felt larger.

Someone else knew about Logan. It changed everything.

I padded down the hallway toward his door, unsure of why. I just had to see it for myself.

I tried the doorknob, and it creaked open.

My heart was in my throat as I peered inside. What would it be like?

This was the room he'd returned to every night he'd visited me. The world he'd kept from me. I don't know why it mattered that I see it, but it did.

I flicked on the lights and the space flooded with a warm glow.

Whisky and coco. The scent was frighteningly strong and absolutely unavoidable. It sent a shiver down my spine, such recent nightmares whispering in my ears.

.   .   .

"How can I take you back to them?" Logan asked. "They deserve better than an omega who can't satisfy. Who can't even make this alpha want you?"

"I don't... understand."

"I can't help you. You're broken, Havoc."

"Let me try."

What had Bane said? Experiments?

At first, I thought I was insane. I believed every word Logan said. I did all he asked, even when it hurt. I was locked up since the moment he left, trapped in that room alone.

"You can't lock me in here."

"You belong to the Mandela pack; Logan ordered you to be kept here."

"I'm not theirs."

"That bite on your neck says differently, girl."

While I was stuck there for months, this was where Logan had returned after every visit. His room was huge, with a few steps leading to a grand bed. One wall was taken up by a long desk, with modern lamps. Couches sprawled before a TV, similar to my room, and a glass window to a grand balcony stretched across the whole of one wall.

I wandered the room, haunted by the memory of him. A laptop sat closed on his desk. Beside it was an empty mug of coffee. The others, they hadn't been in here yet by the looks of it.

I stood at the corner of his bed, resting my head against his bedpost.

He'd come back here, surrounded by his pack mates while I lay curled up, alone and trapped...

Over time at Gavin's, I'd come to realise I was nothing more than a game, one he enjoyed changing... raising the bar, watching me struggle to meet impossible asks.

I shut my eyes, the scents overwhelming me again.

"Logan... I'll do anything."

"Then start by opening that needy little mouth of yours... Prove yourself to me, just one more time."

I made for the deck, needing fresh air. I tugged on the sliding door and blessedly, it came open.

I stumbled out, crossing it in an instant and clutching the railing, my breaths short and sharp. The winter air was bracing against my skin.

I stared out at the city below, suddenly less frightened of it now that I'd faced Logan's room. I twisted the charms on the bracelet around my wrists. It was the last thing in my small handbag. I'd never dared wear it around Logan, knowing he would crush anything I valued.

"You saved us, Havoc. Even if the others don't realise it."

I wasn't alone anymore. Bane got it. Bane *knew* who Logan was. And if he knew, then he could tell the others. It wouldn't be a gold pack omega's word against an alpha like Logan.

I took one more deep breath, a wild smile on my face as I turned back to Logan's room. I needed to return to mine and get that stupid emerald cushion and let it live with my pillows.

I needed to stop being afraid.

Then the blood drained from my face, the smile falling away in an instant. Caspian was seated on one of the low patio chairs against the wall. It was close enough to the sliding door that I hadn't seen him when I'd looked around.

Now I could see the broad balcony shared two doors, one from Logan's room and the other, Caspian's.

I was still as I stared back at him.

He had long dark hair that was tied up, strands of it coming loose to sweep across his sharp pale features. There was a scar across his cheek and black tattoos fought their way up his neck to the edge of his jawline.

He looked rough around the edges with all the tattoos and piercings, but the clothes he was wearing didn't match.

He was wearing a pair of baggy black trousers and a dark silken robe that was much too thin for this cold. Despite that, he let it hang open across his bare chest, revealing the tattoos and muscles beneath. There was a stub of a cigarette between his fingers, but it looked long dead.

He was obscenely attractive. They all were. Since they were my mates, I didn't really have a choice on that interpretation.

Unlike Kai, who had an outright rogue look, Caspian's roughness showed through in glimpses as if designed to surprise. It was a flash of his eyebrow piercing through styled hair, a scar escaping the skin beneath his Rolex, or tattoos peeking from an expensive, silken robe. It was all designed to remind on occasion that something else lurked beneath the surface.

His beetle black eyes were colder than the air that misted before his mouth.

"Bane told you the news, and you came to the most obvious place to celebrate," he murmured.

"I'm not—"

"Logan's pad?" Caspian asked, his eyebrow rising, the metal bar through it glinting. "You are one sick little bitch, aren't you? What happened to wanting to be dropped off at the police station—"

"I *do* want that." But even now the words felt wrong on my tongue, as if Bane had just offered me another lease on life. Looking at the hatred in Caspian's eyes, I realised how stupid that was.

My eyes darted to the balcony door and his gaze followed before flicking back to me. I could see the dare in that look. Then he stood, dead cigarette hanging loosely between two fingers as he stepped up.

All of my instincts told me to run. I couldn't—even if I wanted, he could catch me and there was something dangerous in his eyes.

He was taller than me—they all were. They didn't need Bane's height to dwarf my five-foot four frame, and right now, Caspian was taking full advantage of that as he leered down at me, much too close for comfort.

I didn't take the step back I desperately wanted to. I could feel the balcony railings brushing my clothing. I had about half an inch, if that.

"What do you want?" I asked, holding my voice steady.

Caspian said nothing, and I glanced around, my eyes sliding to the open deck door behind him.

"What could I possibly want?"

I fixed my eyes back on him, steeling myself. "I'm guessing if I don't tell you why I killed Logan, you'll throw me off the side or something?"

"Kai did that once, you know?"

I stared at him. "He... threw someone off the side?"

"Some prick that messed with my sister. Well... that's how the story goes anyway—that it was Kai."

The implication hung like a sharp hook in the air between us.

"That's what Kai does. He takes the fall for the rest of us. He's larger than life, next to him the rest of us...? We become invisible."

I balled and un-balled my fists, each breath grounding me. I could survive this, like I'd survived everything else.

The bite on my neck ached.

I couldn't sleep properly. I needed Logan. I didn't understand what was wrong with me.

A week had passed. I was in pain constantly, and every night it got worse. The bond—the one I'd accepted, that I'd chosen, it was incomplete. But Logan didn't want me. He wouldn't lay with me.

Every night I slept curled up, clutching my stomach, feeling like a piece of my soul had been carved out.

"Please. Tell me how to be what you need," I begged when he visited.

And the next day, when he came, he brought in another omega. "You want to learn how to make me want you? Watch them."

That was when I began to fragment. Every second, the bond on my neck was on fire...

Caspian cocked his head. "I don't care *why* you did it."

His accent, like Kai's, marked him from the streets.

"Tell me what you want or let me go."

His eyes rested on the city below us. "I think I just want you gone."

"I didn't choose to be here." I hated how he was so relaxed and casual while I was pressed up against the cold railing.

He smiled, chewing on his lip. "According to my brothers, best option is to bond you."

"They—" I had to clear my throat. "They said that?"

"We don't get another mate. Not unless..." He trailed off deliberately.

I knew the blood drained from my face. They wouldn't get another mate unless I was dead.

He quirked a half smile as he watched me come to that conclusion. His hand lifted, knuckle grazing my cheek before I could pull away. I clamped down on the flutter of agony.

"Why does touching you feel so fucking good?" he asked. "As if you're designed to ruin us... And it's not the mate bond. None like I've ever heard of." He drew away before pain peaked, his eyes calculating as I tried to regulate my breathing. "If I didn't know better..." he mused. His finger brushed my cheek, and I bit back another whine of pain. "I'd say it hurt you."

My heart rate picked up in panic as he said that. A mirror of my past.

"Make it stop." I begged Logan. I was on my knees before him as he lounged at the table in my room.

"You want me to fuck you when I don't want to?" he asked, amused.

My throat was closing up. I tried so hard when he visited. I dressed up as best as I knew how, desperate to be just like the omegas he brought in.

He took my chin in his grip and I winced as another, stronger prickle of pain shot through my skin. I blinked, unsure of what had just happened. It was like the pain I had when I watched him with other omegas, but sharper, more potent.

"What was that?" he asked, curious.

"N-nothing," I stammered. I couldn't afford anything getting between us. He brushed a finger down my arm, and I flinched.

"My touch causes you pain?" There was a sparkle in his eyes as I stared up at him. I grabbed a hold of that.

"Y-yes," I said. "B-but... I like it."

· · ·

I almost cracked a tooth with the clench of my jaw.

Caspian was waiting, the threat clear in the air. Then he grabbed my arms and forced me to turn so I was looking out at the city beyond.

"See that obscene gargoyle halfway down?" I flinched as his touch found my chin and directed me to follow his gaze. I found it in the dark, but from this distance it was hard to make out the details. "It's missing a horn. The guys back snapped on that halfway down—well... That's what Kai told me, anyway."

Caspian held me tight as my chest heaved. He was crushing me against the railing. "But I always thought it would be better with neither horn at this point, you know? Balance it out. What do you think?"

"Tell me what you want." My teeth were gritted, pain threatening to overwhelm.

He didn't let me go, and I could feel the burn of his touch against my skin, knowing that it must be affecting him too.

"You are too good," he breathed. "It's unnatural how much you can fuck with our heads." Through his touch I could feel the tug, knew that my scent was thick in the air, pain and desperation all at once.

My own mind was getting hazy with desire, bolstered by the shooting agony of his touch.

This was so screwed up.

I had to fight against the way my body wanted to shift back and lean against him.

Still, he hadn't moved, and my breaths were coming deeper. I wouldn't give myself away, not with a sound or a movement. Nothing.

"What do you want?" I asked again through gritted teeth.

"They're going to do what they need to, to survive. But you won't fuck with their minds, you won't twist them up and make this worse than it is."

"I'm... not—I don't want their stupid bond—" His fingers dug into my chin painfully, cutting me off.

His touch traced my neck, slipping beneath the choker.

"What are you hiding under there, Havoc?" he asked. "The bite of another alpha? Is that what you're so afraid of showing us?"

My breath caught in my throat. *That's what he thought?*

"Is that why you killed him? Why you tell us all you want is to be free? That you're happy without the bond."

"It's... not like that."

"You took him from me..." he breathed. "Will this tell me what matters to you, so I can take it, too?" He traced beneath the necklace, searching for the scar. And he'd find it—but it wouldn't be what he thought.

"Stop it!" I grabbed his hand.

He loosed a breath of a laugh, fingers blessedly releasing my neck right before reaching Logan's bite. Instead, he took my hand, grip clamping down on my bracelet.

"Wait—" But saying that was a mistake. In a flash, his grip bit down on my bracelet, and with a painful tug, he snapped it from my wrist.

"No, no just—" I cut off as he held it far past the balcony railings. I tried to tug his arm back, but it was like fighting against stone.

The silver glinted in the warm light of the city below us. Chains and charms. Each one my father had brought back from his travels for me. Each was precious.

"Please don't." My voice was pathetic as I tried to reach for it.

Then I went rigid against him as his teeth brushed my neck, just below the choker. My breath caught and I couldn't speak. I knew it would come out as a whine and I wouldn't give him that, even if my scent was thick in the air.

He drew back just slightly, and I found my voice, my eyes fixed on the glinting bracelet desperately.

"Just... send me back to the police. I killed Logan. The system will deal with me fairly."

"Fairly?" he asked. "The system gave you to us. That means we choose. So, if I bit you in right now, would you consider that... fair?"

His breath brushed down my throat and then I felt the press of his teeth along my lower neck and out to my shoulder.

I gripped the icy railing with all of my might to keep my wits.

Danger.

He was threatening a dark bond right now. The thought was a dousing of cold water on my flushed brain.

"Is that a yes?" he asked.

I tried to move, to duck forward so his teeth weren't brushing my skin, but he dragged me back and I felt more pressure against my flesh.

A whine escaped my chest, low and desperate and I could do nothing to stop it. "It's not—"

"Shh. Shh. Shh." Caspian straightened, blessedly removing his teeth from my skin as he clamped a hand over my mouth. He dragged me back, crushing me against his chest. I was pinned between him and the balcony railing and all I could see were the lights of the city in the cold winter night.

"I won't do it today," he breathed in my ear. "But you will stop fucking around with my brothers. You won't talk to them unless they speak to you, you won't go creeping around our house at night and taking them by surprise and you won't let them touch you—no *matter* what. Do you understand?"

I couldn't move, but the bracelet slipped in his grip, threatening to drop. I nodded desperately, but the truth was, I barely comprehended his words.

He had me all wrong, but it didn't matter. I had to get free of his touch. He shifted, hand dropping from my mouth, and then I felt a slight pressure as he nipped my ear. I cracked, a needy little gasp escaping my throat. He ignored it.

"I want to hear you say it." He tilted my head, looking up at him. He was perfectly intent and controlled while I was practically panting.

I was so pathetic.

"I u-understand," I stammered.

"Good girl." He leaned down and pressed a kiss to my cheek.

Fuck. *Fuck,* I just needed this to be over. I reached for the bracelet. I'd done what he wanted—but then his fist opened, and the bracelet fell.

"No—*no!*" I scrambled uselessly after it, my heart pounding in my ears, gripping the railing as I bent over, watching the flash of silver vanish into darkness. I choked a sob, my throat closing up.

I could barely hear the words he spoke next. "Go on then little omega. Go back to your room and *don't* come out."

Caspian.

We were all so screwed.

Havoc was the most potent fucking omega I'd ever come across. More than I'd ever heard of, even with mates.

I waited until she disappeared from Logan's suite before I finally gathered the strength to move. It was pure agony forcing myself back to my room.

Each step took me away from her.

The images in my head were intrusive, they had been since the moment I touched her. When I'd crushed her against the balcony railing, I'd felt her sweet ass grind against me.

Fuck.

That sound she'd made when I'd pressed my teeth to her flesh —when I'd nipped her ear.

Why had I done that?

I groaned, ripping off my clothes as I turned the shower on.

Pure alpha instinct.

I could see in her confusion that she hadn't realised how damned close I was to cracking.

When I'd stepped back it had taken everything I had not to reach out and squeeze those perfect round ass cheeks.

Who picked leggings like that?

Angel.

Fucking Angel getting the room ready for our omega. Well, here she was, devastating us all.

I'd dreamed of meeting our omega one day. I'd dreamed of it for different reasons than the others, even if that made me a bad pack mate.

I wanted Angel better—of course I did. But I didn't have what Angel and Kai had together. I'd been alone since the day Riley died. The idea of an omega... of... well, romance. As stupid and unlike me that had been, I had dreamed of it anyway, like the fucking idiot I was.

I was a Harpy Alpha, born on the streets. It was enough that me and Kai had got out, life was never giving me more than that.

I'd dreamed of love, and she'd shown up and killed Logan. The man who saved me in the first place...

I needed to wash her scent off me—it was stuck since I'd brushed the scent glands on her neck, which was as good as marking myself. God, she'd melted against me at that touch. The alpha in me didn't want to wash it off, but I turned the water to hot.

And *absolutely*, under no circumstances whatsoever, would I think about her while I showered.

As hot water ran down my skin, I pressed my forehead into the tiled wall.

I absolutely wouldn't think about ripping off that loose top and pinning her against the glass of the balcony so I could fuck her brutally while the others might see.

A growl rose in my throat.

I absolutely would not think about the sounds she would make as her perfect body took me all the way to the knot. I *absolutely* would not think about those perfect lips around my length, as she licked me clean and her golden doe eyes stared up at me from where she knelt.

I groaned, one hand planted on the shower wall, the other gripping the shaft of my cock as I came.

Alone.

Into the hot steam of the shower.

We were all so fucking screwed.

TEN

Angel

Kai was pissed.

He wouldn't say it, but he was fuming.

"Don't you have work?" He asked as I tugged off my shirt and pulled on some silk pyjama pants.

"The firm gave me a few weeks," I said. He knew that.

When I did work, I preferred the evenings, finding it easier to focus when the world was winding down around me. My office was attached to our room, the window facing across the city. I loved to watch the city lights slowly flicker on until there was nothing but lights of gold and red and blue among the ocean of darkness.

I consulted for a law firm on and off, mostly business cases from the expertise my family had left me. I didn't need to; my inheritance was incomprehensible and almost untouched. I didn't have to work a day in my life—to be honest, neither did the others, since I'd never leave my pack wanting for money.

We worked because it was good for us.

One thing I did feel a guilty relief over, though... Logan wouldn't be dragging Caspian into any shady business shit ever again. My family money was clean. Well, as clean as it got with that many zeros involved.

Of course, I knew Cass could handle himself, in fact Logan had preferred him to nearly any guy he had on retainer, but I still hated it. Hated it more whenever Kai had gotten in the mix.

Kai was always full of buzzing energy for weeks after, high from whatever sick crap Logan wanted of him. Never was my connection with him weaker than it was in those times. It wasn't true happiness Kai brought back from those trips; it was an addiction he should stay far, far away from.

He became detached, his discernment of social boundaries almost non-existent. Every night he'd have nightmares.

No. It was good that neither of them would be dragged into it again.

Caspian could build the digital art business he tinkered around with. I knew that made him feel something... healthy. Not just filling a void his stupid family had handed to him. Real, actual fulfilment.

That's what we needed. Miserable fucking bastards the lot of us were, without some direction.

Logan was the most driven of us, even if that came with a slightly... daring streak. But now Logan was gone, I needed to look elsewhere.

I settled down next to Kai in bed. He wasn't curled up watching Grand Prix reruns like he had done the last few months. The commentators had become something of white noise in the background of our bedroom. It did every time anything awful happened.

I grabbed the remote and turned on the TV. The channel was pre-set and the familiar sound of the monotone commentator and engines of cars zooming around the track filled the room.

If you ever want to ground him, just turn it on. That had been Caspian's advice. And he had been right. It soothed Kai every time. This time, however, Kai grabbed the remote from me and turned the TV off.

"Fuck you, Angel."

"What?" I leaned against the headboard, but he shot me a glare.

"You *know* what."

"Because I want her gone?"

Kai scrunched up his nose again and rolled away from me. He didn't say anything more, but then, he didn't need to.

"You know I'm not going anywhere." But I knew my words didn't land. I knew as well as him how important our bond was. Our relationship, sure, but the bond especially.

This bond gave him something he couldn't get anywhere else. I knew what he was feeling, sometimes before even he did. I could identify it when he couldn't, or when he couldn't voice it.

It wasn't a matter of maturity. Kai was... fragments of a person. Shattered and dragged back together by Caspian first, then me and the rest of the pack.

Volatile, unpredictable, borderline psychopathic if pushed. But this bond gave him the ability to connect in a way he couldn't any other way. It gave us the ability to step in when he couldn't, to drag him back from the edge of insanity.

And I was the most important part of that bond.

I sighed, climbing into bed beside him. I reached out to tug him toward me, but he pulled away.

"What about pack lead?" Kai asked.

I clenched my jaw. "Caspian is more than capable—"

Kai flipped toward me, glaring. "You're best for it. Cass knows it too—unless you're suddenly okay with him killing Havoc?" he challenged.

Ice crept up my spine at those words. "That's not going to happen."

"Why, because me and Bane will come around and we'll vote

her back to the cops?" He snorted, and then he slid from the bed completely, standing.

"Kai—" But I cut off as he turned, crossing the room and ripping the balcony door open. I was met by the blast of icy wind before it closed.

Again, with the borderline insanity. He was wearing nothing but sweatpants, and it was the middle of winter. He strode to the edge of the balcony and out of sight, which was enough indication that he didn't want to talk.

I let out a breath. I knew it hurt him, but I believed my vote was for the best.

I wanted what Kai wanted too—so desperately. But I knew Havoc would break us all.

Kai

I wanted Angel to be mine forever.

My mind was a fucking wasteland, and the bond bridged all the gaps I couldn't see. I had blind spots, everywhere, that's what the world kept telling me I had, but they were patched with the pack bond.

Our balconies were all connected—or close enough. I hauled myself over the stone railings that separated them and hopped the short gap to the lounge deck before reaching Caspian and Logan's.

Caspian's curtain was closed and inside I could hear the shower running.

I wanted to be angry at him for his decision today, but it was impossible to ever really be angry at Cass. I'd known him too long. He was his own flavour of important to me, different than Angel. We'd never been sexual, since Cass was cursed with *way* more limited tastes when it came to sex—the poor fucker.

But he was closer to me than blood. He'd been there since the *before* and had known me when I was different. Even then, he'd taken care of me, made himself beautiful for me. He was a man of black and white. Pale skin contrasted by black tattoos. Not a single hint of colour. Cass designed every single piece of art on his skin so that it was as striking to me as it was to the rest of the world.

I passed by the patio table and chairs and the ash tray filled with stubs, then hopped over to Bane's deck—the one he shared with the nest—which was now Havoc's room.

Bane was different since Logan died. His aura had shifted. It had always been strong, but now it was less... contained. It was wild and intrusive and... well... kind of attractive, actually.

I was a sucker for colour, and auras—they were bright when the rest of the world was black and white.

Bane's aura was beautifully bright.

Not that Angel was any less beautiful with a dull aura. Angel was in his own box. Beautiful for so much more than his piercing eyes and devastating jaw and athletic physique.

Even when he was being a fucking idiot.

I lingered on Bane's side of the deck, peering into the room, but his curtains were firmly closed.

Sighing, I moved on to the other side of the deck, the one with pooling warm light. Excellent. The curtains were only half closed.

She was awake.

Not just awake. My bright little Havoc was bustling around her bed, fixing up pillows and blankets. I watched closely, entranced by her. The leggings she was wearing were fatal and skin-tight around the round curves of her waist. Her hoodie was black and baggy, but when she'd reach over the bed, I got a stunning image of the rich olive skin of her tight little waist and the slight gap between her thighs.

I rested against the wall, the cold seeping bone deep. It was bracing in the best of ways. The sheer curtains were bunched, obscuring me from view—though if she looked carefully, she'd see me.

I wasn't worried about that. If she did, her reaction would be educational.

She took a step away from the bed, cocking her head slightly. She tucked her hair behind her ear. An anxious tick, had to be— there were already two thin braids curving around her ear, keeping her hair back.

She chewed on her lip as she examined the bed. The hard edge of her teeth squeezing blood from the plush pink flesh. I was fixated on it.

I'd had my fair share of women. Sharing being a key word when it came to me and Caspian back before the pack. Sharing was a good bet for me. Caspian and I? We liked similar things in bed, but he was better able to identify women who were into it. It had been a good system for me, since there was a lot of inconvenient fallout for being wrong about shit like that.

That was before I met Angel. Love within a pack was unbeatable, and no one had caught my eye after—woman or man. But Havoc... she got my blood hot. And she blazed as bright and colourful as a sunset. Well. I would have to assume, since for me, sunsets looked like a bog in the sky.

Angel's rejection of her still stung. She was the fix for everything. Why were we against her again?

Right.

Logan.

Shit.

Could we just... get past it? How many people had *I* killed? We didn't get all upset about that.

Plus, she was hot—and definitely not a threat. She'd *started* by threatening us, but I could recognise posture as easily as I could recognise true evil. A real threat, it was quiet. It hid. It was why people who crossed our pack never won. Because I was the loud one, the one that drew eyes and set people on edge.

And they never guessed for one second that I was the one on a leash. I wasn't stupid. I knew what the others thought. If I so much as drifted my fingers toward my dagger my pack freaked like I was about to crack.

Last time we'd gone on a *team building trip*—as Logan had loved to call them—Caspian had strung up a guy and gutted him without blinking. Logan had bought him a beer. I know Logan would have loosened my leash if it wasn't for Caspian and Angel.

Angel found all of that sort of shit distasteful.

Then there was Bane... he was quiet and silent and let us do the work, but here and there I saw a darkness in him that outstripped even Caspian. One day, I wanted to know what that looked like uncaged.

No.

I knew darkness.

Havoc was lost. She wasn't darkness.

Whatever happened between her and Logan—it was probably fair game. A bad bet on his part, that was my guess.

Whatever.

Fuck Logan anyway. He played high risk; it was bound to catch up with him eventually. Honestly. He was lucky. I could only hope when my death caught up to me, it had an ass as perfect as Havoc's.

I went back to watching her work. She was now fetching couch cushions and rearranging them on the bed.

Wait... I straightened.

She was nesting? It was unmistakable. Not just by the actions, but now I was focused, I realised how soothing it was for the alpha in me to watch. I was on the edge of loosing a purr, my aura lighting.

But *nesting* meant her heat was near.

"Shit..." I let out a breath.

Havoc in *heat*?

In our house?

My mind went wild. Omegas in heat were on another level. Good thing there were four of us—*if* she'd have us—I shoved that thought away. She would. Of course she would. We were her mates. All this Logan crap was bound to blow over.

Angel wouldn't be able to say no. Cass—well Cass was a stubborn twit on the best of days, but even so...

Fuck...

After the vote I was incapable of dark bonding her in. The vote was two of four, not a majority, which meant it tied my hands...

But none of that mattered. Bites upon an omega in heat were the strongest, and for Angel, I needed as strong as we could get. It meant I had a deadline. I just had to change Angel or Cass's mind before she went into heat.

Structure.

I sighed in satisfaction. My job was straightforward. Get the information Angel needed before her heat.

I watched her until I couldn't feel my hands for the cold, taking in every one of her movements.

I knew I couldn't stay out all night. Dying wouldn't be particularly helpful, not if I ever wanted this dream fuck with her and the others...

She changed into oversized pyjamas—giving me a wonderful view of her perfect little figure in lace as she did. The pyjamas were a pretty colour that suited her, but since the whole blood red debacle I wasn't confident naming it.

Her body was untouched. No tattoos, piercings or scars. Unusual where I came from, not the type me and Caspian would have gone for, but on her, it suited. A blank canvas. If any mark went on that smooth skin, it would be ours.

Her fingers drifted to the black choker around her neck. None of us had missed that particular middle finger to us all. I smiled appreciatively.

She was stuck in a house with a pack of predators who she could only surmise wanted to chain or kill her, and she'd still taken the time to add in an extra fuck you.

Her fingers lingered there a little too long, and it pushed me into daydreams. Of slicing that necklace off and tilting her chin up so her slender neck was open to me.

The longer she paused, fingers pressed against the necklace, the more my thoughts shifted.

It... meant more to her.

More meant secrets... Secrets she didn't want us to know...

Finally, her fingers dropped, and she climbed into bed. It didn't take long before I could see the slow rise and fall of her chest.

My mind began to spin plans.

I could fix everything, with her, with Angel. Sure, she'd hate me for a while, but it would blow over.

I checked my phone for the weather for the day ahead.

Excellent.

Today would be a perfect day to get her to spill all her dark little secrets.

ELEVEN

Havoc

I woke up extra early so I could deconstruct the nest I'd built.

I was too warm, my body feeling like a small radiator. I tried not to think about that as I kicked off the pyjama trousers to cool off and rolled out of bed. It was dangerous to build a nest at all, but my instincts were screaming and there was no way I'd get sleep without it. I couldn't let the others see. They couldn't find out I was close to my heat.

Tearing down my nest was probably one of the most painful things I'd ever done. By the time I removed the last of the cushions, I was fighting back tears, my breaths coming heavy from my chest. But I forced myself back to bed to lay down. Tired as I still was, I managed to grab a few more restless hours of sleep.

I was woken violently to a rough hand over my mouth. Pain spiked at the contact as something pressed over my eyes.

I could see nothing but blackness as I was dragged up, and then I felt a body press against my back. Maple and cinders.

Kai.

For an insane moment I felt a wave of relief. And then the hand over my mouth released, and something was being dragged there instead, a piece of fabric. I tried to spit it out, but the gag was secured within seconds and desperate low sounds tore from my chest.

"The others are out," Kai's voice whispered in my ear. "They need answers, little Havoc. Will you give them to me?"

My breathing was coming in ragged gasps, his skin was still on mine, and I hadn't had relief from that pain.

What would he do?

He waited but didn't move.

When he spoke next, his voice was the faintest breath. "Last chance. Give me a nod or we do it my favourite way."

My throat was bone dry, my chest tight, but I didn't move.

I knew this had been coming. I'd known they would hate me since the moment I'd pulled that trigger.

I just had to survive the day.

He dragged me to the edge of the bed, and before I could let loose a wail of panic, he had me slung over his shoulder.

I *could* survive this.

It wouldn't last long.

I thought he had taken me out to the deck. The winter air pricked my skin, and there was marble beneath my shins where I knelt on bare legs. My hands were bound behind my back. Kai had said nothing more before he'd left.

I tried to collect myself. If he didn't want me to die, he couldn't leave me out here. He'd said he wanted answers. Not that he wanted me dead.

Still, it was awful in the cold and dark. Too many freezing minutes passed, and panicked voices began to whisper foreboding... *What if he doesn't come back?*

I fought my tears, never wanting to give him that. I wouldn't give him anything.

Kai

Havoc wasn't in any real danger.

That boundary was one I couldn't cross. I was playing with smoke and mirrors, even if the real thing called to me. It had been a long time though, and perhaps I had underestimated its allure.

Find the beauty in the world—that was what Angel wanted of me. But in *that* place, I could drag the world to me. There had been a time it was the only way I'd found connection. Until Angel.

He had been hurting, too, and he'd opened up to me—trusted *me* when he trusted no one else.

Curiously, I stood outside beside Havoc, leaning against the cool stone railings.

The cold burned my skin like it burned hers.

It was unusual. I always allowed myself comfort while they suffered. If they were out in the cold, I was inside, comfortable and warm. Torture was painful in many ways, and one was the feeling of hopelessness; of knowing you were alone against the impossible. It was you, and darkness, and pain, and knowing no one was coming. That was the real pain.

But I didn't... *want* to give that part to Havoc. I couldn't leave her like this, her breathing short and sharp, her body tense.

In fact, I didn't *like* the idea of her pain at all. Which was as curious as it was disturbing because I simply couldn't afford thoughts like that.

Mate or not, I'd just met her. Loving Angel and the pack, it was frightening enough. I'd seen the darkest underbelly of the world. I'd seen how fragile we were. Love was a dangerous gamble, one made over and over, for every second that passed.

A black kit was at my feet; one I shouldn't touch. I'd made

Angel promises about that, but I had to pull myself together. I was here to save his aura—to keep him in the pack. So, I reached down and opened it.

When my gaze fell on the things within, my mind began to shift. The items within the bag stared back at me, threatening to seize hold of me and sweep me away...

I couldn't use them.

I wasn't allowed.

... But I could bring them out, *right?* Just to prove I still had the strength. Not just to resist them, but to resist her. She was a bundle of omega hormones and fear, making demands of the alpha within me to protect her.

Focus.

If she saw what was in this bag, it would push her off the side so much quicker... That would be good, right? Angel would be saved, and her suffering would end.

I blinked.

I didn't *care* about her suffering. That *wasn't* what this was about. I felt like I was in the centre of two storms, each trying to rip me in a different direction.

The bag of tools at my feet.

The shivering omega at my side.

But I was here for Angel. That was all.

I waited.

The fear. The unknown. It would get to her soon enough.

Sure enough, after the minutes ticked by low whines began to sound deep in her chest. I ignored the way they hit me.

I inhaled her scent. Rainfall and firewood. Again, it seemed to touch my soul, trying to get me to surface. Instead, I pushed myself deeper into the self-destructive part of me. The black bag and its contents were waiting... I took a breath, trying to dispel their calling.

The choker around her neck... I'd seen her touching it last

night. Could it be enough...?

Well. First let's see if she was done already. It was possible. For some, the unknown was worse than anything I could promise.

I reached out to tug off the gag, and she winced at my touch. She did that every time. At first, I thought it was disgust but... I paused, narrowing my eyes. She couldn't see me. She couldn't anticipate my touch right now.

Once again, I brushed my finger along her cheek.

She jumped away, a low moan breaking from her chest.

Fear. That was natural right now, but... something more. It was physical. It was real—not in her head. She felt pain every time I touched her?

My brows came down, but as I was about to withdraw my finger, the touch changed. It was like a shot of lightning in my veins. It sang to me. I'd not clocked it before, writing it off as some scent matching crap. But it was more than that.

Careful not to touch her skin, I removed the gag.

"*Fuck* you!" she spat.

A genuine smile cracked my mask. "Not done?" I asked.

"No, you psychopathic piece of *shit*!"

Her chest was heaving, lips parted as she panted, plump and red and perfect. She was perfect. All fire and colour. I leaned close, whispering in her ear. "Are you trying to turn me on, sunset?"

A snarl of rage loosed from her chest, and it *did* things to me. Well... this *was* a new experience.

Torture and lust?

I couldn't help the flashes of desire, especially with her wrists bound like that... I shoved the notion away. I'd have her begging for me one day. A day far from now, given what I was currently up to, but I had Angel to taunt until then.

"Alright my stubborn little omega." With that, I tied the gag back around her mouth.

TWELVE

Havoc

When he returned the gag, I began to panic. It had been forever already. How long could he leave me out here?

I tried to scream at him from beneath the gag, but got nothing in return. He was gone already, I was sure. But then... when he'd removed my blindfold, he'd looked just as cold as me. Topless, with nothing but a pair of sweatpants, and goosebumps lit on his skin.

Was he still out here with me? I didn't know why I hoped he was, why the thought settled my heart. His scent, maple and cinders was faint in the air, but it might well be from the mask and blindfold.

As the silence stretched on, my mind began to fray.

He could do this forever, but I could never give him what he wanted. For the first time in my life, I sunk into memories as a solace. Peace. Safety.

A promise that no matter what Kai did to me here, it was nothing to what might be waiting for me. A place I would never return to.

. . .

I was on Logan's lap, my back against his body as his hands rested on my hips. They would occasionally slide beneath my shirt, running across my stomach. Every time, pain would flood my body and I would try to hold it together and not show him how much it hurt.

He continued his conversation with Eli as if I didn't exist. Eli was the dark-haired alpha friend that came with him every visit. He was the one who held me in place while Logan fucked other omegas.

I was starting to realise it was a game for Logan. He was trying to make me jump, being as unpredictable as possible with the way his fingers brushed my skin. But he was also into it. I could feel his hardness beneath me. I tried not to focus on how twisted that was.

"Too much for you, little Havoc?" he breathed in my ear when my grip balled at my dress at another touch.

I shook my head, forcing a smile onto my face. I could feel Eli's gaze on me too.

It was okay. I knew this was the wounded princess bond. We'd have sex once and then it would be fixed. The pain would go away and then he'd change. He'd want me properly once the bond was in place. How could he not?

"Wriggling around like that, you've almost convinced me."

I peered up at him, trying to stifle the desperate hope on my expression. "What do you want me to do?"

Logan contemplated. "Kiss him."

"What?" I turned to glance at Eli. They chatted business late into the night.

"I rather enjoy watching," Logan said with a smile. "I want to see you kiss Eli."

"I..." My cheeks burned as I glanced up to Eli, who's dark eyes were fixed on me with vague curiosity.

"Didn't you say you wanted to become my dreams?" Logan asked.

I leaned close to him, running a hand up his chest like those more experienced omegas did. "I want you."

Logan chuckled darkly, leaning close. "Then go and stick your tongue down his throat."

"No."

"No?" Logan asked.

"I don't want to kiss him." My voice shook. I couldn't take this sort of humiliation. It was too far. And my pack... What if they found out after I met them? What if it meant they didn't want me?

Logan's touch made me jump, firmer this time.

"Well... We can't have you getting me so heated and do nothing about it."

I said nothing, waiting. Then he was lifting me from his lap and standing beside me. He slipped a hand around my waist and before I knew what was happening, he was leading me toward the bed.

My stomach did a flip and my breathing picked up.

Was this all it took?

Telling him no? Was he one of those complicated men omegas chatted about behind the bar sometimes, the ones who wanted to be challenged?

He slid onto the bed, beckoning me and I dropped to the sheets beside him, my breath caught in my throat.

He reached up, taking my chin and leaning close. He didn't kiss me on the lips, but instead dropped down to the bite on my neck. I contained my shiver as the prickle of pain continued with each second.

His teeth bit down again, harder, hard enough that I let out a whimper. He let out a groan. "God, I need release, sweet Havoc."

My touch jumped to his shirt, and I dragged myself close. Despite the pain, I could cry with relief. It was all going to be over...

It had to end soon. How long had I been out here?

By now I was sure he wasn't still waiting with me. No one would suffer this if they didn't need to. Icy air was seeping into my bones when rough hands dragged me up, and my wrists were attached to something high, leaving me to stand on weak legs. I sagged against the bonds when he let me go.

Suddenly, blessed light blinded me as the blindfold was removed.

Kai stood before me, messy white hair fluttering in the breeze, and by the goosebumps still on his skin, I realised he *had* been out here the whole time. Was he trying to prove something to me?

He was mad. He was looking at me curiously, and I noticed he was wearing a pair of black gloves, which explain why his touch hadn't hurt.

Now I was standing, I could see him properly. I'd never seen him like this before, never noticed the way his tattoos tangled with rough bumps on his skin. They were scars that littered his entire body.

"Ready to talk?"

I stared at him. Slowly, *painfully*, I shook my head. It still wasn't a choice.

He raised his eyebrows as he stepped back, and I noticed for the first time that there was a long strip of black cloth laid across the glass top table before me. Upon it were objects that shook me to my core.

A knife.

A lighter and a metal rod.

Corded rope.

A baton-like device with two metal prongs.

A coiled black... thing that looked frighteningly like a whip.

I jumped as his fingers wove through my hair and he dragged me straight, stepping up close, much too close. Then he leaned behind me and unhooked something. I tried to struggle back to no avail. Suddenly, one of my hands was free. The pain his contact brought was almost non-existent, the cold drowning it out completely.

Kai smiled as he stared down at me. Then he dragged my hand up to trace a long ridge on his skin, one that might be hidden by the twists of tattoo along his flesh.

He held my hands against his chest, moving down slowly and I felt ridge after ridge of scars.

"If you're going to walk away with marks, you might as well choose what kind."

I stared at him, horrified as I realised what he was saying.

He *was* insane, I could see that, but he was completely serious about his threat. He wasn't speaking of things he didn't understand. Each one of the scars beneath my fingers matched the weapons on the table.

Why was he letting me see them? Wasn't he afraid of his scars like I was afraid of mine?

He waited for such a long time as tears flooded my cheeks.

Finally, he reached back, and I felt the gag loosen and then fall. I let out a choked breath of relief, then opened my mouth, ready to admit everything that had happened with Logan. But my voice wouldn't come.

Instead, I just stared at him, tears blurring his features.

"Still nothing?" he asked.

"I can't!" I tried, once more, to drown my terror with rage.

Logan shifted further onto the bed, drawing over me, his hands wandering.

What I'd told him about the pain, it was partly true: I did feel surges of pleasure with every one of his possessive touches. A needy moan escaped my lips.

This was it.

How soon before I met the others? My pack. My mates.

Then Logan was straightening, dragging me to my knees as he pressed my fingers to his crotch where I felt him.

"You'll take care of me?" he asked. I nodded as he undid the button to his jeans.

Next thing I was being forced lower until I had to catch myself with my free hand. His fingers wound through my hair.

Sickness coiled in my stomach as I realised what he wanted. His crotch was right before my face.

The mark on my neck burned, demanding what he wouldn't give. He'd offered the princess bond. I'd accepted and he wouldn't... he wouldn't lay with me. I shoved away another burn of tears in my eyes.

He tilted my head up toward him until I was forced to look into his ice-blue pupils, so much colder than I'd thought when I first met him. "Show me you're worth a damn, sweet Havoc."

I couldn't move, bile burning my throat. He still had my hand pressed against his hardness.

I couldn't do this. He was toying with me.

"You know..." Logan let out a low laugh. "I rather think this whole establishment is losing its charm."

Cold panic slid through my veins as I held his eyes.

The threat was clear: he would leave me here, bitten into a half-finished bond.

What would happen?

It took me a long, long time to swallow my pride, and all the time Logan's eyes danced with malice.

Numbly, I fumbled with the button on his jeans, the world blurring in my vision. He halted me for just a moment, forcing me to look back at him.

"You're so beautiful when you cry, Havoc," Logan's voice sang in my head.

. . .

I couldn't go back there.

It wasn't a choice. This was nothing to what Logan had done, and if I told Kai, he could do it to me too. They all could.

He picked up the blade on the table, and I flinched, squeezing my eyes shut. Instead of pain, I felt its tip scrape down my cheek, not enough to break skin.

"We could start by cutting this off..." He murmured, and the knife dipped, catching on my necklace. The one I'd put on when I arrived. The one that covered the scar that Logan had given me.

What?

My heart smashed against my rib cage.

"Isn't it rude? Covering your neck around your alphas?"

I flinched away, gripped by a worse terror than before. "You're *not* my alphas."

He said nothing, and I felt the knife taut against the necklace.

"Wait!" My voice shook. Anything but that. My eyes even darted to the... *things* on the table, desperately trying to figure out what I might survive.

"Why shouldn't I?" Kai asked. He had a smile on his lips now, something victorious dancing in his eyes.

"You're just as sick as he told me you were," I hissed, desperately clutching at anything to stop him.

Kai paused, a flicker of surprise crossing his expression. "Who?"

I shook, knowing I was about to lose everything. Knowing there was nothing I could do about it. Venom rose in my throat at that knowledge. At how very wrong I'd been about them all.

"Logan... told me about you."

Kai leaned back, just the slightest bit, eyes darting between mine as a faint smile edged his lips. "And what did Logan have to say about me?"

Kai is lost. He carried the burden for everyone else far too long. Grew up penniless, ran with the Harpy packs.

"He said… they all pretend around you, but they know you're a nobody from the streets."

They broke him, hurt him for his powers. It made it difficult for him to love the way others love.

"Said you don't know what love looks like so you do the closest fucked up thing you can find."

But beneath it all, he cares so much. Just sometimes he needs to be shown how.

"But they all know the truth. That you're empty, you don't know what love means."

Kai stared down at me for an age, his face completely unreadable. "Do you believe him?" Kai asked. I felt the way my own expression twisted at that question.

"Yes."

He leaned close and breathed in my ear. "Then you aren't nearly scared enough, Havoc." The knife pressed against my neck, hooking under the necklace. I went still. "Now… what's under there that you don't want us to see?"

I bit back my sob.

My shame.

The worst moment of my life, immortalised in a scar. If he saw it, would he know what it was? Would he know who had given me that bite? Kai was a seer, could he see bonds as well as he could see auras?

My chest was heaving in terror. I blinked furiously as I did what I'd done a thousand times beneath Logan's torture.

"Don't you dare look away, sweet Havoc."

Hands held me in place while I shook. Logan drew the beautiful omega against him. It had become agony to watch, the burning bite on my neck spreading poison through my whole body.

"She has what you don't," Logan taunted. "What you never will."

So, I found a way to look, and not look.

Now, in the face of Kai, I tried to fade away into dreams.

I could do this like I had before. Only—

I was jarringly ripped from safety like a cruel punch to the gut.

My chest felt like it was caving in. Because when I'd tried to escape Logan's torture, I'd sunk into dreams of what my mates were like. I'd spun imaginings of what they'd do when they finally found me. Of them loving me and caring for me.

Except I was here.

I had everything I'd ever dreamed of, but Logan wasn't gone. He was the reason Kai had a knife to my neck.

I'd found my dream, and it was a nightmare. The thing I'd used for months to survive was just as bad as the torture I'd escaped.

My chest was tight, and my breaths were coming sharper as I felt the metal against my skin.

There was nowhere to go from here. This was it.

Tears flooded my cheeks. "All that time, I was alone..." I choked. "But you're nothing... like... I dreamed... you'd be."

Why was I saying those words? They were weakness. Damning weakness.

Only, the knife slid away.

"What?" he asked.

But it was too late. It was getting hard to breathe. My chest heaved in terror; my throat completely closed. I couldn't see through my tears, the world spinning. Adrenaline ripped through my system as I struggled for air desperately.

"What are you doing?" Kai's voice was rough, he was gripping my hair and tugging me upright. I cried out and he let me go. The world spun and blurred. Black spots erupted in my vision as I desperately gasped.

I was going to die. I could feel it.

Next thing I was being cut free. I was holding onto anything I could reach, fingers curled around his shirt, the other hand holding my own neck.

I tried to scramble back but hit the railings of the deck, still desperately trying to gasp breaths through a closed throat. I couldn't stop crying.

"Enough, alright." Kai snapped his fingers. "Havoc?" He sounded... different. He shook me roughly, and I was met by his piercing set of eyes, one red and one blank white. He was muttering something, but I couldn't process the words. "Fuck. How does Angel *do* this?" He shook me again. "Inhale. Exhale. Come on."

I was still clutching my own neck, unable to draw breath.

"Come on. *Fuck.*"

But was some stupid breathing exercise supposed to help? My throat was fucking closed, didn't he understand—?

"*Now* Havoc." He seized my chin and this time it was a command backed with alpha energy. I suddenly found myself fixated on his gaze.

"Inhale." Kai breathed in. "Exhale. Slowly."

He had changed completely. He wasn't cold at all, he was intent.

I didn't understand, but I tried to follow his instructions. He did it a few times, tugging my hands away from my throat and by some miracle my breaths started coming again, my airway feeling like it was easing open. He kept it up, holding my eyes with each breath until my throat was clear.

"I wasn't like you dreamed? Tell me what that means." Kai's voice was strange. He sounded... unnerved.

Then it all hit me at once. What he'd done. I broke, in that moment, as I looked into his eyes.

"I waited every night..." I tried to throw the words at him with hatred, but they just sounded as weak and pathetic as they were. *He* was all wrong. *He* wasn't supposed to hurt me... "Y-you were supposed... to save me."

THIRTEEN

Kai

"Y-you... were supposed... to save me."

"Who?" *Who* was she talking to?

I was all over the place right now. I'd never been so jarringly ripped back to myself as I had been when Havoc had begun having a panic attack. Which was stupid, because of course she had. I was literally torturing her, for fuck's sake.

But... it had been like a fist reaching into my soul and ripping me back to reality.

"You." Her eyes were on me. "B-Bane and Angel and C-C-Caspian... I waited..."

Us?

My world was a rigid structure of stone pillars. That made it easy to identify change. I was inflexible. I couldn't bend or adapt. Change came with destruction.

And those words of Havoc's, they were followed by a slow splitting crack trailing up my middle.

"We didn't know about you...?"

"You... should have." Her fierce eyes glistened. It was disarming.

"It's our fault?" I didn't understand, but I could *feel* her belief in it...

As Havoc's expression crumpled, the weak grip her fingers had on my shirt slipped. Then she shook her head. "No... It's my fault."

"Why can't you tell me?" My voice was soft, the question, genuine. She searched my gaze, disarmed for a moment.

A part of me still protested. Why was I being gentle? She'd never feel threatened after this. But then, maybe I'd lost that battle the moment I'd tried to help her get through her panic attack.

"The other pain..." she whispered. "It's worse..." She couldn't finish, but I felt it.

I knew.

Agony ripped me apart, tearing through me, and never once did it change one fact.

I could never agree.

If I did, Caspian would be taken. His life would be forfeit.

Agony split my body apart, over and over. And my mind fractured along with it, the pillar it held onto not enough to stop the edges from burning.

I could never give up Caspian.

The pain of that would last the rest of my life, knowing he suffered because of me...

It wasn't nobility or strength. It was just a choice. There was agony from both sides. I'd just picked one and not the other.

I remembered one last thought before it was all over. That the edges of me, the parts of my mind that burned so I could hold on... they would never heal.

. . .

"It could happen again if you tell me?" I asked. Whatever Havoc was protecting herself from, it wasn't over for her.

The last bastion of my mind fought to hold out. But there were two sides to the tracks of my life. I could take shots at anyone on the other side, and I would die for those on mine.

She wasn't weak or fragile, she hadn't held this information out of spite.

She was a survivor.

And she was frightened of something else, just the same as I had been all those years ago when I'd got the scars that marked my chest.

She nodded numbly.

"You think *we'd* be the ones to hurt you?" I winced as soon as the idiotic question was out of my mouth. I could see the terror in her eyes as her gaze darted to the table behind me.

I could still get her to talk with the tools back there. Enough years had passed for me to know that I would have broken eventually, too. It would have been impossible not to. The pain would have unbalanced in the end. The choice, made for me by reality. Simple fucking math. But even if it wasn't for the laws my brothers put in place—the ones banning me from ever using those instruments again—I didn't want to.

The last bastion crumbled. The realisation hit me like a tonne of bricks. I'd misread everything. We all had. I shut my eyes.

You were supposed to save me.

Those words lingered on my soul, more violating than they had a right to be. I... ached. Not physically... my heart felt... it felt broken. This was worse than the one time I thought Angel was leaving. Like it threatened to do now as his aura got weaker and weaker.

How absolutely unexpected. And thrilling. This was a bigger win than her secrets, which had been for my brothers anyway— though I'd admit a little more interest now she'd kept them.

Yet... looking into her shattered expression, I didn't feel like I'd won.

"We're done," I murmured. "I won't hurt you again." That promise settled the alpha in me, and it wasn't just for today.

Her lip quivered, glittering, golden eyes holding mine, as if she didn't know whether to believe me. I was learning quickly that I found gold utterly irresistible.

To my absolute shock, she just curled her arms around my neck and held on.

Was she... hugging me?

How completely unnatural. Yet, my hands slid around her, drawing her close as she buried her face against my shoulder. We stayed like that on the deck until I became much too aware of her shivers.

I didn't want to let her go, so I didn't.

Hugging me, I knew, was probably a trauma response... but I didn't care. I took her into her room and started running a bath in the huge tub. She needed to warm up.

She stared around, uncomprehending, then her eyes fell on the running water. "I don't... I'd rather a shower." Her voice was strangely blank.

I drained the bath. "You... want help?" I thought it better to offer her a choice in that particular part of the fixing.

She stared up at me for what felt like forever. She was still shaking, her fingers curled on the edge of the bathroom counter. I'd seen her strength today, and if she wanted to get through the shower alone, I wouldn't push that.

I'd push the rest of the shit. Like pizza and Grand Prix and warming her the fuck up, though.

She nodded, though she hadn't said anything. Her eyes were fixed on me, but... it was like she wasn't there. That look was a knife in my chest. All of a sudden, she was me, and I was Angel, watching someone fade away before my very eyes. Someone who was supposed to matter.

And I'd done that to her.

What had Angel done to get me back? Those times were a blur... but he was a comfort. He had always been a pillar for me. But then—he hadn't been the one to hurt me.

So, I ended up seated on the huge shower floor, with her tucked between my legs, facing me, still with her shirt on as I rubbed shampoo into her hair. Hot water streamed around us, and I was still wearing my black gloves so I wouldn't accidentally hurt her.

"Come back," I murmured, holding a hand to her forehead, so the shower didn't run shampoo into her eyes. It was stupid, I knew. As if I could send her packing and then demand she returned.

I also realised I didn't want her to come back just because if she turned up looking like this, Angel would have questions and I'd get in trouble. I *would*—of course. I'd be in deep fucking water if I broke our omega before we even got to know her.

It wasn't that though, which was unsettling—since getting in trouble with Angel was my central compass in life. I needed her to come back because I... I just needed her.

I was rubbing conditioner into her chestnut locks when her eyes found mine at last.

"Why?" she asked. She didn't have to specify.

"I made a mistake," I said quietly.

She waited; gold ringed eyes fixed on me.

I wiped a smear of conditioner from her cheek. "I don't need your secrets."

I had been an idiot, trying to weigh my omegas value through the eyes of others. She was theirs, sure. But she was mine, too, and I'd nearly destroyed her for the sake of the other idiots in our pack.

Then she let out a little breath of a laugh, but it sounded choked. She hunched, shaking, and I realised she was crying.

Tentatively, I shifted her around and hugged her against my chest. It felt like the right thing to do.

She didn't answer, and we sat like that for a while as water rinsed the conditioner from her hair.

Finally, she shifted forward, tugging the shirt over her head.

I blinked, catching it. "Don't." Why in God's name was that word coming from my mouth? If Havoc wanted to strip down in front of me, I should be perfectly on board. But instead, a very unfamiliar stone sunk in my stomach. I knew it—if barely. *Guilt?*

She *was* destroying me.

She finished tugging the shirt off, so she was in nothing but her lacy underwear, staring back at me. "I can... manage from here if you're uncomfortable."

Were my cheeks flushing? *Uncomfortable?*

"I'm fine." I cleared my throat. *What the fuck was going on?*

All those thoughts were wiped from my brain as Havoc leaned back, her perfect, smooth skin pressing against my chest. For the briefest second, she tensed.

"Doesn't it hurt, when you touch me?"

"I'm used to it," she breathed.

Another chill ran down my spine at that. *What* had happened to her?

Could *I* get used to this, though? Heat spurred through my entire body at the touch, it was smothering. Absolute. Nothing else in the world existed right now except for Havoc.

"Did...?" She paused, as if unsure. "Did you love Logan?" she asked quietly.

"No." The answer to that was easy. Angel had. Caspian had. I didn't know about Bane.

Logan had just always... been around. But I'd never liked him much, not when we used to see him at the alpha meets growing up, nor when he'd show up randomly in our side of town to 'drop by', which usually ended up in odd requests.

It made me feel like me and Cass were expendable to him, like he had to come visit the street-side alphas to get away with the shit he wanted. Once he'd even asked for my blood, which was pretty weird, even for my standards.

Havoc released a breath and then took the body wash I passed her, squeezing out some on her hand and then mine. Gently I rubbed it into her arms and across her back, while she did her legs and torso. Her shivering had died down now and her flesh felt warm. Much too warm.

After the shower, she changed into a nightdress—and I took note of that, since it wasn't her usual baggy pyjamas. Then I bundled her under all of her duvets in bed.

I wasn't done. I was soaked, so I left to change and collect the pizza that would have certainly been delivered by now.

The others were all in the lounge. I got strange looks from both Caspian and Bane, and a bewildered one from Angel.

"What are you doing?" Angel asked as I grabbed a box of pizza.

"Hanging out with Havoc."

I turned away from Angel's drawn expression and then marched back down the hallway. I had fresh clothes, comfort food and a dry pair of black gloves.

She deserved it all. She'd proven that today. Havoc was strong in ways I would never have guessed. She was special. I didn't need secrets to know that.

I was going to treat the fuck out of our omega, and I didn't give a shit what the others thought about it.

Havoc

I was desperate.

I understood how crazy it was that Kai was here right now. I understood that it was even more crazy that he was holding me in his arms like he never wanted to let go. Like I mattered.

Had I... seduced him? Is that what it looked like? When the omegas at Gavin's had talked about stuff like this, it never involved torture or panic attacks.

But nothing else had gone my way. Nothing in the last few months, and now... this.

Kai had changed before my eyes.

I'd finally found the price of entry and it felt right because it had been hard. Ridiculously, stupidly hard and painful and awful. And in that, I trusted. I knew now that if I'd fallen into this pack's arms without resistance, I never would have believed it was real.

That was all fucked up. I knew that. I just didn't care. I didn't have anything else.

There was half eaten pizza on the foot of my bed and a car-racing-competition thing was playing on the TV. They were all things Kai had chosen to comfort me. Not something I'd made up or hoped for.

Even now, I wondered if it was real. My fingers traced my wrist, the place my bracelet had been.

Gone.

I swallowed. This *was* too good to be true. No matter what I had with Kai, there were others in this place that would never accept me.

Kai shifted, propping himself up and peering over. "What's wrong?"

I curled up tighter, embarrassment flooding me.

"I'm... shit at reading people." He looked concerned. "Tell me."

"I'm just... afraid this won't last."

He hesitated. "This?"

I nodded. It wouldn't—couldn't—last. What a stupid dream that it might.

His reply soothed me, even if I knew to my core it could never really come true. "Havoc," he murmured. "I'm never going to let you go."

FOURTEEN

Havoc

I peered up into Bane's beautiful silver eyes, daring myself to ask the question that was haunting me.

It was the evening after the whole Kai incident. Kai had only left a few hours ago. He slept with me through the night and then stayed late into the morning.

I'd only been alone for a few hours though. Bane had knocked on my door with a tray hosting two very healthy-looking meals. I wasn't going to complain. I'd spent a lot of my life alone and I hated it.

We'd finished off the rice dish and now I was curled up in his arms on the couch.

"Have... you talked to the others about...?" I couldn't finish the sentence, Logan's name stuck on my tongue.

Bane cleared his throat, his grip on me getting tighter. I peered up to find his eyes closed.

"Not yet. I will... I'm trying. But it's complicated. Logan..." He scowled. "He's still got his claws in. It's not as simple as telling them the truth. I don't hold as much sway as his memory. Not yet."

"Okay." My throat was tight all of a sudden. "What do you think... What should I do?"

"It shouldn't be on you to fix this," he sighed.

"I'm okay," I whispered. I didn't know how true it was. I felt confident enough saying it, but... I was uncertain. I wasn't afraid of Kai doing anything again, not after last night. I hadn't told Bane any of it. It wasn't that I was afraid. In fact, I didn't even know if Kai would keep it to himself, but something about it had felt... private. What Kai had done, what I'd said to him, the way he'd reacted... It felt like it was mine.

It wasn't forbidden, like Logan was. It was just something I didn't want to share.

"You know, I didn't know anything about you from before," I said, changing the subject. "But I wish I had." Sometimes it felt unfair, that I'd spent all those hours dreaming of Caspian, ignoring Bane, when... Well, when this was the reality of it.

Bane turned to me, steel in his expression. "What?"

"The others... I'd heard stuff about them."

"What kind of stuff?" Bane's brows came down, and for a moment I could swear he was nervous.

"Good things. From... him." I still couldn't say Logan's name.

"Caspian's sister is a problem again," Logan drawled. "She sends him into a spiral."

"You calling in a favour?" Eli asked.

I was seated beside Logan as usual, between him and Eli, though I hovered as close to Logan as I could get away with. His request—that I kiss Eli, still stuck in my mind from last visit.

"I don't just want her fired," Logan said. "I want her blacklisted. I want her forced to another state looking for a job."

I blinked, mentally trying to catch up on the conversation they'd been having, Caspian's name drawing me in.

"Caspian has a sister?" I asked.

Logan paused, glancing at me curiously. "You want to know more about them?"

"Yes." Desperately.

Logan dug in his pocket for a moment and then pulled out a folded piece of paper. "This was today. Kai was messing around with one of those instant camera things."

He unfolded it and my breath caught for a second. Five men were in the photo.

They were, perhaps, at a restaurant, and looked to be having fun. One was drinking, one shooting a grin while he flipped the camera off. And there Logan sat in the middle, arm propped on the back of the red booth like he was sitting on a throne. There was a little burn of hatred in the pit of my stomach.

I shoved it away as I noticed the one holding the camera... he was interesting. His hair was white, one eye blank and white while the other had a crimson pupil.

"There's a seer?" I asked, before I could stop myself.

"Kai."

"That's... rare." Seers were alphas or omegas who could see and measure our auras.

"Yup," Logan said. "He's paid the price for that. Our pack is his place. It's where he's safe."

He pointed to the rest of them, giving me their names and telling me a little about each.

"What about him?" I asked, pointing to the last in the picture. He was broad shouldered, with pale skin and dark hair which was shaved at the sides. He was dressed well, with a thick silver necklace around his neck.

"Bane?" Logan asked. "Not much to tell. He keeps to himself."

"You can have it, if you want," he said.

I glanced at Logan nervously. Kindness came at a cost. Still, I *reached for it, but sure enough, Logan took it between two fingers, lifting it out of reach.*

"If you give me something in return." I looked up at him, confused, but then his eyes flickered over to Eli again.

I recoiled, a lump in my throat.

"It's just a kiss, sweet Havoc. You're an omega," he laughed. "He's an alpha. What's the hangup?"

My eyes flashed, for the briefest moment, at the picture in his hand.

My mates. They were my mates. I didn't want anyone else.

I clenched my jaw and wrapped my arms around myself, gaze dropping back down to the table.

Logan chuckled, tucking the picture back into his pocket.

"He told you about us?" Bane asked.

I nodded again. "On good days."

Bane's eyes darkened.

"I..." My chest heaved at what I was about to say. "Please, you can't tell the others."

"Not a word." He held my gaze. "What kind of stuff did he say?"

"Good stuff." It had always been good, despite what I'd said to Kai. I chewed my lip aggressively. "I dreamed a lot about what they'd be like."

"But... not me?"

"He never said much about you."

"Much?" Bane asked.

"He said you had a dark side... love was off the table, but you'd protect the pack."

Bane went absolutely still. Something bitter flickered in the shadows of his bright eyes. I waited, more tensely than perhaps he deserved, and then he loosed a breath with a low laugh. His fingers brushed the silver necklace on his neck as he shifted, leaning back against the couch.

I stared at him, my heart in my throat, hoping for more, though I dared not ask.

We sat for a long time, and I turned my attention back to the baking show, even while my thoughts scattered in a million directions. At my side, I could see the same thing happening to Bane.

Finally, Bane straightened as if preparing to get up. "Do you need anything else before I go?"

"You're leaving?" I tried to stifle my disappointment.

"Do you want me to stay?"

I stared at him, unsure. Had I upset him? A part of me desperately wanted him to stay. I was thinking of being curled up in Kai's arms last night. I'd liked it, but I'd been all over the place emotionally, given the circumstances. But Bane had been good to me since I'd arrived. I couldn't help picturing how comforting it would be, curled up in his huge arms.

He seemed to want to leave though, so I shook my head. "I'll be okay."

Bane tugged me against him unexpectedly and pressed a kiss to the top of my hair. His voice was low, the warmth of his breath tickling my temple. "To Logan," he murmured. "I served him best when people believed I was incapable of love."

Angel

I sat down on the foot of the bed. The Grand Prix was running in the background and Kai was curled up with one of his handheld games.

"So, uh... What's going on with you and Havoc?" I asked. He'd been gone the whole night last night, and I wasn't stupid. Kai wrinkled his nose but didn't look away from his game. There was something else too, something much more worrying.

I'd found his weapon case on the floor of our closet last night. It was his old kit filled with the weapons he used to get information from people on Logan's trips. Both Cass and I had told him he wasn't to use them again—though he'd refused to get rid of them completely.

There was a time none of the pack knew how hurting others with those things drove him to the edge. He had almost detached from the world completely. I almost lost him.

I couldn't ask him about that if I wanted to be sure of the truth. Not until I had him on his knees.

"You should really stop creeping into her room at night."

"How do you know about that?" Kai sounded indignant.

"You told me. Just now." I snorted. I'd suspected, though.

"I didn't, last night," he muttered.

"What does that mean?"

"Means she *wanted* me there." He sounded smug, and my expression soured.

"That's not... a good idea."

"Why not? She's our mate."

"You know why."

Kai didn't reply, his jaw clenching.

"What if I'm just jealous?" I asked.

"Go fuck yourself," Kai snorted. "You wanted her. We talked about this."

It was true. Neither of us had issues with the idea of an omega —a mate, of course. It wasn't an obstacle for me or for him, except... "Not like this."

"I think we can get over it and keep her." He sounded sure, which was just so very... Kai of him. Once he had his mind set on something, rarely did he not get it. But... This was different. I just didn't know if he knew that yet.

"What if I'm just in her room because I'm needy?" Kai said with a grin, a little spark dancing in his eyes. Something came to life within me at that look and I shifted across the bed before I realised it.

"I can meet your needs right here," I growled, my hand closing over his throat.

White and red flashed with desire, a low rumble sounded in his chest and it got me instantly hard.

Kai was too much for me. It didn't matter what he did, I'd be here at the end of the day.

"Are you jealous of her or me?" he asked, his hand slipping down to my crotch. Our connection was never as strong as it was when he had his fist over my rigid cock. He was taunting me— both ways, sliding his palm down my stiff shaft as his words made me scowl.

"You know what I dream of?" he asked.

"What?" I'd regret asking, I was sure.

"One day, I want her desperate between us, taking both our knots at the same time—" He cut off with a laugh as my hand tightened around his throat. He matched it with his grip. "But right now, I want you to choke me with your cock."

I knew he'd felt exactly my body's response to the idea of Havoc.

"On your knees, street rat," I hissed, needing to distract myself.

He released me, shifting easily off the side of the bed where he knelt. The sight of it melted everything else from my brain. Well. *Almost.* I still had interrogating to do before I felt his sweet sweet mouth on my cock.

Kai was the most attractive man I'd ever met. His skin beneath the canvas of scars and tattoos was a dusky tan. His pure white hair lit in the moonlight through the windows, wild and wavy, scattered about his forehead.

He had a razor-sharp jaw and broad grin, behind which was a tongue ring that made me see stars, always with the glitter of wildness in his eyes. That glitter hid shadows of his past. His eyes gave him away. People had used him for that power, and broken him for it, too.

Until he'd met us.

I slid to the edge of the bed, taking his chin and drawing him close, watching with satisfaction at the deepening hunger in his gaze.

"Hands off," I murmured. His lip curled slightly, a sign of delight as he dropped his hands and tucked them both behind his back.

We were both *right* on the edge.

Perfect time to pounce.

"Tell me why I found your case on the floor of the closet today?" I asked, my grip tugging his chin toward me. I didn't have to specify.

He froze, eyes narrowed. But he knew as well as I did, he wasn't supposed to touch the weapons in that bag.

His teeth rolled along his bottom lip, drawing my gaze as he contemplated my question. "I didn't use them."

I shifted forward, watching as his eyes slid to my tenting pyjama pants impatiently. "Tell me the truth."

"They were just for show."

"Show for *what*?" I tightened my grip again.

His chest heaved as he looked at me, eyes darting between mine. But I had him. Our pack bond was wide open, lust lighting it like a beacon. If he lied, I'd know.

I pressed my thumb against his lips. I loved the way our skin paired, my rich mid brown beside the cool tan of his, just a few shades lighter. "Tell me," I pushed.

"I wanted to make her spill all her secrets," he growled. "But I changed my mind."

"Did you take any of them out?" I asked.

His jaw ticked. "Yes."

"And?"

"And she's still in one piece."

Good. That was good.

"Completely?" I asked, unable to hide the twitch of my smile as the resentment flashed in his eyes.

"Not a scratch."

My relief was such that I knew he'd feel it too. I leaned back, releasing his chin.

"Good boy," I breathed.

I slid my other hand toward my crotch, freeing my rock-hard cock. All of his resentment drained away.

I groaned at the first touch of his mouth on my shaft. He teased me, taking the tip only and then sliding his tongue down to my base.

He kept it up until I couldn't take it. "Use your hands."

His fist gripped the base of my cock punishingly and I was instantly rewarded with the feel of his mouth taking me in, halfway at first and then further...

I closed my eyes, leaning back on my palms, groaning. Kai's mouth withdrew, his hand still pumping as he asked, "Do you dream of her pretty pink lips instead of mine?"

I froze, my breath heaving. My eyes snapped open just as he drew his pierced tongue up my shaft and right to the tip.

Fuck. I was close. *Way* too close, too fast at his words. He drew back, reading my expression with mischief.

"Want me to stop?" Kai asked. His hand squeezed on the base of my cock, and I groaned.

I felt the scowl on my own face, blood roaring in my ears, the edges of an orgasm gripping me.

"Say her name," he commanded, letting his aura saturate the

air, dragging Havoc's name right to my tongue. I snapped my mouth closed, lava burning in my veins.

"Shut your filthy mouth," I snarled.

"Make me," he murmured, his lips brushing me with teasing gentleness.

I seized his hair and dragged him down until his fingers were biting my thighs and I could feel the back of his throat squeezing me. The growl in his chest was desperate, and I watched his other hand drop, pumping his own shaft as I drew back, forcing myself down his throat again. He groaned.

For a traitorous flash, it was her. Kai was behind her, grip in her hair and pressing her forward. Her soft, rosy lips circled my shaft, and a little whimper sounded in her chest as she took me all, even if I was much too big for her. Her throat squeezed me, her lips brushing my pelvis, her golden eyes wide and desperate.

In another second, the vision was gone, and Kai was drawing back, the taunting piece of metal in his mouth pressing against the sensitive underside of my shaft. His eyes were dancing with victory, as if he knew exactly what I'd just been thinking—and he might well have got a flash of it through the bond. Fuck him. Once more I gripped his hair, dragging him forward, groaning as I came. He did too, the low sounds of his orgasm pressed out each time I roughly drove my cock into his throat.

After, when I was curled up behind him with my arms wrapped around his waist, I stewed. "That was fucking wrong."

"Isn't that why you keep me around?"

Fuck him. And Havoc.

There was a low delighted rumble with each of Kai's breaths though.

This was all going to shit.

FIFTEEN

Bane

"Hey! Wait up. I'm coming."

I heard Kai's voice behind me. I turned, surprised to see him tugging on a hoodie as he hurried across the living room.

"I'm going to the bookstore," I said, brows drawn at Kai's eagerness. He wasn't the reading type.

Since the others had taken the week off, I'd done the same. I worried they might push me away if I didn't at least appear to grieve Logan. But now I was going crazy without my work, and I was out of books to read.

A few times today I'd considered visiting Havoc, but something had stopped me.

Nerves.

Fucking nerves. Like if I spent any more time with her than I had to, she'd realise what an empty shell I was, or that everything Logan had told her was true. So I needed more reading material.

"Yeh. I know." Kai flashed one of his unnerving smiles.

"Alright." I shrugged, not letting that slightest stirring of hope show on my face.

Did he want to spend time with me?

I was closer to Kai than any of the others. He was up every morning with me, joining me in the office, sometimes to work, sometimes to game. When he was pulled by Caspian to do out-of-house jobs, I always missed the angry clacking of his keyboard and muttered curses. Kai's income came mostly from picking up hacking gigs.

Ethical hacking... I snorted while we waited for the elevator. I didn't think Kai could identify *ethical* if it did a jig before his eyes and then kicked him in the balls. Kai eyed me curiously, but said nothing.

We made our way down to the underground parking in a comfortable silence.

"So..." Kai said as he climbed into the passenger seat. "Havoc."

Right.

Of course, that was what this was about.

"So, uh... you don't mind her?"

My eyes flickered from the backup cam to him. His snow-white hair swept in messy waves across his forehead. His mismatched eyes were fixed on his phone, where he tapped the screen for one of the mindless games he played to keep his brain occupied. His skin was a dusky tan, the familiar silver scar creeping from his ear to just under his eyes. He had a sharp jawline and a strong nose with a hint of a curve to it.

He looked like a street runner through and through. Dressed like it too, unlike Caspian. Right now, he was in hoodie and sweatpants. He wouldn't look out of place slouched on a bench with a bag of spray cans at his feet.

He was a fascinating man, I'd always thought. I knew his history—we all knew why he was like he was, but I'd never had the opportunity to figure out exactly what that meant. I offered the structure he so desperately needed. Caspian was the voice of boundaries. Angel was his compass. Logan had been—well, actually I don't know exactly what Kai thought of Logan. Kai was the only one he hadn't had something on directly. Kai's ties to Caspian and Angel had been enough for Logan.

"I like her," I corrected as I pulled out onto the busy city street. It was noon, so lunchtime traffic was out in full force.

Kai's fingers stopped tapping the screen, and he turned. I could see the bright crimson of his one eye as he regarded me. "You *like* her?"

"Yes." Well, actually I more than *liked* Havoc. She was the centre of everything I had left. The most important woman in the world. That might be an overkill, though, even for Kai.

"Isn't that... wrong?" Kai asked cautiously.

I loosed a low laugh, feeling just a little mischievous. "Well. She killed our pack lead."

Kai narrowed his eyes as if I'd just handed him a difficult riddle to solve.

"So... It's wrong." It wasn't a question and it *was* a question all at the same time.

I didn't answer. Partly because it was amusing not to, and partly because it was hard to explain the truth. It was wrong to them, it wasn't wrong to me, but Kai liked things in black and white. He wanted objective, not subjective.

Kai fiddled with the radio station as we drove, which was unnecessary, since the bookshop was only a few minutes away. This part of town was quaint, with cobblestone and old English style lamp posts. The shops were all made of brick and faintly peeling paint in bright colours. Baked goods peered temptingly from a window of the closest shop.

"Angel gets mad if I mention it, but I think about banging her *all* the time," Kai groaned at my side as the sound of the engine died.

I tucked my keys in my pocket, stifling humour from my expression. "Me too." I got out of the car, and we crossed the narrow road. "But, in case you weren't aware, doing that without asking first *would* be wrong—"

Kai snarled, his fingers closing on my sleeve and drawing me to a stop as we took the steps that led to the bookshop door. "I fucking *know* that!" But the fury drained from his face as he caught the slightest quirk on the corner of my lips. *"Screw you."*

I chuckled as he let me go, turning back to the door.

"You have a sense of humour?" Kai asked as the little bell rang, announcing our entry. He sounded startled. I felt both amusement and a pang of sorrow at that comment.

I was a stranger to them.

We'd been a pack for four years—since we were nineteen, and I was still a stranger.

I took a breath, letting the smell of books soothe me. I was hyper aware how intently Kai watched. And I knew I'd just shown a little darkness. He always seemed extra curious about that.

The bookshop was large, with two floors. The light was warm, Edison bulbs hanging from rafters, and rich oak shelves hosting the books for sale.

A group of young ladies a few isles away glanced over upon our entry, then did a double take. One grabbed her friend's arm, and furious whispers rose unabashedly in the air.

I dealt with that wherever I went, so did Kai. We were alphas. Rare, desired, fought over.

Those titles might have made me feel better, if I didn't manage to sail through life so alone.

It was an irony. Alphas were envied for many reasons, not the least of which was pack bonds. They were supposed to offer a brotherhood unmatched by any bond aside omega-alpha connection. Betas would never experience that with one another—but they could get bitten in by an alpha pack and feel half of what we did.

All of that is what made Logan so damned impressive. He'd managed to foster a pack of alphas, and still keep us isolated.

"So," Kai said as I grabbed a basket and made for the true crime section. "I spent the night with her."

I paused, glancing at him, taking a moment to process that while not allowing an ounce of my envy show. "Anything... happen?"

"Cuddled."

"That's all?" Right. Be more obvious, why don't you?

"Didn't really seem like... the right time," Kai said, evasively.

I scratched my head as we wandered past a few isles. That was unexpected.

"But you seem to know her best," Kai went on.

I snorted at the irony of that after what Havoc had told me last night. I knew her better than the others, and she knew them all better than me.

I began scanning spines.

"She said something about Logan mentioning me..." Kai mused as I plucked out one book, eyes darting across the blurb before tucking it neatly into the basket. "Guess she must have talked with Logan the night they met, before she offed him."

I grunted in agreement, not yet ready to share the truth: that Havoc hadn't met Logan for the first time the night she'd killed him. She hadn't told the others and I would follow her lead on that.

Until the pack was ready to accept that Logan was the villain, I would play this close to my chest. "She said he spoke about us," I said. "The way she told it, she thought pretty well of the lot of you."

"Oh." Kai eyed me curiously, as if something didn't add up.

My thoughts got away from me. What did Logan gain from convincing Havoc the rest of his pack were noble? It sounded as if he was trying to convince her to meet them. Only... When Logan wanted something, he took it. A gold pack omega like Havoc wouldn't have posed a challenge.

"Us?" Kai asked, not missing a word. "What about you?"

"He didn't tell her much about me."

"Damn. Cockblocking you from beyond the grave."

I winced. That bit.

I heard some shuffling and a few footsteps nearby. The group of ladies were clearly trailing us.

I ignored them, but dropped my voice. "I think she wants to stay with us."

Kai perked up. "Why?"

I let out a breath, unsure how to convey that. I couldn't explain. I just... something about the way she'd been hopeful when I'd told her what I thought of Logan. "Doesn't matter. Cass and Angel won't believe me, anyway."

"Okay, but we have the vote power here," Kai said.

I raised an eyebrow. "You say that like it's a good thing. Angel and Cass have a few less screws loose." Well. Actually, I was less and less sure about Cass these days.

Kai smirked. "I don't give a shit if it means we get to keep our girl."

Our girl... Those words warmed me to the soul. Kai was on board, it seemed.

Only... Well, I knew where we were heading. I knew the only bond the pack would agree on was a dark bond. But being dark bonded by us was better than letting her get torn apart by the system. She'd spend her life unbonded, packless, used by a system that would consider her a number.

She could pretend all she wanted, but Havoc was soft on the inside, curious, nervous... unsure. She wasn't like any omega I'd ever met. Safer, higher end establishments wouldn't want her. She'd be handed off to the sharks, sent to the gold pack centres, or used as nothing more than an outlet for alphas in prison to keep the homicides down.

No. If a dark bond was the only choice, I'd agree. But if any of my brothers showed the slightest hint of abusing that bond, I'd fucking crucify them.

"What if we could convince them?" Kai asked.

"What?"

"That she wouldn't leave if she could."

"How?" I asked.

"I have an idea," Kai mused. "But what do you think those two blind pricks *need* to want her like we do?"

They needed to know she didn't have a choice when she'd killed Logan, but that was too close to Havoc's secrets to say out loud. Still, my heart quaked at the idea of what Logan might have done to her.

Logan had tormented me for years, and I'd been a fool. I thought I was the one taking all the blows for the others—so they could have a better life. That I was giving Logan enough control to leave them alone. I was a blind fool. A coward. And that cowardice had cost Havoc.

"She's lost and scared. They think she's got a master plan. We have to show them they're wrong."

"Okay..." he said. "So, if I could prove to them that she wouldn't leave if she could, you think that would do it?"

I shrugged. "I don't know. Maybe? Anything to get them to see her like a human."

Kai trailed me for a while longer, pulling his phone out and tapping away at another game.

It was hard to focus. I felt more connected to him than I had before. More than I'd ever felt to any of our pack. It still took me a while to find the courage to ask the question that was bugging me. "What did you think of Logan?" I tried to make it sound as casual as possible.

Of course, those efforts were wasted since it was Kai. He just shrugged, not glancing up from his phone.

"Bastard, wasn't he?"

"You didn't like him?" I asked, surprised.

Kai finally looked up, fixing me with an intent stare. "I didn't *not* like him. He just never really got under my skin."

I waited, hoping for a little more information on that. He offered me none. "And... getting under your skin is... good?" I prodded.

"Can't care about someone if they don't get under my skin."

"And... how many people have managed that?" I asked.

He considered, lifting his slender, ringed fingers as he thought out loud. "Cass, Angel, you..." He trailed off, his face screwed up in a scowl. I barely noticed it though, my heart suddenly in my throat.

Me?

And... Logan hadn't?

Kai sighed dramatically. "Damn." He flicked up his fourth finger. "She's on there isn't she? Less than a week. Omegas and their scent match fuckery."

At those words, we heard a little squeak of derision from a few isles over, then a curse. The ladies who had been trailing us were clearly doing their best to listen in on our conversation. Well, if anything would dissuade them, it was that.

Kai, it seemed, hadn't noticed.

"Nah. Logan was a good lead. Grounded Cass and Angel, but sometimes he liked to push. Didn't like how he was with Angel sometimes. Got the feeling Logan asked for favours just to make him uncomfortable."

I nodded; half my brain still taken up by being on Kai's list.

"Oh, you know what I *love*? Art... Always watch Cass on his tablet when I can." He plucked a book from the shelf with startling enthusiasm. Kai's enthusiasm was usually restricted to

Angel, video games, or Caspian's discussion of violent jobs. "Watercolour paintings..." Kai flipped it open but then he frowned. "It's like... empty." He looked confused.

I stared at the pages which were bright with colourful paintings. Shit... Kai wouldn't be able to see almost *any* of that.

I cleared my throat. "It's... uh. You won't be able to see them properly."

"Oh." His brows furrowed in disappointment.

Shit. I'd never really talked to Kai about his whole colourblind situation. I'd also never seen him upset about something so... normal.

"They're rubbish anyway," I said.

He shut the book with a sigh, wrinkling his nose discontentedly. "It's fine." He shrugged, slipping the book back and wandering off before I could say anything more.

I skimmed the shelves before picking another book out. In it were charcoal paintings on a white background. No way for Kai to miss the art.

I finished shopping, gathering a larger array of genres than I'd ever bought, since I had no idea what Havoc might like.

As we were leaving, I handed the painting book to him. "Here. Way better artist."

Kai took it, eyes darting between me and the book for a second as if confused, but I was already taking the steps by twos.

The whole way home, Kai didn't turn his phone on once. He looked delighted with himself. At one point, I thought a low rumbling purr might have sounded in his chest. I couldn't help glancing over at him—that sound was damn attractive. I looked straight back at the road, however, when I found his eyes fixed on me.

Something about what had happened in the bookstore niggled at me, out of place. As the elevator took us back up to our top floor apartment, I glanced at him. "You didn't give a shit about the watercolour."

It just... wasn't like him. He didn't need me to buy him anything anyway, he had enough money. *And* he had Angel, for fuck's sake, who was rolling in it.

Kai bit back a grin. "Not one bit."

I sighed. "What is that nickname Angel has for you?"

He began rattling off terms without pause. "Bed hog? Bloodhound? Deep throat *king*"—Kai's eyes flashed, and I felt a flush of heat crawl up my neck—"Psycho brat—"

"That one," I said quickly. Kai's grin split his face; the book still clutched to his chest.

He'd played me. He was holding the book in his arms like a trophy.

I knew how Kai worked. Sometimes he liked Angel buying ridiculous things he didn't need. When he did, he closed his pack bond down—just like right now—as if he didn't want us all knowing how he felt about it. It gave him away, though. For him, I was sure, it was about affirmation.

"What do you think, if we keep her, she seems the type to give you a run for your money?" I muttered as our floor neared.

Kai narrowed his eyes. "There can't be *two* of us."

"Well here, how's this? You can be Angel's. She can be mine."

The elevator pinged, the door opening. I stepped through it, leaving Kai behind, a smug smile on my own face.

At my words, I could *swear* there was a flash of indignance in his eyes.

SIXTEEN

Bane

"Don't tell me you don't dream about her," Kai groaned.

"Shut the *fuck* up," Caspian muttered, smashing his controller aggressively as he leaned forward on the couch. We were all lounging in Kai and Angel's room as we waited for Kai's trap to spring on Havoc. Kai and Cass were playing a racing game. I noticed that Kai's lewd comments were being delivered every time he was on Caspian's tail. Sure enough, Kai managed to get Cass into a tailspin.

"Shit."

"We're alphas. She's an omega—our mate. It's perfectly normal." Angel's voice was clipped. He was leaning back on the couch like me, controller free. I was too antsy to play today, but I never said no to hanging out with them.

"You know what's not normal?" Kai asked.

"Please don't tell us," Cass muttered.

"She always has a gun in those dainty little hands when I picture her riding me."

Caspian and Angel groaned, but I perked up. Consequently, Kai made it past the finish line just at that moment. I chuckled.

"That's fucked up, dude," Angel muttered.

Kai was grinning though as he leaned back on the couch, staring up at the ceiling. "Yeah. It really is. But there's just something hot about her holding a gun."

"*Please.*" Angel growled.

"Maybe because I know she knows how to use it?" Kai wondered.

"Video games are not worth this," Cass muttered.

"Tell me you don't think the idea is hot—Wait..." He trailed off, his eyes catching mine. "Ha. Bane's on my side."

"Bullshit," Angel snorted, but then he caught the look on my face and his eyebrows shot up. "Say he's wrong."

I shrugged, unable to stop the quirk of a smile on my lips. "I put a gun in her hands when I told her she was staying..." I trailed off, knowing there was a flush creeping up my neck. The others froze.

"Not... loaded, though?" Angel asked.

"Yeah, loaded. Made her point it at my face to see if she'd do it."

Even Kai's mouth hit the floor.

"Why would you do that?" Cass demanded.

"I knew she was bluffing." I shrugged again. It was the truth, anyway. "Now I'm not worried about her creeping around and killing one of us at night."

"I feel like there are so many ways between here and letting psycho-killer-omega put a loaded gun to your head, to get that sort of information..." Angel's voice was weak.

"Ah well. Already done." I shrugged.

But then Kai perked up. "Wait—guys! She's out."

I followed Kai over to where his laptop was propped on the bed.

Sure enough in the video, Havoc was passing by the entrance

doorway to the kitchen. The camera didn't show too much of the room itself.

This was it. Kai's plan to let us know if Havoc really wanted to leave.

"Are you sure about this?" Angel asked.

"Tipped off Eric in the lobby. He'll stop her if she gets there," I said. "But she won't."

Caspian snorted derisively; his eyes fixed on the camera. "If she tries to escape, we have another meeting." He seemed completely confident he was about to be proven right; that Havoc would take the first chance to get away from us.

"If she does try to leave, what does that tell us?" Angel asked. "Bane thinks she wants to stay because she... *likes* us?" Angel threw me a flat look. "*I* think she wants to leave because that's literally what she's been saying the whole time."

"No, she wants out, but she doesn't want to be handed back to the cops," Cass said.

"So, you think—?" Angel began.

"She'll make a break for it, won't she? Get away from us *and* the cops."

Havoc curled her fingers around the door, peering out curiously for a moment. Then she turned, her eyes scanning the room, then up to the balcony. Was she checking for us? My heart rate rose.

"She looks shifty," Caspian noted.

"She *won't* leave."

But Havoc had stopped by the door, staring through the gap, absolutely still. A full minute passed, and she didn't move. She shifted from one foot to another. She was wearing a black hoodie and matching sweatpants.

"What's she doing?" Angel asked, impatiently.

Caspian's eyes were narrowed, doubt in them. Kai was just as tense.

Havoc took a step away from the door and I let out a breath of relief. It was strangled in the next second however, when she took one, two, three steps, then slipped through the door.

"Told you," Caspian growled.

"Wait—Keep watching." Kai said, tapping a few buttons and pulling up a different feed. It was the hallway to our floor. The camera was blurred and in black and white, but there was sound alongside the static. Havoc's small frame stepped out cautiously. She was leaning forward as if terrified, her head checking one way and then the other. I clenched my jaw, she was just looking. Nothing more.

"She isn't even wearing shoes," I muttered. "She's not going anywhere."

"Doesn't mean anything," Caspian shot back. "Did we actually get her shoes?"

"Uh..." Angel looked thoughtful. "Actually, no. Just the boots she came in, but they're back in her room."

"So, she just figured she didn't have time to get them," Caspian said.

Havoc was now edging down the hallway. Even from here I could see her wide eyes darting about. She tucked her hair behind her ear as she reached the corner. Kai tapped another few buttons, and the view shifted again. There were two elevators to the main lobby, and Havoc stood before them. Once more she stilled, clearly unsure.

Footsteps approached, and Kai brought up the second feed next to the first. Two people were walking down the hallway. One tall man with dark hair and a blonde woman on his arm. I recognised him, Dan and Allie were in one of our neighbouring packs.

A rumble sounded in my chest and I straightened, making to move, but Angel's hand was on my shoulder. "Let it play out."

"That's an *alpha*—" I began.

"With his omega," Angel cut me off. "Dan's fine. He's not going to do anything."

Havoc seemed to hear the footsteps. She looked panicked, glancing around, backing into the wall as if she might blend into the cream wallpaper.

I could see Dan straighten before he even turned the corner. Allie glanced up at him.

"Alright?" she asked.

My nails bit into my knuckles as they turned the corner, and Dan's eyes fell straight on Havoc. He drew up, and so did Allie. There was a pause.

"Are you okay?" Allie asked.

Havoc nodded, fingers curling around the bottom of her hoodie. Her eyes were fixed on Dan.

"She's afraid—" I began.

"I don't fucking care," Caspian snapped. "We're watching it play out."

Allie pressed the elevator button. The uncomfortable silence was clear even through the cams. Finally, Havoc shifted slightly.

"Do you know how far the police station is?" she asked. Caspian's scowl deepened as Dan and Allie glanced back to Havoc. My throat felt dry. Was Angel right?

I didn't want to believe it. Yesterday when she seemed to want me to stay, I should have.

"Uh... I think there's one just down 7th," Allie glanced up at Dan.

"There's more than one?" Havoc's voice was a squeak.

"More than one where...?" Dan sounded confused.

"In the city?" Havoc asked. I blinked, and I realised my mouth had parted in shock.

"She's not... serious?" Angel asked, looking as bewildered as I felt.

Dan chuckled, as if she were joking. "Yeah, there's more than one police station in the city."

"How would I know which one to go to?"

Allie and Dan exchanged a look. "Are you okay?" Allie asked. "Do you need—?"

"No. I'm fine." But I could hear the edge of panic in her voice. The elevator pinged, and the doors slid open.

"Are you sure?"

"Yes." Havoc was edging along the wall away from them, eyes darting to the elevator like she hoped they'd get in. "I'm good. Just... tired is all. I better get back."

Relief cooled my veins and slowed my pulse as she darted around the corner. Allie and Dan glanced at one another briefly before entering the elevator.

Havoc didn't leave from around the corner. As the doors slid shut, she peeked back at the lobby.

At my side, Angel was rubbing his chin, looking lost. Kai was fixed on the screen, his expression unreadable. Caspian looked icy.

But Havoc was moving again, returning to the elevators.

It took her a while, but eventually she reached out and pressed the button. We were on the top floor, so there was only one. Then she took a few steps back.

"There—see, what more do you need?" Caspian asked.

"We keep watching." But I could hear the doubt in my own voice.

Caspian sighed, still tense.

Finally, the elevator doors pinged open and Havoc edged up to them. She took a few steps in, looking around.

"You'd think she's never seen one before." Kai said quietly.

"I don't think she has..." Angel replied.

"How did you get her up here?" Cass asked. "See how stupid that sounds?"

"She wasn't... really present when I brought her in," Angel murmured. "Couldn't get her to say a word. I doubt she remembers it."

After a moment the doors began to slide closed. Havoc loosed a gasp of panic and then threw herself out of the elevator. She turned, looking around, eyes wide. Then she returned to the button, jabbing it again. The elevator doors, which were inches from closing, instead began to open.

Havoc's hand was pressed to her throat as she stepped back to the elevator, and I could see the way her chest heaved.

"When I got her from Gavin's someone told me she grew up isolated," Angel murmured. "I just didn't imagine..."

Once more Havoc looked around, her fingers tracing the buttons. Again, the elevator doors began to shut.

Havoc tried again to slip out, but she was slower this time. The doors closed around her back leg. Havoc—who was obviously completely unaware of how an elevator functioned—let out a frightened wail and launched herself forward. Of course, because the elevator wasn't rigged to crush her, the doors opened. With no resistance to her full-bodied escape attempt, she went crashing to the floor.

She spun on her back, sobbing as she stared at the elevators, as if one might jump from the wall and swallow her up. Then she scrambled to her feet, breathing ragged as she launched herself back down the hallway in terror. Kai made quick work on shifting the feeds. We were all witness to her stumbling through our front door, spinning on it and slamming it closed, pressing both hands against the door with terrified gasps.

Then she turned, sliding down, clutching herself and trembling.

Kai leaned back from the laptop, chewing on his lip furiously as he turned to us, like he'd just been handed an impossible puzzle and we had all the answers. I opened my mouth, and then shut it again.

"What the fuck?" Angel looked floored.

"She's playing with us. She knows we're watching."

Even Angel shot Caspian a disbelieving glance.

"Well..." As the entirety of the situation dawned on me, I could feel the smile creeping onto my lips. Caspian was wrong about her. Sure, she'd tried to escape, but it was clear she was just afraid. I was more confident now than before; there was no trick or manipulation to Havoc at all. And she deserved better than what we were offering her. "I'm going to go and see if she wants some company."

"Right. Real TLC needed after the battle with the elevator," Kai snorted.

"We should discuss this," Angel said tightly as I reached the door.

"Discuss what?" I asked, turning back to him. "We saw the same thing, right? She's not a snake." I glared at Caspian, who didn't even look ashamed. "I was right, and you lot are *assholes*."

Havoc

I hugged my knees to my chest, still pressed against the front door. Traces of adrenaline lingered in my veins.

When I heard the sound of footsteps, I dragged myself to my feet quickly, glancing around to try to look as if I was busy. But it was Bane. Thank God it was Bane.

My pulse was still erratic, and I knew my cheeks were bright red.

"I um..." I tried to come up with an excuse to be where I was. *Why had I come out of my room in the first place?* "I was just getting a snack."

Bane was tugging the fridge door open, a bright expression on his face. He grabbed out two beers which he set on the counter, a plate of cut up veggies, which he regarded for a moment, and then put back. He scanned the fridge some more and then sighed, shutting it.

He seemed occupied, so I began edging back to my room.

"Stay." He waved a hand at me, even as he was turning away. The command sent a flutter in my stomach. I blinked, and stopped walking. My mind wasn't working right, not after nearly being eaten by that damned metal box.

Elevators were a heavy feature in a lot of movies, including the ones I'd been limited to growing up, but none of those movies came with a manual, or a warning that the damn things did a lot on their own accord.

Bane was tugging a big bag of popcorn from the cupboard. Then he crossed to the living room, popcorn, bowl and beers in his arms. He set them down, emptying out the popcorn into the bowl.

"Uhh..." I wasn't sure what I was supposed to be doing.

He returned to me, taking my arms. "Movie night."

"Out here?" My voice was high pitched.

"Yes. Out here."

"The others will be upset."

His fingers curled around my hoodie, drawing me closer. "I don't care what they think."

I'd never seen him so bright before. "I..."

"Please say yes."

"Okay..." I swallowed.

As soon as I sat down with him on the couches, I regretted it. Not because I didn't want to be with him, or because I didn't like the way his arm was draped around me, but because I kept thinking of the others—of what would happen if they came out and saw us.

Bane began flicking through different movies, reading out the descriptions.

Then a figure moved in my periphery, and someone sat down on one of the other couches.

My blood ran cold at the sight of Caspian, the threats he'd whispered on the balcony sounding in my head. Bane tensed, too. I felt it in the way he was holding me, but he didn't look at Caspian.

Caspian's cold eyes met mine as I glanced at him again and there were threats in that look.

This was a mistake.

"I... should go." I tried to stand, but Bane held me in place.

"No."

I clasped my fingers anxiously as I looked up at Bane. His jaw was set.

"I don't..." I swallowed. "I don't want to upset him." My words were low enough that only he'd be able to hear them.

"Has he threatened you?" Bane asked.

I shook my head on pure instinct. It was *not* a good idea to start creating rifts between them. Bane's gaze slid from me to Caspian. "Have you threatened her?"

Caspian snorted. "Maybe she just knows when she's not wanted."

Bane was on his feet in an instant.

Shit. Shit shit shit.

I followed him, tugging on his arm before anything could happen, ignoring the little flare of pain at the contact. "Please, don't. It's okay. I *want* to go back to my room."

Let Caspian see that I wasn't *trying* to break his rules. "There." Caspian smiled. "See? She just doesn't want to hang out with you."

"That wasn't what I meant," the panicked words slipped from my mouth.

"You're lashing out like a child. Grow up," Bane snarled.

I backed up a few paces.

Fuck. *Fuck* this was all going so wrong. I glanced around. To my dismay I saw Angel on the upper level, watching the whole thing. His narrowed-eyed glare found me where I was wringing my hands. He was going to think I was causing problems in his pack.

Caspian was on his feet now. "And you're trying to make the poor little omega hang out with you when all she wants to do is go back to her room."

"You go back to *your* room Cass," Bane growled. "Jerk off to a photo of Logan alone."

My heart bottomed out of my chest. I felt Caspian's alpha aura explode into the space. His eyes flashed and then his fist was crashing into Bane's face. It was faster and harder than should have been possible.

Bane took the hit well, stumbling only one step, his hand on his cheek. Caspian was shrugging his silken robe off as if prepping for a fight. Once the robe was gone, there was nothing keeping him from looking like a street fighter. His body was nothing but rippling muscles, and now I could see his tattoos covered him from neck to knuckles, right down to the all too defined V that dipped to his waistband. They were made of black lines only, tangled text and drakes, leaping animals and symbols. His pale face was twisted in a snarl, strands of his dark hair coming loose from his ponytail.

There was something dark in the aura that flooded the room. I could feel it. So could everyone else here. What loosed from Bane in response was like nothing I'd ever felt before. It was wrong, and it set my heart pounding in my chest.

Bane straightened, turning to Caspian slowly. Somehow it was worse than if he pounced.

He did, a thousand times in my head. Leaping for Caspian,

eyes dark with rage, wielding his huge form that dwarfed even Caspian's muscular figure... He was fists first, losing it completely. It was something wild and feral and broken...

But I blinked, and Bane hadn't moved.

Caspian was tense too, his fist still balled, his eyes burning with rage. He seemed to be waiting for Bane's response. Had he seen what I'd just seen?

"Years of ignoring us. Playing guard dog, and now you find your voice—now he's *dead*?"

Bane's expression went glacial, and his hand jumped to Caspian's throat. "I'm not your guard dog."

Caspian grabbed Bane's wrist; his expression strained. One look in his eyes told me Caspian had lost the last shred of his sanity. He forced out a laugh. "Then why the collar?"

One single beat passed. Then Bane's full aura crashed into the room like an ocean wave.

His fist hit Caspian's cheek with a CRACK! Caspian was thrown to the side, crashing into the kitchen island with a nasty thud. He tried to pick himself up, his hair out of its ponytail, scattered wildly about the vicious tattoos up his back. He spat blood onto the kitchen counter as he shook his head, a twisted snarl on his face.

Bane, it seemed, wasn't done.

"Hey!" I heard Angel's voice from above, and there was something uncertain in it. I didn't know how I got there. All I knew was the look in Bane's eyes. They were a void. No humanity left.

My fingers curled against the thick muscles on Bane's arms, trying to drag him back as his fist closed viciously into Caspian's hair.

"Havoc!" Angel's voice was frightened as it neared.

As pain prickled across my skin at the contact, Bane froze. His chest heaved as his eyes slid to me.

He faltered, the void stuttering out. Angel was at my side, a hand on my shoulder, but I wasn't letting Bane go.

"We all need to take a step back," Angel growled.

Caspian was trying to right himself, ripping his hair from Bane's grip, the wild look still in his eyes.

"I don't need anyone fighting my fights. Least of all a gold pack bitch." Caspian's words should have hurt, but they didn't.

Bane's eyes flashed, but I reached for him, cupping his cheek in my hand, begging him not to look away. The pain at our touch... it wasn't as bad as it had been before. It was something else now. Bane's eyes held mine, his chest still heaving.

"Take a fucking walk." Even Angel sounded pissed.

The silver galaxies in Bane's eyes never left me as his hand reached up and pressed against mine.

"She's going to destroy us," Caspian snarled. It was followed by the keypad beeping and the door slamming.

Finally, Bane relaxed, his eyes closing for a brief moment, and I thought perhaps, he leaned into my touch.

"I'm..." He glanced between me and Angel. "Sorry." For a moment, I saw a flash of fear in his eyes, as if Angel was going to reject him.

"Are you kidding dude? He asked for it." Their voices were faint, and I realised I was backing up.

I needed to get back to my room.

"Havoc—" Bane's voice cut off as he caught my expression. I didn't know what it looked like, all I knew was that I had to leave, now.

I turned and fled back down the hallway. It didn't matter how I felt about Bane.

I would never be wanted in this house.

Caspian

With every punch delivered to the swinging bag, I tried to drown her face from my mind.

The gym on our floor was shared with three other packs, but no one was here right now.

She'd ruined everything. My brothers. My house. Racing games. *Wanks* weren't even fucking safe—didn't matter if I tried to jack off to butterflies in Sumatra, I'd travel the globe and end up in the room opposite mine, pinning her to the bed.

A smatter of red appeared on the wrap of the punching bag before me.

The way she'd glanced at me from beneath Bane's arm on the couch... She was terrified. And then Bane questioning *me?* like I was the villain when *she'd* put the bullet in Logan's skull.

How had everyone forgotten that?

Angel even... he was softening.

They were going to want her bitten in. I'd have to live with her for the rest of my life. The worst part was how I'd felt guilty when she'd looked at me in fear.

Guilty? For threatening the fucking woman who had killed my best friend, and lived in *my* fucking house, and melted my brothers' brains, and haunted my fucking dreams—*"Fuck!"*

The patch job split, and the fluffy grey insides of the bag bulged out. This one needed replacing an age ago.

"Didn't we get that in new last week?" Kai's voice made me spin.

"Fuck off." I wasn't in the mood.

"Nah." Kai swaggered over instead, dropping down on one of the weight benches beside me, idly checking out his reflection in the mirror that spanned the whole wall.

I scowled as I unravelled the wraps on my fists.

"Congrats," he said.

"For what?" I asked, knowing I'd regret it, but too hot headed not to take the bait.

"Bane's a tough nut to piss off."

I scowled. "You're all traitors."

"Yup."

"Why?"

"Have you *seen* her ass?"

I turned on him, cuffing him on the cheek before he had a moment to react. He blinked, his eyes flashing with delight before he launched at me.

He got a few good blows in, the pain matching my knuckles and split cheek from Bane's fist. It was all a fucking relief. I had Kai pinned to the mat in no time. He was better with weapons than hand to hand, always had been.

"You know we *both* owe him for getting out," I snarled, my forearm biting down on his neck. The Harpy's didn't let go of their own. Not ever. Not until Logan. He was a force unto himself, claiming what he wanted from wherever he wanted it from—and lucky for Kai and I, we were one of those things.

"Owe?" Kai cackled. "How many times have we paid back that debt in blood?"

He was right of course. It was why Angel had been able to bargain Kai out of those jobs in the last few years.

The problem was, what I owed Logan—it could never be paid back.

"He's six feet below mate," Kai breathed. "You need to see it? We'll all be wearing black tomorrow."

My stomach dropped, but I shoved away his taunt.

Logan's funeral.

"Then you can get the fuck over it," Kai went on. "And *under* her. Come on. She wants us. You saw her today."

I released Kai with a hiss. My heart pounded in my chest, the reminder undoing every blow I'd delivered to the split bag.

I had to get out of here before I did something I regretted.

SEVENTEEN

Havoc

I curled up in my bed all evening, ignoring the knock on the door, which meant Angel was leaving me food outside. I wasn't hungry. I was a fool, and even now I clutched the photo in my grip. Caspian held his middle finger out at the camera, that sullen look on his face. It had broken me before.

I'd wanted the chance to get him to smile. Of being the omega Logan told me he secretly dreamed of. I had felt surer about him than any of the others. Kai and Angel had love. Bane didn't want it—or so I had thought. But Caspian? He was waiting for me.

The little black heart I'd scribbled beside his face blurred in my vision.

He hated me. He hated me as much as he did the day he tore my bracelet away and whispered threats. It would never change.

The night stretched on in silence, and when sleep finally found me, the nightmares pounced.

"How soon can you get rid of her? Caspian's efficient when his sister isn't hanging around all the time." Logan appeared at my side as the

nightmare swept me away. He wrinkled his nose in a scowl. I paused, tuning back into the conversation between him and Eli.

"What's... what's wrong with his sister?" I dared ask. I hadn't said anything for a good while, not since Logan had folded and tucked the picture of the pack into his pocket.

Earlier they'd been talking about getting her fired, and it was stuck in my brain.

Logan glanced at me, amused. "Nothing. He loves her. But when she's visiting all the time his work declines. Drags up the past too much, I think."

Work? Logan wanted to take Caspian's sister away for the sake of his job?

"But... she makes him happy?" I asked.

"He'll get over it." Logan shrugged. "How soon do you think—?"

My fingers closed around Logan's arm, swallowing the jolt of pain. "Don't..." I whispered. "Don't do it."

Logan froze, turning to me. "What did you say?" The amusement in his eyes was dangerous, now.

My fingers were still curled around his arm. Something inside me quaked with fear at what I was about to do, but... They were my mates, and he was toying with them like he toyed with me.

I leaned up, my words just for him. "I'll... I'll do what you want, if you don't make his sister leave."

A cruel smile crept upon Logan's face. His finger curled under my chin and I stifled my flinch. "That's your price, is it?"

My pulse was thready as I nodded.

He leaned even closer, his words a breath. "I will, if you can convince Eli to do more than kiss you."

I felt the blood drain from my face as he leaned away.

But with the request, came an unexpected thrill. Logan would take my bargain, and for the first time in forever, I felt the faintest glimmer of control. It was more thrilling than his request was frightening.

"If-if I do that." I steadied my voice. "She gets a promotion."

The flash of delight on Logan's face was, perhaps, the most genuine thing I'd ever seen from him. He leaned back, his hand dropping from my chin.

"Done."

It took me a while to build the courage to edge across the booth to Eli. He wasn't hostile toward me, but his expression was often impassive, and I found him hard to read. I started by trailing my finger along Eli's arm with just the gentlest touch. It didn't hurt like Logan's touch did. It also wasn't bold or confident like the other omegas I'd seen in Gavin's, but his response was instant, all the same.

The eyes he fixed on me were curious. Dark chocolate curls fluttered around his olive skin.

He was a good-looking man. He just... wasn't my mate.

How... was I going to go from here, to a kiss?

He must know what I was doing, but did he want me to take the conversational steps, anyway?

Or could this be a prank, and he might throw me off, not wanting my advances at all. If that was the case, I was fucked anyway. I wasn't going to give Logan the satisfaction of seeing me bumble about. He taunted me enough about how I was a terrible omega.

I clenched my jaw. I was an omega, and Eli was an alpha.

He was packless, though his aura wasn't gone. He had been his pack's lead, but after one of his brothers had died, two of the others had developed aura sickness, their alpha auras slowly waning to nothing. The last of them had cut the pack bond himself, leaving Eli alone.

Logan had told me the story once, on one of the few nights Eli left early.

As far as I knew, Eli had never had a mate, and I'd never seen *him with the omegas Logan brought in. In fact, I'd never seen him interested in much at all aside from the business talks.*

I took a breath. If he was going to reject me, I should get it over with.

I stood, slipping between him and the table so it was easy to slide onto his lap, straddling him. Adrenaline hit my veins as I held his gaze. Still, he barely changed, his dark eyes holding mine. They were brown, I could see from here, just so dark they almost looked black. He had a strong nose that was perfectly straight, and his face was slim and angled. He sometimes wore a strap of a dark beard, and it suited him well.

As I settled onto his lap, his grip closed around my waist. It wasn't urging me on, but also wasn't a rejection. I was so close now, and I could taste the faintest trace of bourbon on his breath. His eyes had shifted, something hungry in them as I stared up at him. He smelled like sage and something earthy.

He almost looked like... like he wanted me.

Something warm and pleasant coiled in my stomach. Suddenly, reaching up to cup his face was easy. He didn't speak, waiting for me.

I drew closer, fear and anticipation fire in my veins... and then I pressed my lips to his.

His soft lips parted, moulding with mine easily. It was a shock when he pushed his tongue between my teeth, pressing deeper, exploring my mouth like he couldn't get enough. His grip was firm as he dragged me against him. One of his hands moved to my hair, holding me against him possessively as he deepened the kiss further, tilting my head slightly. I could hear the faint vibration in his chest.

That was want.

Want from him in a way Logan had never wanted me, and at his touch, all that passed between us was warmth, not one flicker of pain.

My hands dropped from his face, instead curling around his shirt as I pulled myself closer to him.

When he broke the kiss, I was breathless and there was heat in my core.

"More." My whisper was longing and desperation and victory. This is what Logan wanted from me, and perhaps it was supposed to be a punishment, but it wasn't.

Eli dragged me against his chest, standing and the next thing I knew the bed was at my back and Eli was caging me in.

Never once did I turn back to Logan.

"What do you want me to do?" My question was breathless and amateur, but Eli didn't seem to notice. His hands still pinned me to the bed, his kisses exploring my neck, collar, grazing the skin of my breasts.

He drew back up, a smile on his lips as he leaned close, speaking too low for Logan to hear. "I want to give you what you deserve, little omega."

His touch brushed my leg near the base of my skirt, and I tensed, unsure. Then he lowered himself down, slowly pressing my skirt up. My breath caught in my lungs.

I glanced at Logan once and wished I hadn't. He was leaning back, his fly undone, gripping himself as he watched us. The chill in my bones was quickly wiped from my mind as Eli pressed my knees further apart and tugged me closer. Then his mouth found my centre and every coherent thought I had died.

When I found release from Eli, it was bittersweet. The surge of pleasure was drowned by an aching pain. A need.

I knew it in my soul. I knew it from the burning mark on my neck.

It was because it wasn't Logan who'd given me that release, when he was the one who'd claimed me. The one I'd chosen.

I fought tears as my body shook with pleasure and pain.

He frowned as he took me in, tilting his head. "It wasn't good?" He sounded wounded.

But... if he said anything to Logan...

I nodded, cupping his cheek. "It was. I swear it was. I just..." I trailed off, and for a moment his gaze slid to my neck. His eyes darkened for a moment as if he could see the pain it delivered. "It wasn't you." I needed him to understand.

It was me. Just like Logan had said all along. I was the broken one.

I returned to Logan's side, and he drew me close, his breath hot on my ear. "Sweet Havoc, that was perfect."

I shut my eyes, trying not to ball my fists. "When you came," he went on. "I felt your release like pure fucking bliss."

My eyes snapped up to him, blinking in shock, my chest heaving. I jumped as Logan pressed something into my hands.

When I stood before the bathroom mirror that night, I realised the princess mark on my neck had turned a deep black. I swallowed, wondering if it was worth it. I glanced down at the piece of paper he'd given me. The photo of my mates blurred in my vision as tears crowded my eyes.

Had I betrayed them today, by wanting Eli?

I curled up in bed, the photo in my trembling grip, drinking in each line of every face except Logan's.

If they met me, would they even want me at all?

Kai

Havoc was having nightmares tonight.

I could see the problem. It was obvious. Her nest was, to put it bluntly, pathetic. It was in my DNA to recognise that. She didn't have enough... well... anything.

I could fix it.

So, I hurried out of her room and down to the hallway to the living room. Cass had been a real dick to her today, and I'd found that Caspian's dickishness was a great way to get people to forget *quite* how bad I was.

I gathered up all the blankets and cushions I could carry and headed back.

It was a bit of a challenge to slip into her room silently with an armful of nesting material, but I managed.

Then I got to work, quietly and gently tucking the cushions into place around her.

If she wanted a safe nest, I could give her that.

I tried to put myself in her shoes as I dragged cushions in from all over the living room.

She was worried about Caspian, I knew that, but she didn't understand something. The more you pissed Caspian off, the more likely he was to fall in love with you.

... Or kill you.

Actually, now I considered that theory... it could go either way. Maybe I was just lucky. Hmm... Caspian had probably killed dozens more people than he'd loved. Come to think of it, maybe I wouldn't mention that to Havoc, after all.

I dropped the last bundle of couch cushions onto the floor. This was hard work. I was exhausted.

Right.

One last touch and then I'd go to sleep.

I found the remote and turned on the TV, making sure it was muted. Then I flicked through the settings until I found the Grand Prix reruns saved to our account. I found one over eight hours long, which was more than enough to get Havoc through the night.

Good.

Extra good.

I turned the volume up, so it was a low buzz in the background, and then I curled up at her side, easily dropping off to sleep.

Havoc

I woke up to the most soothing sound I'd ever heard. It was accompanied by the faint vibrations and warmth pressed against my back. It was a deep, low purr.

My eyes opened, my vision bleary. I froze.

There were arms around me. Heavy and hot, holding me against a broad chest.

Maple and cinders filled my nostrils.

Kai.

I let out a squeak.

"Shh, it's okay..." Kai's voice was drowsy, and he tugged me closer in response.

But... Why wasn't I hurting? He was touching me... And... my eyes flew open. What the fuck was going on? I was in a large dark box.

I bolted up in terror, startling Kai awake.

"Hey wait—!" He grabbed me back against him. I was just about to loose a terrified scream when I finally realised where I was.

I could hear the TV... The blankets were familiar and covered with *my* scent. I was in my room.

"Don't freak out. I just helped out with the nest a bit." He pulled me closer, as if he could squeeze the frightened breaths right out of me.

But I was still processing what he was saying.

He'd... built me a nest? I had to bite my lip to keep it from trembling.

Kai had built me a nest—and then climbed in without warning... But still.

He'd... built me a nest, and it was ridiculous and over the top and didn't even make sense... but... I could smell the whole house in this nest. Not just Bane's leathery apple scent, but that sweet cinnamon smell that was Angel, and the rich roses and cranberry of Caspian—though less of that, as if Kai had tried to avoid it.

My breathing slowed and for a moment I had to fight the tears pricking my eyes.

Slowly, Kai loosened his grip, and I turned to him, though he still didn't release me completely. The light was dim, mostly getting over the towering walls of the nest from the TV.

His crimson eye glowed dully in the dark. "I can take it all down in the morning—if you still want to keep it secret."

I stared at him, unsure of what to say to that, so I just nodded. It hurt, taking down my nest. It was like a wound gouging into my soul.

"Why are you crying?" He looked startled.

Shit.

One traitorous tear had escaped. Before I could do anything, he was wiping it away. I furrowed my brow, staring at his fingers before I realised he was again wearing thin black gloves to protect me.

"Are you scared of me?" he asked.

"No." It was the truth actually. My tears were not nearly that rational. Still, I wasn't afraid of him. Not like I should be.

I was just... overwhelmed and... happy. Which made me an idiot, because the last time I'd felt hope like this was Logan. And I needed to rein it in.

Logan would have never made you a nest.

"You should try to get some more sleep," Kai murmured, clearly intending to stay. And I wanted him to.

Kai's touch lifted to my neck, and he began massaging a spot just beneath my jaw. The motion made me melt against him, and an unfamiliar low sound came from my chest.

"Are you purring for me, little omega?" Kai breathed.

I couldn't find words to deny it, but I did try to catch the traitorous sound.

"Your heat's coming," he murmured.

I stiffened, terrified at any notion that they might discover that.

"Do you want to keep it away?"

That question caught me off guard. I nodded, unsure.

"Then you have to relax," he murmured. "Don't startle it along."

Relax? How was I supposed to do that? The pressure of his fingers deepened, and a little moan escaped me.

"That's not going to help," he told me.

"What?" The word was breathless.

"Thinking about what it would be like if I knotted you."

Holy hell. "I'm *not*."

Okay. But now I was. *Fuck.*

Another sound escaped me, this one much more needy. I was pressed against him, which meant I felt the way his body responded to that sound.

A flutter of panic set me on edge. Was this really happening? Kai was holding me in his arms, whispering taunts in my ear.

And I was responding. As in—it wasn't a dream, and that meant real life Kai was going to hear whatever stupid things might come out of my mouth as he teased me.

I *had* to act normal. "You..." I gathered myself. "Aren't making that very easy."

Okay, good. That sounded like a normal thing a normal person would say.

He let out a low laugh, his fingers still massaging that pressure point on my neck. "Maybe I'm motivated by different things."

"You *want* me to go into heat?"

He paused, and then his next words sent my head spinning. "I want you. Forever."

I swallowed, grounding myself before I made another colossal mistake. These were sweet words from an alpha. I knew that was my weakness. "Life's not that simple."

"You are," he breathed in my ear. "They'll see it too. Cass and Angel... Bane doesn't need convincing."

"I don't *want* you." I realised at that moment, how much of a lie it was.

I just didn't want a dark bond.

But these men... Even now, pressed against Kai... God I was such a fool. I was giddy with the attention.

Starved of it for months, I was a wreck. Vulnerable and easy to please, I felt helpless at that realisation. It was dangerous and I could never give into it.

"I could help you relax some more?" he offered, ignoring what I'd said.

What did that mean?

His grip tightened and his hand brushed my stomach, sliding down to the edge of my top.

"I can't..."

"Why?"

Because if I said yes to this it might just make me insane.

"Something tells me you follow the rules about as much as I do." He seemed to be reading my mind.

This was wrong—but I was quickly forgetting all reasons as to why.

Maple and cinders. It was enough to drown me. I knew he'd be able to all but taste the hormones slicking off me right now.

"Let me in Havoc." Kai was pulling me tighter against him.

He was wearing gloves, his whole body covered—just to protect me. It was more than madness. He recognised my pain and tried to avoid it. Around us, ridiculous walls of cushions towered, carrying scents from across the whole house. From all the others.

All of them except Logan.

He'd done that for me. What if... just for this moment, I let myself have the dream I'd clung to for so many months?

He was offering.

And it was safe. The lights were off. Not like it had been with Logan. That room had been so bright, he'd always been able to see me. Always been reminded of who I was.

"What use is an omega who can't seduce their alpha?"

My lip quivered.

But this was Kai. Not Logan. *My* Kai. *And he was the one offering.*

I shut my eyes, shifting my mouth against his forearm, the corded muscle that held me against him. I pressed my teeth against his flesh, pure instinct driving me on.

I bit down. A demand. A little whine rising in my chest.

He loosed a growl and then his fingers moved below my panties, finding me soaked.

Then he slipped two fingers into me. I let out a moan of shock and pleasure.

He flipped us both so that my face was pressed against pillows, and he was behind me, then pushed my shirt up. He crushed me into the nest but for my hips, which he tugged upwards against his own body as he began to fuck me with his fingers, holding me down with a tight grip on my hair.

"You're pure addiction, Havoc," he breathed in my ear. "Since the first time I saw you, I've not been able to get you out of my head."

I writhed beneath him, my pleasure building too fast—so much faster than it had with Eli.

I let out a needy moan, louder than before.

He ground against me, and I felt his hardness, his desire and that alone—the feeling of him wanting me—it was enough to send me over the edge.

EIGHTEEN

Angel

"Are we sure we should let him come?" Cass was in the passenger seat, a scowl on his face as I drove. "I say we drop him at the side of the road and call it."

Kai snorted from the back seat, and I could see his smirk in the rear view. I didn't voice the agreement I was feeling, since someone had to hold it together.

This was fucking miserable. We were all tense, all wearing black, and on our way to Logan's funeral.

Kai had been gone all night, which made me angry—because dude, pick your fucking days.

Bane and Cass weren't speaking, not something I'd usually notice, since Bane didn't talk much at all, but it was obvious from the tension in the air. At breakfast, the testosterone was so thick I could have spread it on my toast.

And Kai wouldn't shut up with his stupid comments about Havoc. He was on overdrive, and I'd caught him trying to put on a black t-shirt with 'Rainfall and Firewood' written across it this morning. I'd had to literally wrestle it off him.

When had he found time to get a t-shirt with Havoc's scent printed across it?

It even had a graphic of a campfire in the rain. I'd have thought it didn't need explaining that Logan's *funeral* wasn't the place to start testing boundaries. If it was anyone else, I might have strangled him.

Cass *would* have lost it though, and I was starting to realise that was the entire point.

"He's not going to say this shit once we get there," I growled.

Kai mimed zipping his mouth and Bane snorted. The two of them seemed to be getting closer, which was good, but I just wished it didn't involve disrespecting Logan's grave.

Havoc

The pack was at Logan's funeral this afternoon. Bane had visited to let me know they'd be out, and there were snacks in the fridge.

I hadn't seen him since he'd lost it on Caspian yesterday, but this didn't really seem like the time to bring it up either.

Something about knowing I was alone in the house changed things. Normally I could never be completely sure Caspian wasn't lurking in an armchair, ready to pounce again.

I found myself wandering their rooms, well, all but Caspian's, because even though my scent may not linger, I wouldn't risk it.

Bane's room was excruciatingly clean. I couldn't help the smile on my face as I looked around. It was dim, with cool lights above, and the colours were all dark. His bed was made of sleek black wood with deep green bedding. The couches looked frankly clinical, and I couldn't help taking one of the little decorative cushions and knocking it to the floor. Actually... next thing I knew I bent to pick it up, brushing my chin along it, marking it with my scent. The air was thick with leather and applewood and I wanted to be part of that. I froze, cushion clutched between my fingers.

What was I doing?

That was flirting. *Heavy* fucking flirting. With a guy I couldn't have... I stuffed the cushion hastily beneath two others and backed out of the room quickly.

Instead, I wandered up the stairs to the rooms beyond the balcony overlooking the living room. I was in Kai and Angel's room when I felt it. The distinct, vicious twist of my stomach. I doubled over, my hand coming out to grip their bedside table.

Fuck.

No. Not now. Not yet.

My heat... Please... Please be a false alarm.

I sank to my knees, shaking as I tried to reject it. My skin felt like it was on fire and a low whine rose in my chest.

My first thought was panic, because they were all out. My mates were all out, and I was about to go into heat.

"Get a grip," I hissed. Even if I did go into heat. I needed drugs to knock me out like my father had always given me. An IV in my arm with a soothing cocktail so I could sleep it out.

Not four men.

Four beautiful men.

I whined again.

"You aren't wanted," I choked. "Get a grip."

I clutched the wooden side table, desperately praying for a false alarm.

It would pass.

It would pass.

I shut my eyes, but that was a mistake. Memories slammed into me of the last time I'd felt this.

. . .

A text popped up on Logan's open phone on the table before me. He was at the door, arguing with Gavin about some arrangement or another. My eyes slid to the screen of texts as I recognised the name.

> Kai: It was his mothers. We were drunk playing video games. Don't know who broke it.

Kai sent a photo. It was the smashed pieces of something ceramic.

I stared at the texts and the photo, my heart racing.

They were right there.

I could reach out and tap a few buttons and talk to them. I glanced up to see Eli watching me calmly from the other side of the table. I swallowed. It was too risky.

More texts popped up.

> Kai: It's his prayer angel thing. His mum gave it to him.
>
> Caspian: Did you just make a chat to talk behind his back?
>
> Kai: He won't say how upset he is.
>
> Bane: Can we make it up to him?

I furrowed my brow, reading and rereading the text on the screen. Prayer angel?

I had a pair of those. One was my dad's, and one was mine. They were some of the few things I'd been able to bring.

I slipped from my seat and made for my bed. The first opaque sapphire blue angel was sitting on my bedside table. The other I found in the drawer. They were both ancient, and the one I held had part of the hands missing and a chip in the halo.

Logan was seating himself at the little cove, checking his texts when I set the angel down on the table.

"Give it to him?" I whispered.

Logan stared at me, then glanced at the little figure on the table. He picked it up, turning it in his hand with a sneer. "You want me to give him junk?"

My throat tightened. Another text buzzed.

Caspian: Alright. Can we get him another one?

"It's not junk to me," I breathed.

Logan laughed, but the phone buzzed again.

Kai: It's not about the money, damn thing was old as sin, anyway. It's about what it meant to him.

Logan glanced at his phone again and then back to me, considering. "Okay."

My heart lifted.

"After the omega leaves today, I want you playing with Eli. If you're good enough I'll consider giving that to Angel."

I blinked, my heart in my throat at the thought of a little piece of me leaving this room... taken out into the world, falling into Angel's hands... What would he think of it? Would he put it beside his bed like I put it beside mine? I had its partner at my bedside right now. He... would be with me when I slept.

My angel, watching over me.

I nodded too quickly, and Logan grinned, reclining back and tapping a few buttons. I saw the text as he placed the phone down.

Logan: Don't worry. I have the perfect gift.

It was a promise to me.

Just like when I'd bargained for Caspian's sister, I felt a little thrill in my veins. I could tolerate the evening, knowing what I'd won.

The omega he brought in tonight was beautiful, with pale skin and midnight hair. She was in heat. I knew it the moment she entered. There was a certain buzz to her scent, a flavour of energy on top of the sweet, fruity aroma about her.

She walked in on steady feet, which meant she was in a down spell, but her pupils were blown, sliding between Eli and Logan with desire.

This, I realised, was going to be awful. I felt Eli's arm tighten around my waist. I hadn't noticed how I'd shrunk down against him.

"Come," Logan commanded. Her eyes were fixed on him, and she slinked over.

The moment Logan took her hand in his, I felt it, discomfort twisting my stomach. I tensed in Eli's arms, but he was still holding me tight. It was like this every time.

As I watched the two of them, I sunk into my dreams. I imagined Angel getting my gift. What would he think? Would he think it was trash?

Logan joined the omega on the bed. The pain on my neck grew, seeping into my blood and bones. Still, I remained in Eli's arms, forced to keep my eyes on Logan.

No. Angel was the type to appreciate a gift like that—I was sure of it. The beautiful omega was on top of Logan now, her hands running desperately up his chest. His head was tilted back, eyes fixed on me as the omega pressed her hips down over him. My pain spiked and my stomach twisted. I was shaking.

My gift for Angel, it wasn't expensive, but Logan said he'd grown up rich, that money didn't mean the same to him as it did everyone else.

I blinked as I felt another stronger twist in my stomach, shattering all my dreams. It was familiar. I was on my feet in a moment as I excused myself to the bathroom. Logan would be pissed, but... God I couldn't—I shut the door, fumbling at the counter as my stomach twisted again. The other pain—the pain I felt when I saw him with another, it died down though, letting me focus.

"Fuck," I hissed. "Fuck fuck fuck."

My heat... No. No, I couldn't... But then a thought struck me.

What was I thinking? The hormones slicking off that midnight-haired omega out there were intoxicating.

If I went into heat, would Logan... would he want me? Would it be enough?

A flutter of fear accompanied the next twist. I sank to my knees.

I let the waves of warmth wash over me, my body shaking until the ache passed.

My heat wasn't here yet, this was just a warning. A warning that it was coming soon.

I stood, anxiously flattening down the creases in my dress. My scent would be thick in the air. There wasn't anything I could do about it, though. If I spent any longer in here, he would be too angry...

I crossed back to Eli, and he tugged me onto his lap, his eyes on his phone as the other two in the room made ungodly noises. The pain returned, each beat of my heart shooting it through my veins.

The moment my eyes found Logan again, he groaned, climaxing. He'd waited on purpose, I knew it. Anything to make me suffer. My fists balled in my lap, trying to keep my breathing even. Keeping Logan from seeing the amount of agony he caused was the only power I had left.

But sex during heat wasn't a one round thing, and it didn't take long before they were back at it.

I pressed back against Eli, my voice low enough that only he could hear. "If I'm in heat... Will it be enough? Will he...?" I swallowed. Would he end this at last? I didn't need to finish the question.

Eli's fingers bit down on my waist and he stroked my hair gently. There was something sad in the motion that set my nerves on edge.

Then he tapped his phone and opened up a chat, searching it for a while before leaving it open on my lap. I stole intermittent glances, not wanting Logan to spot me looking away.

The dark-haired omega he was with right now was clutching him desperately, moaning loudly as Logan gripped her waist, his head thrown back with pleasure.

> Logan: She's going to be rabid when she's in heat.

> Eli: Planning on holding out on her?

Logan: She doesn't deserve me. How many times do you think a gold pack slut should have to get on her knees to make up for that? Anyway, drug in the fucking air if I make her watch. Tell me I'm wrong.

> Logan: Probably have to leash her to the bed though.

> Logan: How close do you think she is?

I felt bile burning my throat.

"Knot..." The omega's voice was a desperate moan. "Please... knot me."

My nails dug into my palms.

My heat would not be like that. It would not be my salvation. I stared at the desperation of the omega before me. I could feel the pheromones in the air—could practically feel her need as if it were my own.

This was what heat looked like, desperate and feral. Logan's text had been clear.

She doesn't deserve me.

This wasn't going to end. The torture I went through every visit would be nothing compared to what was coming.

I jumped as Eli pressed something into my palm. I glanced down briefly and found I was holding a tiny white pill.

"It will keep it away a little longer," he murmured in my ear.

I clenched my fist around it.

Eli was helping me?

With my eyes still fixed on Logan my fingers found Eli's arm and I squeezed it briefly. Enough to say I was grateful.

The heat was dissipating, the pangs of pain dying down. The world came into focus. The first thing I saw was the galaxy duvet cover draped on the floor beside Kai and Angel's bed. I straightened, catching my breath, removing my hands from the coffee table I'd been clutching.

I took a steadying breath, and then froze.

Before me, on the tabletop was a half-finished glass of water, a small tin of mints and a cracked blue angel.

My... angel.

My breath caught.

I reached for it.

It was familiar to my touch, something I'd held countless times in my life as I'd gone to sleep.

Logan had given it to Angel, and Angel kept it here beside his bed, just like I dreamed he would.

Then a hateful voice sliced across the space.

"Put. That. *Down.*"

NINETEEN

Angel

"Put that *down*." My voice cut across the space, shaking with fury. I'd returned to find Havoc in my room. In her hand was the blue prayer angel.

The last gift Logan had given me before he died.

From a man who wielded money like it was water, who bought only the newest, most expensive things, that cracked blue prayer angel had been the most precious gift.

I remember not thinking anything could replace the one that broke. And then he'd handed me that, and something about the imperfections, the cracks... it *had* to be important if Logan had kept it.

Now Havoc had it clutched in her fist as she stared over at me, her expression tight.

I'd left the funeral early. I wasn't ready. Not for the casket, not for the condolences. Not for the moment one of his aunts had approached us. "Tragic, how it happened. So violent."

At which point I heard Kai whisper to Bane, "Shot in the head by the hottie I finger banged this morning."

Aaaannnd that was it.

I had to leave.

And I wish that was really the reason. I was the only one of us who'd seen Logan the night he'd died. That memory replayed over and over every minute I was there, and all I could land on was her.

She had been kneeling beside the bed, covered in blood as she stared at him. Unable to move, unable to run.

When she looked up at me, there was one brief moment where her eyes had gone wide and she reached out, a desperate sound coming from her chest. Then she pulled her hand back, a shadow crossing her expression as she looked back to Logan, tears flooding her cheeks, tracking salt through Logan's blood.

Why had she shot Logan, and then stopped Bane attacking Cass?

That was all I could fucking think.

So, I left, because Logan deserved better.

And now here *she* was, in my room, taking his gifts while soil smothered him.

Had they buried him yet?

Was it done?

"How *dare* you," I snarled, taking another few steps forward. Her fist tightened around the precious thing. "Put it down."

"It's... important to you?" she asked. For a moment, the question was desperate, like the answer meant something to her. But the words... They were a taunt. She was holding something of mine, and she wanted to know if she could wield it as a threat.

"Cass is right. You're playing us."

She'd messed with Bane and Kai. And now Kai defended her, spiralling and going after Cass in her defence.

"Playing you?" She said the words slowly, as if testing them out. "You *took* me from the police."

She *had* tried to leave when she'd seen our door open, even if she'd failed. But what if she had known we were watching? What if this was all a trick to make her seem like such a damsel? Lost and gentle and sweet.

Well, there was only one way to find out. "You want me to take you to the station now?" I asked. It was a bluff. I couldn't, the vote we'd taken made it impossible. She was staying.

She opened her mouth, glancing between me and the angel in her hand. *My* angel.

"Y-yes," she stammered.

"Okay." I dug in my pocket for my keys, but she flinched at the sound, backing up a step.

I felt my hackles rise. "What's the problem?"

"What about the others?"

"They're still at the funeral. I can get you to the station by the time they get back. Close the door on Logan and you." I had to refrain from staring too long at the angel she still had in her fist. "Are you worried they'll miss you?"

I wish the flash of pain in her eyes didn't seem so damned genuine. She shook her head, furiously chewing on her bottom lip. "Just... Maybe we wait until they're back, talk to Bane and Kai—"

"They don't *like* you, Havoc. Not really. You just"—I waved a hand at her—"Smell good. That's all." It was crueller than I'd meant it to be, but hearing Kai's name on her lips set me on edge.

"Kai... built me a pillow nest this morning."

God, did she have to look so pathetic saying something like that? There was a little flash of hope in her eyes, as if I might tell her what that meant. I clenched my jaw. "He wants to bang you."

She shook her head.

"Right. He didn't touch you then—I'm sure. He just wanted to have a pillow fight and cuddle you to sleep, all platonic and shit?"

I might have slapped her, by the way she flinched.

That was low—I knew that. But I was sick of this facade. I needed to see her crack, to see that vicious, raging woman who'd arrived the day Logan died. That woman had been easier to reconcile with.

"He said you were the nice one." Her words were so quiet I almost didn't hear them.

My blood chilled. "Who?" My voice was a low growl.

"Logan." When she said that, her knuckles went white around my angel. My pulse quickened.

"Don't say his fucking name," I breathed.

"He was my mate. I can say his name."

"You didn't deserve him, just like you don't deserve Bane or Kai or—"

I cut off at her reaction. He eyes went wide, the blood draining from her face, then she let out a strangled scream. Before I could do a thing, she flung the angel at the marble floor.

It shattered with the last dwindling shreds of my sanity.

I closed the distance, grabbing her by the arms, catching myself before I shook her. My chest was heaving as she glared up at me with a twisted expression on her face.

"Why would you—?" I cut off, knowing how stupid that was. She didn't give a shit.

She looked like she was about to spit something back at me when her expression slipped to horror. She buckled.

"Havoc—?"

A low moan slipped from her throat and her scent hit me like a truck. The world was ripped from around me. There was, in that moment, nothing else but her. She clutched her stomach, her breathing heavy as if she were in pain.

I wasn't aware of lifting her in my arms until I felt the blankets beneath us.

What the fuck had happened? Had I done something?

I was tilting her to face me again, and she loosed another low sound. It set my veins on fire. I had to take care of her. What did she need?

I felt a tug and looked down to see her fingers curling around my shirt, holding tight. She whined again.

That sound, her touch, the scent in the air, it was like an ocean wave crashing into me and sweeping me out with it. All rational thoughts gone from my head, I leaned down and pressed my lips to hers, dragging her closer. Her hands became more insistent, wrapping around me as she panted into my mouth. Little mewls were escaping her now, needy and desperate.

I was red hot, but I leaned back as she wriggled beneath me.

"What do you need?"

"Too... Hot..." She whimpered. "So hot."

It was true, her skin was on fire. I leaned back as she fumbled for the waistband of her sweatpants. Right. I helped her slip them off, my veins alight at the sight of the perfect, smooth golden skin of her legs. She was tense, pressed into my pillows, chestnut hair sticking to her pink cheeks.

"I'm..." Her voice cracked, but I was already leaning close, holding her gaze.

"What?"

Her eyes were glistening. "I'm s-scared."

"No." My voice was a low growl. "I'm here."

That was when it hit me. Heat. She was going into heat.

And I was the only one in my house.

Because all my brothers were out at Logan's fucking funeral.

It was as if a bucket of ice water was dumped on my head.

I was pressed over her, palms against the sheets of my bed. Mine and *Kai's* bed. She was staring up at me, chest heaving in terror and need... And I'd just lost myself so much I'd told her I would help her through her heat.

She was ruin.

Unadulterated destruction.

We couldn't kill her. If this was a *fraction* of what Bane and Kai felt—we were never taking her back to the police.

I hadn't realised until this moment how impossible that was. We had no control left.

There was only one answer.

Havoc let out another whimper that almost wiped my mind completely blank, but I held on. The air... it wasn't so thick with her scent anymore—or I was getting used to it.

Good. Good, I needed to.

She froze beneath me as I wound my fingers into her hair and tilted her chin up. Her golden eyes darted between mine, uncertain all of a sudden. I felt a fissure crack across my heart, but I didn't care. I didn't have room to care. I needed to do this so none of the others had to.

"W-what are you doing?" She was frightened. Her fear rattled me. I didn't answer because I didn't trust my voice. Instead, I lowered down,

I could do it. By deciding on the act, I swayed the vote to a majority. Bane and Kai had said yes already.

We needed some control back. This was the only way.

My teeth pressed against the skin just beneath her collar.

"Don't..." Her voice was thick. "P-please don't."

The fissure grew, scoring too deep. What I was about to do was an evil thing. It was wrong. It was wrong and completely necessary, and we were done for without it—but it went against everything I'd ever thought of myself.

This was our right. A dark bond was our right to claim for the life she'd taken. The life that was being buried right now.

I tried to convince myself of that.

We decided her fate—that was the law. And no one would blame us for this.

What if I didn't do it, and Kai had to? Would it destroy him? What about Bane? He seemed to care for her, truly care, and while I didn't understand how he could, I wanted that for him.

I was the only one who could shoulder this. I had to open the dark bond, so they wouldn't have to.

Havoc

I couldn't move beneath Angel.

I shook my head just the slightest bit, as if begging him not to dark bond me was a fucking option. Logan had told me once that Angel was the kind of man who would do the right thing, no matter what it cost.

I felt pain as his teeth bit down and he broke skin. Something shifted within me, making my breath catch. It was Angel. I could feel his presence through the bond, just like Logan had been there after he'd bitten me. Only this connection made my soul ache. It was only a fraction, though, not a full bite—not even close.

Angel was absolutely still. Nothing else happened for the longest time and I dared not struggle, not wanting his teeth to cut anymore.

Tears flooded my cheeks.

This was it. I would be bonded to them like a slave. Every dream of them would shatter in the face of that.

Then he shifted away from me. I was still pinned by his weight, but his teeth were gone. He leaned away just a little more. I could see his face, the set to his jaw.

For a moment the world stilled as we stared at one another, faces inches apart. His chest was heaving, and there was a true war within the deep forest green of his eyes. The freckled, warm brown of his skin was flushed, full lips parted in a snarl.

"Run." His voice was a husk. I stared into his eyes and realised it wasn't a game he was playing, or a dare. He was strained, absolutely warring with himself not to do this.

For a moment, I was too frightened to move. His hand closed around my shirt, and he leaned in closer.

"I said. *Run*." It was a command. The strongest command I'd heard from him, outstripping what I believed his aura capable of.

It ripped me free of the heat haze. He didn't fight me as I threw him off, then I was ducking from beneath his arms and staggering from the bed. I didn't look back as I tore through the door, my breaths heavy as I took the spiral stairs down to the main living room.

Only then did I look back up to the balcony. He was there, eyes following me as I backed up, his grip taut on the railings.

I turned and fled down the hallway and didn't stop until I had locked myself in my bathroom.

TWENTY

Caspian

Elliot fucking Kingsman was coming over tonight. He'd cornered me and Bane at the end of the funeral and all but invited himself over. For the good old times, he'd said. We'd known him for too long to deny him, and he was apparently helping Angel sort out Logan's estate.

I'd say at least when he knocked on the door, he'd brought booze, but it was pink and in a tall glass bottle, so it didn't count.

Angel, Logan, Bane and Elliot had grown up together. Me and Kai had met them when we were in our early teens, but none of us had realised we might be destined for a pack until we were sixteen. By that time Elliot had found another set of brothers. Bunch of pricks, the lot of them, and I was glad when I'd heard it. The years since hadn't been kind to him or his choice.

I hadn't seen him in a while, and he looked tired. Some of his cockiness had faded, the smile on his face a little more rigid than I remembered. He still had his ponytail, a few loose chocolate waves framing his cheeks. He had olive skin, with an all too straight nose that had always just looked so... punchable.

One day.

He sat himself down on our couch where Kai was running through channels. Angel was making his way down the stairs.

Bane's eyes flickered up from his book, but he said nothing as he eyed Elliot. It was hard to read Bane, but I thought he might have gone a bit tense at the sight of his childhood friend.

"Damn Kingsman, didn't mention you were coming." Angel clapped Elliot on the shoulder before taking a seat beside him. I joined them, settling down on my armchair, flicking through emails on my phone.

"How are you holding up?" Elliot asked.

I saw Angel shrug out of the corner of my eye.

"Losing a pack mate never leaves you," Elliot said, quietly.

I grunted, looking up. Maybe I thought he was a pretentious prick, but he knew this pain first hand and it was nice to hear someone take it seriously.

"Hey, Bane. You think uh... you could check on her?" Angel looked shifty. Bane's eyes snapped up. "I caught her in my room earlier. Thought she might uh... be in heat."

"*In?*" Bane asked. "Like now?"

Kai straightened as Bane jumped to his feet.

Elliot's eyebrows rose as he poured himself a glass of wine, clearing his throat.

"Well, no one mentioned we were having visitors," Angel muttered.

"How long ago?" Bane demanded.

"End of the funeral." Angel looked more sullen than I was used to seeing.

"Shit." Bane was striding down the hallway.

There was no way she was in heat this whole time. We'd know. We'd have to know. Not that I wanted that complication in the mix, but I knew she'd find a way to pull some mind-fucking-crap on my brothers.

"So..." Elliot glanced between us. "She's part of the pack?"

"No." I said, much too aggressively.

"We're... not sure what to do about her," Angel added.

There was an awkward silence in which I could practically see the sulk on Kai's face.

Brat.

"It's fine," Bane said, returning down the hall. "She said it was a false alarm."

"Thank god," Angel muttered. I agreed.

"Means it's soon, though," Bane said. "We're going to have to make some decisions.

"Not tonight." Angel leaned forward to pick up Elliot's offensive pink contribution to the night and pour himself a glass.

The conversation went on for a long time. Enough so that they began getting into discussions of Logan from their youth, most of which I wasn't familiar with. Bane was unwillingly dragged into a few.

They finished the bottle off as they talked, and Angel went to the kitchen for another.

"You guys mind if I kip here for the night?" Elliot asked. "My pad is so far away?"

"'Course," Angel said. "Logan would never turn you away. Neither will we."

Well great. The last thing I wanted was having to see this asshole in the morning. I'd be sleeping in late.

"So. The elephant in the room," Elliot said, leaning back. "She's gold pack. What are you getting upset about?" He asked. "Dark bond her so she's not a problem, and have some out-of-bond-fucks if you ever want annoying little alpha shits running about."

"We don't want her bonded," I growled. Well. Half of us didn't.

"Understandable, I suppose." Elliot shrugged. "But dark bonds are different. You run the show. You aren't going to get in trouble for it—so why not?"

I snorted, leaning back in my chair.

That sort of cowardly thinking process summed up Elliot Kingsman perfectly well.

Havoc

I locked myself in my bathroom all evening, curled up in the corner and clutching my throat. Bane had knocked on my bathroom door at one point. "Havoc, are you...? Angel said something about heat—"

"I'm fine!" I squeaked back. "False alarm."

Just a warning of my heat this time. But it wouldn't be for long.

I battled with tears all evening, my mind going over it again and again. Angel had been there, and for a moment everything might have been alright.

Then his teeth had clamped down on my neck.

I could still feel the echo of it. Of him across the house right now as this wound sealed up. It wasn't a full bite; I'd know if it was.

I hadn't realised, until that moment, how frightened I was of a dark bond. Everything I'd ever gone through with Logan—they'd be able to hurt me, just like that. I'd return to a world where I had no control.

Then... what had I been thinking? Talking Angel out of taking me to the police?

He'd literally offered. It was supposed to be everything I wanted. And I'd panicked at the idea.

Stupid. I couldn't be with Bane or Kai. I couldn't save Angel's aura with a regular omega bond, and they'd never offer me the princess bond.

That's all this pack wanted me for. A dark bond to save Angel.

I was a mess. I didn't know what I wanted anymore. What waited for me in the system was cold, and Bane's arms... Kai's... they were warm.

At the same time, Caspian and Angel didn't want me and I couldn't... I couldn't ever be bound to someone who didn't want me.

Not again.

"Are you afraid of me, Havoc?" Logan asked. He was on top of me on the bed, pinning me down, his hand around my neck.

I warred with the tears that were so close to ruining my makeup. That—that would make him upset. He had threatened to take away one of the gifts I'd given to the pack, and I'd challenged him. My cheek ached from the blow he'd given me.

I nodded, desperate for him to let me go. This was worse than it had ever been. Eli was out—he'd left to take a private call.

Logan's eyes creased with delight. "Would you still let me fuck you?"

My eyes widened as his grip closed tighter. I tried to swallow, but his hand crushing my neck was too much.

"Would you, Havoc? To end your pain? To be with them?"

My stomach did a flip. With loathing I nodded again, closing my eyes.

"Say it."

My breathing hitched and his grip became crushing.

Then I heard my drawer slide and glanced down to see him fumbling in my bedside table. He pulled out the picture he had given me. The one with the others. Angel, Caspian, Kai, Bane and Logan.

"What would they think if they found out how obsessed you are with them?"

I didn't reply, my eyes wild as he held the picture out before me. It was everything. The most important thing I owned.

"And besides, what is the point of me coming here at all, if you don't want me? I'm doing this for you, aren't I? For them. To see if you can become good enough to make me want you."

"Please don't..." I swallowed back the horrible words trying to come from my mouth.

Don't stop visiting...

I needed him as much as I feared him. Without Logan, I could never meet the others.

"Say. It," Logan spat.

I choked on my breath. "I... I do..." I stammered.

"Do what?"

"Want y-you."

"Want me to what?"

"T-to..." I couldn't look at him. "To sleep with m-me."

His grip relented at last, and I sagged, choking on lungfuls of clear air.

"Good little omega," he breathed in my ear.

Then he crushed the picture in his fist and tossed it onto the bed. I choked on my sob. As soon as he stepped away, I dived for it, unwrapping it and flattening out the creases.

Logan left, his laughter fading as the door slammed behind him.

I didn't realise Eli had returned until I felt the bed move as he sat down, lacing an arm around my waist and tugging me close.

"Do you know them?" I whispered.

Eli tensed, then nodded curtly.

My heart soared, the sensation tangling with my terror at what I was about to do. Eli could betray me. He could tell Logan what I was about to ask. But I trusted him. He came back every time. I dreaded the day Logan would walk through that door without Eli at his side.

Eli was gentle and kind and understood how much pain I was in. He did everything in his power beneath Logan to protect me.

"Could you tell them... about me?" I held myself absolutely still, my eyes darting back to Eli.

"He likes to keep his circles separate," he said. "He doesn't allow me near them anymore."

"Please." My fingers closed around Eli's hand. "Find a way to tell them."

He shut his eyes. "If I could, I would."

I curled up, tears forming in my eyes. "Where are they?" I choked. "Why... Why won't they come?"

"I'm here, Havoc." For the first time Eli pulled me into an embrace that had no other meaning than comfort. I clutched him desperately, holding onto the only good thing in my world. "I'm here and I won't leave you."

On the hard bathroom floor, I hugged my knees for hours, racing through my remaining options, hitting dead ends over and over until I heard the faintest knock on my bedroom door.

I waited for a while, but the knock sounded again.

I approached, much more cautious than I'd ever been before. But, if Angel was coming to bite me, he wouldn't be knocking. I creaked the door open, hoping for Bane. Instead, I found myself looking up into dark eyes framed by chocolate curls.

My mouth went dry as I stared up at him.

"Eli?"

TWENTY-ONE

Havoc

"What are you doing here?"

"I thought we could talk."

"And if you get caught?" I asked.

"I'm known for my silver tongue. I rather think I could talk my way out of it. Besides, it's only a chat."

"R-right."

Crossing the room, I tugged the curtains closed and then locked the balcony—I knew Kai entered through there sometimes. There was a flutter of nerves in my stomach as I saw Eli sitting on my couch.

I approached, suddenly aware that I was still in my black sweatpants and hoodie. "I'm not really dressed for..." For what? A date? Is that what I thought this was? My cheeks heated as he glanced up at me. I saw the faintest hint of a smile curve his lips.

"You are lovely, Havoc. As usual."

I couldn't explain why my throat went dry.

I liked him.

But it was more than that.

"You're not..." My voice was thick. "Angry?"

"Angry?" Eli's brows came down. "Why would I be angry?"

"I... I killed him."

Eli reached out from where he sat, catching my wrist and tugging me toward him. He took both my hands in his, staring up at me curiously. I swallowed, lacing my fingers into his, unsure why I was doing it... But his touch was familiar and comforting.

"Why on earth would I have done what I did, if I hadn't wanted that?"

Eli pressed his lips to mine, something he didn't do as often as I would like. Sometimes Logan got frustrated when we were too sweet.

He drew my touch to his jeans unexpectedly, and I froze as he slipped my finger into his pocket. He drew away, his own expression not wavering as I stared at him in shock, examining the smooth metal thing in my grip.

It wasn't until later that I had been able to take a proper look and discover what it was.

A bullet.

Eli had been the only one who saved me.

"You *wanted* me to kill him?" I asked.

Eli tensed and there was a storm in his eyes. "I wanted you to have a choice."

I couldn't look at him all of a sudden, shifting my eyes to the ceiling to gather myself.

"And you *did*." His voice was a breath.

I nodded, something lodged in my throat.

"None of them understand," he whispered. "They don't know what you went through."

But... Eli didn't understand either. I thought I would crack a tooth with the clench of my jaw.

"They don't know how strong you had to be."

I broke. Not able to let him continue spinning these tales. I shook my head, finding it in me to look at him. It *was* weakness in the end. Everything was my fault. "It didn't... after you left..." My voice broke. "It wasn't strength," I whispered. "He... he didn't need to die."

"What do you mean?"

None of it had gone the way Eli thought.

"Talk to me," he whispered. He tugged at my hands, still tangled with his, and I sunk down, guilt weighing at my heart as I let him hold me.

"Talk to me Havoc. I can see how much it's killing you."

The cool metal of the gun was pressed into my fingers. I stared at it in shock. Numbly, my fingers checked the chamber indicator. It was empty. For show. Except... Suddenly the gift from Eli made all the sense in the world.

"My sweet Havoc knows how to use a gun?" Logan asked. "If that's not a turn on I don't know what is. You might have me."

I'd heard that taunt before, though.

I was alone with him. Eli was gone, left early for a work emergency. I wasn't alone with Logan often and it made my skin crawl.

"What would my little omega do with power?" he asked. "You think you can wear it with enough beauty that you might finally seduce me?"

"I found a way to load your bullet without him seeing..." I whispered. "And then I held it to his head. I didn't even know what I was going to do..." A million things had gone through my mind. "The second he learned it was loaded, I could have made him do anything. I could make him take me to meet the others..."

"But...?" Eli asked.

There were goosebumps along my arms as he held me against him. It was a dangerous thing, thinking of the many ways that night could have ended. Of the million possibilities, each was one slight misstep away from leading me down darker roads than I had yet trodden.

I dug my nails into my palms, grounding myself. "But he changed his mind," I whispered. And when he had, it changed everything.

"He what?" Eli asked.

"He wanted me. I could see it in his eyes... It was everything..." My breath caught. "He offered me everything I wanted."

He was going to do it. This was real.

My heart was slamming into my ribs. That was elation, right? Because my pain was about to be over.

The sting of Logan's touch ran up my arms, a low growl in his chest, the one he saved for other omegas. Never for me.

I was going to be free.

"What went wrong?" Eli asked, but I just shook my head, still trying to find a way to explain.

"It was my fault. All that time I begged him..." My breath caught. "And then... When he did..."

The truth hit me too late, turning my stomach.

I was going to be free, yet it meant...

I backed up a pace, my breath caught in my lungs.

"N-no."

This was the man that had tortured me for months. And now he wanted to use me—my body in one final way for his own stupid satisfaction?

Logan laughed.

"What do you mean, no?" He stepped toward me. "This is what you begged me for over and over. I can feel how much you want me; I can taste it in the air every time I step in this room."

I lifted the gun again and levelled it toward him, my grip shaking.

He stepped right up to it, much too delighted. He took my hand and tilted it so that the metal was pressed under his chin, then he caged me in. "Is this part of the game Havoc?" His words were a breath. "Are you baiting me so I can't change my mind?"

What?

I stared at him, sickness rising in my throat as I realised what he was saying.

He was much too close. "I don't like being told I can't have what's mine," he breathed. "Is that what you finally figured out? Is that the game you finally use to trap me?"

Trap him?

I was trapped. Not him.

My breaths were coming sharply up my throat.

The truth was like a beacon though, freeing and fucking terrifying. "I don't want you."

He took my chin in his grip and pain speared through my body.

"You do want me, Havoc. You're a pathetic little gold pack wreck who's been crying over me sleeping with other omegas for months now. You don't have any dignity left. You scream my name when Eli makes you come. You get on your knees and use your desperate little mouth to wet me so I can knot other omegas, while you beg me to give it to you instead."

"No." The word was a war to spit out, as I shrunk beneath the power of an alpha in his voice. It felt as though he was trying to force his very words upon my brain as truth. But they were... they were *true, all of them. They had been.*

But they weren't anymore. "I. Don't. Want. You."

It was a violation of every one of my instincts. My stomach roiled with sickness at the thought of it, at the darkness in his eyes as I dissatisfied him. My mate.

"Yes, you do." His words were gripping. It was all I could do to shake my head. "Get on the bed, Havoc." He sounded dangerous.

"No."

He was regarding me with a frightening glint in his eyes. It was something new. Something feral and ravenous and unhinged.

It was in that moment that I understood how screwed I was. He grabbed me, tossing me easily onto the bed before his weight came down on my back. Somehow, the gun was still in my grip.

I scrambled over to face him, terror lighting my veins. His scent hit the air and my stomach did a flip, demanding I listen to him, the pain in my stomach urging me not to fight him on this. To take what I had needed for so long.

I couldn't though. With shaking fingers, I pressed the gun to his head.

"Get off." My voice shook.

He just laughed. Pressed up against me as he was, I felt the way his body responded to the threat. The way he loved it.

That was when the last, thin flakes of denial finally burned away like ashes in the wind, revealing the horror beneath. He was a monster, and I'd been fighting that truth, desperate to find a way to rationalise it.

He was evil, and to him I was nothing more than a toy.

"There can't be anything more beautiful in the world than a frightened omega hiding behind the barrel of an empty gun."

His fingers closed around my chin and another spear of pain shot through me. Pain he'd given me. Pain he loved and used as a taunt to make me nothing.

I didn't know, in that moment, if the decision was conscious or reactionary, but my shaking fingers steadied.

I squeezed the trigger. It shouldn't have been possible. The pain of violating my nature should have been too immense.

An omega should not be able to kill her alpha.

But I lived with pain every day. I was broken and poisoned and twisted into something unrecognisable. With a world-shattering bang, I destroyed the last thing that made me an omega.

Eli held me tight as I wept, even after I'd dragged the last, ragged word out.

"I don't... understand," I whispered, finally.

"What?"

"Why aren't you angry?"

"Why would I be angry?" he asked me again.

Because he'd thought, I was sure, that I'd shot Logan for not taking me to the others, for not freeing me. Not because... "He's dead because I changed my mind," I choked. "You saw me beg for him again and again, and then when he said he—" I cut off as Eli's hold tightened.

"No." He forced me to look up at him. "It is *not* your fault. He deserved what was coming for him."

We sat for another long while, his fingers rubbing along the skin of my arm soothingly. It was so nice to feel his touch. Real touch that didn't hurt.

"I *knew* you'd be strong enough to do it," Eli breathed.

"Why *did* you help me?"

"Because no one else was coming."

"I... You saw it from the start," I whispered. "I'm no good as an omega, he never wanted—"

"Logan made himself *ill* over that bond he made with you."

My heart tripped. "What do you mean?"

"I mean he lied about how much he wanted you. He was sick once, out on the street after. Denied why, but it was obvious."

"Why would he do that?"

"Because Logan wanted power more than he wanted pleasure."

I shut my eyes at that, and Eli shifted closer, tucking my hair behind my ear. "Don't linger on it. Now... I heard the others talking, not that I meant to eavesdrop, but your heat...?"

I winced. "The pill you gave me, it's wearing off."

"Do you want another?"

"You... have one?"

He nodded, pulling a pouch from his pocket. "You can maybe push it off one more time."

I stared at him as I took it. "You brought this with you?"

Eli smiled as I took the white pill from the pouch and placed it into my mouth. "Havoc. The only reason I'm here is for you."

"But..." I swallowed. "I'm—"

I cut off as his hand cupped my cheek. "You're worth protecting." He tilted my chin to him. "I'm just sorry I haven't been able to do it more."

I didn't know what to say to that. My heart raced, and I squeezed my hoodie with anxious fingers.

"How is it here?" he asked.

I bit my lip. "It's fine." I thought to Bane, to Kai. "They're... nice." Half of a lie.

"Are they treating you right?"

My fingers wrung my hoodie a little. "They don't know why I killed him, some of them are upset. But I don't blame them."

"Are they planning on biting you?"

My breath caught at that. "I d-don't know. Today..." My touch drifted to the small nick on the base of my neck. "I thought Angel..." I swallowed. "I don't want to be dark bonded, Eli." I hated the plea in my voice. I hated how foolish that complaint was because he could do nothing about it. Legally, they were completely in their rights. Morally, the world would even side with them.

"I know." Eli drew me closer, his other hand weaving through my hair as he pressed a kiss to my forehead. I gripped his wrist. "I wish I could do more."

"Thank you for coming." I hadn't realised how much I needed this. Someone who understood fully. Who knew I wasn't crazy for the pain I still carried.

Before I realised what I was doing, I was drawing up and my lips met his. He kissed me back, fingers curling through my hair.

I was taken off guard by the thrill of it.

Eli wasn't my mate. He was my choice. And he had come for me.

"Do you want release?" he murmured. "Just for you, without him getting any pleasure out of it at all." I couldn't find my words at that offer. He smiled. "I'll beg, if you need me to. There's nothing better in the world than tasting you, Havoc."

A breath of a laugh slipped from my lips. Eli was already on his knees before me, easily dragging me to the edge of the couch.

"If they find us—"

"Fuck them, Havoc. I know your value..." He paused. "I've missed you." He pressed a kiss to my thigh over my thick sweatpants. I couldn't help the smile curving my mouth. But the light he shed on my soul dimmed a little.

"I'm... Nothing can happen between us after tonight..." My future was uncertain, but none of the paths before me had room for him. I wasn't a fool.

"And yet..." He tugged me closer still, his eyes bright. "I still want to bring you release. Please. Don't. Deny. Me." He kissed me again between every word, and a giggle bubbled up my throat.

"Okay..." I couldn't remember when I'd last smiled like this.

He barely paused, tugging my sweatpants all the way off and

pressing my legs open and forcing me back onto my palms. He pulled my panties aside and I let out a gasp as I felt his tongue against me. He teased a finger at my entrance.

"Please," I breathed. I needed him. Slowly he pressed the finger into me. It was torturous. "Please Eli!"

I could hear the contented rumble in his chest at my heavy breaths and he sped up, filling me over and over, his tongue teasing me until I saw stars.

Tumbling over the edge of this orgasm was different than I remembered. Before it had been painful. Yesterday Kai had brought me to a climax, and I'd felt no pain at all. This one was somewhere in between. I moaned in pleasure while I still felt a jolt at my neck as if somehow, Eli wasn't as detached from my past as I wished he was. It didn't matter. I'd long learned to ride an orgasm like this, a part of me finding ways to enjoy the pain it brought.

He returned to the couch, pulling me against him as I caught my breath. I clutched his arms, which were wrapped tight around me, resting against his chest, a smile on my face.

I wanted it to last, but as the quiet minutes passed I realised I wasn't nearly as settled as I wanted to be. And I didn't know when I would see Eli again after tonight.

"I need... I need to understand," I whispered.

"Understand what?" he asked.

"Why he did it."

There was a long pause before Eli sighed. "Logan was as straight forward as any narcissist," he said. He seemed to contemplate for a moment before going on. "He was addicted to power, born an exceptional alpha with money and influence, but it was never enough. He allowed no one—*no one* into his life he couldn't control. Sometimes they didn't even realise. Not until it was too late. Not until they'd lost everything that mattered, and he was all that was left."

"He hated being beholden to others—and you were the worst threat to that because a mate is not something you choose. And you are gold pack, something he despised. You had so much power over him, and he pushed back against that as hard as he knew how. Keeping you in that place wasn't just about power over you. It was power over all of them. Every night he returned to his pack with a secret. A fix to all of their problems. A fated omega—and not just any omega, a gold pack omega with an accepted princess bond, ready to be claimed at any point."

"Would he have ever taken me to them?" I asked, my voice hoarse.

"If the power you offered served him better with you known. He was likely waiting for Angel's sickness to get worse. To have more control, so that his offer of a fix was the best it could be."

"But then they'd have *known* what he was doing to me."

"No." Eli breathed a laugh. "He trafficked in secrets and blackmail. Why do you think he let you give them gifts? He was learning your weaknesses, building control. He would never have taken you to them unless he could ensure you would never tell. Then he'd have taunted you with it, watched your relationships with the others build with that secret suspended between you. And the sweeter those relationships were for his brothers, the darker they would be for you. He would have been there in the centre of it all, always. He'd have loved every second of it."

"He wasn't worried it might all come crashing down?"

"I think that was part of the thrill. Sometimes I even think he wished for it. The payoff for holding something over someone's head for years and years, a trap they don't know existed, a puppeteer behind the scenes controlling their life in ways they didn't know. No, I think Logan needed it to shatter, eventually. That would have been its own payoff. The moment they realised how he'd been manipulating them all that time."

I couldn't explain why it was cathartic, hearing all of this from

Eli. Perhaps it was validation. That Logan was evil, and I wasn't crazy. Someone else saw it too.

"He played too many games at once," Eli said. "He wanted to play you, play his pack and play me all at the same time."

"You?" I asked.

"That, I think, is why he loved me coming. We were always even growing up. Both well off, both clever enough to grow into that money and use it properly. It's why I never wanted to be in the same pack as him. We were born to clash. But then I lost my pack and that meant you gave him the power over me he so desperately wanted."

"Me?"

"A gold pack omega with a princess bond. You would have been able to anchor me into his pack. With him as lead."

"You wanted that?"

"Not... at first. I saw through his game, using you to taunt me, and I humoured him. I meant to make a few favourable deals by giving him the illusion of control and then get out. He never quite understood my pride. I would never have joined a pack under him. Except..." Eli rubbed his chin. "I never expected..." He trailed off.

"What?"

"I never expected how much I would want you."

My heart skipped a beat as he watched me. "You what?"

"Logan underestimated one thing. If I was to truly reach the point of wanting you, I wouldn't be sharing with him."

"That's why you gave me the bullet?"

"I knew you would do it."

But... something didn't sit right with what he'd said. "You wouldn't share me... with him?" I asked.

"Never."

"Eli, I'm... stuck with them. I can't be with you." I tried to turn, but he pulled me closer.

"That's not true, Havoc."

"It's—"

"Logan was right about one thing. You're gold pack. You are strong enough to anchor me in."

"You can't give me the princess bond. And the others, they never will."

Eli paused and I could feel his breath tickling my ear. "I know."

I blinked, unsure of what he was saying.

"Best time to make a bond is surrounding connection. You let me in Havoc. Your blood is alight with my gift."

"What?" Again, I tried to pull away and again his grip tightened. I felt his touch upon my neck. "Eli—what—?" But I cut off as I felt his fingers tug at the necklace. "Stop it!" I tried to pull him off, but he dropped his hands, crushing my wrists with one hand and then using this other to unlatch the necklace. "Eli—"

"Don't fight me on this, Havoc." His voice was cooler than before. "It's everything you wanted, is it not? I saw the photo you cared so much for; I saw how you removed him from it. I fixed the stain upon your dreams. Instead of Logan, you can have me and the others."

"It'll be a dark bond."

He sighed. "Havoc, you're gold pack. What Logan offered was a farce, you will never get a princess bond from them. I'm not your mate, I can't offer you one."

But if I was given to the system, I wouldn't be bonded to anyone. I had two options. Be a slave to the system, or a slave to a pack.

"I don't want *any* bond!" I spat.

I just wanted to be free. He said nothing, instead tilting my chin up so my neck was open to him. For the second time today, I was at risk of losing everything.

"Why are you doing this?" I choked.

"Because I need a pack, and your pack is lost without a leader."

"That's not how it works." If he bit me, he didn't have a pack. It would just be me and him.

"Exactly," he murmured. "I'm not biting into Logan's pack. His pack will be biting into mine."

TWENTY-TWO

Angel

I woke to ecstasy like nothing I'd ever felt. It was wave after wave of pleasure that washed over me in the dark of my bed that felt like no orgasm I'd ever had.

What.

The.

Fuck?

Yet somehow, I knew it was Havoc. I tried to get up, but I was almost paralysed by it.

I staggered from my bed, careful not to wake Kai. Then I grabbed a nightgown and hurried down the hall to discover what the hell that crazy fucking omega had done to me this time.

Havoc

"That bullet I gave you," Eli hissed. "It was a path to both of our dreams. I won't let you throw that away for the fear Logan gave you."

I threw the full weight of my body against his embrace. "No

—" But I gasped as his grip became painful. Then I felt his teeth brush my neck. *"Don't* do this!"

My struggles paid off, my elbow catching his ribcage hard, enough to get a grunt from him and loosen his grip. I tore from his arms, breaking into a run over the coffee table, toward the door. Bane or Kai. I had to get to—

Eli's weight winded me as he caught me with ease, slamming me to the floor on my front. A choked sob escaped my mouth.

"Eli *please*—!"

"You're gold pack. Not an omega duchess who can take her pick. Logan, me, Angel—we are more than you deserve to *dream* of, and you spit in our faces. Logan spoiled you with that offer."

"Logan tortured me for months!" I spat.

Again, I fought his grip, but his aura was out, bolstering his strength. Fighting him was like warring with stone.

"And who was there for you that whole time? I was. And you'd still rather be with them than me?"

"I don't want *any* bond!"

He forced me up, so I was on my knees, back pressed against his chest as he once again lowered his mouth to my neck. He clamped his other hand over my mouth. I tried to struggle, to get my teeth around the edges of his grip, but he clamped down harder and pain shot through my jaw. I screamed deep in my throat, desperate for someone to hear me, my nails scraping his face and neck and arms, getting barely a flinch.

This was it. I was as helpless here as I had been against Angel. I couldn't do anything to stop him—CRASH! The door slammed open.

I looked up, hope lighting my veins as Eli froze. If it was Bane or Kai—but another sob wracked my chest as I stared up at Angel in the doorway.

No...

"What the fuck is going on?" Angel demanded.

I tried to scream through Eli's hand. Angel's eyes were dark with fury, and he took a step forward.

"Let me bite her." Eli's words drew Angel up and I could see him re-evaluating the picture before him, his gaze dropping to my neck as he understood what was happening. I tried to shake my head, tears slipping down my face.

"I get a pack," Eli said. "You get a brother. I will take responsibility for her—for pack lead—everything so you don't have to. She's your mate. She's too close to you. You *know* that."

My breaths were coming ragged. His words were too perfect. This was everything Angel wanted.

"Think of it. Your aura will be safe, and your relationship with Kai. And you can keep the bond with her, but you don't have to take any steps until you're ready."

No. This couldn't be happening.

I threw my weight against Eli once again, low wails coming from my chest, my eyes fixed on Angel, but he wasn't looking at me.

"You left a mark on her neck today, Angel. You know it's the best way."

Still, Angel's gaze was locked on Eli.

Angel had never wanted me. All he wanted was a way to fix his aura. I knew he hated that I was in this house, knew he hated it more when Bane and Kai chose to let me stay.

He was going to let this happen to me.

In his eyes, I could see his dawning realisation that what Eli was offering was a solution to everything.

TWENTY-THREE

Angel

Havoc looked up at me from where she was trapped against Eli. For the briefest moment in her frightened eyes, I saw hope. I didn't just see it; through the waning connection of the faintest bond between us, I felt it.

I got an image like I sometimes did in my bond with Kai, but this one wasn't half healed like his were. This was raw and stomach turning. Kai was always one of two things. The shattered child with pieces unfound, or the thing it fled: a vicious monster.

But in this unwanted connection I had with Havoc, I didn't find a monster. I didn't even find anger. There was just... a creature in a cage, desperate and bloodied, betrayed by each bond of trust she'd given. It was weary with the effort to scratch through the walls, and its waning song of hope was the faintest rough whisper.

And I was the last thing to silence it. She looked at me, and it was as if the life shuttered out in her soul.

I knew the truth. Havoc believed I would watch as Elliot stole her freedom away.

Silence swallowed the bond between us as the light died in her eyes.

When reality crashed in, though, the truth was clear. I had heard the words she'd said just before I'd opened the door.

The ones I tried to reject.

"Logan tortured me for months."

I knew what I had to do.

My alpha seeped from aura to flesh and bone, saturating me, adrenaline crashing through my veins as the world vanished but for the woman before me.

My mate.

I had failed. I had failed my mate.

I grabbed the bond to my brothers, ready to tear it open and sound the alarm. But then that burst of energy and life, the storm I could call that marked me an alpha—it vanished.

No. *No no no.*

The world was still. My bond to my pack collapsed to the thinnest thrumming thread. My brothers were now just the faintest trace in my soul. I couldn't reach them.

The agony of that ripped through me, grief colouring the world—but... Elliot still had her. He was frozen, watching me intently, waiting to see what I would do.

Havoc

"If your teeth touch my mate's neck Kingsman, I'll remove every last one," Angel snarled. Eli stiffened behind me.

It took a moment for the words to sink in, then I reacted on instinct. I threw my head back with all my might and heard Eli grunt behind me as pain exploded in my skull. His grip loosened, and I launched myself out of his arms.

Something grabbed my ankle, and a cry tore from my throat. A shadow flashed across my vision and Angel crashed into Eli, ripping him off me.

I could hear them behind me as I scrambled to my feet, making for the door.

"Shit!" Angel grunted, and a sharp pain shot through our tenuous bond. It almost stopped me, but the hallway was ahead, and I was so close.

The door slammed shut before I could get through. A figure was at my side, their weight holding the door closed. I turned, knowing it was Eli.

"NO!" Angel collided with Eli, breaking his grip. "Get back!"

The words were tossed at me, the sound haywire in my brain, half panic, half command. I listened, backing up a few paces, trying to understand what was happening.

Eli's alpha aura was dominating the space, flooding my senses, and from Angel... there was almost nothing. The faintest pulse of strangled energy.

He... he couldn't fight another alpha without his aura. There was something else off about Angel. Eli threw him away with ease, and he staggered. Angel was off balance, his hand gripping his side. I backed up a few more steps, blood pounding in my ears as I tried to understand. And then I saw the flash of silver in Eli's fist.

A knife.

"You'll crawl to me once I claim her," Eli snarled, stalking up to Angel. Angel was between me and Eli, his hand trailing the wall to steady himself.

I saw red blossoming across his shirt.

Blood. He'd been stabbed.

I made for him, but his command cut between us.

"Stay back!" The desperation drew me up. I had to get to the others, but Eli was between me and the door. He was rounding on Angel as he backed us into a corner. His aura was strong, and with Angel wounded, he could take us both with no issue.

Shock still rang in my head.

Angel had saved me.

After everything, he had saved me.

"Where's your aura?" Eli hissed. "This is why you need to let me bite her."

Eli stepped toward me as I backed into the wall. Angel threw himself between us again, but Eli drew up, fury etching his face.

"Don't make me hurt you more." Eli was half feral, and there was murder in his eyes.

"If you want to bite her, you'll have to kill me."

Eli didn't hesitate, going straight for Angel, blade out.

My blood turned to ice.

Angel caught his wrist, and the two struggled enough that the knife was thrown to the floor. Eli hissed in rage and managed to punch Angel in the stomach. Angel let out a grunt of pain. "Better be fast, they're coming," Angel rasped. "They're going to gut you."

Eli paused, eyes darting to the door. I saw the first flash of nerves in his eyes. He was afraid of the others.

I took that moment to reach for the blade. Eli struck another blow into Angel's cheek, this one harder than the last. He looked feral, something unhinged in his eyes as his aura offered strength and speed Angel couldn't match.

His hand clamped over Angel's stomach wound, and he twisted into it with his fist. Angel let out a roar of pain.

"Enough!" I cried, holding the knife in both fists as I stepped toward them. Eli froze, glancing at me with calculating eyes. I knew how to use a gun—even a bow and arrow —but the knife was unfamiliar in my grip. I was shaking, too, knowing that Eli could move twice my speed and might get it from me without a scratch.

But Angel was bleeding. His rich skin, which was usually golden, was ashen. That wound could be deadly.

This had to stop.

"Let him go."

Eli's face was twisted in a snarl. "Drop that and come here. Then I'll stop."

I lowered the knife just slightly, even as Angel tried to throw his weight against Eli's hold.

But if the others were on the way, I just had to stall him.

Eli lifted his arm, slamming it against Angel's mouth and then twisting again against his wound. I jumped at the low sound of agony from Angel. My heart jolted in my chest, and I let one hand drop from the knife.

"I'll do it." The words almost tripped over themselves on their way out of my mouth. "Let him go and I'll do it."

Then a bang sounded from outside and Eli froze. The mania in his eyes flickered. I returned my grip on the knife, spurred on by my confidence that someone was coming.

Another beat passed and then Eli released Angel, but the look in his eyes told me he might just risk it all, anyway. I was close enough that he could pounce, and fast enough to take the knife I clearly didn't know how to use.

After another second that seemed to last forever, he finally stepped back, turning and fleeing toward the deck. He ripped the sliding door open and was gone.

I turned to Angel in panic. He'd sunk against the wall, clutching his stomach. *Fuck*—he could have been stabbed anywhere.

Then the door burst open. Relief saturated my veins, and I spun.

"*You!*" Caspian spat the word with hateful venom, his beetle black eyes full of fury.

What? Why was he staring right at me?

Oh. Shit.

All he could see was me, facing a wounded Angel with a knife clutched in my grip.

"No, wait—!" but I cut off as Caspian launched himself at me.

I dropped the knife in panic. Anything to show him the truth. Right before he collided with me, Angel was there. Again.

"No!" To my shock, Angel had Caspian by his neck. "No one touches her!"

"Angel—" Caspian's eyes darted between us.

"Swear. *It!*" Angel's chest was heaving, blood pooling more rapidly against his shirt.

"Fucking hell, *alright.*"

Angel let out a breath, his hand dropping, his body shaking. Caspian grabbed him before he fell, this time letting him slide down the wall. At that moment, Bane and Kai arrived through the door.

"What's going on?" Bane asked.

"Eli." It was all I could say through the shock.

"He got out... on the deck," Angel hissed.

"No..." Kai was pale. "He passed me in the hall, told me he was getting help."

"Shit."

"Kai. Stop him." It was all Angel had to say. Kai was backing up and darting down the hallway.

Bane had turned, making for the bathroom while Caspian pulled his phone from his pocket.

"No fucking ambulance," Angel snarled.

"Angel—" Caspian began, but Angel cut him off.

"No hospitals. No cops."

What? I stared between them both. But Caspian just dropped the phone and instead peeled up Angel's shirt. Bane scowled as he returned with a red kit, which he tossed to Caspian.

"Don't be a fucking idiot—" Bane began.

"No hospitals. No cops. No fucking arguments." Angel glared at Caspian, who was roughly wiping blood away from the wound. "Can you deal with it?"

Caspian wrinkled his nose. "It won't be pretty, but looks like it."

"Do it—explanations *after*," he added, catching Bane who looked poised to snap at them.

Caspian rolled his eyes. "Help me get him onto the bed."

Bane didn't need Caspian's help. He just hauled Angel to his feet, and all but carried him over. In a second he was lying on my duvet and Caspian was cross-legged beside him, rinsing his hands with sanitizer. "Explanation better be good," he said darkly.

At that realisation that Angel was going to be okay, all the strength drained out of me. I hugged myself, glancing about the room, suddenly unsure of what to do with myself. Before I could consider that, Bane was at my side.

He nudged my chin to face him ever so gently, eyes holding mine. I swallowed, as if that might keep at bay the wave of emotions that suddenly swept through my chest. All I could do was shake my head, jaw clenched, and then Bane was drawing me into his huge chest, arms around me. I was swallowed by the scent of leather and applewood.

No tears came, but I shook all the same, everything from the night crashing in.

He said nothing, just holding me as he led me to the far end of the bed and sat down. For a minute, the only sound was the low grunts of pain from Angel.

The front door slammed open to a furious looking Kai. Angel looked over.

"Nothing?"

"Not a trace. Too fucking late," Kai hissed, crossing the room to him. "What happened? Your aura—"

"*Later.*" Angel's voice was tight, and for a moment, I saw a flash of panic in his eyes. His fists clenched and unclenched at his side. Kai shifted, clearly just as unsettled, but didn't argue.

Caspian used a pair of scissors to cut a piece of thread from a suture I was trying very hard not to look at. Then he was covering the wound.

"That's all?" Angel asked. Caspian nodded.

Kai was glancing around, as if finding something to snap at, but when his eyes fell on me, he froze, and his lips parted in shock.

"What?" Bane asked, looking down at me. I realised much too late that my choker was gone. Eli had taken it. My hand jumped to my neck, covering it desperately.

"What?" Caspian demanded as he snapped the medical kit shut.

"That's a dead princess bond..." Kai said.

All of them froze.

No... This was too much right now.

"Only mates can offer those. How—?" Bane asked.

"Out. All of you." Angel's voice made me jump.

"What?" Kai demanded. "Tell us what—"

"I need to speak with Havoc." Angel's voice was clipped, but there was an edge to it, one that held just the slightest tremor as if he were on the brink of cracking. I stiffened, not sure what to make of any of it. My mind was still split in a million directions.

Kai's eyes narrowed. I noticed Caspian and Bane glance to him in silent communication. I'd never seen Kai as tense as he was right now. Then he flicked his head to the door in the smallest increment. He turned and left.

Caspian got to his feet, following Kai as Bane brushed my cheek. "You okay?"

I nodded quickly.

"Ten minutes," Bane said to Angel before he followed. "You aren't the only one who needs looking after."

The door shut, leaving us in an awful silence. Angel was still ashen as he fixed his forest green eyes on me from where he was propped on pillows.

"Logan?" His voice was quiet. I hugged myself, unable to break our gaze. Slowly, I nodded.

Angel stared at me for a long moment, and then he lifted his hands to his face, holding them there as he breathed out slowly. Then he pushed himself up.

"Don't—" I began. Caspian had just finished stitching him up. Angel winced, but didn't stop, and I was crossing the bed before I could stop myself, grabbing his arm as he dragged his legs over the edge, sitting up. His scent, sweet cinnamon, was tangled with blood.

He tugged me to him. "Are you hurt?" he asked, his voice rough.

Me...?

"You... Just got stabbed."

He was shaking his head, as if taking a knife for me was of no consequence. "He attacked you in our house—*we* let him in."

I didn't understand how we'd got to this. From him nearly biting me, to this wildness in his eyes at the idea of me hurt. But Angel's affection was a dangerous thing to consider, the crackling flames of hope—of dreams that had seen me to sleep when I was trapped in my darkest nightmares. Just as quick as they flared, those flames could leave me burned. "You didn't know," I said instead, afraid to linger on it. "I never told you—"

"This room was meant for you." His voice cracked. "You should be *safe* here." He searched my face, tucking my hair behind my ear as if worried I might fall apart before my eyes.

I grabbed his sleeve. "You're going to hurt yourself—"

"You shouldn't give a shit about my pain, Havoc," Angel said through gritted teeth. I paused, withdrawing my hand as I stared up at him.

"You stopped him from..." I trailed off, unable to finish that sentence. "How did you know?"

If Angel hadn't come, I would be dark bonded to Eli right now. That sent a flutter of horror through my stomach. My thoughts were under threat of coming apart.

"I woke to... Something odd." His brows were drawn. "I just... *knew* it was you."

My mind raced back to what I'd done tonight. Back with Logan, he'd felt it when I'd found release with Eli in bed. Had Angel got a flicker of that same thing, with the trace of the bond he'd made on my neck today?

"I heard what you said right before I came in. You said Logan..." he said, pulling me from that thought abruptly. He took a breath. "... Hurt you."

I couldn't meet his eyes suddenly, grip clutching at my hoodie. I was glad for how long it was, since I wasn't wearing my sweatpants from when me and Eli—I cut that thought off abruptly.

I forced myself to look back to Angel, nodding.

"How long?" he asked.

For a moment, I considered that the door to the bathroom was wide open, and if I ran to it, Angel would never catch me in time—not with that wound. And then I could curl up and hide until... Well, until when?

Angel had overheard Eli. Kai had seen the bite.

I couldn't hide this anymore, and for a second, that didn't seem so terrifying. Angel had just taken a knife for me.

I cleared my throat. "Three..." The word was so quiet even I couldn't hear it. "Three months," I tried again.

"The day you... the day he died. It was because he hurt you?"

I squeezed my eyes shut in reflex, shuddering as that world shattering bang rang in my head again. That seemed to be enough of an answer for Angel.

"Fuck." His curse was a low breath. I didn't dare look up at him, but I saw the way his fist clenched at my side. "I... screwed up. This whole time."

I glanced up enough to catch the strained muscles along the smooth, mid-brown skin of his throat. I saw the way his Adam's apple shifted as he swallowed. I still didn't dare look up into his eyes.

"We failed you Havoc. *I* failed you."

Those words sunk in slowly, like ice melting in my throat, the cold seeping into my veins and the rest of my body. My chest felt tight all of a sudden, and breathing was suddenly more difficult. Without warning, burning hot tears spilled down my cheeks. Before I had the chance to flee or curl up, Angel's fingers wound through my hair, and he dragged me against his chest. His other arm wrapped around me, impossibly tight. It must have been painful for him, yet he didn't flinch.

After a long moment, he spoke. "You were going to give up that knife for me when Elliot asked."

I held onto him, finding no way to answer that.

"I don't understand," he breathed.

I shut my eyes, drawing back from the embrace, only to get swallowed up by his forest green gaze.

"I..." I frowned, not sure there were words that could explain it to him. To any of them. So instead, I unwound his arms from me and crossed the short distance to the bedside table. I opened the top drawer and reached in. I hesitated and then I slipped the drawer closed, returning to Angel.

Angel stared down at what I held out to him, his brow furrowed. He reached out and took the blue prayer angel, the partner to the one I'd smashed less than a day ago now. He turned it delicately, as if it might burn him.

"It was from you?"

"He um... told me about you. Even when he didn't want me to meet you... yet," I added, still not ready to reveal the true nature of that time. My voice was hoarse. "But I wanted a piece of me to be with you."

Shit.

I don't think I should have said that. It was too much.

"What would they think if they found out how obsessed you are with them?" Logan's voice cut, but I squeezed my eyes shut as I tried to shove it away.

He'd saved me. *Angel* had saved me just like I'd dreamed he would. I could try right now. For him. "I had two. The one I gave you was dad's."

There was such a long silence as he stared at it, and I could see the horror etched on his face. I could see his despair. I hated it because I knew, no matter how much I had begged the universe to let them save me, that it wasn't their fault. That they couldn't possibly have known.

He pressed the angel back into my palms roughly.

"You should take it," I said. "I smashed yours."

"I don't deserve it." The words were so broken that I couldn't argue. Instead, I set it on display on my bedside table for the first time since I had arrived.

"How?" His voice walked a thin line between hollow and hateful. He ran his fingers anxiously along his buzzed black hair—then winced at the pain in his side. "How did he keep you from us?"

I almost shrunk down again. "I…" I swallowed. "I can't say it more than once."

Angel nodded. "Will you… tell us?"

I chewed on my lip, considering that. Considering what it might look like. I wanted them to know—I knew they needed to know. Logan had toyed with all of them the same as he had me. The longer the truth was kept from them, the longer he had power. But still, at the same time, I'd already had this conversation with Eli once tonight. And he'd offered me the perfect support until it had turned to poison.

"Could I just tell you, and you tell them?" I asked.

Angel looked startled. "Me? I could ask Bane—"

"No." I couldn't say why, but it had to be Angel.

Slowly, he nodded. "I can do that."

TWENTY-FOUR

Caspian

We waited outside the room for what felt like an age.

"A princess bond has to be given by a mate." Bane's eyes fixed on Kai, who leaned against the wall, tense as a cat. He said nothing.

I didn't reply. I couldn't. We all knew what that meant. Kai was a seer, and he could confirm Logan had given that bite.

Yet, I clung to that silence. It was the one final string of denial to keep me from breaking like I knew I would the second we went back into that room.

"Angel's almost gone." Kai said after too much time. His gaze darted between us, and he might look expressionless if you didn't know him. *I* could see he was one small fracture away from disconnecting completely.

I swallowed my own pride as I tried to dig up ways to get through to him. Angel's aura had almost completely vanished from the pack. Right now, he was the faintest flicker in my mind; he'd closed the connection down, not wanting any of us to feel what he was feeling. And I didn't blame him.

I walked over to Kai, not capable of offering words. Instead, I squeezed his shoulder until he looked up at me. He responded to touch better than anything else, besides.

Self-loathing didn't absolve me from my job as his big brother, and it never mattered how old we got.

It didn't matter that I'd met Kai for the first time when he was seven and I was eight. Or that all I'd been able to offer was my shithole of a home. The home I ran while my mother worked hard to wipe out every last brain cell with as many drugs and drinks as welfare checks afforded her.

Kai turned to me and I tugged him into my arms before he could protest. The only thing that gave him away was how tightly he held on.

"He's not going anywhere," I murmured. Angel had said once he would give up his aura rather than let the pack suffer. The foul, twisted part of me clung to that. It was easier to watch someone lose something they had faced up to and made peace with. It was a different story when they didn't want to lose what was taken.

"*Cass... I'm s-scared.*"

"*I know. I know. But I got you.*"

"*Swear t-to me.*"

"*I swear it. Course I swear it.*"

Bile rose in my throat at the memory, and I buried it fast. It was a testament to how off balance I was today if shit like that broke through.

The latch of the door clicked, and Kai tugged away to look over at Havoc, who was peering out. She looked sick, her olive skin was drained of all colour. She'd put on a pair of leggings—thank fuck. I didn't think I could handle my rampant fucking alpha hindbrain getting away from me tonight. The image of Havoc in an oversized hoodie, sleeves to her knuckles and bare legs tucked beneath her as she clutched Bane. It was haunting. She'd looked so scared. Tonight, it hadn't even been screwed up thoughts—I'd just wanted to be the one holding her, which was arguably worse. Instead, Havoc had shot me terrified looks as I wielded bloodied surgical gloves and a 3-0 vicryl to stitch Angel's wound. I was also sure he'd taken that wound for her—which really shouldn't make me *jealous*.

"He's ready," she said.

Kai was slipping through the door in an instant, Bane quickly after. It left me out in the hallway with her. She was watching me wearily, but she didn't need to, not anymore. Angel had protected her today.

Something had changed, something major. But it was like when someone you trust recommends a movie. You know the journey is coming, but the nature of it is a mystery until you turn it on and watch for yourself.

Something told me Havoc was about to take a pick axe to my world, even when I didn't know how. And there was absolutely nothing I could do to refuse to turn this movie on and watch it play through.

When I entered, Kai was sitting cross legged beside Angel, their fingers laced. Bane had taken a seat at the foot of the bed. The mattress was huge enough, if I wanted to join them—it was designed for the pack, after all. Still, I leaned against the bedpost.

My hackles were up the moment I crossed the doorway. It was worse now I knew Elliot had been the aggressor. I could smell blood and hormones in the air. Her fear lingered in like a thick fog. My omega's fear.

The rampant rage boiling in my chest was hard to ignore, not caring how much I desperately wanted to hate her.

Attacked in your own home while you slept. Your pack. Your brother. Your omega, in her room. The one you'd helped build for her before you'd even met her. My grip bit down on the wooden bedpost, one burst of my aura away from splintering it.

Havoc remained by the door, apparently not planning on entering. Angel spoke first. "After Havoc, you'll need to come back in. There's a lot we have to discuss. But I promise you something. I'm going to find a way to fix this."

Havoc nodded, glancing one last time at us nervously, and then leaving.

This did not bode well.

"What's going on?" I asked.

"She wants me to tell you what she just told me," Angel said. I realised, now I was closer, that he looked worse than before. "There's so much shit we missed."

I braced for whatever was coming, but it wasn't enough.

Nothing. Nothing could have prepared me for Angel's recount.

By the time he was done, I was numb.

"He... betrayed us." My voice was a rasp. Logan had betrayed the pack, and he'd destroyed our omega. A shadow had crossed Bane's face, and Kai looked ready to commit murder.

"It's still fucking her up," Angel said. "She kept saying shit like..." He grimaced. *"What if Logan was right, and she's just no good as an omega? That he might have been doing what he thought was best."*

"But... Why *would* he do that?" I could hear the denial in my voice. "Not just to her, to us? He knew you had aura sickness?"

"Because that's what Logan does," Bane said quietly. "Fucks around with shit that makes him feel powerful."

I stared at him. "You trusted her right from the start."

"I guessed."

"How?" I asked.

"Because I knew the same Logan she did, alright?" Bane's tone made it clear that was all he would say on that, but I felt like someone had a fist around my heart. "And she deserves better than what we've given her."

This was wrong, all fucking wrong. This had been Logan's pack. He had been the centre of us all, holding it together.

"She was going to give herself to Eli to protect me," Angel said quietly.

My heart twisted at those words.

Shit.

None of this was right. How had we got here in such a short time? Where Havoc was the victim and Logan the enemy? When Logan saved me—had saved us all in one way or another.

Bane was the outcast taken in by his family, Angel the orphan. I'd been destined to the streets, and Kai would have been used for his powers for the rest of his life.

Logan had been the force to drag us together. Havoc had been the one to kill him.

Yet, I couldn't argue with them—I couldn't even convince myself that there was another reason for what he'd done. And the smallest part of me knew there wasn't. We all had dark thorns in our souls, and I'd seen Logan's once or twice, on jobs when the others weren't around. But it had been his outlet, and the fallout was people who deserved it.

Or so I'd thought.

"I still don't know how we never felt her through the bond," Bane said quietly. "He bit her."

"Logan was lead. He was completely in control of our pack bonds. We never felt it because it never went through. Not properly. He never... consolidated it."

I knew it was a part of princess bonds that were rarely talked about. While a bite was the largest piece of the puzzle, the physical connection between alpha and omega was necessary. It wasn't discussed much because... well it wasn't usually an issue. Most bites were given *during* sex anyway—it was preferable to most people.

"What he did was barbaric," Angel said quietly. "He left Havoc with a bond on her neck that demanded completion, and when it never happened, it hurt her."

"It's why it's..." I trailed off. "When we touch her..." I didn't need to say any more. We all knew that her touch was like a siren's call. As if her bond was trying to fix itself.

"And it causes *her* pain," Kai growled. "Fucking poison."

"Makes sense in a twisted way," Angel said quietly. "She said it didn't happen straight away, but after he brought in other omegas."

And made her watch...

I blinked, suddenly feeling as though my mind was snared in a spiderweb, struggling to get out, struggling to escape the truth that was smothering me from all sides. It threatened everything I'd ever known.

I reached toward an ancient pain. My anchor. And I was freed of that web by one simple fact: it didn't matter what Logan had done to her.

I could not be with the woman who had killed the man I owed everything. I owed Logan a debt that I could never repay, it wouldn't be offset by anything. Not even what he'd done to Havoc.

And I understood that she deserved better than that. She deserved my brothers tripping over themselves to fix this.

But not me.

I realised, in that moment, how absolutely foolish my dreams of an omega had been anyway. I had nothing to give her now and I never would.

What had I dreamed of? That she might offer me something? She might shine light on this broken husk of a human? One so far deserving of love that sometimes I had to close my bond to my brothers so they wouldn't know I loathed myself that I even had them.

It caught me mid laugh, or games night, or when Bane would cook my favourite meal, snatching me from the moment.

And you smile, while he lies still and silent and cold...

No.

It had been a selfish dream.

Havoc had been broken, and she didn't deserve the burden of fixing anything. I couldn't allow myself to love her for what she'd done to Logan. I couldn't even tell her I would choose her over him if I'd known it all.

But... the others—they *had* chosen her. I could feel myself retreating in my bond, as the only real solution came to me. Kai glanced over, his eyes narrowed in confusion as he felt my retreat. For a moment, I felt guilty. Angel had already almost been ripped from us entirely tonight.

"What about Eli?" Bane asked.

Kai's gaze snapped to Bane at that, his eyes glittering with fury. "What are we going to do about him after tonight?"

He looked between me and Angel, as if he hoped we might loosen his leash for this. It would be a lie to say I wasn't tempted.

What Elliot had done tonight—that at least, was a safe place to fuel my hatred.

"We'll discuss that when she's back," Angel said. "From now on, everything else goes through her. We've been treating her like a criminal when she deserves the fucking world."

"So we give her that," Kai said. "We fix it."

"We're going to make this up to her as much as we possibly can." There was something cautious in Angel's voice. His expression was stiffer than before.

"How?" I asked.

"Come on." His voice was hoarse. "There's only one way we can fix this, and you know it."

Kai and Bane tensed. As I realised what he meant, it was as though a stone dropped into my stomach.

TWENTY-FIVE

Havoc

I turned on the TV to a music channel, not that I'd be able to focus on anything, anyway. I checked the cupboard I'd seen Bane open the other day and found another bag of popcorn.

I clutched it on the couch, eating furiously while scantily clad men and women danced across the screen. My mind unravelled.

This was insane. *Why had I told Angel?*

It was going to go so wrong. *What will they think?* They might still be so angry, and then—if they were, *and* they knew, I didn't know if my heart could take that.

But then... maybe... maybe things were going to change?

Don't be stupid. They still need you to fix Angel's sickness, how can you do that without a dark bond?

When the popcorn bag depleted enough not to be huggable, I swapped it for a cushion, clutching it to my chest as I tried to focus on the words of a sappy song about lost lovers.

Not helpful.

"Havoc." I jumped violently at Bane's voice.

Popcorn sprayed everywhere. I'd been so focused on watching

the dancers and cramming another handful into my mouth that I hadn't noticed the scent of leather and applewood drifting in.

He was leaning against the corner where the hallway met the living room. I swallowed my popcorn in one grating gulp. "You're all done?" I asked, voice strained. There was something in the way he was looking at me though, that told me the answer to that question.

He knew.

He knew everything.

I was on my feet in a second and crossed to him, both terrified and so pathetically desperate. Then I was in his arms and he was holding me so tight I couldn't breathe.

When he finally released me, I drew back. "Has it changed anything?" My voice was a rough whisper.

"You're perfect, Havoc. All that's changed, is they can see it now too."

There was a strange stillness in the room when I returned. I sat on the bed beside Bane, huddled up at his side.

Caspian was leaning against the bedpost with his arms folded, his posture rigid. I met Kai's gaze. He was on the edge of the mattress, looking as though he wanted to reach for me, but wasn't sure if he should. Their scents were enough to mostly bury the faint scent of Eli that lingered.

"Right," Angel said. "We have to talk about Kingsman—*Eli*, I mean." He glanced at me.

Bane drew me closer. "We aren't going to just roll on what happened tonight."

"No," Angel said. "But he didn't get what he came for, and he won't."

"Why no police?" I asked, wondering if I was missing something. "Isn't that what they're for?" They always were in the movies.

At my side, Bane seemed like he agreed. "He stabbed you, Angel, he'll have no defence—"

"That's not what I'm worried about," Angel said. There was a pause, and I didn't miss how everyone's gaze fell on me. "Eli's a Kingsman. His family has major influence in the GPRE."

I stared at Angel, goosebumps pricking my skin. The GPRE—Gold Pack and Rogue Enforcement was the government branch that had final say upon the fate of gold pack omegas and rogue alphas.

"Fuck." Caspian was scowling. "And we have a gold pack omega who was found holding the gun that killed his best friend a week ago."

"But... Logan was your pack mate, you get to decide..." I swallowed. "What happens, right?"

"Sure, that's protocol," Caspian said. "But rules go out the window if the GPRE opens a case for unusual circumstances."

"So... Eli could do that?" My voice was hoarse. Would he try to come for me again?

"Doesn't matter." Angel straightened, his forest green eyes fixed on me. "Because there's an obvious solution."

"What?"

"We make you untouchable."

"How?" I asked.

I noticed how Kai went ashen.

Angel's next words caught me off guard. "We're going to offer you the princess bond."

I stared at them, my mouth popping open. None of them said anything, leaving me to scramble for an answer to that insanity. "If you offer me the bond, I could walk." That was the thing I should have done when Logan offered. Bane's arm tightened around me, as if the idea upset him.

"We know," Angel replied. "And we fully expect you to. But when you do, you'll be protected."

When I did?

When I left them...?

"What about your aura?" I asked. It was all but gone. I noticed how Kai squeezed his eyes shut, nose scrunched.

Angel snorted, though the humour in his words was brittle. "Least I deserve, I think."

Panic began to simmer, though. It was stupid and irrational, but enough to set me on edge. Were they kicking me out? What was I going to do? If I had to choose this *now*—

"We're just going to ask one thing," Bane murmured.

"Yes?" I looked up at him, and my voice was paper thin.

"There's a ball in a week," Angel said. "Our pack is expected to attend. It's huge, a major public event. It would be indisputable if we were to offer the princess bond there. Too many eyes for Eli to worm his way around."

Relief flooded my system. "Oh. Okay, yeah." A week? Somehow, that was enough to soothe the panic brewing in my chest. I'd be able to stay here until then, right?

I didn't have anything. All my father's assets had been seized, and being gold pack meant I didn't have much. No money—no bank account, no passport. If I walked away from a princess bond, I'd be able to get all of those things, but I'd still start off with nothing. And I'd be on my own. And I really didn't want to have to make a decision on a bond because of that.

"But, the ball wasn't the ask," Angel said.

"Oh..." I trailed off, waiting.

"We can't expect you to do anything but walk if we offer you the bond. It's not just that we deserve it, but right now it's the best choice for you."

I nodded, my heart in my throat. I couldn't take my eyes from Angel, couldn't risk looking at Bane or Kai.

"You stay here until then. Give us a week to change your mind."

Havoc

"Kai, help me to my room?" Angel asked.

Bane and Caspian were gone, and Kai was getting rid of the bloody shirt and med kit from the bed.

"Wait," I said, frowning down at the dressing on his torso. "You shouldn't. I can go sleep somewhere else." I could take the couch, or even their room.

Angel, however, was already sitting up with a wince.

"Really," I said quickly. "I'm fine."

"*Idiot*, lay back down," Kai growled from behind me. Angel scowled. "And you—"

I squeaked in surprise as Kai picked me up from behind, marched me around the huge bed, and tossed me easily onto the covers. "Aren't going anywhere."

He was beside me in a second, tugging me between his legs where he sat, pulling me against his chest.

"But I—"

"No choice."

Angel grabbed a pillow and tossed it at us. "Go fucking easy, it's been a long night."

"Fine." Kai buried his chin in the crook of my neck. I was surrounded by maple and cinders, engulfed by his arms and pressed against his chest. My breathing came easier right now than it had all night. "Say yes, little omega," Kai breathed. "He did take a knife for you. He'll sleep better and heal up faster with you safely between us all night."

Butterflies took flight in my stomach at that.

"*Guilting* her isn't what I meant." Another pillow caught Kai in the head, but I knew Angel had already seen the smile tugging at my lips.

"Is that a yes?" Kai asked, peering down at me.

"I don't mind staying," I said. Kai's grin was worth it. "But I'm going to change." I was exhausted, but I didn't want to sleep in this damn hoodie. Not when I'd been wearing it with Eli earlier.

I showered, brushed my teeth, and changed. The scar of Logans bite was clear between the waves of chestnut hair that tumbled around my shoulders. Two dull crescents. I took a breath, leaving them in view.

This was it. Facing a world that could see my scar.

I could do this. *Kai* wasn't afraid of the marks marring his chest.

I paused at the door. It was just a crack open, and I could hear Kai and Angel outside.

"Probably past their expiry date, but they'll get you through the night," Kai was saying, and I heard the sound of pills being shaken in a bottle.

"Don't push her tonight," Angel said.

"Take the damn narc," I could practically hear the grin in Kai's voice.

"When I said she gets an honest choice to leave, I meant it. You get that?"

"She won't."

"Tell me you get it." Angel's voice was low.

There was a long pause. When Kai replied, he sounded rough. "Yeah. I get it."

I stepped away from the door, chewing on my lip. The chill that seeped up my spine was somehow the worst thing of the night. This pack had just handed me everything I'd ever dreamed of. But the world was so twisted up that I couldn't just open my mouth and say I wanted it.

Somehow, acknowledging that Kai and Bane's arms were the safest place I could imagine being, was wrong. It was the worst thing Logan had done. I knew that now. He had broken me so thoroughly that I couldn't take my dream if it was handed to me.

But I was so tired tonight, and I just wanted to feel that safety, even if I had no idea how long it could last. So, I pushed the bathroom door open.

I almost choked up at the sight that met me. Kai had grabbed all the couch cushions and stacked them in a semicircle around the bed, then tucked blankets around them. His eyes lit up when he saw me, and I noticed he was wearing those black gloves of his.

"The pill Eli gave you?" Angel asked as I switched the lights off before heading toward them.

"It worked," I said, feeling the change already, my impulses dampened. Not enough that I didn't appreciate what Kai had done.

I'd slept in this bed with Kai before, but somehow it was completely different with Angel here. Especially since I knew they were together. But Kai pulled me into bed without pause and hauled me up to the pillow, so I was laying between them, Kai at my back. The curtains were still parted, and I could see the edges of Angel's face in the moonlight. He had settled down between the covers, arms over them, a slight wrinkle in his nose every time he shifted.

Kai held me tighter. "I'm sorry," he whispered. "That I was never there." I heard the pain in his voice, and somehow it felt like he'd been holding those words in for too long.

I turned to him, staring up into his one white, one glowing eye. I didn't want him hurting over that, not with what I realised after tonight.

I pressed my forehead to his.

Then I blinked, something finally sinking in. It was something that my brain had been too wired to realise until now. I lifted my hand and pressed it to his cheek. He flinched away, brow furrowed, but a smile was spreading across my face.

"There's no pain," I whispered.

"What?"

"It's gone."

"Here, touch Angel. See if it's just me,"

"I'm not going to just—" But I cut off as he grabbed my hand and pressed it to Angel's shoulder. Angel, who had been trying to tuck a pillow under one side of his torso, glanced at the two of us.

"Nothing."

Something loosened in my chest, my heart filling. I knew what it was. I turned back to Kai and took his face between my hands.

"Well, sorry Havoc, but your touch still feels like sin," Kai said, his voice low and rough.

I grinned, and before he could say anything else I pressed my lips to Kai's. He reacted instantly, shifting over me, his tongue pressing between my lips as he dragged my waist against him. Maple and cinders smothered my senses and briefly, I thought I could just live in this moment forever, with Kai's arms around me.

Then the kiss broke off as another pillow collided with Kai's head.

"Told you to take it fucking easy," Angel hissed. Kai drew away, leaving me catching my breath.

"*She* kissed *me*." Kai's voice was indignant.

"Both of you," Angel replied.

I couldn't help my breathless laugh.

As Kai curled up behind me, I drifted off with peaceful ease. I knew what this was, this unfamiliar thing that settled my nerves and allowed his painless touch upon my skin.

This was trust.

TWENTY-SIX

Havoc

I woke a few times throughout the night, feeling warmer and safer than I ever had. Kai didn't let me go, and one of his arms was draped over me so he could both hold me and tangle his fingers in Angel's.

I slept peacefully, though when I woke, Angel was gone. There was still a low rumble at my back, Kai's slender fingers clutching my waist as he held me against him.

Carefully, I tried to slip free of his grip, but he tightened it. I tried again, but he only groaned and then both his arms wrapped around me tight. "My little sunset," he breathed. "I can't think of anything better than waking up to you wriggling against me." I felt his exact bodily response to that.

Kai loosed a groan as he pressed a kiss to my neck. My skin tingled with the touch, heat spearing my core and a smile tugging on my lips. But... I'd just been thinking something important. "Where's Angel?" I asked.

Kai, who was kissing up my neck hungrily, paused. "Shit." He sighed. "I suppose I have to care, since he's stabbed up and all."

He loosened his grip on me and sat up, peering around the

room. I was shocked at how disappointed I felt once I was out of his embrace.

I needed to get a grip. I had some big decisions ahead of me.

My stomach twisted anxiously at that thought as Kai shifted to the edge of the bed.

I eyed him as he stretched; it was impossible not to. He was only wearing sweatpants, and the smooth, dusky skin of his torso, decorated with rippling muscle, scars and swirling tattoos, was on full display. More heat seeped into my veins as he shot me a sly smile and stood.

"Coming?" he asked, holding his hand out. I took it, following, then second guessed myself as he led me to the door.

Last night, I had chosen a baggy top as usual, but I wore it with a pair of silken shorts. I was an omega after all, and I had just been invited into bed with two of my alphas. Who could blame a girl, really?

But now I'd slept, and the fog of last night had passed... "I... should change."

"Don't you dare." Kai swept me off my feet in an instant, holding me easily in his arms as he marched us out into the hallway. I had to wrap my arms around his neck to balance myself.

The smells of breakfast met me instantly, smothering the soothing scent of maple and cinder I was discreetly huffing from the crook of Kai's neck.

Kai set me down as we entered the kitchen. The aroma of fresh coffee, sizzling bacon, and pancakes filled my senses. On the table, I could see eggs, toast, and a bowl of fruit. Caspian was lounging on one of the chairs, scrolling on his phone.

"Oh, don't—!" Bane was in the kitchen, holding a pan with one hand. He was leaning across the kitchen island to snatch a bowl and mixer from Angel's grip. "Sit the fuck down and chop apples."

"Cass did them all. And I'm fine." Angel grumbled from where he sat on one of the bar stools, facing away from us.

"The third dressing of the day says differently," Caspian grunted.

"Good morning!" Kai announced with a stretch.

Caspian spared us both a glance. "It's 3pm."

"Well. Late night—" Kai was shrugging.

"Sit!" Caspian cut him off as Angel tried to get up. "Dude. I'll nail your leg to the chair."

"You sleep alright?" Angel asked, eyes fixed on me as he lowered himself back down.

I nodded, glancing around and trying to place my nerves.

"We, uh, haven't done a pack breakfast in a while. Thought it might be called for."

I could read between those lines. "Right, of course," I said, taking a step back. "I can go back—"

Kai's arms caught me as Bane turned, brows furrowed.

Angel huffed. "I didn't mean that. We want you to join us."

I couldn't help a nervous glance toward Caspian, who was still not looking up at me. I knew things had changed last night, but I didn't know how much for him, and that old threat still lingered.

"What these idiots don't want to say"—Caspian finally shot a glance between Angel and Bane—"is that they made breakfast for you."

My cheeks flooded with heat, my chest suddenly tight as my gaze swept across the breakfast table again.

Bane waved his spatula at Caspian. "You helped too."

Caspian set his phone down and crossed his arms with a scowl but said nothing else.

I stepped up beside Bane in the kitchen, watching what he was doing. My breakfast-making skills were limited to cereal, toast, and bacon and eggs.

Pancakes were Luther's favourite, but my brother hadn't been in my life for over half a decade, and I hadn't had the heart to make them after he left.

"Doing alright?" Bane asked as he flipped the pancake. I was glad for how casual he was acting. Tentatively, I brushed his arm with my fingers. He shot me a confused glance, but I was smiling and reaching up to cup his cheek.

"No pain?" he asked.

"Nope."

He set the spatula down and regarded me for a moment. "Well, that changes everything."

Before I knew it, he was lifting me by the waist and setting me on the kitchen island. His touch was at my jaw, tilting my head up until I got lost in his silver eyes. His thumbs brushed my cheeks as he leaned against the counter, my legs caught around his hips.

I grinned, my fingers curling into his shirt so I could hold myself against him, enjoying the scent of leather and applewood. It happened in a moment of pure instinct.

Bane's lips captured mine, passionate and firm. His fingers wove through my hair, his other hand at my waist, crushing me against him. And in this room, before the others, it felt like a claim.

When we broke away, I was breathless and there was a low rumble in his chest. His eyes were a roiling storm, and then he shifted, brushing his jaw gently along my temple. Indisputably, a mark.

My stomach fluttered as his hand slipped to my chin, his thumb caressing my cheek again as if he never wanted to let me go.

I didn't dare look around at the others.

Kai was quick to tug me to my seat when Bane let me go, his eyes narrowed as he shot dirty glances at the huge, smug alpha.

"I'd like to make an announcement," Kai declared, firmly

holding me at his side like I was a trophy. "I was right. And you were all wrong."

"I wasn't," Bane muttered as he sat down.

"Fine. Bane wasn't."

"Bane got there before you," I whispered in Kai's ear.

"Bane was good. Okay. I was still right."

Angel was clearly suppressing a grin. Caspian... Well, he looked less cold than usual, but he wasn't warming up.

All thoughts vanished from my head as Kai hoisted me up onto the dining table.

"What are you—?" I cut off as he hopped up after me, lifting me by the waist. I was pressed against him and then he began to drag me right into the centre.

I let out a little squeak as plates, bowls and cutlery were scattered across the table beneath me.

"Oh, what the fuck, Kai?!" Angel groaned.

With absolutely no thought given to the plates, condiments, dishes of pancakes or eggs benedict, Kai dropped me down into the middle of the feast and then crushed my lips with his.

"Fuck me," Angel grumbled. "We spent ages on this."

I could barely concentrate, because Kai was driving his tongue aggressively into my mouth, his hands wandering down to my waist.

His eyes glittered as he broke the kiss, a grin on his face. "I was right."

"There's syrup in her hair," Bane noted.

"Guess that means I'll have to take her to the shower," Kai replied, picking up a sticky strand of my hair and dropping it onto my face. Then he leaned down and licked all the way up my cheek —which I should, perhaps find gross, but instead I giggled.

His fingers bit down on my hips and he dragged me back towards him.

"I wanted to eat this," Caspian muttered.

"There are far better feasts in the world," Kai replied. Then, without warning, he shifted lower and took my nipple between his teeth, biting down.

I let out a gasp, my back arching as heat flooded my veins. I thought a plate might have cracked beneath my back. My fingers bit into the corded muscle in his arms and all of a sudden I could see no one else.

"Kai..." I hissed, my cheeks burning.

"Why not carry on right here?" Kai asked.

"I am putting my foot down." Angel's voice cut through the magic. "You cannot fuck our omega on the dining table *during* breakfast."

Kai's pout was delightful. When he let me up, I managed—with difficulty—to extract myself from the table.

Luckily, Kai had dropped me over a bowl of uncut fruit and a plate of pancakes. It was easy to take the first layer off so I hadn't ruined it all. When I made for the spare seat, Kai dragged me back onto his lap. I didn't argue. Even when it involved his hand possessively biting down on my thigh.

"Actually," Angel said pointedly as he loaded his plate with pancakes. "You can't fuck her at all."

"Wait. Why?" Kai asked, indignant. His arms wrapped me tight as if Angel had threatened to take me away.

"Heat's too close. Don't want to push it before the ball."

Right. Of course.

That was fine. It wasn't like I'd been planning sex with them, anyway. I caught a slight smirk on Bane's face as he caught my expression. I checked it to make sure I wasn't pouting as much as Kai.

I ate until well past full, and didn't regret a thing. "Thanks!" I said, glancing between the others as Kai poured me another glass of orange juice.

"Bane did most of it," Angel said.

"Yeh. Though I gotta go to the grocery store," Bane said. "Text me anything you need."

"Like... now?" I perked up.

"Yeah."

"Can I come?" I asked.

"Uh. Sure?" Bane shrugged. "Can't promise it'll be very exciting."

But he could speak for himself. I'd never been to one of the city shops before.

Bane

"You don't have to..." I swallowed. "I'm not going to push like Kai. You don't have to spend time with me."

"I know," Havoc said as we made our way down the hallway.

"Tell Angel or me if he's too much."

"I will," she said with a smile. "But he's not. He's not pushy in a bad way. It's kind of nice."

Okay. Good.

I was quite surprised, actually. Kai didn't often know his boundaries so well. But there was something fascinating about watching the two of them together, they had similar energy that seemed to bounce off of one another.

As we approached the elevators, I noticed Havoc shifting nearer. Taking clear note of the fact she'd just told me she didn't mind Kai's boldness, I slipped my arm around her waist and tugged her closer. She stepped into that touch, glancing up at me with equal amount delight and nerves.

Her chestnut hair hung in waves that reached her mid-back. Today it was fully down, without even a braid behind her ear. I'd noticed there was always a hint of a tangle or two in those waves, as if they refused to behave, but it was quite charming.

As we waited for the elevator, her golden gaze found me from beneath her dark eyelashes, the olive skin on her cheeks just a little rosy. She was wearing an oversized zip up hoodie today—the sleeves reaching her knuckles, a pair of black leggings, and the worn leather boots she'd arrived in.

Casual and cute was a far stretch from the typical appearance of omegas, who were most often seen in upscale clothing as a sign of status, but it suited Havoc perfectly.

Always with an aura of chaos, she was unconventional, unkempt and frankly, everything Logan—who strived for nothing less than perfection—would hate. Which meant in my eyes, Havoc was as perfect for us, as her name was for her.

She remained close to me for the duration of the elevator ride, and seemed to breathe easier as we stepped into the parking garage.

I smiled to myself as I dug in my pocket for my keys.

She'd done it. She'd broken down our walls. We had a chance to convince her to stay, and I surprised myself with a sense of genuine hope.

TWENTY-SEVEN

Bane

"What the fuck? This is so good."

"What are you doing?" I asked, startled. I'd turned to find Havoc with an open Sweetcrisp bar in the shopping aisle, already having devoured half of it.

She paused, staring at me, then glancing down at the bar. She covered her mouth. "What?" she asked. "Did I do something wrong?"

"Um..." I scratched my head. "You're not really supposed to eat it before we pay?"

Kai, I knew, would do something like that on purpose just to piss me off, but she looked genuinely panicked.

"Oh. Uh... I can go wait outside." There was something tense in her expression, as if expecting me to snap at her.

"It's fine." I didn't really care what anyone thought. She didn't relax. "I want you to stay."

Havoc swallowed her bite, eyeing me wearily. "I didn't go anywhere. Ever. With Lhevus, he'd take me out. But not really around people. We'd go on walks and stuff, but he wanted to hide me."

"Lhevus?" I stopped in my tracks, staring at her, a pack of noodles halfway to the trolly.

"Yeah. My dad?"

Angel had given us a run-down of Havoc's history when we'd arrived. We'd all been a bit out of it, though, fresh with the wound of Logan's death. I remembered him going on about her dad being a gold pack sympathiser, but... "Your *father* is one the most notorious researchers in the gold pack regime?"

"Was." She shrugged. "They killed him."

I just stared at her, then cleared my throat. "I'm sorry." I was being slow. She'd just told me about her father's execution. But I couldn't get my head around any of it.

"Don't be. He didn't... care for me. Not *really*. It was more about my title than anything."

Havoc was already drifting from the conversation and eyeing a bag of haribos with interest.

"So you were stuck there?" My brain returned to the whole... elevator incident, to the fact she'd not been familiar with something so common.

"It was a big place, lots of acreage. It was fine."

"Did you *ever* leave?"

"A few times. Every birthday until I was twelve, he took me to a local farmers market. But after I perfumed, it was over. He didn't want to risk anything."

"You perfumed when you were twelve?" I asked.

"Yeah." Havoc glanced down at the half eaten Sweetcrisp bar as if trying to figure out what to do with it.

That was young. Explained her powerful aura—well, that and not registering. The injection the institute gave to omegas was to keep their auras in line with society's laws, but it dampened their powers, too. Gold pack omegas often had stronger auras.

My mind was in a spiral. This was why Logan had lost his

fucking mind. His mate was the daughter of someone his family actively sought to destroy.

And here she was, standing in the aisle of a grocery store, cramming the rest of a Sweetcrisp bar into her cheeks like a guilty hamster. Her gaze darted down the aisle as she scrunched up the wrapper and tucked it into her pocket, her eyes watering slightly as she swallowed the last part.

"I've seen lots of movies. But they don't usually go over shopping etiquette. I'm a bit lost."

"You're fine." But my eyes fell on the box of bars she'd torn open. I bit back my smile as I dropped it into the cart. Then I turned to grab the bag of haribos.

When I looked back, she was reaching over the cart to examine a bag of spicy crisps. I was met by the full sight of her round butt hugged by black leggings.

Who gave her clothes like that?

Right.

Angel.

Hadn't he considered she'd also look like that for everyone else? I caught a beta male do a double take down the aisle and swear I let out a growl in my chest.

Havoc straightened, turning to me in alarm.

"What?"

"Uh. Nothing." I faked a cough. "Sore throat."

Havoc

"Where are the others?" I asked. We were unpacking the groceries in the kitchen, and I was trying to memorise where everything went.

"Caspian's probably in the second office." Bane nodded up the balcony to the end of the hall. "Texted saying not to disturb him since he's getting back into work. Angel and Kai are out."

"What are they doing?" I asked, curiously, handing Bane the milk for the fridge.

"Wednesday, so it's date night. They were thinking of skipping it this week, but I think Angel wanted to keep some routine."

"Oh, nice. What do they do?"

"When Angel's not in recovery... Go karting, paintball, the range, rock climbing, buffets—you name it. Angel lets Kai come up with the crazy ideas—he had no shortage of those—then they go all in. Today they'll probably just go to a restaurant. Weekends are usually pack stuff if one of us organises something. Otherwise we go to Jeremy's Burger Joint down the street."

"That's... nice, actually." I remember when Luther lived with us, Lhevus would make us all have Sunday roast together every week. I think my dad just appreciated structure, but I always enjoyed helping Luther cook everything.

Bane was flattening all the grocery bags and tucking them in a cupboard. "I'm just glad they went. I get you all to myself."

He straightened, turning back to me with a charming half smile. I had just slipped onto one of the bar stools, unsure of what to do with myself.

"Oh." I tried to stamp down my over-eagerness at that. I really wanted to keep spending time with him, and the idea of being alone in my room—well I'd had enough of that for a lifetime.

"Our last movie night got interrupted," he said. "Unless you want to do something else?"

"No. Movies are great."

I loved movies. I even more loved the idea of new movies, instead of the same fifty I'd grown up on. I joined him on the couch, eager to be close. I tried not to loose a little purr as he tugged me into his arms.

Why did he feel so safe?

256

He tilted my chin toward him. It was hard to put into words how good it felt that he could touch me without pain, as if Logan's claws were falling away. It was like that now with Kai, Angel and Bane. But Caspian had brushed by me while I loaded the dishwasher yesterday and I'd felt the familiar prickle of pain on my skin. He'd shot me a strange look, but I hadn't been able to read it.

I was convinced now, that it *was* to do with trust.

"A lot happened yesterday. How are you holding up?"

"I'm..." My brows furrowed, unable to escape the way he was looking at me, as if he truly wanted to know. "I'm okay." But the truth was, my anxiety was hiding under every rock, oblivious to my excitement or my wants.

"But?" he asked.

"I'm nervous about the ball thing," I said quickly, before I could second guess myself.

"Why?"

"I don't want to take the bond just because I haven't got any options after."

"You won't." Bane sounded so sure. "Tomorrow Angel's going to take you out. I promise by the end of the day, you won't have a single doubt about the options you have."

I stared at him, unsure what it meant, but I nodded anyway, trusting his faith.

He leaned closer, and I closed the gap, pressing my lips to his, that swooping sensation in my stomach again. He drew me closer, and my eyelash brushed his cheek, his soft lips so full of comfort.

Next thing I knew I was on his lap, fingers brushing his chin and neck, the kiss getting deeper.

He was perfect.

Only... that made me so anxious.

"Would they want you if they knew how you've debased yourself to convince me you're enough?" Rough fingers gripped my chin with a painful touch. "It doesn't matter how much you try."

I broke from my kiss with Bane in a flash, my chest heaving.

"Are you okay?" Bane was asking. I could barely hear him, my arms coming around my chest, goosebumps erupting across my whole body. I couldn't look at him. I had to get away, but I couldn't move—"*Havoc?*"

He'd straightened where he sat, hands on my arms.

"Talk to me."

"... I know what I am..." I trailed off, unable to find the words.

"Our omega," he said quietly.

I winced, shutting my eyes.

Their mate. Their only option. I balled my fists around my hoodie, hating how I was hiding from the words here as much as I did in my mind.

"You can tell me," Bane said gently, still so patient. I looked up at him at last, trying not to let the spark of resentment lodge into my soul. Tried not to think that he might be being deliberately obtuse. That wasn't who he was—at least I didn't think so.

So instead of that, I tried to find the words that refused to come.

"I'm not..." I took a breath, knowing I had to say this so it wouldn't destroy me. And besides, Bane knew. They all knew. It was only me pretending it was a secret. "I'm no good at being an omega."

Bane stared at me, confusion not slipping. "Tell me what you mean by that."

I couldn't look at him. Was this pity? Pretending he had no idea.

Just like Kai and Angel... a little voice whispered.

"Logan bit me..." The words slipped out in a breath. "And I wanted him so much. I could barely be in a room with him and not feel it. But he didn't... I wasn't enough to..."

I was a failed omega.

I knew what Eli had said about Logan faking it, but that didn't undo anything. That feeling was like a cold vice around my heart as I gave everything, just to be met by coldness.

"I was never trained." Not like other omegas. "And I'm gold pack. And I don't know, what if I'm just... broken? Angel and Kai —they know I can fix Angel's aura. So now they're—"

"You worried we're *faking* attraction?" Bane sounded stunned.

"You're all stuck with me. I'm your scent match, and I'm gold pack. I know I'm a good solution, but I'm not appealing like other omegas. I just wish everyone would stop pretending."

"I... want you," Bane murmured. "And so does every other member of this pack. The problem isn't that you aren't... hot? *Appealing*? It's the opposite."

I stared at him, uncomprehending.

"You have no idea how badly it *kills* me to be in a room with you and not just..." He let out a breath. "You really have no idea. I —we *all* want you to know you're more important than that, so we're killing ourselves fighting it."

"But the others—Caspian—?"

"I promise you there hasn't been a PG dream in this apartment since the night you got here. Caspian included."

My cheeks burned as I stared at him.

"Tell me you believe me. None of us have met a woman who's screwed us up like you have."

A small giggle bubbled up my throat at that, both at the words and at the daring part of my heart that clung onto it, believing it.

Then I felt like an idiot. Should this be what I was worried about? Not my freedom, but whether I was attractive to a pack I knew I had to walk away from?

Is that what Logan had turned me into?

Bane shifted closer and tucked my hair behind my ear. I looked into those beautiful eyes, silver storm clouds ready to break. It matched the silver chain around his neck, the one that always looked out of place. My eyes traced the faint stubble along his angled jaw and the set of his straight nose. His heavy, dark eyebrows were knotted just slightly. Heat flooded my veins.

"I could show you how much I want you—?" he began, but cut off as my fingers closed around his wrist.

"Yes." I wanted that so. Fucking. Badly.

His pupils blew. The scent of new leather and apples filled the air. His lips pressed against my neck and I sunk against him, letting my scent mark him with a wild thrill. His fingers wound through my hair as he shifted me up and he fumbled with the zipper on my jacket with his other hand.

"Wait, right here?" I asked, my voice high.

"The others won't be back for ages."

"Caspian?"

"He's busy."

"But he could come out," I whispered.

"I mean... he could." There was a half-smile on Bane's face as he tugged on the zipper of my jacket. A low growl ripped from his chest. It wiped all arguments from my head. Okay. So, I'd been sly when I'd dressed this morning—I wasn't wearing a shirt, just a thin black lace bralette.

"Fuck, Havoc I'm going to ruin you."

At first, I didn't identify the chill that raced down my spine, all I knew was that my hands took his cheeks firmly. He paused.

"Wait." I... I wasn't ready to be that vulnerable again. Not after Eli, who'd given me that, and then tried to use it to steal my freedom. "I want..." I swallowed then lowered my hand down to his waist to find the bulge against his jeans. He cocked his eyebrow. "I want you."

Another low rumble sounded from him, and I felt it through our contact. With his grip still in my hair, he dragged me into another kiss with such roughness that I had to press my hands to his chest to steady myself. When he broke the kiss, my breaths were heaving.

"I want it like that," I whispered.

Bane stilled, eyes calculating. He straightened, so I was pressed against him, my head tilted up to meet his burning gaze.

"Let me get this straight," he breathed. "You want me holding you just like this...?" he asked, still gripping my hair.

I nodded just slightly as his grip tightened. I let out the slightest breathy moan. Somehow, the fact that we were still here, in the middle of the living room, made my blood run hotter.

"Tell me pet, you want it rough, or gentle?"

My breathing hitched, the answer coming instantly, a thrill in my veins at the idea. "Rough." My voice was faint and needy.

Logan had taken every piece of control I had over my life—all but for one thing. He'd let me watch those omegas and try to figure out everything for myself. And then, when I tried to live up to them—insecure and floundering—he deemed me not good enough, and left me locked up. And I had blamed myself.

How many times would I replay his reactions, to me and Eli, or when he let me touch him? I would desperately try to figure out why he was so cold with me and so into the others.

I knew now, it was all a lie. And it changed nothing.

Right now I wanted—*needed*—Bane to show me that everything he'd said was true.

I needed passion.

He lifted me higher until I could feel his breath against my lips. "And you want me to use that pretty little mouth of yours until I'm all done?"

My fingers curled around his shirt, my voice nothing but a whine. "Yes."

TWENTY-EIGHT

Bane

Rainfall and firewood.

Havoc's perfume filled the air.

Her touch trailed my torso as she sank to her knees between my legs. It was the most incredible sight I'd ever witnessed.

My chest was heaving at the sight of the sheer dark lace and the press of her nipples against it. I tilted my head back, trying to collect myself—or I'd be done before we even started.

I looked back down in time to see her freeing my cock from my jeans. When she saw my size, her eyes went wide, her mouth popping open.

I almost laughed.

Guess that meant Logan and Eli were average at best. Fucking pricks.

When standing, Havoc came barely to my shoulders. Her frame was slight, especially when compared to mine. Right now her delicate hand circled my cock, not at all nervous like she was so often. Instead, I watched curiosity clash with the heat in her eyes as she ran her tongue along the underside of my shaft.

My grip instantly dug into the cushions beside me. Her eyes flicked to them, delight sweeping away everything else.

That's what she wanted to see. What Logan had denied her. Passion. Need. Not from her, she had so much to give, I'd already seen that over and over.

She needed to see it returned.

Not a tall order; I'd been fighting exactly that since I'd met her.

But then Havoc pressed her lips over my tip and that was enough to wipe all thoughts from my brain.

She started working my shaft, and it felt amazing. I almost forgot myself until her nails bit into the back of my hand, dragging it toward her. For a moment she was glaring up at me.

"Are you sure you can fit me all?" I growled, taking her hair in my grip and shifting my position just slightly. That sight was deadly; her lips pressed halfway along my length, and it looked too big for her. Heat speared my core.

She didn't look away, and those golden irises beneath dark lashes flashed with molten fury at my words. I grinned, my hormones spiking, the alpha crashing free with a burst of my aura.

Then I held her in place as I slid my length forward, groaning with lust at the sight of my huge shaft forcing all the way into her tight little throat. I could see the way her fingers, covered to the knuckle by her jacket, bit down on my jeans as a low moan rose from her chest. My gaze slid to the olive skin along her neck and collarbones, down to the curve of her breasts. Her nipples pressed against the black lace, and her body seized over what I was doing to it.

"Too much?" I asked, holding her there as I leaned back. She couldn't nod or shake her head, but her wide eyes held mine, not panicked, but... sultry.

"You're mine, pet," I murmured as I slid out so slowly. Once I was out, she was taking little panting breaths, clutching my thighs to stay up. Then she composed herself and ran her tongue along my shaft again. Her grip found where my hands were still tangled in her hair.

"Don't stop," she breathed.

Havoc

I was more turned on than I had ever been.

Bane was almost feral with desire. Even as he held me in place, choking me roughly, I could see he was fighting to hold back.

A part of me wanted to know what it looked like on the other side of that self-control. They were all dangerous in different ways. Angel's threat was smooth, a threat like water—slipping through every crack. Kai and Caspian, they had sharp edges. But none of them matched the roughness Bane had. And he boxed it all up in routine and sharp cut shirts and kept quiet so no one would know that when he spoke, he wielded power.

And right now, with his fist in my hair as he choked me with his cock, I was witness to the side he tried so hard to hide. My body shook, my fingers digging into his jeans, white with the effort of taking him so deep. His knot was swelling with each thrust and every time my lips brushed it, a shiver ran down my spine.

I watched the tick of Bane's clenched jaw, the furrow of his dark brows, the little part of his lips as he tilted his head just slightly back, taking pleasure in me.

I realised, in that moment, what set me on edge. I knew what I was looking for.

They knew all of my secrets.

I wanted theirs.

I heard the sound of a door closing and my heart rate spiked.

Bane tensed just as he pulled his cock from my mouth. My eyes darted to the balcony behind him.

Shit.

Caspian was frozen, eyes fixed on me and Bane as he stared down from the balcony railings into the living room. And there I was, kneeling on the floor before the couch, Bane's tip hovering before my lips. I saw the smile on Bane's face out of the corner of my eye—as if he knew exactly who I was looking at.

Bane shifted me closer, grip still on my hair, lining his tip up to my mouth. I looked back to him in shock as I realised exactly what he wanted. "I didn't say stop." His voice was low and rough.

I didn't take my eyes from Bane as I parted my mouth. With no hesitation, he slid his length back down my throat until my lips brushed his knot. He held me there.

"Good girl," Bane murmured as I let out a groan. Slick pooled in my lace panties and I knew my scent had just choked up the air. I didn't dare look away from him, knowing my cheeks were flaming red at the idea that Caspian was watching. I let out another whimper in my chest at that thought, something feral and... and fucking pleased.

At the sound, Bane started to pump out and in, only withdrawing halfway before slamming back into my throat.

"Touch yourself." His words were laced with a command.

I dropped one of my hands, slipping it into my panties and rubbing my clit. The heat that was already in my system lit up.

Finally, I broke, my eyes darting back to the balcony.

Shit.

My gaze locked with Caspian, his fists balled around the railings as he stared down at me, his jaw clenched. My brain, melted by hormones, went haywire. Caspian was as beautiful as Bane, his dark hair tangled over his shoulders, tattoos reaching to his sharp jawline. His beetle black eyes were so dark I couldn't tell if the pupils were blown like I knew mine were.

Why was he still watching?

I couldn't help the little sounds I made with each of Bane's pumps. He sped up, and my gaze returned to him, entranced by the corded muscle on his neck that was taught, and the low feral noises he was making each time my lips met his knot.

"Fuck... Havoc. Come for me."

My name on Bane's tongue, the command, the heat in my veins at knowing Caspian was watching, it all sent me over the edge. I shuddered as Bane gripped my hair tight and drove all the way in. His hot seed hit my throat.

My lips parted slightly over his knot as he came and my body trembled with wave after wave of my orgasm.

But when he drew me up into his arms, running kisses along my neck, Caspian was gone.

TWENTY-NINE

Havoc

The trip I was supposed to take with Angel was postponed by a few days. Caspian had taken one look at his wound after their date night and ordered bed rest. (And banned him from being alone with Kai.)

"Don't *tell* me it's not his fault," I'd overheard Caspian snapping at them both in the dining room. "Can no one keep their dick in their pants around here?"

The smirk on Bane's face made my cheeks burn red hot.

I had spent the last two days either cuddled up demanding Bane show me all his favourite movies, or watching Kai and Bane play video games while Angel sulked on the bed.

I almost lost my mind when I saw the racing game they were playing. It was a newer version of the one I'd grown up on. My dad had an old console in the house.

I kept my mouth shut, however, wanting to take my time to make sure I knew every change in rules or items.

I'd spent my childhood playing against Luther, until he was bored with it, and then the NPCs. I was good. Stupid good, Luther had said. But I decided to keep that to myself for now while I studied their racing styles.

Finally, Angel was well enough to take me out, even if no one was clear on exactly what that meant.

I'd spent tonight curled up in Bane's room on his couch. Now, ready to turn in, I stood with a stretch.

I wanted to stay, but I was nervous to ask. It wasn't because I thought he'd say no, or even be bothered by it, but I was still anxious at how safe this house was getting.

The question remained suspended between us all.

Would I take the bond?

Angel had said it was a bad idea—and I got that. But with every day that passed it became more and more clear what I wanted.

And that terrified me, because I'd done it before, and what had that got me?

Nightmares of Gavin's swept me away, even sometimes with Kai there. He'd wake me in a cold sweat, holding me tight.

But I wanted them. Wanted it so badly even when I knew what a fool that made me.

Bane kissed me goodnight, and I took my mug with me, wanting to get myself a cup of tea before I went to sleep. It was something Bane did, and it helped settle my dreams. Kai had been switching between his room and mine, and wouldn't be there tonight.

When I neared my room in the hallway, I heard voices. I halted when I heard my name.

"Can I go out with Havoc tomorrow?" That was Angel. I crept closer until I saw a glimpse of Angel and Caspian on the couch in the living room. Caspian was checking his wound.

"Yeah, should be fine."

"Good," Angel said. "And I need help with something." I stepped away, about to head back to my bedroom—since tea wasn't worth Caspian's cold stare, but the next words made me pause.

"I'm not getting on board with your Logan vendetta." Caspian's voice was clipped.

"I know. This isn't about that."

"What then?"

"You know much about the place she was at—Gavin's Treasures? The club that was keeping her?" Angel asked.

There was a pause, and I heard Caspian sigh. "Heard of it."

"I need—"

"I know what you need," Caspian cut him off. "I'll do it."

There was a pause. "Why?" Angel asked.

"I'm paying his debts."

"And what are Logan's debts?"

There was another long silence before Caspian replied. "She is."

My pulse quickened. "What does that mean?"

"Means," Caspian replied. "The least I can do is clear his slate. I'm not an idiot, I know what he did. I fix it, then she can take the bond with you guys."

A beat past, and then I heard movement. I dared peer around to see Angel had taken Caspian's wrist with a scowl. "What do you mean, 'with you guys?'" Angel's voice was low.

I could see Caspian's jaw was clenched from here, and the loose strands of his dark hair swept across his pale face. "Logan gave her that bond, she should get it. But when she does, I'm cleaving."

My hand jumped to my mouth, and I shifted out of sight, my throat dry. I heard Angel's low growl. *"Cass—"*

"Don't," Caspian spat.

My heart was slamming against my ribs. Cleaving was the term for the excruciating process of a pack member severing themselves from the bond. It was volatile, painful and destructive.

Sometimes the aura wound it left behind never healed, leaving the alpha unable to form bonds permanently. Sometimes, it killed the alpha who tried it.

"This is bullshit. You're making this an ultimatum? Havoc or you?"

"No!" Cass sounded angry. "Because you won't tell her, or the others. Her choice has to be honest—you *know* that. It's why you're doing what you're doing tomorrow. The ball is what—four days away, you can convince her—?"

"That's bullshit. What about the rest of us? What about Kai—?"

"Stop! It's not about you. It's about—" Caspian broke off.

"Your sister?" Angel asked. "Is this what Halley would want—is this what *he'd* want—?"

Caspian cut Angel's words off with a snarl.

Once more I dared glance around. Caspian's fist was curled around Angel's shirt. "Don't talk about shit you can't fucking fathom."

But I was backing up, having heard too much already.

I slipped into my room and leaned against the door, unable to move. This was worse than his threat on the balcony.

Caspian was serious, and that meant I could never take the bond.

A chill slid down my spine at the thought of it. At the thought of joining their pack and then being the reason Caspian left.

Kai wouldn't be able to forgive me. I knew how much Caspian meant to him—they were practically siblings.

They would all hate me, and I could never again be bonded to someone who didn't want me.

Havoc

I woke to a knock on the door. I was glad it was Kai's night away because I'd cried myself to sleep and I didn't want questions.

It was Angel on the other side with his sweet cinnamon scent.

Why did he look even more beautiful now I knew the truth? I could never have him. He was in sweatpants and his dressing gown hung open, showing the white bandage upon a rippling torso of golden-brown skin.

More importantly, he was holding a fresh mug of coffee.

"We'll be leaving in 30," he told me with a smile, pressing the mug into my hand.

"Thank you," I managed, trying to measure my expression. He couldn't know what I'd overheard last night.

I changed and washed and double checked my eyes weren't red from the night before, and then hurried out to meet him.

I didn't realise how nervous I was about spending the day alone with Angel. Usually, when I was with Angel, I was with Kai, who was high energy and acted a bit like a social shield. Angel was quieter, more intense, and I had the impression he was highly tuned in to each of my words and reactions.

The day was not what I expected. Angel took me to some high-end place that looked like the law firms I'd seen in movies. The people there seemed to know him, smiling and chatting, and all the while giving me funny looks. The strangeness of feeling as though I'd stepped right into my childhood movies, was enough to distract me from my dread at what I'd overheard last night. If the conversation with Caspian had bothered Angel, he was hiding it expertly.

"You should have told me to dress differently." I huddled close to him, watching anxiously as the elevator doors trapped us in. Luckily there was no one else in the awful metal box with us.

I was tagging along at his side in a hoodie and leggings, but Angel looked right at home in a sleek grey suit.

He was tall, and of the pack, he was dwarfed only by Bane, but while Bane was built like a lumberjack, Angel was much more athletic. The way he held himself in a suit had me ogling—and I wasn't the only one. He chatted to people like he owned the place, pinching the middle jacket buttons between his fingers with a charming smile the whole time. It was a different smile than the one I knew, as if he were hosting it only for show.

"It's unlikely the reason they're staring," Angel told me. "What happened with Logan got out, and our pack is quite well known around here."

Right. Of course. So, everyone looking at me right now knew I was a killer.

Luckily, Angel ushered me from the elevators into a private room. "Right. Havoc, first we're going to take some pictures."

"Of me?"

"For your passport, there's a bunch of documents we need to get the ball rolling on. Then we'll set up a bank account, and I need to check your AORN and make sure it's updated correctly."

My AORN, or alpha-omega registration number, would have me listed as gold pack. It had been given to me the moment I'd been sold to Gavin's. But a passport and bank account? "Don't I have to wait until after the bond goes through?" I asked.

"I want it all set up. Some of it will go through anyway, bank account and passport is something you can have regardless of whether you accept or decline the bond."

"Right."

"And there's something else," Angel said.

"What?"

"If you'll let them, I want pictures and a legal check on Logan's bite."

I stared at him, swallowing. "Why?"

"He never declared it, but it's important. I don't know what it means that it was never consolidated, but I'm putting one of the firm's legal teams on it."

"Okay."

"It does mean bringing in one of the seers on retainer, and photos. Are you comfortable with that?"

"You'll be here?" I asked.

Angel frowned. "I'm not leaving you."

"Okay then..." I swallowed. I had to do this. "Yes." I'd heard what Caspian had said yesterday. I knew the truth, that I couldn't say yes to this bond no matter what I wanted.

I had to accept what Angel was offering today.

THIRTY

Havoc

"How did you and Kai get together? Was it before the pack?"

We were done for the day, and sitting in a little coffee shop. Angel had bought me a peppermint mocha which was, I'd decided, a tier up from coffee.

"Yeah." Angel thought for a moment, something darker crossing his eyes. "My parents died seven years ago. Brutal murder, happened right in our house, through security and everything. For a long time after I was paranoid, never felt safe, even in my own house."

I stared at him. Those words had been spoken casually, but there was a weight to them, as if it were much harder for him to say than he was letting on. "I'm sorry. I didn't know."

"It's alright." Angel shrugged, but he was tense. "One of the first times I spoke to Kai, I remember talking about everything. Never talked about it back then. Not to therapists, not to friends, not even Logan or Bane, even though they'd been my friends my whole life, and were even there when it happened. But Kai... I trusted him the first time I met him, and I know how insane that sounds. So... That night he broke into my house, and I woke up to him in bed next to me."

I almost choked on the drink I'd just taken a sip of.

"That was my reaction too," Angel snorted. "Next day I hired a bunch more bodyguards to secure the house. Next morning, same thing. Five days he did it, and each time I was going crazy installing the latest security tech, getting the best in the business. None of it stopped him, every morning I'd wake up, and he'd be there next to me."

"That's just... completely normal," I mused.

"It was his way of telling me that I'd always be safer with him."

"Oh... right." I guess that made sense. In a weird Kai way.

"Well. That's what I tell myself."

"You never asked him?"

"Ruins the magic a bit, don't you think?" Angel grinned.

I snorted. "Makes me feel better about our first meeting." Kai was nuts, but at least it was evenly distributed.

"Wait." Angel asked, brows knotting. "What does that mean?"

Right. Shit. "Uh... Nothing. We worked it out."

There was an edge of concern in his eyes. "If you don't tell me, I'll get it out of him."

"Don't." But Angel didn't take his blazing eyes off me. "He just... took me out on the deck and left me in the cold for a bit to get me to say why I killed Logan."

Angel stared at me, his mouth working for a moment.

I hugged my drink to my chest, thinking for a way out of this. "But you know, you almost bit me, and Caspian threatened to throw me off the deck, so... If we put it in perspective—"

"Cass did *what*?"

"I don't think he meant it." Well. That was a lie, and Angel could see it plain on my face.

Angel wrinkled his nose, jaw ticking as he lifted his coffee to his lips.

"I'm going to have a word with—"

"Don't. Please don't."

Angel sighed. "It's not just about you, Havoc. We're a pack, but we aren't acting like it."

"You... need a leader." I meant it as a question, but it didn't come out like one.

"Yeah. It's something we're coming back to after the ball." But he looked thoughtful for a moment.

I nodded, sipping my mocha again. "How does Caspian know so much about wounds and shit?"

"Oh, yeah. He grew up in the Harpy district with Kai. Was involved with some street gang. He had a knack for stitching people up and got taught by their on-call doctor. Not exactly formal or even legal training, but he does a good enough job."

"But you'd rather him than a hospital?"

"Hated them ever since my parents died."

There was an awkward pause for a moment, and I drummed my fingers on the wooden panels of the coffee table. "What um... What can I do to get Caspian not to hate me?"

It was a long shot, Angel hadn't sounded hopeful when he was talking to Caspian last night.

"You're talking like you're going to take the bond."

I swallowed. "If we're talking options today, I want to know the pack is an option, too."

That was another lie, but a guilty part of me wanted Angel to give me hope. I still had time left with them. Was it possible I could drag Caspian from this ledge?

That shouldn't be your job.

I clenched my jaw, burying the thought. It wouldn't hurt to *ask* about Caspian.

Angel nodded, considering. "You haven't done anything wrong, Havoc. Caspian's problem isn't *with* you."

"But it's because of what I did?"

Angel nodded.

"And he can't forgive me?"

"I don't think it's a matter of forgiveness..." Angel considered. "His relationship with Logan got tangled in a whole lot of trauma. He *thinks* he owes Logan a debt he doesn't believe he can ever pay. Accepting you would mean rejecting that."

"He... thinks?" I asked, not missing Angel's emphasis on that word.

"He'll swear up and down its debt that plagues him, but it's a lie."

"Then what?"

Angel set his coffee down, rubbing the bridge of his nose. "Look. I think he might come around—"

"You do?" I asked.

Angel paused, brows furrowed. I could see the pain in his eyes and wondered what he made of Caspian's declaration last night.

"Caspian is complicated and stubborn. If he thinks we're talking about him behind his back before he's ready, it won't help."

"I get it."

"But it's not on you Havoc. If we can't fix ourselves, we don't deserve you anyway," he said. "I do want to talk to you about the bond, though."

"Yeah?"

"Look, Bane has connected with you in a way I've never seen him connect with anyone. Kai's infatuated, they are both going to do whatever they can to convince you to stay. But I'm sure you know it's not that simple. You can't choose us because you don't have options. Money. Independence. You are worth more than that—and so are they."

I nodded, my heart in my throat. I knew the truth. The best thing to do would be to prepare them for it too. "I mean... I think I have to..." I swallowed.

"Reject the bond?" Angel asked.

I nodded again, fixed on the mocha before me. "It's just... after Logan. I said yes to him and then..." I couldn't finish. I'd heard what Caspian had said last night, and it made everything clear, but I didn't realise until now how true this was too.

Panic fluttered in my stomach every time I thought of taking the bond, every time I settled into happiness or hope...

"I know."

I glanced up at Angel.

"I mean... I don't want that to happen, but I get it. We all knew when we offered it."

Angel

"So. Tell me about your plans for after?" I asked, trying to shove away the heaviness in my heart.

She knew she had to reject the bond. That's what she'd just said. My sickness would take me from the pack, but that wasn't what worried me right now.

I almost closed my eyes, thoughts turning to Caspian. I couldn't believe what I heard last night. But then, if she didn't take the bond, that wouldn't be a problem because he wouldn't have a reason to leave.

No. It *would* be a problem.

I'd missed this.

We all had.

Caspian was so much further gone than I'd ever realised, and I didn't know if I was too late. Even now he was distant, closed off within the connection to the pack.

I'd left Caspian's healing to Logan, and given what he'd done for Cass, it had seemed like the right choice. But the last few days had taken my whole life and shaken it. What I'd learned was that all of my foundations were made of porcelain.

Logan wasn't what I thought, and a dark whisper warned that he'd been ruining us for a lot longer than Havoc. What had Caspian's healing truly been? Outlets made of nothing but blood and violence?

He needed more than that, but I was worried I was too late. That he was so drowned in false coping that he wouldn't know how to take a step in the right direction.

I felt lost.

I didn't know what he needed or *how* to help him. I didn't even know where to start.

Pushing that can of worms away, I focused on Havoc. This part of the conversation, it was why I was really here in the cafe.

"My plans?" she asked, chewing on her lip. She clutched her coffee cup with both hands. "I don't know. I don't have many skills. I was thinking..." Her nose wrinkled in the cutest way and she couldn't meet my eyes all of a sudden. "Logan used to talk about omegas who walked away from princess bonds. He said they were like... royalty. But I don't know how or why—"

She cut off as she caught the slightest smile twitching on my lips.

"What?" she asked.

"Sorry." I shouldn't be smiling, but... I blew out a breath. This was exactly what I'd hoped to convince her of. She'd got there on her own, but still, she had no idea. "The moment you reject a princess bond, you become a duchess. If you claim that title, by my reckoning you'll be the most sought-after omega in the city."

Havoc froze, staring at me as if I were crazy. "That doesn't make sense. Even if I'm protected by the institute, my eyes will still be gold."

"It's exactly your eyes that will work in your favour. There are —I think, only two gold pack duchesses in the city."

"And they do... Well?"

Again, I fought my smile. "They are deadly."

"And you think I can do the same?"

"You're gold pack, your scent is earthy—"

"That's a good thing?" she asked.

"Most omegas have floral or sweet scents. It's rare—gives you an air of danger, matches the gold pack brand."

"What does that mean?"

"The reason gold pack omegas are feared is that they break the institute's constraints on alphas and omegas. They are considered..." I winced at the words I was about to use, but she had to understand the power she was about to wield. "Wild and feral."

"Which is... bad," she said, as if trying to convince me of something.

"Unless you're a duchess. Packs want duchesses on their arms because it provides an illusion of power. Duchesses are omegas who have done the thing that most would never dare do. They rejected their own scent match, they rejected the strongest and most coveted bond that barely gets offered in the first place. They are the greatest fuck you to everything society is told to value. Contract one in, take her to the biggest events the city offers, get spotted taking one out—it's a status boost like no other. And gold pack duchesses? Think about that Havoc. Take everything that makes a duchess valuable and double it. Getting the offer of a princess bond in the first place when you're a gold pack—it's almost impossible, but to reject it? No, you will be fighting off half the alphas in the city the moment you list your name. Not to mention your aura is powerful, and—let's be honest, people will know what you did to Logan."

It was kind of screwed up really, but that was often the case with alpha-omega laws. We dealt with a lot of things amongst ourselves. The bonds that could connect us, could shatter us, and they were considered justice on their own.

"That doesn't sound good either." Her voice was high pitched. She tucked an imaginary lock of hair behind her ear.

Again, I had to stifle a grin. This humour was much more twisted than before, but it was the only way I had to cope with learning what Logan had done. And it was bringing me infinite satisfaction that this petite, adorable omega with rosy cheeks and a deathly fear of elevators, had executed Logan Mandela. Had shot him in the face with a gun he'd given her.

In cold blood.

It just warmed something in that not-so-golden heart of mine, knowing how much he would have hated headlines that splattered the newspapers only weeks ago at his death.

At the time, I'd had to look away, but yesterday I'd found myself scrolling back through Hound's Weekly website to update myself on how savage they'd actually gotten.

And she had no idea. She had no idea that the man she'd killed was a rising star in the city, who was quickly gaining a reputation, able to create waves skyscraper to street side.

The branding for her would be... Well it would be like no other. Havoc. Mandela's killer. Duchess open to offers.

"Havoc," I said. "You are going to start alpha wars in this city. I swear it."

"But... what will I have to do?" she asked, nervous.

"Let some rich alpha pack take you on dates, flaunt you at balls and events." For the first time, the high I was riding this entire conversation, crashed.

Telling Havoc how much power she had, telling her that she could walk away and seize the world by the neck, was thrilling. The brightness in her eyes as I painted this picture, as if she had hope... it was the most beautiful thing I'd ever seen.

Yet, the image of her in the arms of another pack, even if she wouldn't belong to them—my heart felt like it was caving in.

"Will I have to *be* with them?" she asked. That question ripped me from my thoughts.

"*You* will set every rule. Tell them you'll only attend if they all wear ballet dresses, and they'll probably turn up with toe shoes to boot."

Havoc giggled, and the sound sent butterflies through my stomach. But as soon as the humour appeared, it vanished. She chewed her lip. "I wouldn't ever be able to... to pull that off."

"Nonsense. One of the firms I'm with represents some of the highest class omegas in the city. I'll make sure they take care of you. And the top PA's in the city will be clamouring for you as a client the moment the ball is over. That said, you need anything—anything at all, Havoc, I'll be there. All of us will."

A long silence passed between us and for a moment, she looked hurt.

"What?" I asked.

"You aren't supposed to be... supporting this... You're... my mate."

My brow came down as I tried to work out the source of the tremor in her voice.

"Don't you...?" She trailed off, fingers curling around the edges of her coat. She couldn't finish.

Oh.

Fuck.

"Havoc..." I blew out a breath. "It's not—God. I don't *want* you gone." Doing this was like twisting a knife in my chest.

"Then—?"

"This is what you deserve. Logan said I had a heart of gold, but he liked to forget my vengeful streak."

"Vengeance on who?" She sounded startled.

"On him." I snorted. "Logan wanted to give you a princess bond? Havoc, I'm going to make sure you walk away a fucking princess."

And she had no idea. This—this was only the half of it.

THIRTY-ONE

Caspian

"You have cameras." I knew it was true. I'd not only scoped out Gavin's Treasures myself, but it was illegal for a club like his not to. Too many alphas in a small space.

"My clients pay good money to have the surveillance deleted."

"And?" I asked casually, turning the knife in my hands. It was two days until the ball, until all this Havoc crap would be over, and I was here tying off Logan's loose ends.

I leaned back on the huge desk in Gavin Shephard's office. The man himself was cuffed to his own desk chair, trembling. He was scared, but he hadn't cried or begged, which was all the information I needed to confirm what I already suspected of the sorts of business he truly dealt in.

He was the owner of Gavin's Treasures. The establishment that had held Havoc hostage for all those months.

I'd met men like him before. Where I'd grown up. On trips with Logan. They were chameleons in society, this one was dressed up well, a slightly fatherly look to him—in his mid-fifties, with silvery hair and a neat beard. Draw weapons though? Then the mask would fall away.

Gavin Shephard had been on the sharp end of a weapon like this before, enough times he could tell he had no way out. I'd got past his security without blinking, my clothing was saturated with scent dampeners, so he'd not identify a thing, and he'd not get a glimpse of my face. Not unless things were going poorly for him.

There was a long pause. "The footage gets deleted in cycles."

Perfect.

I wondered if he could see the cold smile in my eyes as I drew his laptop closer, tapping a few keys.

"Password?" I asked.

The whole process took about twenty minutes. I was careful to take every tape I could, so Logan's wasn't singled out. Then I was tossing his laptop on the couch.

"Excellent," I said with a stretch. "Now. You're going to sign these."

I had him sign a number of waivers, purchasing contracts, perfectly forged for each of the clients who had visited in the last month. I wouldn't single out Logan. And Kai would have a field day sifting through the rest, digging up dirt. Money would be in Gavin's account in the morning, too, validating that.

While Gavin was signing, my phone buzzed in my pocket. I only had one chat unmuted, so I slipped it out to see what the pack wanted.

> Angel: Was thinking we need to show Havoc the local cuisine. Jeremy's burgers tonight, everyone in?

> Kai: Will Cass have time before his date with Havoc?

I scowled.

Bane: I'm in. Also, Cass, she's asking if she needs to wear anything special? What's the setting—wine and cheese? Rollerblading? Or should I find her something that's easy to wash the blood from?

Neither Kai nor Bane knew what I was doing with Havoc tonight.

Gavin was still signing papers, and I noticed out of the corner of my eye, the slight tremor in his hand. Good. It meant he didn't know who I was, and a man like him was likely to have many enemies.

I dared slip my glove off to type a reply.

Me: It's not a date.

Me: I don't give a shit what she wears.

I paused, then added.

Me: Yes to burgers.

My real job for the night didn't start for a few hours, and I had to make an appearance. I didn't want Kai suspecting what I was going to do if Havoc took the bond.

I looked back to the man in the chair, forcing his hand back into the cuff.

I'd been watching him for a few days before I'd come, and I was confident that we wouldn't be disturbed.

"Th-that's everything?" he asked.

I rested against the desk, folding my arms. Gavin's Treasures, the place Havoc had been trapped in, wasn't the only business he owned...

I was on edge, I knew that, and I couldn't let that influence my decision. I was here to pay Logan's debts, and to do that, my payment had to be damn good. Even if it meant being alone with her for the evening.

The idea of that twisted me up just as it gave me a guilty thrill.

But Havoc wasn't just dangerous because I couldn't fight my need for her. I lived my life in darkness, taking every step blindly, never knowing where it would lead and not thinking of where I'd been. There was a place I could never return to.

Havoc was dangerous because she was a flickering light in that dark, a siren calling me, leading me onward, and I couldn't stop following.

And I knew she was taking me right back to that place.

For a moment, I heard the sound from my nightmares.

"Think twice..." The lyrics of an old song, one of Halley's favourites, played on the radio.

The darkness was coloured by flashing streetlights. It was late. I was driving. "... You and me in paradise..." The road ahead was quiet.

Until it wasn't.

A scream sounded as blazing headlights came from nowhere.

Then there was nothing but agony as a thousand iron claws ripped apart my flesh to the sound of metal exploding against metal.

Then nothing.

Pain tore up my arm. Warm tarmac stuck to my cheek—my skin —my flesh.

In the blackness I could see flaming orange. The world had stopped, but the song hadn't. "... It's just another day for you and me... in paradise..."

I couldn't move.

Not until I heard her screaming.

. . .

I wrenched myself from the memory, shaken. I realised I'd been staring at Gavin for a long time. He was even paler now.

I *could* manage one damn evening with her. I could do what I needed to do and get the fuck out.

Thoughts of Havoc and Logan were bad for my sanity, but it was too late. My aura stirred like leaves in a jittery wind.

Gavin Shephard had trapped Havoc.

My mate.

This man had kept her locked up for months like she was property.

And Logan asked him to...

I clenched my jaw, burning that whisper away, my anger peaking. When I spoke, my voice was a low growl. "I don't know if I'm done with you yet."

I rolled the edges of my balaclava, knowing that if I peeled it up, it was lights out for the filthy fucker before me.

Angel

Tonight was the night Caspian was taking Havoc out.

We had two days until the winter ball, and I held out a selfish shitty hope that something would happen, and he'd come around. Havoc had a way of getting to us all. Caspian was not immune. But it's also why I suggested the diner. He needed to be reminded of us at our best—and not just because of Havoc.

My dreams were impossible, though. I wanted it all. I wanted Havoc to stay, and I wanted Caspian to fall for her just like the rest of us were. To realise that she wasn't his demons.

Right now, Kai was slipping into the booth in Jeremy's so Havoc was seated between both him and Bane. She was watching him from beneath the flutter of loose brown hair that swept across her face, chewing on her lip to hide her smile.

Kai was falling hard for Havoc. He knew she might walk away, but it wasn't in Kai's nature to do things by halves. He was much more open with the pack bond than any of us were, and that meant his passion was—quite literally, infectious.

I wondered what Caspian thought of it.

The job he was doing today made Jeremy's burger joint comically light in comparison. I was surprised he'd come at all to be honest, especially now he was sitting a space away from Bane, drumming his fingers and watching other patrons as if he were bored.

I got a list of what everyone wanted and went up to the front with a smile.

Jeremy's was the 'line up at the front to order' kind of diner, with gaudy red booths and fake wood tabletops. We'd always voted, Jeremy's had always won, and Logan had always hated it.

I jumped as warm fingers slipped into mine, and looked down to see Havoc joining me in line.

"You alright?" I asked, eyeing her. She had become much more comfortable with me since our outing two days ago.

She was, I thought, just as tactile as Kai. Which was good, because Kai couldn't keep his hands off her. She *was* an omega, after all. I shouldn't be surprised.

Right now, the fingers of her other hand were curled around the edge of her hoodie, which meant she was anxious.

"Yeah, it's just... these are more expensive than a coffee." She glanced up at the menu.

"That they are."

"I still... don't have any money."

"First off," I chuckled. "That coffee was about half the price of the burgers"—Havoc visibly paled—"second, if *four* guys can't cover your meal at a burger joint, your prayers tonight better be demanding a refund on your mates."

I squeezed her hand and watched as she relaxed slightly. The smile on her face at my words was still tense, as if she wasn't sure. Sometimes, when I looked at her, my heart broke.

She'd been alone at her dad's house for years. Omegas weren't built for a lonely life. No one was, but omegas more than most.

Had Logan *known* that when he met her?

I wondered sometimes, about the boldness of his offer—a princess bond the first day they'd met. Yet, it wouldn't have taken long for him to learn her truth.

Havoc was vulnerable, ignorant of the world in all the worst ways, but more than that, she was a touch-starved omega. He had been her *mate,* and Logan could be—when he wanted—the most charming man I'd ever met.

The perfect storm.

And now here we were, a bunch of degenerates trying to pick up the pieces in the wake of his destruction.

Not enough. No matter how I saw her light up when Kai tugged her into a hug, or Bane drew her closer on the couch. She might be ignorant to the world, but that wasn't her fault. Havoc wasn't a fool.

She knew she couldn't take our offer. Not as we were. Not with how she'd been hurt.

When her burger arrived at our table, Havoc was unable to stifle her beam.

"What?" I asked. "You've had burgers before, *right*?"

Tell me she'd had burgers? *Everyone* had eaten burgers.

"I was just thinking, Logan told me even if he *did* bring me home, he'd never be able to show my face at parties or take me to restaurants." Her laugh was darker than I'd heard before as she speared a fry with a fork.

I froze, and so did my brothers. I saw the darkness flash in Bane's eyes, Caspian looked ready to crack a tooth and Kai's nose wrinkled in a hateful scowl.

She looked up at the quiet, then her fork slipped in her grip. "I'm... sorry..." Her voice was weak. "I shouldn't—"

"You have more right to talk about him than anyone," I said before she got any further.

There was a beat and Bane took a breath, obviously trying to relax. "That being said"—he reached over and snagged a fry from Havoc's plate—"I'm inclined to agree with him if you keep cutting fries with a knife and fork."

Havoc dropped the cutlery instantly, her cheeks blazing. "My house was a bit strict on meals."

"How is it you know your way around a gun, but you don't know fries are finger food?" I asked.

"You said you were raised on a bunch of movies," Kai put in. "Movies have people eating at burger joints."

"They do," Havoc replied indignantly. "But it's up to me to figure out if they're roughing it or not."

I choked on the cola I'd just taken a sip from.

"But back to the guns. I want to hear about that," Kai added.

"We had a range out back." Havoc shrugged. "Mostly used it for archery, but Lhevus used to show me guns too. Told me it was for safety."

Again, there was a strange pause at the table as she name-dropped her dad—the gold pack sympathiser and branded terrorist—as if it were nothing at all.

"You don't call him dad," I noted before she spotted our reaction.

"Yeh... I mean... I do like to..." She poked at the peas on her plate. "But he'd get real upset when I did that."

"Why?"

She dropped her voice in that mocking tone again. "'*No use in getting attached, Havoc. Never know what tomorrow is going to bring.*'" She snorted. "Well he wasn't *fucking* wrong." She jabbed a pea with her fork a little too aggressively. Instead of being impaled, the pea shot off her plate and caught Caspian right in the eye.

Her mouth dropped open, her face blanching. Bane and Kai, however, roared with laughter and I thought as he rubbed his eye with his fist, I might have seen Caspian fighting his own smile.

"Sorry." Havoc dropped her fork again, returning to her fries.

Caspian cleared his throat. "You did archery?" His question caught me by surprise. He didn't look at Havoc when he asked, instead focusing on his fork as he cut his burger.

"Halley's into archery, isn't she?" Kai prodded.

I contained my wince.

"Your sister?" Havoc asked.

Caspian froze, cold eyes snapping to her. "How do you know that?"

Havoc bit her lip. "I just heard her mentioned by—" She cut off. "Just in conversation, that's all." Her voice was low, and I hated the hint of fear in it. I spotted Bane's hand slip to her thigh comfortingly.

It seemed to be painful for Caspian, to un-clench his jaw, but he managed it, his expression relaxing.

"Best treat ever growing up," Kai said cheerily. "Getting to go on a trip to the archery range, right?" He elbowed Cass.

Cass, who was still watching Havoc with a strange look, nodded curtly.

"Why uh... Did you stop?" Havoc asked, glancing between them.

Caspian shrugged. "Impractical."

"Bullshit," Kai snorted. "And you *loved* it."

Caspian looked like he wanted to tear Kai's throat out. I knew Kai well enough to know he was fully aware of that.

"Yeh. Well not anymore," Caspian muttered. "Useless hobby. Better weapons to practise."

No one but Kai had the balls to prod Caspian when it came to this, but we all knew the truth of it.

Caspian avoided everything from his childhood.

His brother's death was his before and after moment. I'd lost my parents growing up. It had been sudden and terrible and it had broken me, but even I didn't envy what had happened to Caspian.

I just needed him to stop laying it at Havoc's feet.

"Come on." Kai, it seemed, wasn't letting it go, and Caspian looked ready to strangle him. "We all know you only stopped archery because—"

"So." Caspian cut Kai off loudly. "Havoc. What's with the gold pack shit?" He waved at his own eyes.

I opened my mouth and then shut it, suppressing a sigh. Even Kai scowled. Havoc's gaze darted between them both, clearly confused.

"Uhh... What do you mean?"

"You don't have to answer that," Bane said, glaring daggers at Caspian.

"Why are you gold pack?" Caspian, it seemed, was buckling in on his choice to ask her the uncomfortable question. Havoc, however, didn't look phased. She shrugged, once more looking from him to Kai as if trying to discern the tension between us.

"Dad didn't want me enrolling with the institute because it *'wasn't what nature intended'.*" She air-quoted that last part, her voice low and mocking as she rolled her eyes.

"Wait..." I couldn't help myself. "*That's* why you chose gold pack?" The question came out before I'd thought it through, but there was a chill creeping up my spine.

I knew her answer before she gave it. "No. He just... wouldn't take me. Never taught me to drive either or anything."

My heart was racing.

"But..." Caspian was the only one who dared ask, and for a

moment, he looked like he regretted the belligerent change of topic. "You *would* have enrolled?"

"Heck yeah." Havoc laughed. "I was kind of lonely, and the institute offers training—with other omegas, right? I kind of always wanted a 'girlfriend'"—she finger quoted—"You know?"

Once more, the table fell still, stunned into silence.

She... hadn't chosen it at all. She'd been *kept* from being a normal omega.

I felt my hairs stand on end, my aura threatening to burst out in the middle of the restaurant. But those golden eyes were a fucking violation. Didn't matter if you grew up where Kai and Caspian had, or where I had, there were few things worse than blocking an omegas enrolment. They could refuse—become an outcast, but it was a *choice*.

That golden ring around her eyes damned her, it would follow her forever. The worst of the world would come for her, and she'd have no protection.

It should *always* be a choice.

She glanced around at our faces and I could swear she visibly shrunk. She looked to me desperately, and I'd seen that look before. It was Kai when he couldn't figure out what he'd said to upset someone.

"I'm... sorry." Her voice was a breath, her eyes dropping to her food and for a moment I thought she was going to burst into tears. Bane shifted closer, slipping his hand into hers. "You're fine," he murmured. "It's *not* you." He did shoot Caspian a dark look, and Cass—to his credit—had the decency to look uncomfortable.

THIRTY-TWO

Caspian

I hummed to myself as I slipped out the back door of Gavin's, the bag on my back light as a feather. My mind was too, even if it wouldn't last.

I smiled. The night air was bracing.

Shame Kai couldn't come, how he loved explosives, but being entangled with Angel brought strict rules.

Poor fucker.

I tossed my phone cheerily as I exited the property.

Everything was ready. I'd first considered making this a quick job, but... No. I was going to do this job thoroughly—and get some answers about our omega while I was at it.

Havoc

"So, uh... What are we doing?" I asked.

"You'll see," Caspian grunted.

Right. Unhelpful.

It was dark out and I was in the passenger side of a huge

truck. We cruised through the city streets, the air inside warm. Caspian's scent was stronger here than I was used to, roses and cranberries. How did a scent like that seem somehow deadly?

I was alone with him for the first time since he'd threatened to throw me off a deck railing. No longer was I plagued with such a fear, but a different sort of nerves had me tonight.

The ball was days away, and I wanted to find a way to convince him not to leave the pack if I took the princess bond.

I was still working out how to pose that question without making him mad. I wasn't supposed to know about it at all. I knew he didn't like me, but we could come to an agreement, right?

Or something.

I knew now what my future could look like. I wasn't afraid of it anymore. I think... I think I would make it, saying no to the bond.

But Bane and Angel and Kai made that more heart-breaking by the day.

Caspian drove the car up to the top of a multi-story parking lot. It was empty at this time, the city bright with golden lights against the winter night.

The clock on the dashboard said midnight.

He pulled up to the edge, and from the height of the truck I could see the city beyond.

"That building over there?" I had to strain to see what he was talking about. "It's isolated, huge, got the red billboard just to the left—"

"Yeah. I see it."

"That's Gavin's Treasures."

I tore my gaze from the building, shocked. "What?"

But he was swiping through his phone. Something popped up on it right before he handed it to me.

I stared down to see a red button on the screen. "Press that, and..." He thumbed toward the building he had just pointed out —the one I'd been trapped in for months. "Boom. Whole thing goes up."

"What?" My throat was suddenly dry. Had I heard him right?

"Old Gavin Shephard is tied up inside, surrounded by explosives. Press it and it all goes up."

I couldn't be hearing him right. "Are you kidding?"

"Why would I be?"

Right. He was as mad as Kai, it seemed.

"A... big red button?" Even I knew how cliche that was.

"Kai's joke, really—not that he's allowed near this shit anymore."

"A... joke?" My voice was weak, my mind racing. Caspian just shrugged.

"Why are you doing this?"

"Look. I get that gold pack shit has other rules, but Gavin had no right to keep you there like that—no matter what Logan asked. You might be out of union protection, but that means the institute decides what happens, not any old prick on the streets."

"No I mean... why are *you* doing this?" I asked.

"This settles the debt."

"What debt?"

"The one Logan racked up when he did..." Caspian winced. "What he did."

"Does it?" I asked, my heart pounding in my chest. I stared back down at the phone.

"You don't think so?" Caspian asked. "What else do you want? Name it. I'll get it done."

"I want..." I trailed off, biting my lip. I knew what I wanted, but did I dare say it? "I want his pack."

"They've offered it to you."

"They did... you didn't." I wanted to be careful around this topic.

"I don't want you, Havoc."

I blinked, trying not to let that cut. "It's what he promised me."

"He promised you Angel had a heart of gold—and now he's on a vendetta. And look at me? This pack's a mess. Logan didn't promise you anything real. Rainbows and wishes aren't going to change that."

"I think that promise is worth something." My voice was nothing but a whisper. I couldn't meet his eyes.

"Right." Caspian snorted. "The omega afraid of elevators. I'm sure your judgement is sound."

My cheeks flared. "How do you know that?"

"We were all watching to see if you'd leave."

I swallowed, my heart pounding a million miles a minute. *Was that true?*

Well.

Obviously.

I bit my lip aggressively as I stared down at the phone in my hand, then I turned back to him. "Why are you so horrible?"

"The way I am."

"It's not. Logan said—"

"Logan *lied,* Havoc. He lied about everything."

"What about your sister?" I asked.

Caspian's eyes went dark. "What about her?"

"You care about her. Does she think you're a monster?"

For a second, Caspian's lip curled. "Anyone who knows me, Havoc—*really* knows me—thinks I'm a monster. My sister is particularly aware of that fact."

"I don't believe you."

Caspian just snorted.

"Is that what she would say?" I asked.

"Yes."

Infuriatingly, he closed his eyes, leaning back against the seat as if bored.

I glared at him, my nose wrinkling. I'd decided he didn't deserve to be that attractive. Not with his stupid perfect chiselled cheekbones, the slight ridge on his nose and dark brows with that dumb eyebrow piercing. How was his dark hair always that *perfect* messy, when *my* hair was always an unmanageable heap of buffles? Right now, wisps escaped his bun, swooping down to his jawline where his tattoos ended, even his hands were fucking attractive, knuckles and bones stark, tendons clear as he flexed them at his lap in patiently.

Still, he didn't look at me. A flare of anger lit in my chest.

I glanced from him to the phone.

He had to be joking about the bomb thing right? He was testing me. Honestly, I didn't know anymore, but it was easier to pretend right now.

Carefully, and without making any noise, I swiped from the edge of the screen. I tapped it until I found a list of contacts.

I scrolled through them until I found what I was looking for. 'Sis' was listed near the bottom.

I pressed the phone button, a swoop in my stomach as the phone flashed with a dial pad. It began to ring.

"What are you doing?" Caspian's voice was sharp. But it was too late. The screen shifted and then I heard a voice coming from it.

"Hello?" the female voice rang out.

Caspian froze, his eyes wide.

"Hi?" I asked.

"Is... everything okay? Why do you have Cass's phone?"

"I'm uh..." I began, but Caspian lunged for me, eyes blazing with fury, but I twisted in my seat, getting my feet up and managing to lodge my boots against his chest as I held the phone to my ear. "I-I'm Havoc."

He tried again, and I all but buried my head in the crook between the seat and the door, both hands clutching the phone.

"His... mate?" Something in her tone perked up, curiosity in her voice. "You've worked things out?"

"I—" But I swore as Caspian dug a knife from his belt and waved it at me with silent fury.

"What?" Halley asked.

"He uh…" I paused as Caspian violently gestured at me to give the phone back. "… Has a knife."

"What?" The melodic voice vanished for something sharper. Caspian dropped the knife so fast it might have burned him.

"I don't," he rasped. For a moment, all of his sharp edges melted away for panic.

Something about it got a huge grin from me. Caspian, on the other hand, looked deadly. "I don't, Halley. She's just messing about."

"Cassie? What's going on?"

Cassie? My grin widened.

"It's fine. Really," Caspian said. "We're in the middle of something."

"You've been ignoring my texts."

"I know. Been busy."

"I know what the news is saying, I know what it can be like. Does this mean she's…? Well I was worried, I know what you can get like about Logan—"

"Halley!" Caspian's voice was a snarl.

"Come over, alright?" She was much too cheery. "Bring her? You know, I met a pack—"

"Wait—what? Alphas?" Caspian's eyes were wide.

"Yeah... Well... It's complicated. They're good—"

"Halley—"

"I miss you, Cassie. It's been ages."

Caspian paused, something wounded in his eyes. "I know." His voice was thick. "I'm sorry. I'll catch you up."

He stopped trying to get the phone from me, instead resting his head back, eyes closed.

I lifted the phone to my ear. "Bye…" I said.

"Bye. And… thanks for getting him to call," Halley said. "Do it again." I pulled the phone away and tentatively tapped the red phone symbol.

The phone cut off.

I peered at Caspian. He didn't move.

"She… doesn't seem to think you're so bad."

"Don't…" Caspian's voice was dangerous. He didn't answer, his fists balled on his lap. "Don't ever do that again."

I held the phone out to him. He glanced at it. "What?"

"I… Don't know how to get back to the button…" I said with a shrug.

He snatched it from my grip and tapped the screen until the big red button was back.

"No more fucking about," Caspian growled. "You want revenge or not?" He shoved the phone back into my hands aggressively. My heart sank.

"I d-don't know." I clutched the phone, fear returning as I stared at it. "This… this is how simple it is for you? You just let me blow up Gavin's and it's over?"

"Yes. That's exactly how it works."

Sickness rose in my throat. "It's… it's not that simple for me."

He didn't look at me, just gazing off over the lights of the city. "Then I can't help you."

"You… Wouldn't have."

He paused, glancing at me. "What?"

"You wouldn't have helped me."

He gave me a funny look, but I was frozen, ice creeping up my spine as I stared at him.

"That night, I had this whole plan. The second Logan knew there was a bullet in that gun, I could have made him do anything." Caspian's eyes had gone glacial. "Before he tried to—" I cut off, my voice shaking. "I had this whole plan. I was going to get him to unlock his phone, and then sit far across the room and call one of you and explain everything."

And... that plan, which had lit so briefly in my mind was something I sometimes returned to.

"Right." Caspian looked sour. "And you would have called me." He snorted. "How fucking convenient."

I felt a flare of rage, then I was digging in my bra and tugged out the picture I'd got from Logan. I pressed it against his chest.

His lip curled as he looked at me, leaning back just slightly, his chest heaving. Then he took the paper. I bit back the prickle of pain at his touch.

He looked down at the picture, the photos of the pack with Logan scribbled out. And in the corner, beside Caspian's name, was the little black heart I'd drawn.

The storm in his eyes broke for a moment as he stared at it, his brow coming down.

"If I'd done that, if I'd called you...?" I couldn't finish the question, something stuck in my throat. Caspian's dark eyes found mine, and as he looked at me, it was as if I could see something flickering out in them.

I had to get out. I couldn't be in this space anymore with his stupid deadly scent of roses.

I fumbled for the door handle until the ice cold air of the night smothered me. I slammed it, staggering to the ledge of the parking lot, gripping the stone as my throat began closing up.

No.

No, not now.

I squeezed my eyes shut, imagining Kai was here with me,

telling me to breathe. My fingers were white knuckled on the phone I still held.

The door slammed behind me. I heard his footsteps, but I couldn't turn.

Then he was holding the photo out to me, standing at my side. I looked up at him, my hair billowing across my face in the ice-cold wind.

He looked as empty as he had in the car. "I can't be what you need."

It was all he said.

"What would have happened?" My voice was a cracked whisper.

I had to hear him say it.

He didn't answer. His expression just twisted slightly, upper lip curled as if I made him sick.

My blood flashed red hot. "Tell me what would have happened?" I demanded again, shoving him. He barely moved, his expression stony. "If I called you and you'd come and it had been me and him in that place?" I jabbed my finger to the building in the distance. The one he'd pointed out. The one he'd brought me here to destroy. "Would I still be there?"

And what would Logan have done when he realised I'd called the one pack mate who was loyal to the fucking grave? Would he have laughed at me?

Caspian said nothing, and he was blurring in my vision as hot tears burned my eyes.

"*Tell me!*" I was screaming now, shoving him again, needing him to react—to say or do anything but look at me like that.

When he finally spoke, his voice was low. "I don't know."

"You don't—"

Caspian's grip closed around my arms. "That picture is a lie, alright?" he snarled. "There's nothing for you to love."

I stared at him wildly, adrenaline coursing through my veins. "You... *don't know?*" My voice was shattered.

That wasn't good enough. None of this was good enough— Not this trip or that stupid fucking button, when I wanted—

"There's nothing left of me, Havoc. There's nothing to love. I'm only here because Kai and Halley don't deserve to lose another brother because of me—and Halley..." His voice shattered, his fingers digging into my arms, pressing me against the stone as if it was all that was holding him up. His eyes were blazing with a storm of fury and pain. "She's only here because of him."

I stared at him in shock.

"Logan?" But I already knew the answer.

Of course it was Logan. Everything always came back to Logan.

He let me go, stepping back as if I'd hurt him, fingers running through his hair.

"I don't... I don't regret shooting him," I whispered. His eyes darted to me, swirling with threats, but right now I wasn't afraid. "If I'd called you, I would still be in there right now. There's... no consequences. People like you and him, you can just... get away with whatever you want."

"We're not... *I'm* not..." But he couldn't get the words out.

"That's not good enough!" My voice was raised, panic surging through my system. "None of this is good enough. How many other omegas have to deal with what I did?" I demanded.

For a moment, he looked afraid as I waved the phone wildly in the direction of the building. My sanity was cracking like it had the day I'd shot Logan. When I'd pulled the trigger. When I'd met them all for the first time.

I was such a fool, falling into their arms for comfort, for scents, for their promises of safety that they could take away in the blink of an eye. "How many others suffer?" I demanded. "Because of men like you?"

"Havoc—" But Caspian cut off as orange light split the dark sky. It was followed instantly with an earth shaking BOOM.

I spun, my whole body tense.

My mind was racing, eyes fixed ahead at the huge plume of flame and debris that was erupting into the sky. I looked down.

My thumb was pressed against the phone screen, holding the red button down.

I'd pressed it.

A low moan escaped my throat as I dropped the phone.

It hadn't been... intentional.

Had it?

But he'd said Gavin was in there. "I... killed him." My voice was a husk. This... this was all wrong. "I... No..." Panic gripped me, my breathing short and sharp. "With Logan... I d-didn't..." Tears flooded my cheeks. A low, wounded sound came from my chest. My knees hit the concrete. I was clutching myself. "I didn't have a choice."

"Havoc." Caspian was there.

"It... w-was real?" The words were dry in my throat.

It wasn't until this moment that I realised how much I hadn't believed it. But now... Gavin was dead.

I'd just killed him without a second thought. Without pain or consequence. Nobody was crumbling over me, blood spilling into my eyes and nose and mouth. No pale, lifeless face stared back at me... Gavin wouldn't have a body left.

"Hey!" Caspian was there, kneeling before me. "Look at me, Havoc."

"I..." I couldn't breathe. "I shouldn't have..." I felt sick.

"He wasn't in the building."

Those words drew me up. "What?"

"He wasn't in there," he said again. "No one was in there."

"But why—?"

"I thought..." He looked a little on edge. "I wanted to know..."

"If I was a killer?" My voice was hoarse. "This was a—"

"It wasn't a trick. I wanted to know if you actually wanted him dead. I do know where he lives. I can get him for you if you—"

"No!" I shook my head quickly, fingers closing around his shirt.

But I felt like my throat was opening up.

Okay... Okay... I hadn't killed him.

That was good.

My panic was settling, and I still couldn't look away from Caspian.

THIRTY-THREE

Havoc

We got home around one in the morning. I wasn't really sure how I felt.

I hadn't killed Gavin, which was good—I thought, anyway. But I had blown up the building. Which was insane. I wasn't going to lie, a smile tried to fight its way onto my lips every time I thought about it.

Caspian was silent as we entered the dark living room.

"I..." I caught his arm before he left. He stared down at me, his eyes still hardened. A part of me wanted to bring up the conversation I'd overheard, to ask him about cleaving. But I was a coward.

When I said nothing, he stepped away. I watched as he took the stairs and then disappeared into their second office.

I was at the sink in my bathroom, washing my face when I felt a dreaded twist in my stomach.

Uh... Not the time.

I blinked at my reflection, gritting my teeth as if will power might make it go away, but in the next second I was on the floor, clutching my stomach with a moan of pain.

Fuck.

It was a scare. It *had* to be a scare. Last time Eli's pill lasted much longer than a week. But scare or not, this was so much worse than what I'd felt before.

My skin was clammy, pain spearing my stomach. I just had to ride it out.

Heat was rolling off me in waves, the sudden lust making me heady. The door to the bathroom was shut, thank god. I could wait it out.

When the first wave of pain died down—and I was sure it wasn't over—a wild plan came to mind.

But... would I have time?

I didn't have a choice. If the next wave was like this one, I couldn't swear I wouldn't find myself crawling to Bane's door.

Why wouldn't I want that? The thought was frantic and absolutely fucking delusional.

The ball was in a few days.

I *had* to make it to the ball.

Caspian

I set the coffee down on the table in the second office, preparing for a long night. My laptop was open before me, green bars marking a few of the recovery's I'd run.

Usually Kai would do this sort of job. The files were corrupt here and there, but I knew enough to recover them. I wouldn't do that to Kai; it would be cruel.

I wasn't blind. Havoc—as much as she was my demon—had slipped right past the walls of this group. Kai... Well Kai loved her and there was no way I would ask him to watch any of this.

Me, though? I'd be gone in a few days, and my loyalty to Logan wouldn't be affected by anything I saw here.

Havoc's words kept replaying in my head. She'd been furious, tears spilling down her cheeks as she shoved me, as she demanded that I become more than I was capable of being.

"... *men like you.*"

Why did that stick with me? As if I didn't know I was a monster.

I realised my fingers trembled as I hovered the space bar to watch the first video of surveillance footage.

I had to pull myself together.

It was fine. I just had to cut the parts Angel needed. Whatever he took to lawyers for her, it would be kept quiet anyway, I wouldn't be *defaming* Logan's name.

I had to prepare myself. Logan was a complicated man, and he'd decided that Havoc was an outlet. It was fucked up, I got that, but I'd known he was fucked up.

Only... Just as I predicted, the walls I'd so carefully placed in my life began crumbling as I tried to cling to my conviction.

"There's one option, but it's a long shot." I was on my feet in a moment in that bright, sterile room.

"It's a trial. It could save them." The doctor didn't sound hopeful, but he didn't know how strong they were. Riley and Halley had survived things this pompous white-coated prick couldn't conceive of.

"What do I have to do?"

"Look son..." I flinched from his touch. I was eighteen and I could take care of my little brother and sister. *"... It's expensive."*

"How much?" It didn't matter. I'd get it.

The doctor handed me a stack of papers.

Beeps echoed into the room for forever, sounds I'd never forget as I fixed on the black print.

Riley and Halley qualified.

Right age. Blood relatives of an omega. An alpha sibling—the doctors could have as much blood from me as they wanted.

They qualified but for one thing... The dollar signs and zeros stared at me like taunts.

The videos began rolling one after another.

I could do this. None of the others had known the truth, that I'd needed Logan and his trips. I needed fucked up outlets just like him.

They always deserved it, though... I shoved the thought away.

But the tapes went on and on...

I had three weeks' worth, and the closer we got to the moment Havoc killed him, the more frequent his visits.

I remembered how he'd been gone more often during that time... I hadn't questioned it.

Somehow, being able to place days in my life, to timestamps on this tape—to moments she suffered... It was like a knife in my throat, threatening to steal my breath.

Angel needed this, but they could never see it.

Never.

My throat was tight. But I had to go back, to see what happened. It could be relevant.

I steeled myself, my nails digging into my palms.

But I'd opened the floodgates and so I reran the memories I'd sworn to lay to rest as I watched, clinging to my conviction.

My phone went to voicemail again. I'd screwed up. I shouldn't have said the amount of money in the other voicemails.

"Loven?" My voice shook with rage into the answering machine. "Pick up. I need..." I swore.

That wouldn't work. "Pick up and I'm yours for the rest of my

HAVOC KILLED HER ALPHA

life." I had to calm my breathing, my aura was thick in the air. My throat was tight. The beeping went on like a clock, counting down.

I was running out of time. "Listen. You owe me, you piece of shit. I'm there every time you snap your fucking fingers. If you don't pick up this phone, I'll—" I cut off as the phone beeped, marking the end of the call.

I whipped it across the room, and it exploded on a med cart. Kai jumped to his feet at the sound, his eyes wide as he stared at me.

He hadn't said anything yet. He'd just stared at Riley and Halley upon hospital beds, covered in tubes and machines, as if he didn't understand what was happening.

Then the door crashed open, and I jumped. It wasn't Loven or his thugs. I was staring into the crystal blue eyes of the last person I expected in this Grich District back alley fucking hospital.

"Logan?"

I jumped out of my skin as Logan struck Havoc across the face. It came out of nowhere, ripping me from the memory. I slammed the space bar, pausing the video and shoving the chair back before I realised.

I'd seen the power behind his fists.

On *thugs*. On people who deserved it.

Not an omega as small as Havoc.

My breathing became ragged, my thoughts scattering, latching onto her—she would be in her room right now.

Why would he *dare*? That was our mate—he'd known that, hadn't he?

It was one thing, hearing what Logan had done, another to see it.

I rewound the tape, *needing* to hear or see something that might explain it.

If it were Halley, in that room, would there be anything that would make it okay?

The unwanted thought shook me to the core, yet still, I pressed play.

"Come on, little Havoc. Do as I say or maybe I'll get Eli to take back that promotion I offered Caspian's sister."

I froze.

What...?

What the hell had Logan just said?

Havoc straightened, a ferocious expression on her face even from the poor camera angle. "I did what you asked. You can't take it back."

"I can do whatever I want." Logan laughed.

"I'll never make another deal with you again," she hissed. "You won't get anything from me. Not ever—"

I slammed the skip button, adrenaline setting my veins alight. I couldn't watch it again. The video now showed Havoc on her knees, clutching her face.

My gaze fixed on the wall behind the computer screen as, out of the corner of my eye, Logan moved, and then Havoc was against the wall. Logan's voice was tinny through the recording.

"Do I come here for me?" he snarled. "Or for you, and my poor fucking pack brothers who will have to deal with an omega like you?"

Havoc said nothing.

"Answer me!"

"D-don't send his sister away."

"Answer me." Logan shook her.

I was on my feet, stepping back from the laptop, even when I heard Havoc's frightened answer.

"For them. You c-come for them."

I slammed the laptop closed and backed out of the office. I was at her room before I caught myself. I clutched her doorknob in the dark hallway.

Why did I need to go to her? Nothing... nothing had changed.

Only... her scent was in the air. Rainfall and firewood, but there was an edge to it, as if she were scared. It was leading to the end of the hallway...

I made for Logan's room, not at all prepared for the sight that met me.

"What the hell are you doing?" My voice was weak. Every fucking thought was obliterated from my mind.

Havoc was on Logan's huge bed, clutching a pillow to her stomach as she let out low whimpers of distress. She was in nothing but black lace, her discarded clothing on the bed.

She looked... Well, she looked like a goddess, all silken olive-gold skin in black lace. Despite the pillow, I could see one breast pressed against her bra, a perfect fit. Her chest heaved, and it was just full enough that the light curved around it with every breath.

Her chestnut tangles swept across the sheets around her, one lock tumbling past her cheeks, one golden iris holding mine through it.

I had to leave. But even as the thought crossed my mind, the door clicked shut at my back. And it would have been a physical impossibility for me to tear my gaze from her at that moment.

Why the hell *was* her underwear so... damned lacy?

Bit of a stupid question, really. Not like Angel had left her a large collection of granny panties. But the heavy scent of dying embers in heavy rain—the sight of Havoc panting on the bed—was sending my brain cells fleeing in droves.

"What do you think I'm doing?" she hissed. "I'm trying to... Turn myself off."

Damn.

The underwear clicked. This was... "Is it real heat?" I asked, stirrings of panic in my chest.

Please—please be a scare.

Angel had said it had been a scare the last time.

"I don't know. Stupid... fucking omega bullshit!" she groaned.

She *really* needed to stop using that needy voice. "What—what did you do before?" I demanded. I... I should get the others. Or... should I? My mind wasn't clear, I could feel the leashed animal inside of me ripping through its chains.

"IV and drugs from my dad."

"That's so *bad* for you—"

"Do you have a better idea?" she shrieked. "I don't see you getting your dick out."

Don't say things like that. "You're not thinking straight."

"Are *you*?" she demanded, her eyes wild as she glared at me, and I realised I'd crossed the room halfway without noticing. I drew myself up, heart slamming into my rib cage.

"Logan wouldn't—and now you lot, *my mates*, and not one of you—FUCK! *What's the point in you at all, if you won't fuck me?*"

She loosed another of those low siren moans and I didn't

know how I got there, but I was ripping the dumb fucking pillow from her arms and dragging her body against mine.

Shit.

The last thing I did was slam the door on the pack bond.

This was going to end badly.

Havoc

Now he was here, his skin on mine, my thoughts were settling just enough to process what was happening.

The first thought was that I knew I wasn't going to stop this.

I want to want you, Havoc. I just don't.

Those were Logan's words, ones I'd been told over and over.

And right now Caspian caged me in, the opposite of all of that. His aura was smothering the room and his pupils were blown.

Caspian didn't want to want me, yet he did.

And I wanted that raw, alpha energy so badly. I couldn't take anything clinical or calculated ever again. I wanted him to claim me, even if he hated it—even if I knew it was wrong.

"Fuck me," I moaned, my fingers closing around his top. My voice was a whine and I could see him warring with himself, betrayed by the need he felt just like I did. "I need you."

Those were the words that sent him over the cliff.

"We have to leave this room—" His voice was low, each word strained. I cut him off with a snarl that surprised even me. My hand shot out, clamping around his throat.

"You're going to fuck me *right here*," I hissed.

I wasn't going anywhere. For the first time the lingering scent of Logan wasn't a taunt or a threat.

It was a damned trophy.

He was dead, and I was alive. Here. On his bed. With *his* guard dog.

And I needed to know Caspian wanted me enough to do it.

There was a twisting sneer on Caspian's face and I knew he was thinking the exact same thing as me.

"Then leave," I hissed, my fingers still clamped around his throat. My chest was still heaving, my skin burning, and every inch of my veins was alight with lust. But if he left, I *wouldn't* follow.

Those beautiful dark eyes seethed with the collision of fury and lust. He wasn't going to leave. I knew it, in that moment. But he hated that he wouldn't.

"You wanted to give me vengeance?" I asked. "Fuck me on his bed."

The tiniest wisp of a voice tried to warn that this was a bad plan. *The ball... your heat...* It was snuffed out as his fingers dug into my waist, making promises of what he had to offer. But I didn't want gentle or kind. I wanted his fury.

His touch still stung, but through this wave of heat, it wasn't... It wasn't bad at all. It was making me need him more.

THIRTY-FOUR

Havoc

Caspian was above me, pinning me to the sheets as he tore off my lace underwear. I moaned something I couldn't even hear. I think I was asking him to hurry up.

The first touch of his tip against my entrance was torture. My body was hot with need, and I was so wet. My fingers curled around his cheeks, so he was looking right at me.

He was so beautiful. The pale skin of his face was marred only by a scar below his eyes. His dark hair was coming loose, trailing over my cheeks. This close I could see the pupils of his beetle black eyes were blown with need.

I pressed my lips to his. He kissed me back, something feral and passionate in that touch. He gripped my hair, holding me against him as he slid in. I moaned through our kiss, nails digging in as he filled me. Every nerve was on fire with that age old pain that was—right now, tangled with the pleasure with each inch I stretched around his length. I could feel every muscle of my body clenching over him.

He broke the kiss and leaned up as he slid out. I grabbed the sheets as he drew away, so he was caging me in, eyes roaming my body as my legs tangled around his hips.

Caspian began driving into me and I arched up. I could feel his knot swelling every time he slammed into me.

I didn't take long before I raced toward an orgasm the likes of which I'd never felt. One more stroke and—

"Don't come." Caspian's low command slammed into me, his aura bursting into the room. I gasped, my whole body seizing in protest.

He *hadn't* just—But the fucker had the gall to groan, his hand slamming to the headboard as he toppled over that cliff he'd just ripped me away from. With each stroke of his cock, ice shot through my veins, a low snarl tearing from my throat.

Every nerve in my body was alight, and goosebumps spread across my flesh as I panted, my lips still parted in shock.

All I could see was him, and cranberry and roses tangled in the air around us, slicking off him in waves.

Okay. Well. The *only* good thing about what had just happened was that it had sent this wave of heat fleeing. Yet, I was no less frustrated.

His finger tailed from my collarbone to my breast and I let out a whine. Each touch was a flash of lust. "Beg me, dove," he murmured.

I stared at him, chest heaving. "No."

Caspian flashed a cruel grin.

"I can get Bane..." I hissed. Or Kai or Angel. Any of them would... Would fix *this* if he wouldn't.

Caspian looked amused, his grip digging into my waist as he tugged me close.

"You could try." There was a dare in his eyes. "But I'm not done."

He leaned down, his kiss trailing where his finger just was, until his teeth bit down on my erect nipple. I let out another whine.

My hands were in his hair, my body arching toward him. He was gone in a flash, palm pinning me back to the bed.

"I said. Beg."

Caspian

I should have left.

I knew that.

Some of the haze in my brain was fading now I'd found release, but not enough. Right now, her body trembled with the denial of her orgasm. I flicked her nipple and her nails bit into my arm where she clutched me. Every single shift of that touch was molten lava. I'd just come, but my cock was stiffening already.

The hatred in her eyes was worth how wrong this was. If she was going to ruin me, I'd return the favour.

It wasn't enough, though. I couldn't match what she'd done— what she was currently doing to me. *His* scent still lingered, impossible to ignore.

Traitor.

I took her wrists and lifted her hands to the headboard, curling her fingers around the wood.

"Let go of that and it's over. Make a single sound, unless it's begging, I stop," I breathed.

Her eyes were wide as she stared up at me, but I wasn't buying the innocent act. She might be a chaotic disaster day to day, but here, in the bedroom, she was a lynx.

I lowered my hand, cupping her heat. She was soaked.

She let out a moan of desperation that had my cock twitching.

I withdrew my hand instantly. She glared at me, teeth biting down on her lower lip. That sent me back to what I'd seen in the

323

living room. Those plush lips taking Bane to the knot. I almost came again right then.

I refocused on her, brushing her clit. Her back arched, but she stifled the noise she so clearly needed to make.

"Better," I murmured, leaning down and capturing her nipple between my teeth as I circled her clit. I felt her shudder with the effort of keeping quiet.

I slipped a finger in, leaning back to admire her efforts. With one hand I held her down by her hip, with the other I slid in and out slowly.

Her eyes were deadly as they held mine, her perfect breasts heaving, the faintest glisten of sweat along her collarbone. I thought she might draw blood from the ferocity in which she was biting her lip now, her nose flaring each time I drove my finger in.

"That doesn't sound like begging," I taunted as I switched to two fingers. She tilted her head back, eyes wide and desperate.

I forced myself not to look at the scar on her neck.

Instead, I dipped down and found her clit with my tongue. Sweet sin, she tasted amazing. She jolted against me, her breaths desperate and ragged, but to her credit, not even the slightest whine broke from her chest. She was trying so hard.

I played with her clit until she was writhing, working herself over me. Then, when I could feel her tensing beneath me, I released her clit and shifted, pressing my hand over her throat, drawing my fingers out of her.

"Beg." I'd dropped my alpha command.

Her mouth parted just slightly, her breaths still heavy, but her eyes remained determined as she glared.

I pressed in slowly. A whine finally sounded from her chest. I drew my fingers away in an instant and she grabbed my arm where I still held her throat.

"I can't... help it," she whined.

There were goosebumps rippling across her flesh again. Every part of where her skin met mine became hotter. She was a drug, her scent of firewood and rain drowning the room.

"That's not begging."

She snarled at me, nails becoming vicious, but I just laughed and let go, tossing her on her front before she could protest. I curled my fingers into her hair just like Bane had. I pressed her down, cheek against the blankets so she could see me out of one, furious golden eye.

My cock was harder than it had ever been with her like this, presented beneath me. She was shivering with need, back arched, delicate fingers gripping the sheets as she waited, full lips parted.

I pressed my tip to her entrance, and she moaned, fighting my grip on her hair to take me further. She was soaked. Sliding into her was effortless. I went slow, enjoying the feeling of her hot core clenching around me. She loosed little whines, fists balling, back arching further.

I drew out just as slow. Then I waited.

A long second passed, and her brow furrowed, cheeks growing pink as she realised what was happening. She wriggled against my grip on her hair again, trying to shift back.

"*Fuck* you!" she hissed.

I grinned, pressing my tip to her again before drawing away. Her next whine was half snarl, and it made me even harder, if that was possible.

"Magic word, little omega." My words came with a low rumble, almost a purr of satisfaction.

"Please." It was half beg, half snarl and I'd never heard anything so arousing.

"Please *what*?"

She bucked against my grip, getting another laugh from me.

Her chest heaved, and then she said the words that set my veins alight. "Please... fuck me."

I drove into her without mercy, setting a rhythm that drew out the most ungodly sounds from her with each thrust. Her knees shifted as she presented herself to me more, her eye fixed on me.

"Knot me." Her low whine was just as demanding as she'd been when she'd told me I was going to fuck her on this bed.

Lava seeped into my veins, but knotting her *was* where I drew the line. Whatever had happened with her heat, it seemed to have passed. If there was any chance I wouldn't send her into heat, knotting her would destroy it. Even if I wanted to so damned badly.

I wanted to feel her everywhere. I bent over her, releasing her hair and closing my grip around her slender wrists instead, drawing them up the sheets until her back was pressed against my chest.

"Please knot me, Caspian."

Shit. My name on her tongue was like a shot of lightning.

I had to keep my head. *No* knotting. *And* making sure she felt every piece of humiliation she made me feel. These were Logan's fucking sheets.

I was so close, and her body was weak beneath me, trembling more as she neared a climax once more. I released one of her wrists and closed it around her throat, dragging her tighter against me.

"That tight little body of yours is going to squeeze me for every last drop." I felt her clench over me as a desperate mewl escaped her lips. "Come for me, Havoc." I threw every ounce of my aura into the command.

She cried out, fingers scrabbling desperately on the sheets, as if doing so might shield her from the orgasm that crashed in.

The way her muscles tightened over my cock was bliss, and I came right after, slamming into her while I filled her with my hot seed. Each of my thrusts got a shattered moan from her as her body gave out. My fist around her throat was the only thing holding her against me.

Havoc

There were stars in my veins. It was taking much too long for me to catch my breath. Caspian was on his back at my side, sounding just as wrecked. I'd replaced my underwear and the sweatpants, but I left the baggy top for now. I wasn't ready to relinquish the power I had over him when his gaze trailed the black lace hugging my breasts.

I slid closer to him, a little unsure. I didn't really know what I wanted, but the cold gaze he'd been giving me since I arrived wasn't it. I gently touched his hand, and he glanced over at me.

He gave me a calculating look, and I felt a flutter of fear, bracing for the rejection. It went deeper at this moment, a thousand wounds from Logan leaving a bitter taste.

If he was going to reject me after that, he better leave fast. I'd rather he didn't see my tears.

Then Caspian drew me against him, his arm around my shoulders. I couldn't help the little purr that rumbled in my chest, even if it made him tense.

Then he shifted, and I wasn't quite sure what he was doing until another wave of rose and cranberries filled the room.

Oh. My cheeks heated. He... was marking me.

That was good. I thought so, anyway.

"Was it uh..." I swallowed. "Good?" I almost winced. But now I was coming down from the heat and sex high, a little ball of anxiety was growing.

He'd done a lot, and I had just... sort of reacted.

Caspian raised an eyebrow at me. "I don't believe you don't know the answer to that."

"Uh..." How to put this? "It was my first time."

Caspian froze. "No... It wasn't."

I didn't answer for a while, mulling over all the potential

responses. But Caspian played rough. I could too. "You don't really think Logan would want Eli's seconds?"

He stared down at me, lips parted.

"I mean. I did enough *stuff* with Eli that it's not, like, a big deal..." I trailed off at the true flutter of panic in his eyes.

He sat up, rubbing his face. "No."

Then he got off the bed and began pacing. "No. That wasn't... No." He seemed to be talking more to himself. He glared at me. "Why didn't you tell me?"

I just shrugged, still trying to catch up to his reaction.

"But we... But I..." He looked wild. His fingers ran through his hair. At some point he'd lost the hair tie completely, leaving the dark waves to brush his tattooed shoulders. "That wasn't... romantic."

"Romantic?" I scoffed the word. He just gave me a look like I was mad.

Oh.

He was serious.

Some movies like to make first times a big deal, but it hadn't seemed like that to me until now. I didn't really understand. "It was really good..."

"They're going to kill me," he groaned. To my surprise, he dropped to his knees beside the edge of the bed and dragged me toward him, so I was straddling his torso. Our touch was still the... *better* kind of prickle, not anything jarring like it had been before. "Havoc. Look I know you're pissed. I know you want to get back at me, but if this is another game...?"

Well. It wasn't. But it could be. I felt a smile tugging on my lips. His eyes narrowed. "So..." I said. "If you took my v—"

He clamped a hand over my mouth in a flash, eyes wide. "Don't. *Say*. It."

He withdrew his hand tentatively as if I might bite him. "Does this mean you can't cleave if I take the bond?" I asked, before he could stop me.

His mouth worked silently for a moment, eyes flashing. "Angel—"

"I overheard," I said, quickly. "But I can't... take it, if it means you leave."

"Fuck..." He looked furious. "I shouldn't have—*we* shouldn't have..." He swallowed. "This was a mistake."

For the first time I realised I maybe *did* feel a little sentimental about this being my first time, because those words were like a punch to the gut.

I shoved him off me, eyes burning. I had to get out of here.

"Come on..." He was on his feet and then he caught my wrist. "Havoc, you know—"

I spun on him, holding onto my rage so I wouldn't cry.

It wasn't working.

"It's not okay for you to be rough my first time—but it's fine if you say it's a mistake?"

Caspian had been my first time. Once, that would have been a dream. It... it still was. And he was ruining it.

I grabbed my hoodie and the wrinkled photo on the bed from when I'd removed my bra.

I'd never seen him as vulnerable as he had been in this room, but even now, as I left, I saw the ice sliding back behind his eyes.

THIRTY-FIVE

Caspian

I was fucked.

I was completely, totally and utterly fucked. Havoc had vanished down the hall to her room, but I hadn't missed the glittering tears in her eyes as she'd left, tucking that stupid picture into her bra as she'd gone.

Why did she keep insisting I was someone I couldn't be?

Yet, you fucked her. Like a total idiot.

I'd known it was a mistake before I'd realised my absolute clown act was her first time.

I couldn't face my silent room, so I headed down to the fridge to grab a beer, trying to dislodge the feeling of a stone in my throat at the sight of her tears. Why had I touched her? Like there wasn't enough to unpack tonight. There was a faint voice in my head, still screaming at me that nothing on those tapes mattered, nor did her tears.

Traitor.

I was a fucking traitor.

. . .

"Fuck." Logan was pale as he stared at me. Somehow, in this horrible sterile room, beside my brother and sister, who were barely clinging to life, I'd managed to explain.

"How did you know?" I asked.

"You left me a voicemail I think meant for someone called Loven? Here, just—" He was scrolling through his phone. "In my bank right now—I think I have enough..." At his words, my heart soared. "But... only for one." Logan was glancing across the papers. "I'll call my father, see if he'll open my account early. It's less than six months till I'm eighteen, I can't see... it should be doable." He was dialling. "Look, I need a solid reason to be asking for this. Can I tell him..." Logan winced, shifting uncomfortably.

"What do you need?" I'd give him anything for this. I'd give him everything I had to my name and every minute I had left to breathe.

"Can I tell him you're pack? Sell it better."

Logan had been scouting me and Kai in every alpha meet since we were twelve. It had been gentle prods until now, and I'd always laughed him off, telling him he didn't want the fallout of snapping up two harpy alphas.

"I'm in." The words were out of my mouth without thought. I glanced to Kai before I could catch myself.

"I'm going where you're going," Kai said quietly.

Logan nodded, clapping my shoulder as he got to his feet, his phone ringing.

I froze when I stepped down the hall and caught sight of Angel lounging on the couch.

"You're back?" he asked. I had told him I'd be up all night working on the videos.

"Yeah." Shit. Was it too late to turn around?

"So...?" He pressed.

"It was fine." I closed the fridge, eyes darting to the hallway.

I couldn't do this, not now.

Angel cocked his head. "That's Havoc. Like... a lot of Havoc. Did you...?" A grin spread across his face.

"It's not what you think."

"This alpha's nose begs to differ."

"It was a mis—" I cut off, scowling. I shouldn't have said that to her at all. I wouldn't be repeating it to Angel. Even if it had been a mistake, it wasn't because of her, it was because of me. "She had a heat scare, alright?" I needed to diffuse this. "And I... Well, you know what she's like—? I mean, I'm not saying it's her fault. I just... lost it."

"Wait..." Angel trailed off. "How far did you go?"

I was sure my expression gave everything away.

Angel was on his feet in a second. "What the fuck, dude?" Oh... he looked pissed. Like rare *Angel* pissed. "Her heat—"

"I didn't trigger it," I said.

He breathed a laugh. "You're *lucky*... But... wait, this means... you've changed your mind?"

Of course, he would think that.

Because that's exactly what sex with your mate should have meant, you fucking idiot.

Angel's eyes flashed and the scant remains of his aura hit the room. "Then *what* are you doing, messing about with her like that? She fucking cares about—"

"I *know*." My teeth were gritted.

"You're the one saying she had to go. You're the one who threatened to cleave if she took the—"

"*What?*"

The voice startled us both. My blood ran cold as I looked up at the balcony railing. Kai was closing his fist around it, staring down at me, eyes wide.

Shit.

I glanced between Kai and Angel. "I..." I swallowed, lost for words.

"He's lying," Kai said.

I took a breath, setting the beer down, pressing my fist to my palm as I watched him. "I... can't—"

"You're joking..." Kai cut me off. Then he was taking the stairs by twos, then crossing toward me. His fist closed around my shirt as he slammed me into the fridge. "Tell me he's *lying.*" He spat the words with venom.

"I don't have a choice. You know—"

"You're full of shit," Kai spat. "You use Logan as your excuse for *everything*—and now he's your excuse to leave me?"

Angel had been about to move forward to intervene, but paused.

"I'm *not* leaving you." This was exactly why I didn't want him to know.

"This bond is the only thing that keeps you with me. Without it, I'll be the same as Halley."

"What does that mean?" My voice was a low growl and my grip closed around his wrists.

"You aren't..." Kai paused, searching for the words. "You just... *protect* her. You aren't there. Not really. She tries so hard, but *I* even get her better than you do—"

"What would you know?" I spat. "As emotionally fucking stunted as you are blind."

Shit, I shouldn't have—But Kai reacted in a flash, his fist catching me in the face. Pain split my cheek. Anger at everything today crashed into me like a train.

I returned the blow twice as hard, and Kai staggered. My aura was out of control, and I was after him in a moment. Then Bane came out of nowhere, ripping me back and shoving me against the front door.

Where the hell had he come from? But the bond was wide fucking open, a battleground of emotions right now. It must have woken him.

"What the hell is going on?" Bane demanded. Angel was at Kai's side, eyes blazing as he glared at me.

Kai spat. "Cass fucked Havoc, and now he's cleaving."

I'd only felt Bane's aura lose control a few times, but once again, with Havoc involved, his aura all but obliterated mine and Angel's from the room.

His eyes were dark as he looked at me. I saw him pounce in a flash, no control left in those eyes, and then I blinked and he was still standing stock still. That had happened last time, too.

"You did what?" His voice was dangerous.

"We all need to take a step back." Angel placed a hand on Bane's shoulder. He never took his eyes from me.

"He's not cleaving. You"—Kai jabbed a finger at me—"*Can't,* not after doing that. And what the *fuck?*" He was off balance. "You've been treating her like shit, but *you* get her first?"

"I had no clue, alright?" I spat. "Never would have if I'd known she hadn't—" I cut off, realising my mistake too late. Kai had meant first out of us. Not first... *first.* I scrambled for a way out, but Bane's eyes had gone dark.

"She hadn't *what?*" Angel's voice was low, the last word a snarl.

Shit.

There was nothing to say. They'd be able to read it all over my face.

Bane lost it. I didn't see his fist coming. My world burst with white, pain exploding along my chin as I was slammed again into the wall.

"Bane—!" That was Angel's warning shout, but Bane was upon me. His aura was smothering, but I shoved mine out in time to get my arm across my face for the next blow. I grunted at the power behind it.

Someone else shouted, perhaps Kai. I tasted blood, the world was spinning. Bane's fist closed around my throat. I could see nothing but raw, unhinged fury.

I welcomed it.

This is exactly what I fucking deserved.

Kai was there, his aura competing with ours. He'd leaped right onto Bane's back, trying to get his arm around his neck. Bane barely blinked. He was a fucking monster right now.

A laugh choked from my bruised throat as Bane threw Kai off. "She ruined us," I rasped.

"*Logan* ruined us," Bane snarled.

"I'm... so sorry Caspian."

I couldn't look at any of them. Not Kai. Not Logan. Not the struggling bodies of my brother and sister in blue gowns. Tubes and wires remained the only thing between them and death.

A death that would find one of them...

I'd been driving. This was my fault.

"I... drank before we left." How many beers? Maybe... two over a few hours. It was my party we were going to. My graduation...

"No." Logan's voice was firm. "We aren't doing this. Not now, alright? And they checked you—you weren't over the limit, you said the truck came out of nowhere—"

"But if I hadn't..." Bile burned my throat. "I'd have reacted faster."

My throat was tight, but then I felt a warm arm crook in mine. Kai's head rested against my neck as he clutched me, a low rumble in his chest. My breathing settled, enough that I could focus.

He was safe.

My eyes burned. Kai was okay. In the face of losing Riley or Halley, that meant the world.

"Caspian." Logan sounded strained. "I'm sorry, the doctor said we don't have much time."

"I don't..." I swallowed down the vomit threatening to come up. I found the strength to look up into Logan's eyes. My voice was a brittle rasp.

"I have to choose?"

I cracked; unhinged fury shattering me all at once. At what I'd seen on those tapes. At what I'd just taken from her—even though I had no right. At the memories that I would never be free of. That night had been my fault, and then it had been my choice.

Him or her.

"Cass... I'm s-scared."

"I know. I know. But I got you."

"Swear t-to me."

"I swear it. Course I swear it."

I was bound to a man capable of hurting Havoc—a woman who deserved the world. Who deserved everything my brothers wanted to give—and I was incapable of betraying Logan, because if it hadn't been for him, they would both be gone.

Bile rose in my throat, and I grabbed Bane by the shirt, needing to send him over the edge, needing him to loose that rage. *I* was the one who'd screwed up. "Logan saved her—"

"He didn't save her!" Bane roared, slamming me against the door. *"He let Riley die."*

Bane

Silence followed my words.

Caspian stared at me in shock. *"What?"* His voice was a rasp.

Reality was sinking in. I'd lost it the way I did in my nightmares.

I released him like I'd been burned, my aura dropping away, glancing back at the other two. Kai was closest, and Angel was on the other side, between us and the hallway. Between us and Havoc's room.

Shit...

Havoc.

She was still in the house. I had to get a grip.

"Bane. What the fuck does that mean?" Caspian rasped. I dared glance back at him. Blood trickled down his chin, and a bruise was blossoming across his cheek. He needed the kitchen island to stand straight.

But I'd opened Pandora's box, and there was no closing it now.

"Do you think..." I had to clear my throat. "Do you really think *Logan Mandela* didn't have access to thirty grand?"

I was about to lose them all. But they didn't deserve to lose each other because of Logan. Havoc deserved better than to watch her tormentor destroy her dreams from the grave.

"He said he didn't have the money—"

"He fucking *lied*," I snarled.

"Why would he do that?" Caspian sneered, as if it were a joke, but there was no light in his eyes.

Again, I glanced between Angel and Kai, years of secrets about to crest, about to take everything I cared about.

"He had us *all* marked—Eli too, but he never got enough leverage on Eli to make him appealing."

"What does that mean?" Angel asked.

There were some things Logan said that I would never forget.

"My dad thinks the only way to build a good pack is to pick from

the upper crust. You want power? Look at the harpy district. More mutts than they know what to do with. I want harpy alphas with blood on their hands and debts they can never pay back."

"He didn't just want a pack of the strongest alphas he could find. He wanted us at his feet. He had his vision, and it involved us following his commands blindly."

"I don't—" Angel began, but I cut him off.

"You and Kai were perfect." I looked at Caspian. "Kai's a seer, and your aura is strong. He knew you'd come as a pair. He knew the Harpy's didn't want to deal with the money you were asking for. So he gave you the money to save one of them. He texted me the day of your accident, said..." I winced. "Watch me. By the end of the day I'll have a perfect leashed mutt. He'll be so fucked in the head he won't even know it."

I'd deleted the text, but it had never left me.

"That's..." Caspian's voice was dry. "That's a bunch of crap."

"It's not."

"Why would he tell you that?" Angel demanded.

"He told me everything. It was his only way to brag. He knew I'd never tell."

"Wait." Angel caught my arm. "*Why* are you telling us now and not then?"

"Because..." I paused, taking a breath as I met Angel's eyes properly. "He knew what I did."

This was it.

This was the moment I lost them.

"It can't be that bad. Not bad enough you'd keep something like that...?" But Angel trailed off at the look on my face. "Tell us."

I couldn't take my eyes from him. "I'm a rogue."

I'd never known my parents. I knew they were well off, and they'd left me a decent inheritance—enough that I was deemed of high enough status to be adopted by the Mandela pack.

Rogues were alphas with a gold pack omega parent, but they didn't have the same golden-eyed tell like Havoc did.

"How do you know?" Angel asked. Angel's brows came down as he regarded me, something calculating in his eyes.

"How do you think?" I asked.

There was one easy way to tell a rogue alpha. Their aura could smash through the protections society had in place, allowing them to go into a rage. The institute did everything it could to keep that from happening; the injections they gave to omegas meant that their alpha offspring were bound by those laws. Laws designed to keep regular citizens—betas and omegas—safe.

Betas and omegas just like Angel's parents.

"I didn't... I couldn't control it." I didn't remember much of that day. I remembered seeing red. A haze taking over as Logan taunted me.

"Logan knew what was happening. He ran. I don't... I don't remember much. Just them coming in—"

"Who?" I stared at Angel. My pack brother.

That day I'd been visiting Angel's house.

"Your... parents."

I remember them stepping into the room and seeing me. I remember Angel's dad pushing his mother behind him. Then... nothing... I'd woken with blood across my body.

Angel was stepping back, his brow knotted as he stared at me.

Kai was ashen. Caspian—I couldn't bring myself to look at Caspian.

"You never said anything," Angel rasped.

"Logan... hid me. Said if I was found they'd take me away, but it meant I could never tell."

"You think you know what it's like to be lonely? Wait. Wait until you see what they do to rogues who kill."

"And then... I didn't know..." I didn't know that I'd fall for Angel. That he would become one of the few lights in the dark.

And, when losing his parents had pushed Angel closer, Logan had recognised the benefit of one friend who leaned on him during the worst trauma of his life, while holding the secret of the one who'd caused it.

Power.

It had always been about power for Logan.

THIRTY-SIX

Havoc

I clutched my knees as I leaned against the wall beside the crack in my door. It was close enough to the living room that I could hear their raised words.

I was shaking, tears tumbling down my cheeks. I hadn't recovered from Caspian's words when the shouting had started.

It was my fault.

"You can't do this to her!"

Luther's furious shout sounded in my head. I had tried to close my ears that time, terrified, but their argument had echoed across the whole house.

"She's my daughter. I can do what I wish. I took you in, Luther. Sheltered you, but I didn't ask for your input when it comes to my blood."

"You'll ruin her life," Luther spat. *"There's days left before she turns gold pack—"*

"I think it's time for you to leave. You're sixteen. Old enough to manage."

"I'm not leaving her."

"You will. You'll leave and you'll not speak a word. Not unless you want the world to know about your ailment."

"I don't give a shit if the whole world knows I'm a rogue. I'm not letting her suffer the same—"

"Send the institute my way, boy, and they'll find my gold pack omega daughter just as curious as they'll find me."

That had been the last I'd ever heard of my brother.

Right now, I could hear the same desperation in Bane's voice. Then Angel left, slamming the front door behind him.

I sat in silence for a long time.

This pack had been together for years, and now they were falling apart. When I arrived...

Slowly, I crept down the hallway. There was no one in the lounge, but I saw movement out on the deck. A swirling plume of smoke and Caspian's figure, slouched in the chair out in the cold.

I crept forward, daring myself on.

I had to know what happened. Caspian would give it to me straight.

He looked up at the sound of the deck door unlatching. His eyes were dark as they found me. My heart dropped in my chest.

"What happened?" I asked, slipping out beside him. "Is Angel okay?"

Caspian just stared at me, and then a laugh escaped him as he shook his head. "None of us are okay."

I didn't say anything, not missing the hostility in his tone. After a long silence stretched, I stepped closer. "Why?"

"Why do you think?" Caspian wouldn't look at me, instead taking another long drag.

"Is it my fault?" I had to know. I had to know the truth. "If I rejected the bond, would... would everything go back to the way it was?"

He shut his eyes for a second.

"Why are you here, Havoc? Why are you so intent on saving us?" He dropped the butt of the smoke on the floor and stepped on it, not looking at me.

He moved to pass me, but I caught his arm, making him look at me. I opened my mouth but couldn't find an answer.

It's not your job to save us.

Those were Angel's words. But... that wasn't what this was. I didn't want to be a lone gold pack duchess, I was *done* being lonely. And I'd never felt what I had with Kai and Bane and Angel in the last week.

They didn't *have* to be perfect.

"There is no fixing this Havoc." He left me out in the frigid winter air, hugging myself.

I couldn't move. I wanted to wait until Caspian was long gone, and then... then what? I didn't know what to do.

"Hey!" I heard Kai's voice from inside. "What the fuck was that?"

I turned to see Kai gripping Caspian by the shoulder.

"What?" Caspian asked.

"I heard what you said."

"Nothing that wasn't true."

"Bullshit," Kai spat. "You're just upset because you trusted the wrong—" Kai cut off as Caspian seized him by the collar.

"You don't know shit, Kai. You're an empty fucking shell, with all the human tortured out of you. You're the last one who gets to tell me what to think about all of this."

He released Kai, who had a dumbstruck expression on his face, making for the front door.

"He's angry." I heard Kai muttering after the door had slammed. "Because he doesn't know how to deal, and I do."

Kai looked manic, picking up everything left on the floor and tossing it into a pile in the centre of the room. I thought he was just cleaning until he grabbed a lighter and a can of something that looked suspiciously... flammable.

"Hold up!" I crossed toward him before he could do anything stupid—like light the whole apartment on fire. "What are you doing?"

"I can't fucking think straight with all this crap in here."

"I don't think *this* is the solution." I put my hand over the lighter.

"I can't think straight with this crap around." He repeated, tugging from my grip. "Angel won't want to come back—he *hates* mess—"

"Angel's not leaving you."

"He already fucking did—" I grabbed his shirt as a flame flickered above the lighter.

"Kai!" I tried to get him to look at me, my voice thick. "He's coming back."

"You don't know that. You didn't hear what Bane said—"

"He won't leave you." I didn't know if I had the right to believe that, but if I didn't, then Caspian was right, and there was nothing left of them.

Kai's fingers closed around my arms tightly, too tightly. His eyes were wild. "Did he come for you when you needed him?" Kai demanded. "When you begged the universe every night? Did any of us come for you?"

I stared at him, panic stirring in my chest.

"Why do you trust us, Havoc? When we never came?"

I tried to step away, but he didn't let me go. "When we can all crumble so damned easily, and here you are trying to put us back together—and for what? So we won't leave you next time?"

I could feel the tears welling in my eyes as I tried to pry his grip off. I could feel my own panic swelling, my throat getting thicker. "Let me go."

I felt like he was staring right into my soul, seeing how absolutely empty I was.

But... no. He was wrong. And Caspian was wrong. This *wasn't* about saving them, it was about family. A real place that I belonged, with people who maybe... just maybe could love me the same way I wanted to love them.

Kai's dark expression broke. "I'm sorry." He pulled me into a hug, clutching me desperately. "I'm sorry. You don't deserve that."

I held onto him, shaking still.

"They're coming back," I whispered again.

THIRTY-SEVEN

Angel

Late that night, when I'd driven city streets to the point of insanity, I entered my room to find Kai and Havoc curled up in my sheets.

My heart ached at the sight of it.

I tried to back out of the room before either of them woke, but Havoc was already stirring, rubbing her eyes as she crawled out from Kai's arms.

"Angel?"

I couldn't answer.

"Are you okay?" That was genuine concern in her voice. Behind her, Kai was sitting up in bed, his eyes fixed on me. He didn't move.

He could spiral so quickly with fights, and the pack had never had one like tonight. He looked so wounded, as if he had worried I wouldn't come back.

Havoc wrung her hands as if she wasn't sure what she was supposed to be doing. "I'll... leave you two..."

She tried to edge past me but I caught her. She looked up at me with frightened eyes. I couldn't help thinking, at that moment, that she and Kai were too alike. And that was a dangerous thought... Her fingers curled around my wrist, as if it were the only thing she dared do.

"You can stay," I said.

"I should... go... check on Bane..." Her brow furrowed as if she wasn't sure why she'd said that.

For a moment, I thought of her leaving here for Bane's room. That darkness crept in. But I shoved it back. I'd thought of nothing else tonight. What Bane had said... What he'd done...

It had opened old wounds that wouldn't close again for a long while, but I wasn't ready to see the pack fall apart for it.

There had been a moment during the fight, when Bane had slipped up, when he'd opened the bond to us. For a brief flash, I'd felt what he did.

It wasn't like anything else my pack brothers experienced. His piece of the pack bond was cold and wounded and afraid. Bane had lived like that for years, terrified of a truth that ate him alive.

I wasn't ready to shoulder him with everything from last night. I had been surrounded by support, Caspian had had us all, but Bane had been alone. He'd suffered this whole time, and I'd missed it. We had all missed it.

"We'll be alright," I told Havoc. I couldn't yet mean it as much as I wished, but I would.

We *would* be fine.

When Havoc slipped away, I turned to Kai. I could see he was relieved, as if he needed those words as much as Havoc did.

Havoc

I crept through the lounge, but it was empty. I was glad Kai had Angel to comfort him.

Caspian wasn't in, but Bane?

Earlier, after I'd talked Kai out of burning down the apartment, I'd tried Bane's door to find it locked. But I couldn't stand the idea of him alone all night.

I crept up to his room, raising my fist to knock, and then thinking better of it. I turned the door handle slowly and was surprised when it opened. I paused, considering that. Did that mean he didn't want to be alone?

When I peered in, a lamp was on in the corner, but when my eyes found his messy bed, there was no one in it.

I searched the room until I spotted him. He was sitting with his back pressed against the glass, out on the balcony. There was a half-drunk beer in his hand and his head was buried in his arms.

I clenched my jaw, fighting a wave of sadness as I padded out to the balcony. I sat down at his side, taking the beer and slipping my fingers into his.

He looked down at me, brows furrowed as if trying to figure me out.

I didn't know if I was good at this. My understanding of love mostly came from the movies I watched growing up. Now though, I was constantly tugged all over with nagging instincts, and I had no idea if I was crazy, or if it was an omega thing, or if it was because they were my mates.

"You... Alright?" I whispered.

Bane didn't meet my eyes; his were bloodshot and ringed with red, but I didn't mention it.

"I'm sorry, Havoc."

"For what?"

"Everything tonight. It was my fault. You just got here, and I've fucked everything up. You deserve better."

My heart ached. I didn't want him feeling like this, but I didn't know what to say. I didn't even know much of what the fight had been about.

I didn't believe him, though. I knew how much he loved the others. He would never hurt them, not on purpose.

"Angel said... we'll be alright," I said.

Bane stared at me, his eyes sad. "They will. You will."

There was a lump in my throat. "I'm not going to sleep tonight," he went on. "But you need to rest. The ball is two days away."

"I can stay up with you."

He shook his head, but I was already moving. I clambered onto his lap without regard if he wanted it or not. I took his face in my hands. "I'm not going to bed until you carry me there."

He huffed a laugh, but there was still pain in his eyes. "I don't deserve this."

"You do," I whispered. "You were the first one who saw me."

He held me, burying his face in my neck. The strong, firm arms that encompassed me trembled as he clutched me close.

"If um... If I say no to the bond," I whispered. "Can I still... Will I still see you?"

It wasn't something I'd asked the others. I didn't know how complicated it would be with Kai and Angel. But Bane had always been simple for me. Easier to trust. Easier to speak to.

His embrace tightened. "Of course you will," he breathed. "But, that's not going to happen. They'll have a chance to heal now." His laugh was low and void of humour. "They won't want me around after tonight."

"That's a bunch of crap," I muttered. "And besides. I don't want a pack without you in it."

After a few more minutes of silence, he stood and carried me to the bed. I clutched him, not letting him slip away, tangling my legs around him until he had no choice but to pull the blankets around us both.

"I'm a rogue, Havoc," he said.

"I know." I'd heard enough of the fight to know that. "And I'm gold pack."

"It's not the same. I could be dangerous."

I actually smiled at that. "You're the only one who's never threatened me."

He frowned, not finding an answer to that.

I wanted to give him peace so badly, I wanted him to be able to rest. I held him close, nudging under his neck as a gentle rumble sounded in my chest, a low purr—different to one I'd heard before. It was something of instinct, something of comfort.

Bane relaxed around me, his breathing loosening bit by bit. When I looked up, he was asleep, and the frown creasing his brows was gone.

THIRTY-EIGHT

Kai

I found Havoc in a mighty battle with the coffee machine the next morning. By the time I rescued her, she was trying to get coffee grounds out of the steaming jug, spoon by spoon. The problem: she hadn't used a filter.

"Dad drank instant," she muttered as she caught my grin.

I took over brewing another pot while she crossed her arms, a flush and pout on her face. She was just so fucking cute—especially the morning after cuddling up with me and waiting until Angel was home safe.

And now she seemed to be trying to fix us breakfast? My eyes snagged on some singed crusts in a pan. I nudged the garbage lid open and spied some truly blackened eggs that had been abandoned.

"It gets too hot too quickly," she said. "Didn't have an open flame at home…"

"It's gas—takes a bit of getting used to."

She nodded.

"Bane alright?" I asked, redirecting the conversation away from the breakfast massacre.

Her sad expression was enough of an answer. "I don't know how to make him feel better."

"He'll still be better for you being there," I said. I wasn't usually good at comfort, but this one was easy. No way could any of us not feel better with Havoc here. Even with Angel holding me, I'd noticed when she'd left.

"Caspian never came home."

"Already texted him." And he'd sent back a couple of middle fingers. That was that, which probably meant he'd be getting drunk until tomorrow morning.

"He's... okay then?"

"As okay as pissed Caspian can be," I replied. "He'll be back when he's back. Today, tonight, tomorrow, who knows?"

The bastard better.

He had to get a grip.

Angel was back, he'd had a bomb dropped on him last night too, a worse one. Well. I don't know which one was worse.

But I couldn't believe Cass was still hung up on choosing Logan over Havoc.

First off, Logan had never had mesmerising doe eyes, like the ones fixed on me right now. She was still concerned for us, even though we didn't deserve that. I stepped up to her, catching her chin with the crook of my finger.

"Don't worry sunset." *My* sunset. Beautiful and bright and full of colour when the rest of the world was dull. I gazed down at her hungrily.

Secondly, Logan hadn't had two pert little breasts with nipples teasing me from beneath a silken pyjama shirt. I tugged her closer, leaning down, pressing my lips to hers. She kissed me back with so much passion.

I squeezed her butt, deepening my kiss and pressing my tongue past her lips. What a stupid rule that we shouldn't fuck her. If Caspian had broken it, so could I. I wanted her and she clearly wanted me, We needed each other, just like we'd needed each other last night when everyone else was being stupid.

I drew away, breaking the kiss. "You're too perfect," I breathed in her ear, slipping one hand up to her chest where I caught her nipple between my fingers and twisted. Her plush lips parted and her head tipped back just slightly.

That was it.

Screw the others and their stupid rules.

"I'm going to spread you across this counter and fuck you 'til you come for me," I growled. Her grip on me dug in, nails cutting at my skin, and a needy moan rose in her chest.

I felt something shift at my hip. I froze.

"You will absolutely fucking not."

Angel's voice was a cold bucket to reality. Fingers wound through my hair and jerked my head back with little dignity. The cold edge of a blade pressed against my neck and his breath was hot in my ear. "Let her go, you degenerate."

A grin spread on my lips. I hadn't been sure last night, even with him in my arms, but my Angel was back. Properly back if he was playing games like this.

Havoc's eyes were wide as she stared between us. She might have been more panicked, but she could feel the full force of my hard on. It had appeared the moment I felt the blade at my throat.

"Why do you need your knife at breakfast?" Angel asked.

"I need my knife anytime I don't know where my pack is."

Angel snorted. "Havoc, would you pour me a cup of coffee?"

I wrinkled my nose as Havoc slid from between us. I tried to move, but Angel wasn't having it, pressing me up against the counter to which I'd just had Havoc pinned.

"Do we need to leash you?" he asked.

"If she's the one who puts it on." I noticed with delight, that Havoc froze for just a second at my words as she was reaching for a mug from the top shelf.

Her pyjama top slid up, revealing a slice of her perfect waist. More molten heat slid into my core.

"You've made her nervous," Angel growled.

"I like her nervous," I replied.

Angel leaned back slightly, and I spun to him.

Havoc, who was filling a mug with coffee, let out a breathy sound as Angel pressed his lips to mine, tongue driving into my mouth with passion, blade still between us.

When he broke the kiss, I was out of breath. "You came back."

"I did," Angel said. "And we don't need to buy a new apartment this time." Though his eyes slid to the pile of mess Havoc had talked me down from burning last night.

I could have put it out. Probably. "Thank her."

Angel returned the blade to its sheath at my hip.

Havoc, who was much too fixated on opening the carton of milk, jumped as Angel stepped up behind her.

"Is that true?" he asked, leaning down and littering kisses along her neck as he wound his arms around her waist.

"Cold hands!" she squeaked, all but dropping the milk, her palms coming down on the counter. My hard-on just got worse.

Angel relented, instead turning her, picking her up and setting her down on the marble top. She had that shy smile on her face that she got whenever one of us got too sweet, like she wasn't sure if she was dreaming. Her lips quirked up, her bottom lip caught in her teeth just slightly.

"Are you alright?"

I kicked myself inwardly. *I* should have asked her that. Then she'd be giving me those golden-ringed doe eyes she was giving Angel right now. She nodded.

"What about what happened with Cass?" Angel prodded.

My thoughts turned dark at the mention of Cass. What Bane had said last night... Well, it was haunting me, too. I hadn't been close to Riley or Halley like Cass, but they were a huge part of my world. Hearing that of Logan—Well, I hope the asshole was burning in hell.

But Cass had threatened to leave me. I just... didn't understand. He'd sworn to be my pack brother since we were ten. We'd bled for each other. He needed me, and he knew I needed him.

"Caspian?" Havoc spoke much too quickly. "What about him?"

"Heat?" Angel asked.

"Oh. Yeh. Nothing. Ball's tomorrow, I think I'm good."

"Good..." Angel's touch lingered on her waist. "Anything *else* about what happened with Cass?"

"Like what?"

"Did he... hurt you?" I don't think Angel believed Cass would hurt her on purpose, but we all knew he had spines in places he wasn't even aware of.

Right now he had one lodged right up his—

"Oh—no. Nothing like that," Havoc said.

Angel raised an eyebrow.

I had to admit, I was curious. Imagining Cass with Havoc was both hot and... well a little frightening. I'd seen Cass fuck. It was like trying to imagine a teddy bear face off against a monster truck.

A teddy bear with a fear of elevators.

"It was fine. Really. Hot, actually." Her cheeks went instantly red.

Okay. I nixed that image. Either Cass had discovered a soft side, or Havoc was more dangerous under the sheets than I'd pictured.

Who was I kidding? Cass didn't *have* a soft side—and *that* was a wonderful conclusion to come to.

"Alright." Angel nodded, seeming satisfied, though I'd been hoping he'd prod her a little more about the Caspian fuck. Instead, he leaned down, capturing her lips with his.

"So... You're okay?" Havoc said after Angel leaned away. She sounded as hopeful as I felt.

He poured himself a coffee and made his way to a bar stool.

"Look. Logan did one thing right," Angel said, looking down at his coffee with a contemplative expression. "Kept Bane's secret. And it's going to stay that way."

"That... he's a rogue?" Havoc asked. Angel nodded, looking unsurprised. If she'd spent the night with Bane, she would know by now what the fight was over. "My brother was one."

I paused, glancing over at her. "Your brother?"

"Kind of. Adopted. Lhevus took him in when he was young to keep him from the institute. He said it's more dangerous if they go into a rage younger, they're... harsher on those. Even though... Even though it's not their fault. He said the institute doesn't offer support or help. They aren't interested in fixing the problem, they just lock rogues up?"

"He's right on that," Angel said. "They take it case by case, but if there're deaths... Well, it's harder to fight. Did your brother... hurt anyone?" There was a tightness to his voice.

"Yeah..." She chewed on her lip. "He was on a playground."

Angel shut his eyes, grip tightening around his coffee mug. "It's not..." He swallowed. "It's not their fault. I get why Bane was afraid to say, especially if Logan's been holding it over his head all these years."

Caspian

The drop to the ground was deadly.

The only consolation was that death would be quick. The fact was, I'd looked out of my balcony every night, and I knew exactly where my target was.

Right now I was on a bulky stone platform on the edge of our apartment building. It was night, and I regretted not wearing gloves. How many stories up again? I'd lost track. I'd got out of the elevator at thirty-five.

It had been a challenge to reach it, using a lot of emergency stairs attached to the outside of the apartment block. It was a blessing the wind wasn't too strong. The drinks from last night left my head pounding. I'd spent a freezing night in my truck, shivering and sinking into self-hate.

I was done with denial. I'd been sick all night. I felt... undone.

I placed my earpiece in and dialled Halley's number before returning my phone to my pocket.

"Cassie?" I heard her light voice hit the headset. My nerves instantly calmed.

"Hey."

"Oh, it's actually you this time. How's Havoc?"

I swallowed, crouching down and reaching out to the frigid ridge of stone before me. I made sure not to look down.

"We... I..." I couldn't lie, but I couldn't find the words to explain.

"Cass..." Her voice was quieter. "Are you okay?"

"Yes." My answer was instant. But suddenly Kai's blazing mismatched eyes flashed in my vision. Challenging me. Telling me I didn't really even know my own sister. "No. I'm not." My voice was hollow.

There was a pause. "Where are you? I could meet up—?"

"I can't." I gripped the next ridge of stone and pulled myself up. The city street that lit up the night was so far below.

"Okay... Talk to me."

I'd reached the edge of the stone. Beside me was nothing but a steep drop off on either side of the gargoyle before me. Ugly fucking thing. Overgrown demented pigeons, the lot of them. Which I supposed was the point. They were so much bigger up close than I'd imagined. This one was three times my size, but I wasn't complaining. Now I just had to hope it was as steady as it looked.

I blinked, focusing again on Halley. "I... fucked things up."

"With Havoc? Or the pack?"

"All of them."

There was another silence as I hauled myself on top of the eagle-like creature's back.

"You'll fix it. They love you—"

"Can you... tell me what you thought of Logan?" The words broke through clenched teeth, and it wasn't the cold. My heart was thundering in my chest. I blamed it on the fact that the cars below were the size of ants.

I edged further up the stupid stone statue.

"Caspian—"

"The truth." I braced for it, knowing nothing good came when she used my full name.

"He saved my life."

"I know." The words were thick in my throat. "I know he did, Halley. But I need the truth."

"I..." She trailed off. I could hear her breath on the other side of the phone. "He's dead, Cassie. It's not right to—"

"I *need* the truth. P-please." I never let her hear me like this. Not even after Riley. But Kai was right. She deserved better.

An icy breeze suddenly picked up, and I tensed, sinking against the frigid stone. As the breeze died, the silence stretched. The streets spun below me.

I gritted my teeth, reaching out to the gargoyle's panther-like head. It had tusks and one horn left—*"He was cruel."* Her words were barely a breath.

My footing slipped, and I lurched to the side. In a moment of terror, my aura burst free, and my left hand—which still gripped the stone back, sunk in, steadying me.

I recoiled, rebalancing myself, heart thundering in my

ears, adrenaline coursing through my system. "How?" I rasped. There were scores in the stone where I'd dug my fingers.

Her words just made me more determined, though, and the danger was like a drug, burning away everything that threatened in the dark corners of my mind. I reached for the crumbling shoulder blade of the stone creature below me.

"You were already pack," Halley said. "And he seemed to care for you. I didn't want to... create trouble."

I waited, needing her to say more, while wanting to run from it all at the same time.

"I don't know, he just..."

"Tell me."

"Came to me after I recovered. Told me I was lucky he was there, but you were destined for better things. Said I was nothing but..." The slightest beat passed. "A worthless beta who would hold him back. I should keep my distance so I don't get in your way."

"You never told me."

"He saved me, Cass. If it wasn't for him, I'd never have seen you, ever."

I couldn't answer. The city blurred, all the bright gold and red and green lights mixing together into a jumble. "I'm sorry, Halley."

"Don't."

"You're the only good thing I have left."

I heard her breath. "Don't be stupid, Cassie. You have Kai and Angel and Bane—they're *good*. And maybe... Havoc, too?"

My throat was thick. I couldn't answer.

"Go fix it with them, alright."

"Yeh."

"I love you."

"I love you more." The light giggle was enough to lift my heart.

And then the phone beeped, and I was left with nothing but the sound of the city street below.

I took a breath, then reached out to this stone monster's one remaining horn. Upon it hung a silver bracelet.

Havoc

I couldn't sleep until Caspian was home. I didn't know why.

Perhaps because tomorrow was the ball, or maybe it was guilt. No matter what they said, I was responsible for the fight. What if something happened to him?

My stomach clenched every time I thought about it. Long after the others were asleep, I sat up in my room, the TV on low and my door cracked open.

I didn't know what I'd do. I just knew my time was running out and everything was fixed with all of them except Caspian.

It was 2am before I heard the front door open. I wrung my hands, now unsure of how to proceed with that information. I was so tired. Perhaps I'd just make sure he was alright.

I didn't hear his footsteps pass my door however, so eventually I slunk down the hallway in the dark.

The lounge was lit by the low orange glow of the city beyond, the curtains not closed all the way. I scanned the room before I found Caspian. He was sprawled across the couch, completely passed out.

I stared at him for a long while before deciding what to do. Then I headed back down the hallway to his room.

I grabbed the duvet and pillow from his bed, then stopped by my room to grab one last thing; the last bar in the box of Sweet-crisps. I snatched it up and headed back to the lounge. Setting everything down beside the couch, I grabbed a glass from the kitchen cupboard and filled it with water.

I set the glass on the floor beside where he lay, then draped the duvet over him. Next, I carefully tucked the pillow under his head. He groaned, rolling over, and I froze, ready to dart away if I woke him.

I withdrew my arm slowly, satisfied he was comfortable.

Before I could take a step, I was halted by a sudden grip on my wrist. Next thing I knew, I was being tugged beneath the huge fluffy duvet, with nothing but the scent of roses and cranberries. Caspian's scent. Even if it was mixed with a trace of tequila.

He wrapped his arms around me and held me tight. It took me a moment to realise he was shaking slightly. Probably just had too much to drink.

Then I felt something cool against my palm, and something slipped over my fingers.

I peered down and my heart tripped.

My charm bracelet. I stared at it for what felt like forever.

On it was a charm that hadn't been there before.

A silver hound.

"I'm sorry Havoc," Caspian whispered. "None of it was your fault."

I clutched him, not sure what to say.

"Please..." His voice was rough as gravel. "Don't leave them." He buried his face in the crook of my neck. I realised in that moment, that with his touch, came no pain at all. "Don't... leave us."

THIRTY-NINE

Havoc

It was hard to contain my excitement in the car on the way to the ball. The pack was nervous though, and it took me a while to clue into why. I'd slept in Caspian's arms, and when I woke, I was sure of what I would do today.

"I'm going to take the bond," I said when the radio music lulled. Bane, who was driving, turned around to flash me a huge grin. Angel let out a sigh as he relaxed in his seat, and Kai whooped.

"Fuck yes," Caspian growled, tugging me against him in a firm embrace.

I was grinning all the way until we parked.

The ball was like nothing I'd ever experienced. It was hosted in a huge room with a dark marble floor and an open expanse of space in the middle, surrounded by circular dining tables. The ceiling stretched way above, allowing for a few overlooking balconies, and at one end was a broad stage with two sweeping light curtains tied to each side. There were great crystal lights gently twisting above, and the decor was blue and white for the winter theme.

When we stepped in, I felt myself shrink down at the amount of people. I huddled up to Bane, his massive frame something of a shield to the masses.

There was a slight mist in the air above with the vaguely familiar taste of scent dampener. That was definitely necessary given that most of this ball was host to alphas, omegas and formed packs.

Angel led us over to our table, and I was pleased to see it was along the wall. We received stares with every step we took, and I could hear whispers rising. Some blatantly pointed in our direction.

Right now, I wore the off-shoulder wine red dress Angel had helped choose. It had long sleeves that I now clutched anxiously.

The evening began with live music and a buffet. Guests took to the dance floor as chatter rose around the room. The stares of passers-by got worse as the evening went on, as if people were piecing together who I was.

The scar on my neck was visible. I didn't want to be ashamed of it, but it was hard to stick to that conviction when it seemed the eyes of every alpha and omega in the room were drawn to it.

It was no one's business, and I couldn't understand why these people—who I'd never met—were so invested in who I was.

Finally, it came to a head.

Midway through the evening, Kai joined me at the buffet beside the dance floor so we could snack while we watched the dancers—mostly couples with much more elegance than I could ever imagine having. He'd just turned away for a moment to grab another of the cream puffs I couldn't stop eating, when someone bumped into my shoulder. It was hard enough that I staggered. A firm hand grabbed my arm to steady me.

"Oops." It was a tall alpha with hair tied in a bun with shaved sides. His hooked nose just managed to suit his face, and he had a rich tan to his skin. I was caught by his scent—clove and spice, with a much too harsh edge to it. On his arm was a beautiful omega with silky black curls. The smile on her face was as sickly sweet as the aroma of peaches that surrounded her.

"Careful, babe," she said, rubbing her alpha's arm. "It'll take forever to get gold pack reek out." She leaned forward and spat in my plate. I had just been opening my mouth to tell them it was okay, when I froze. I tried to tug away, but the alpha still had me by the arm.

"Let go." My nerves were alight all of a sudden.

"Why is your hand on my mate?" Kai's voice was low. The grip on my arm vanished, and Kai was between me and the alpha, a growl in his chest that set my hairs on end.

I grabbed him. "Kai." I didn't want the attention of a fight. My cheeks were already burning, something tight in my throat.

There was fury simmering in his eyes, and I could practically feel Kai fighting with his alpha aura. If it came out, we'd be kicked from the ball. That could be exactly what these two wanted.

"Let's go." I tugged him harder.

"She's a coward, too," the omega taunted. "What did you do, kill him when his back was turned?"

The blood drained from my face, my mouth parted in shock. How could she so easily speak about that? The echoing bang from my memory shattered my thoughts. The gun recoiled in my unsteady grip and bruised my ribs.

I didn't realise I'd moved, but all of a sudden the plate of cream puffs and drizzled chocolate was in my palm. I shoved it right into the omega's bulging cleavage.

Good thing too, since punching her would have also got us kicked out. Actually, I didn't know *this* wouldn't.

Her mouth dropped open, her eyes jumping to her alpha for a moment, flashing with fury.

Then the others were there, Bane and Angel and Caspian, all tense, as if expecting a fight.

I scrambled for my composure. "I slipped." I spoke with the same sarcastic edge as she had. "So sorry."

Kai released the alpha's wrist, taking a step away, his arm winding around my waist. I felt a thrill at his touch, imagining how we might look right now. As if I belonged with him—with all of them. A part of their pack. Their family. Kai cocked his head as he watched them, as if daring them to do anything.

The alpha was still tense, seeming even more angry, his glare directed at Angel now.

"Percy, Kendra, are you *trying* to start a fight with my pack?" Angel asked quietly.

"You're the ones with the balls to show *her* face here."

"Our pack is our business. Your pack is yours." His eyes slid coldly to the omega—Kendra, whose hand was up, covering the smear of chocolate and cream across her chest. It was all rather stark against her baby pink dress. "And it seems to need tending."

The omega's grip bit down visibly on Percy's arm, as if she wanted to leave. If the rest of their pack was in attendance, they weren't appearing like ours had. Percy took a step away, shooting me another glare before leading his omega away.

"I'm—" I began.

"If you dare say sorry, pet," Bane growled, "I'll squish a cream puff on *your* chest."

As Kai led me to the table, he leaned down and whispered, "I still think we should do that later."

I giggled as we sat back down.

"You alright then?" Caspian asked.

"Yeah... I guess. Were they close to Logan?" I asked.

"Our pack has been well known among these circles for a long time. Logan was big on keeping us relevant," Angel said. "His death made headlines. Percy's right, it *is* a bold statement to attend like this."

He seemed to deliberate on something. "I wasn't just planning on offering the princess bond tonight. I am going to denounce Logan publicly. It's clear it might not be received very well. It might be prudent to leave right after."

Kai, who had been fidgety the whole evening even before the confrontation, rolled his eyes. "What makes you think any of us would want to stay here an extra second?" He shifted his chair closer to mine and gave me a peck on the cheek. "We're going to have an omega to take care of."

They'd all come to my defence just now; Angel had even spoken as if I was part of the pack. The warmth that seeped into my veins at that thought—what the rest of the night might look like once we were out of here—it was enough to settle my nerves.

Later, Angel gave me a warning when the speeches and announcements were about to begin. I was grateful, as it gave me a chance to head to the bathroom and collect my thoughts.

I stared at myself in the mirror, and a daring smile crept on my lips. I'd been too nervous to look in the mirror at home. I'd just told Kai to swear it looked good. Since he hadn't been able to stop ogling me, I'd believed his reassurance.

I looked like I could really be an omega.

The wine red was a perfect compliment to my olive skin. The thin golden necklace drew attention to my slender neck. The dress itself was silky, scrunching in at my waist before flaring out at my hips. It was open backed, which wasn't appropriate for the weather, but with how near I was to my heat, my body temperature was higher than usual. I'd left my shawl in the car.

The black stockings were shiny, and they left only the slightest slit of skin on my thigh before the dress. My hair was down; light, loose chestnut ringlets were glossy and tame for once as they tumbled to my mid-back. I didn't wear much makeup, but the deep red on my lipstick matched the dress. The silver charm bracelet stood out, but I didn't care.

If I was on the street, I'd totally pass if people realised I was an omega. At the ball, the standards were a bit higher. The beautiful, sweet scented women who sashayed by wore elegant dresses and pointed heels. But I didn't mind.

I passed. I passed. I passed. And besides, Angel had picked the dress just for me. I knew I was enough for them.

I took a calming breath, knowing I would soon be up on that stage before a thousand people. I just had to take the bond.

And then I could go home with them all and start making a *massive* nest for the heat that had to hit in the next few days. Caspian hadn't pushed me into it, but it had been looming on the horizon ever since we'd had sex.

I balled my fists, taking another deep breath and closing my eyes. Someone stepped up to the sink beside me for a moment, but I ignored them.

This was it.

Footsteps vanished from the bathroom and when I released the breath, opening my eyes, I was alone.

I didn't stifle my beam this time as I looked back at myself. I wanted *this* woman to become the familiar face in the mirror. Not the one with eye bags and nerves, spending hours on makeup in my bathroom at Gavin's, just so Logan could tell me to wash my face.

But I was free of him.

I'd made it. My home was waiting, and all I had to do was go on that stage for less than a minute.

My smile faltered for a moment as my eyes dropped down to something that hadn't been there before.

A folded piece of paper sat in the sink, its corner soaking up drops of water. Upon it, 'Havoc' was written in a scrawl.

Ice crept up my spine.

A warning voice told me not to look—to just throw it away and run to the others.

Instead, I picked it up, unfolding it carefully, my heart in my throat. Within was a message and two photos printed in black and white.

The photos were blurred. The first was in a large room that looked like a home office. In it were three people. One lay on the floor, and the other two were against the wall, looking to be in a struggle. My hand jumped to my mouth as I looked at the second photo. It was the same, but zoomed in.

I knew who it was.

He looked much younger, but the set to his jaw, his eyes— even furious as they were—his larger build. It was Bane. It was the day he'd gone rogue.

My eyes jumped to the text beneath.

"Reject the pack and leave the ball by yourself. Tell anyone about this, fail to leave, and your lover's affliction will be leaked by morning."

FORTY

Havoc

My world was cracking into pieces.

It took three attempts to exit the bathroom. I kept freezing at the door and backing into one of the stalls in case I had to throw up.

All I could think of was Bane being taken away. From me. From the pack... When he'd just found freedom from Logan.

By the time I walked back to my seat, I was numb.

The piece of paper was folded and tucked into my bra, as I was too afraid to throw it out.

It had taken me too long to compose myself. Even now, I fought tears. My eyes were darting around the ball, trying to spot... *What*? What was I expecting to see?

I knew who the note was from.

Eli wanted me to leave, which meant he wasn't in here. He was outside, waiting.

My fingers gripped the hem of my dress under the table.

"Havoc?" Kai leaned close. "What's wrong?"

I looked up to him, trying to measure my expression. "I'm fine. Just... nervous."

I couldn't tell them.

Bane was leaning back in the seat beside me, chuckling at something Angel had said. My stomach plummeted.

If the truth got out, he'd go to jail, or worse even. The institute sometimes claimed criminal alphas for labour.

Bane caught my eye, his eyes lighting up as he saw me looking at him. I had to force my smile, but it felt as though a knife was lodged in my throat.

No.

I couldn't risk it. I already knew that.

It was over.

I felt sick, and time moved in a blur. Announcements started, noting celebrations and achievements of different packs around the room. It was being broadcast live. Packs of this status held a lot of power, and their news was city news.

Before I knew it, Angel got to his feet. He would make the announcement for the pack.

Bane's touch slipped to my leg. I usually loved his touch, but right now I almost jumped. I placed my hand on his, my vision blurring for a moment. I squeezed his hand in mine and he squeezed it back.

I broke, unable to help glancing at him. Those beautiful storm-cloud eyes were glittering with hope and he leaned close, just as Angel stepped to the stage. He pressed a kiss to my temple.

"I love you, Havoc," Bane murmured in my ear. My breath caught as I spun to him. "I wanted to say it before the others got to you."

I couldn't speak as he reached up to his neck. As I watched, he undid the silver chain necklace. "You freed me," he breathed as he set the necklace on the table.

I stared at it, then at him. A tear splashed down my cheek and he lifted his thumb, brushing it away. My eyes burned with the effort of not breaking down completely. I tried to smile, tried to make it look like happiness. He tugged me into his arms, and I clutched him, blinking more away.

"I love you, too." *So fucking much it hurt.* My voice was thick, the words almost sticking to my throat on the way up. He just squeezed me tighter until it was almost impossible to breathe.

What was waiting for me on the other side of this?

I couldn't think about that right now. These arms around me... he had offered me faith when no one else had. He had seen me when everyone else had seen a killer.

I had to protect him, no matter what happened.

This had all been an impossible dream, anyway; how many times had I pinched myself, waiting for it to be over?

I'd known. I'd known all this time.

Focusing was impossible as Angel stood upon the stage, speaking into a microphone, and his speech passed in a blur.

"You all heard about the passing of our pack lead, Logan Mandela... Truths have come to light... While certain details are private, our pack is denouncing Logan for his betrayal..." Whispers and breaths of shock rose around the room. I tried to keep my gaze on Angel, tried not to look at the others, afraid of getting swept up by their loving gazes. "We want to publicly offer Havoc Saint the princess bond."

Silence followed those words as shock fell upon the room.

I felt Caspian brush my shoulder, encouraging me to go up there like I was supposed to.

My legs were leaden as I crossed the huge ballroom, each step a damnation as silence smothered me like a blanket.

These people watching, what would they think? Would they be happier that I rejected this pack?

I took the steps, refusing to look out at the crowd as I approached Angel. My legs felt like they were going to give out.

"Our pack, the Mandela Pack, offers you the princess bond." He took my face in his hands and pressed his forehead to mine.

"Though. I think we need to consider renaming." He whispered those words, just for me. He was smiling and I couldn't look away. His forest green eyes held mine, the faint scattering of freckles across his mid brown skin looked, all of a sudden, like constellations I hadn't taken enough time to name. His touch was warm and comforting, and I wanted it forever.

With a declaration, physical connection and the authority of the pack, I felt the offer settle upon me like it had that day with Logan.

If I accepted, the bite was next. A bite from all of them this time. I almost squeezed my eyes shut at that thought.

A dream.

One I wasn't destined for.

We wouldn't have done that part in public, of course. All I was supposed to do here was speak the words.

Angel slid his hand around my waist and nudged me toward the mic. Until now, I hadn't taken my eyes off him. Looking out into the crowd was a mistake.

It was a sea of eyes, all watching, all judging. Invested in a moment that I wished was just mine.

I cleared my throat, and the sound echoed around the room. It was dizzying. I could still feel the offer of the bond pulling at me, needing an answer. The breath seemed to leave my chest as I felt, in entirety, how much I wanted to take it.

It wasn't just Bane.

I loved them all. I wanted a home with them.

Loneliness was a dark shadow that, for a few brief hours, I thought I was done with. But the folded piece of paper in my bra —tucked beside the photo I carried everywhere—was ever present.

I found our table in the crowd and could see all three of them. Bane, Kai and Caspian. I glanced to Angel as if pausing might change things.

I shouldn't have.

It made everything worse. He was looking at me, his brows drawn, as if he could see something was wrong. He took a step toward me, but I held my hand out in just the slightest motion. He halted.

"I..." I had to take another breath. *How long had I stood here in silence?*

"I..." Again, the word was a husk, inaudible. I had to do this now, before I wasn't strong enough.

"I reject the Mandela Pack."

The weight of the princess bond, hovering between our auras, vanished. There was nothing but silence ringing in my ears.

I began to walk from the stage, but Angel caught my arm. I pulled away, unable to look at him. I could see nothing but the panels of the platform beneath each step.

I had to hold my tears. They couldn't know there was something wrong. Let them think I had lied, that this was revenge for Logan.

There was movement. I didn't look up enough to see, but I knew my pack was on their feet. Security was inching into the room as if concerned. I could swear there was more of that scent dampening mist in the air.

A princess bond was surrounded by etiquette. It was absolutely expected, if not woven into magical law, to respect the decision of rejection.

I stepped past tables on the opposite side of the hall, finally lifting my eyes to the double doors.

The exit.

I quickened my steps, needing to be through before my fear overcame me.

Then my grip was on the handle and I was turning it, pushing it open and—I broke, turning back to look at them.

Angel was off the stage, halfway between me and the pack

table. He looked lost. The others did too. I could see it from this distance.

"Good girl, Havoc," the familiar purr sounded from beyond, and I spun.

Eli was right there, as if he wanted to be seen by the whole world, because it was more than just the people in this room watching. Cameras had followed my exit.

My heart was in my throat as I stared at him, finally losing my battle to fear. I couldn't move. I couldn't take a single step. His fingers laced in mine, and I was through.

The sound of the door slamming shut behind me marked the moment the last of my hope died.

FORTY-ONE

Angel

I'd seen two things.

Eli at the door, and Havoc—her mask cracking as she gazed back at us, a flicker of fear in her eyes.

I'd seen it, and so—it seemed—had the others. And I knew, in that moment, on a primal level, that Havoc hadn't rejected our bond because she wanted to.

If Bane's aura had been a shock wave, it would have obliterated every last crystal chandelier hanging high above our heads.

What followed was utter chaos as was warned about to children before bed, when parents explain why the institute places strict laws upon alphas. The only blessing was that Bane didn't devolve into a full fury—possible, given he was a rogue. He just... lost it. Like any normal alpha who'd watched his mate stolen away by her worst nightmare.

The first problem was security had seen it coming a mile off. And the second was that tension had been taut in the room since the moment I publicly denounced Logan. That, and the abandonment of control over an aura as large as Bane's, was a stimulant to every alpha near their rut without a partner to settle them. What followed was similar to what would happen if someone was to light a firework in a truck full of other fireworks.

The last—and arguably worst problem of all was that the room was full of omegas—most of whom were in heels.

There weren't enough hormone dampeners in the world that could have settled the absolute riot that followed.

I didn't have time to get back to my brothers, not when they were so conveniently drawing the attention of security. With murder in my veins, I launched toward the doors, which were already crowded with fleeing packs, heels in hands—or just the whole omega, tossed over a shoulder.

FORTY-TWO

Havoc

Eli's fist was vice-like around my wrist as he tugged me down the steps from the grand hall.

It wasn't long before I heard the chaos behind me. I glanced back to see people spilling from the doors. Eli turned for the briefest moment, a ghost of a smile on his face before he continued tugging me toward the street edge.

Where were we going?

There were cars everywhere, some with doors open and drivers waiting. We seemed to be making for a dark limo, but I couldn't tell—

"HAVOC!" Angel's shout drew me up and Eli stopped, too, spinning. His eyes narrowed for a moment. He was calculating as we both spotted Angel throwing his weight through the crowds of people.

"Give me permission to dark bond you." Eli's words caught me off guard.

"What?"

"If I bond you, he can't touch me. Unless you want me to

finish the job I started in your room? His aura isn't any better, is it?"

I tried to pull from him. "You can't dark bond me—I-I rejected a princess bond—"

"Which means it's illegal *unless* you give me permission."

"No!"

He dragged me to him, taking my chin in a painful grip. "Give me permission now or that picture of your rogue mutt is everywhere by breakfast."

I stared at him in shock.

I heard Angel shout my name again.

"Tell me how it will look to witnesses if he reaches us?" Eli spat. "Was I the aggressor, or was he? You just rejected him, Havoc. Whatever I do might well be self-defence—even *protecting* you."

Blood roared in my ears as I tore my chin free of Eli, looking to Angel. He was free of the crowds, taking the steps in leaps. There was ferocious rage in his eyes as he reached for me.

I let out a sob, almost reaching out too, so desperate to feel his touch like I just had on the stage, to feel the safety of his arms.

Eli's grip on my wrist became bruising.

Angel had taken a blade for me once, and no matter what happened here, Eli still had the evidence of Bane.

"Give me permission!"

"Okay." The word was nothing more than a rasp. I didn't have time to look to Eli before he'd grabbed my hair and yanked my head back. I let out a cry of pain as his teeth sunk into my neck.

Angel

My heart smashed against my rib cage as I reached for her. I saw the briefest flicker of hope before Eli closed a fist in her hair and dragged her toward him.

As he sunk his teeth into Havoc's neck, she let out a whimper of pain.

"*NO!*" My roar echoed across the street, but it was too late. Claws attached to my brain, forcing my body to draw up without permission. I halted right before them, as Havoc sagged in his arms.

Eli had bonded her.

It was one of the laws that we—alphas controlled by the institute—were bound to follow. If an omega rejected a princess bond, her fated pack couldn't challenge her future packs.

I couldn't take one more step toward her. I couldn't touch Eli.

Tears were streaking Havoc's face as she looked at me. It was the moment I felt the first crack in my heart.

Then my eyes slid to the bite on her neck. There was something wrong with it. The blood wasn't bright red. Darkness leached into her skin like an infection.

Not just a normal bond. A dark bond.

As I looked to Eli, I'd never felt hatred as raw. He was vile scum, and for the first time, I knew that calling that ruined Kai.

I wanted him dead.

I wanted to be the one to do it, to see the blood seeping from his cold flesh.

Eli took a step back, dragging Havoc with him toward a dark limo behind. A door was open, waiting. I caught a glimpse of another alpha within. A pair of yellow pupils were watching me with a curious, blank expression.

I didn't have time to process that I knew those eyes, because Eli was grinning, spreading his free arm. "You should have taken my offer when I visited. Then she would belong to both of us, and you wouldn't be an auraless mutt."

He shoved Havoc toward the door, not looking away from me.

She almost fell, grabbing the door to steady herself, and a growl ripped from my chest. That sound, somehow, steadied her. She finally tore her gaze from me, her fist balled around her sleeves, and she turned to the open door.

She didn't want me to see her suffer.

My heart shattered as, with a shaking step, she climbed in. I could do nothing but watch.

Eli ducked in behind her and the door slammed. The moment it did, I felt the claws in my mind loosen.

"I'm coming, Havoc!" I'd find a way.

We would find a way.

But her heat... It was near. I turned, staring wildly out at the chaos around me as if it might hand me solutions.

I had to find the others. I didn't care what it took. I didn't care about broken princess bonds and the laws that surrounded them... Bane... *Bane* was a rogue. He would be able to break those laws.

I launched myself against the tide of fleeing packs.

I'd get her back.

Havoc

What came next was a blur. I tried to take a seat in the corner, away from any of the others, but Eli instead tugged me onto his lap.

His touch was familiar, and I hated it.

I tried to calm my breathing, the sight of Angel's horror-struck face burned into my mind. It took me a moment to take in the people in the car. There were three others and their scents all tangled.

One was younger, with black, buzzed hair, bright yellow eyes and piercings scattered across his face and ears. He had taken the corner seat with a dark expression and was looking out the window. The other two couldn't take their gazes from me.

One was rugged looking, with tanned skin, a strap of a beard, and styled raven hair. He looked older than the others—perhaps mid-thirties. I glanced at the last. He had a strong nose, was built like Bane, and had dark auburn hair tied in a ponytail. Both were watching me with intent curiosity. The raven-haired alpha's eyes dropped down to my neck, to Eli's fresh bite.

What were they here for?

That thought was full of dread.

"She's got Lhevus blood?" The raven-haired one asked. Eli nodded, and the other chuckled darkly.

I couldn't think straight, and I hated how they were looking at me.

"We waited out here for a first look." That was the one with auburn hair and a strong nose. "So, let's have it."

Suddenly, traitorously, I shrunk into Eli's arms, afraid of the others in the car. Afraid of how different they were to everything I'd ever known. Eli tucked my hair behind my ear, and I flinched from the touch.

"They're going to be your pack. Make a good first impression."

They were going to be... *what?*

I couldn't move.

These men were strangers.

"Hey. You think we can make it seven?" the raven-haired man asked before I could find an answer. His tone suggested he wasn't at all paying attention to the conversation. "There's been more interest now her rejection's public. I just got an offer for 1.6."

Eli tensed.

"Will she manage seven?" the auburn-haired one asked. "I'm not sacrificing my bond for a bit of extra cash."

"Only you'd call 1.6 million a little extra cash, Lain," the dark-haired man grunted.

"She's gold pack," Eli said. "She'll anchor seven. I wouldn't be worried about eight."

I couldn't help glancing about, my stomach twisting. Were they talking about what I thought they were?

Eli had a *buy in* for the pack?

But omegas were rare and aura sickness was indiscriminate when it came to the rich or poor...

Don't cry, Havoc.

Not now.

If Eli intended to forge a pack, there was only one way to do that with an omega. If I was at the centre, if each of them bit me like Eli had, they would be bonded as brothers.

I caught the shifting gaze of the quiet man in the corner. His eyes traced the way I anxiously gripped my dress. He had a twisted expression as his yellow eyes met mine, and then he was looking out the window again, face completely blank.

"Come on Havoc. Show some interest." Eli shifted me until I was between his legs, hands cupping my upper arms on each side, so I was facing the opposite seat. I ducked my head as Eli pulled more of my hair from where it tumbled before my face. "It's really not that bad. Once your heat comes, you'll be asking for them."

I couldn't look up, couldn't see the way I knew they were staring at me, as if I were a fancy piece of art they'd purchased.

The auburn-haired one—Lain, stood and crossed the limo to sit at our side.

I bit back my fear as he touched my cheek, turning me toward him. "You *are* special, aren't you?" he murmured. I grabbed his wrist as he began turning my chin one way and then the other, but his grip was too firm to fight. "The omega who killed Mandela." He smiled, and it was something wicked. "How I'd like to hear about that sometime."

"My claim is highest," the quiet one with yellow eyes spoke for the first time, tapping his phone screen. "I get first bite. I don't want anyone else putting a filthy paw on her until I'm done."

Lain's eyes narrowed. The tension in the car was palpable. "There's no way—"

"Here's the thing," the yellow-eyed alpha said. "I had twice the buy in, and I have my aura—while you don't. Which means I can bite in any time. Eli's already in. So, she's mine until heat."

There was a nasty pause. I felt sick as they discussed me like I wasn't here.

"How long until her heat?" The raven haired one asked, leaning forward in his seat.

"It was delayed twice," Eli said. "Next week, if not sooner. First heat, too."

"First?"

"She was drugged for the others."

The red hair one grunted. "Means it'll last longer, right?"

"And you won't get a stronger bond than if you bite in during," Eli said.

There was a pause, and then Lain reached out, as if to touch me again. Eli caught his wrist. "You heard him."

Lain's expression was deadly, but he ripped his hand away.

"Why don't you go and introduce yourself to Viper," Eli murmured in my ear.

The fresh wound on my neck throbbed at the command and I was pushing myself upright before I realised.

This wasn't like a regular alpha command—those lasted moments and could be resisted. This dug claws into my brain, not letting go, pushing... pushing... pushing...

"No." I forced myself to stop, forced myself to cling to Eli's arm and not do as he told me. A familiar pain rose in my chest, rippling across my skin. It was the same as the pain I used to feel at the touch of my alphas. Only it was worse—*much* worse, and it spread across my entire body as Eli's command again seized my mind. My breathing picked up as I tried to suppress my gasp of pain.

This was what a dark bond felt like.

"Don't fight me, Havoc," Eli murmured. "It's not worth it."

I stared at the floor of the limo, chest heaving as the pain continued, the command still gripping my mind. But I'd felt this pain before and I held on, managing to shake my head.

Then there was movement. My eyes darted to the side in time to see Viper waving a hand, not looking up from his phone. "I'm busy. Send her to my wing when we get in."

There was a pause, and then the pain vanished. Eli must have released the command. I tried not to sag against him.

There was nothing left of the man I had once thought he was. Someone much gentler than this. Someone who would never have dark bonded me. I fought tears once more. I didn't know if I would survive what was coming... Losing my family.

And the pain... Why was it so familiar?

Princess bonds were artificially made by the institute. My father had always said dark bonds were the result of us challenging nature, the equal and opposite reaction.

"She meets the others first," Eli said at last. "Then I'll send her."

Once more I looked to Viper. He was completely expressionless as he replied. "They get ten minutes."

Angel

I was outside the police station with Kai, waiting for them to process Caspian and Bane. Kai, it seemed, had been able to slip out without getting caught. The other two shouldn't be long.

While I waited, I scoured old contact lists desperately, trying phone number after phone number.

It was our only chance to find out where Havoc had been taken.

"Fuck!" The last number I tried didn't work.

Before I could turn back to Kai however, my phone began to buzz. *'Unknown number',* the screen read. I hesitated only a moment before picking up.

"Angel." I almost dropped the phone in relief as I recognised the voice.

"Viper. Listen to me—"

"How's the pack doing?" Viper cut me off. "Must have been rough since old Logan took a bullet to the brain."

"Fuck yourself, Viper. We aren't going to pretend I didn't just see you in that limo with my mate."

Kai froze at my side, his eyes wide.

Through the phone, I heard a breath of amusement.

"He's forming a pack?" I asked, even if I was terrified of the answer. I'd spoken to Havoc about her value as a gold pack duchess across the city. Her value only increased by her rejection of us, of her public history with Logan. All of that—*all of it*, made her equally valuable in a pack like the one Eli could form right now.

"You don't want to know the buy-in cost, Angel. Wildest thing I've ever seen."

But why would Viper want in? I hadn't heard he had aura sickness. "Did your aura—?"

"My aura's *glowing*."

"Then why?" I spat. I'd known Viper on and off since I was a child. He was the rebellious kid of a family that put mine and Logan's wealth to shame. He was a year younger than us, though he hadn't liked Logan one bit. He had always been... different, but I'd never believed him cruel. "You *know* she doesn't want to be there."

There was a pause. "It's quite clear she doesn't."

"Eli *has* something on her."

"The most likely explanation." Viper sounded like he was speaking through a mouthful of something.

"Have you—has anyone…?" I couldn't finish that thought, let alone the words that came with it.

"Only Eli's bitten her." I heard a slurping sound. Was he eating fucking noodles during this conversation? *He'd* called *me*, the piece of shit.

"But you will?" I asked, unable to stop the growl in my voice. What was this call? *A taunt?*

"Daddy wants me to," Viper replied. "He believes it's a *uniquely* fitting pack for me."

All the violent threats that were rising in my mind, died at the tone in Viper's voice. "*You* don't want to?" I couldn't help my hope, even knowing Viper was the kind of man to pounce on weakness.

"Rather tasteless by my reckoning, biting a scent matched omega."

"Tell me where she is. I'll give you anything, Viper. Fucking anything if you tell me."

Viper sighed. "Fine. But if you come, burn it all down. I want this to fall apart, and I'd prefer if my old man can't blame me for it."

"Stall them. Don't let *anyone* touch her."

"Already on it."

"You knew I'd ask?"

"Angel." Something in his voice changed. "She's your mate." He sounded different than I'd ever heard him. "I'll text you the address."

"Thank you."

"If you come, I promise my security won't see a thing, but *I'm* not getting my hands bloody here alright? Can't afford it."

"I get it. Just… stall them. That's all."

FORTY-THREE

Havoc

"If the Oxford cunt wants to keep her until heat, I need a good look."

"Keep it dignified, Lain," Eli snapped as he dropped his coat on the couch. We had arrived at one of the largest mansions I'd ever seen—even in movies.

"I paid enough money for a gold pack bitch, I can do what I want." Lain, the auburn-haired one from the limo, was scowling. My throat went dry.

"*Don't* keep it dignified and you'll bite last. I'm not running a frat pack."

We were in what looked to be a large living room. It was sprawled with couches, glass tables, a liquor cabinet, and a pool table.

Viper was gone, but Lain and the raven-haired one called Kent had followed us in. Eli had led me in, his touch on the small of my back until I was standing at the edge of one of the couches. There were two others, one seated on an armchair in the corner, reading a newspaper with no apparent interest. The other was a brute of a man with blond hair and blue eyes, who was peering at me curiously from where he was seated on the couch. He looked halfway through his dinner.

Kent was pouring himself a drink, while the foul, red-haired Lain was still hovering close. "You weren't kidding about the earthy scent," Lain noted. "Can't stand a sickly-sweet omega." He brushed my hair, and I stepped away quickly. Now we weren't in the limo, I was starting to identify scents. Lain's was a bitter apple scent. Too strong.

I could barely breathe. This was like Gavin's but worse. So much worse.

I wanted to run, but Eli was right there at my side, that pain one word away. The truth hit me then, at last: I was right where I had begun. Eli had taken me right back to my worst nightmare. I was at the whims of alphas, terrified of the pain they could bring.

"You're going to save us all, aren't you?" Lain was still talking. I couldn't process the words properly, the world spinning in my vision. "Do a turn for me, that's a sexy little dress." I stared at him unmoving, my nails biting my palms as he grinned. "That's alright love, I'll be having you do more than turns for me once I bite in."

"You've gone through no formal training, correct?" The blond brute from the couch asked. "We'll have to fix that."

"You knew that when you bid," Eli snorted.

"It was too good to miss, been on the lookout for a while. The omega that *killed* Mandela—that fucker was untouchable at the table. But I'm not showing her off at poker games until she can hold herself better."

"Not curious, Ry?" One of them was asking. My eyes followed his gaze to the man on the armchair in the corner.

"I can see the golden eyes from here. Don't give a fuck otherwise, never met an omega who couldn't please." He turned another page of his newspaper.

"Right, Lain, if you're done sniffing, I'm taking her to Viper."

"Bunch of crap, that is."

Eli shrugged. "You want more of a say, pay up."

Eli took me by the arm, his grip firm as he led me from the room. "Try to run and the institute will bring you right back to me." He said, not looking at me.

With the voices and scents of the alphas fading, I could focus better. "Eli," I whispered. He looked down at me with cool eyes. "Please don't do this."

"You were with your pack for what? A few weeks, and you were ready to fall into their arms. You'll find your footing here quick enough."

"I don't know them."

Eli huffed a laugh. "You didn't know Angel or the others either, you just convinced yourself you did."

I swallowed, mouth dry.

They were my mates. More than that, they had cared about me. Enough to offer a bond to hand me back all the power Eli had just stolen.

"This pack is powerful and wealthy," he went on. "You'll be taken care of for the rest of your life."

"I'm nothing to them, I never will be."

Eli's expression was pitying. "None of this is out of the ordinary for an omega with eyes like yours, no matter what your delusional pack of pups might have promised—"

He cut off as I seized the front of his shirt, heart in my throat. "They're going to come for me." The bold statement made it to my lips without thought.

Even so, panic gripped me. It was as if my world was tumbling back in time, all of my old fears returning. I thought Eli might be seeing it in my eyes. Or he could feel it. We were connected through the bite on my neck. He was a presence I was trying so hard not to acknowledge.

A cold smile curled his lips. "You rejected their princess bond.

I'm your new pack, none of them can touch me. They aren't coming for you now, just like they didn't then."

At those words, a low snarl rose in my throat.

"Havoc." Eli pried my grip from his shirt with ease and shoved me away. "I'm lead. Behave, and I'll keep them in line. But these men aren't patient, nor are they here to be challenged by a gold pack omega. Act like a child, and I'll give them free rein."

Those words sent a chill down my spine. He said nothing else as he led me through the rest of the house.

He knocked and then pushed open a door to a living space three times the size of my nest. Viper was slouched on a sofa, boxes of takeout sprawled before him. The scent in here was cool; mint and mist.

He barely glanced up at us as Eli spoke. "The others won't disturb you, but I'll be in and out. She's *my* omega, right now. You won't force yourself on her if she doesn't want you. You can spend the time letting her get comfortable, but bite her however you need."

With that, he slammed the door and left me alone in the room with Viper.

I didn't know what to think when he said nothing. Eventually, he set his phone down and glanced over at me.

"Come here."

I thought of running to the bathroom and locking myself in. Eli was gone. He was the only one who could hurt me with commands. But finally, Viper stood, peering over at me and scratching his chin. He crossed to the bed and picked up a bundle of black fabric, then approached.

He was tall and slender, his dark hair was buzzed short, allowing all the ridiculous chiselled edges of his face to speak for themselves. He looked like a magazine model, only with tattoos across his hands, and piercings in his ears, including black ear gauges. His yellow eyes were unnaturally bright, and I wondered if that's why he'd been named the way he had.

He pressed the bundle of black into my arms and then touched my shoulder, nodding toward the couch.

Did I dare not listen?

A part of me just wanted to huddle by the door until I was forced to do anything. But, nothing about him seemed aggressive, and the scent of mint and mist was strangely soothing.

He began toward the couch, not seeming particularly bothered if I listened or not, again on his phone.

The TV sparked on, and something began to load. I peered down at the thing in my hands.

A... dressing gown?

I blinked, letting it unravel to make sure.

I didn't understand, but I was tugging it on, relieved to put a layer of thick fabric between me and prying eyes. I followed him cautiously.

I sat at the far end of the couch. Before us, was a bunch of takeout, open boxes of dumplings, rice and noodles. He used a slippered foot to nudge a folded noodle box toward me. It was still steaming from the corners. Whatever the TV was trying to play still struggled to load.

Viper said nothing, relaxing back and returning to his phone.

Once more, I had no idea what to make of it as the seconds stretched on. Now the pack of men weren't here staring at me, the weight of everything slammed in. The fear came with twinges in my stomach. Not good.

Not good at all.

I hadn't thought about that, but my dad had told me once that fight-or-flight response could also trigger heat.

I buried another wave of tears and grabbed the box of noodles. Anything to distract myself.

I felt Viper's eyes on me for a moment.

This room, even this man, wasn't as frightening as everything else, but I had to remember that he'd bought into a pack to bond me. Nothing he was doing here was out of the goodness of his heart.

That's what I thought, anyway, until the TV finally won that battle with the loading screen. As I prodded chopsticks into my noodles, realising how *not* hungry I was, a familiar sound came from the TV. It was the zooming sounds of cars around racetracks and the low hum of commentators that I knew so well from when Kai spent the night.

I looked up, and the words at the bottom of the screen confirmed it.

It was a rerun of the Grand Prix.

FORTY-FOUR

Havoc

I looked at Viper properly for the first time. "You know Angel?"

"Sure do. He's going to owe me *big* time."

"They're coming?" I'd said it to Eli, but the hope was still tangled with all those nights in Gavin's when my wishes weren't answered.

"What is wrong with the lot of you?" Viper gave me a strange look. "You're their mate. No force on this earth could keep them away."

The fist around my throat began to loosen for a moment. "Can I talk to them?"

Viper shook his head. "Won't be long till they're here. Let them do their thing."

Something in my chest loosened at that, allowing me to breathe.

Viper picked up a piece of cloth from the table, sprayed it with something from his pocket, and then put it on his face. It was a black mask with a broad white fanged smile across the whole thing.

"What are you doing?" I asked.

"Scent dampener. You're perfuming like crazy. I have no intention of joining your heat. They better hurry up."

I hugged my knees to my chest, anxiously.

Another long time passed, and I felt more twists in my stomach. It worried me that it wasn't sharp and fast. That usually meant this might be real heat, not a warning flash.

The door banged open, making me jump.

"I was exploring when I caught the loveliest smell in the air." It was Lain, the foul-red haired alpha with the scent of bitter apples.

"Get out." Viper didn't even get to his feet as he glanced to the alpha at the door.

"Nah." Lain took a swaggering step into the room. "*You* said you wanted her until heat began. Seems like you're out of time."

Viper tapped his phone, still not looking up.

"You're nothing but a spoiled trust fund baby," Lain went on. "Once we get our auras, you'll be bottom rung."

"Right now, I do have my aura, so unless you want me to put you through the wall, fuck off." Still Viper didn't look up.

But then Lain drew a gun from the back of his belt and clicked the safety.

Bane

My aura was contained by the barest thread. Caspian was at my side in a small dull room with a pane of glass along one wall. Angel's lawyer was on her feet, having a vicious argument with a cop—or whatever asshole that had locked us in here.

"Last I checked it wasn't illegal to release an aura in public," she snapped.

I couldn't focus. On the next seat along, Caspian looked just as dazed. My body ached. We'd been at the centre of the brawl, but I was glad for it. It was the only thing keeping me grounded.

Havoc was gone.

Taken.

Eli had her.

"It was a room full of—" the cop began.

"Footage shows Lilac-Gate security were the first to throw punches. My clients were trying to *leave* the building. Unless you have any valid charges, they're free to go."

Angel had got out, Kai too—he'd managed to slip through the crowds the moment the fighting started.

They'd better be going after her.

Before I knew it, my hands were being uncuffed. I didn't need prompting to leave. The moment the door opened I was taking the hallways and stairs of the police station at a run, Caspian at my side. Angel and Kai were outside.

Why were they here?

"Havoc—" I began.

"Get in." Kai opened the door to Cass's huge truck.

"Thanks, Jos," Angel said. The woman who'd been arguing with the cop had followed us out. "Email me the rest."

"Get out of here quick," I heard her say as I climbed in.

Angel had already jumped into the driver's seat and in moments we were ripping out into the street.

"Fill us in," Caspian demanded. "Why are you still here?"

"We need you. Anyway, only just got the address."

"You know where she is?" I asked. "We have to—before—"

"Eli bit her."

My blood turned to ice, a low growl rumbling in my chest.

"How do you know?" Cass asked.

"Did it right in front of me. He's forming a pack. There's a buy in."

"What?" My voice was dry, blood roaring in my ears. "No.

She's not..." Something cracked in my soul. It was Havoc. Our omega. Sweet and off balance and shy. The one who didn't know elevators, or shopping etiquette and still found a way to stick with us even when we were at our worst. She was fierce, but... She wasn't ready for a world like that. She had just started to climb out of the hole Logan and her father had dug for her. Just started to see her own value and find her footing. "He can't."

"He can—" Angel began.

"We *can't* let that happen," I snarled.

"Where do you think we're going?" Angel asked.

"Do we need people? I could contact—" Caspian began.

"No. Not enough time—and she just rejected our bond on live TV."

Fuck. Right. My mind was catching up. It wasn't just because of our auras we couldn't touch Eli, the laws around it were just as brutal. If anyone got caught working with us to sabotage Havoc's pack... No. To find people willing to risk that—even for the right amount—it wasn't time we had.

"Only Eli has bitten in. It's a buy-in—mostly alphas without auras. They'll have to wait for her heat."

For a moment, I felt a rush of relief, but Cass's jaw ticked.

"It's not far off, and she'll be terrified."

"That's not the only problem. He's bonded her, he's her new pack, so we—"

"Can't touch him," Cass finished. "Shit." He kicked the glove box hard enough to crack. "We need hires, Angel—"

"No. We... We have me," I said.

I was a rogue. My omega parent—who I'd never met, was gold pack. I could break the laws that held the others back. I'd hidden from it for years, but Angel was right. There was no time, Havoc could be going into heat right now. I shoved that thought away. "I can deal with Eli. We go and do as Viper says. Burn it all down."

I could feel Cass and Kai's eyes on me.

"I'm not leaving her," I said.

"You know that was blackmail back there." Angel's voice was low. "You know what he might have on her—on us?"

Cass glanced between us, comprehension dawning in his eyes. "He knows about Bane?"

I nodded, but I didn't feel a flicker of fear. "I don't fucking care." All that meant was that she was in a dark bond because of me. "And before you say it, I know what has to happen."

If we wanted Havoc free, Eli had to die. As did any other alpha fucker who'd laid a fang on her.

"You're... okay with that?" Angel asked, forest eyes fixed on me in the mirror.

For a moment, my memories flickered. The world was crimson. Blood soaked my hands. I could hear them screaming. But it was gone as fast as it had come.

This was different, and that was easy to see. Eli deserved it.

He'd taken her from us, had stolen her freedom. I'd seen her strength, but right now she would be terrified.

"We never saved her last time," I said. That would *never* happen again. "Get me in a room with him."

FORTY-FIVE

Viper

I heard the gun click.

Every sense soared to high alert as my aura lit. It was a muscle I had trained to oblivion and back.

The world burst with life. Colour, sound, scent, the blood rushing through my veins, it all crescendoed to a roar. Every hair on my body stood on end as I navigated it all, instincts warring for priority.

The first was Havoc.

That instinct was first.

She was an omega. I knew where she was without looking, as if her scent and aura was a lingering shadow in my mind. I could sense her fear even with the mask on. Before I'd made a conscious choice, I was on my feet and in front of her in one motion, sweeping her behind me as I turned to the armed alpha at the door.

"Drop it," I spat.

The alpha—Lain Voger, paused as he sensed my aura. I'd moved so quickly to stand before Havoc his eyes couldn't have followed.

My aura wasn't potent enough to justify what he'd just seen, and I could see his confusion. That look was familiar. Someone with an aura my size shouldn't be able to do what I could, but most people with an aura my size hadn't broken themselves over and over to be able to convert the energy like this.

And it still isn't enough...

Not the time. Havoc was my focus and right now it didn't matter that she wasn't my mate, my alpha demanded I protect her.

Lain approached, a sneer on his face and I felt Havoc try to peer around me. I nudged her back, sinking deeper into my aura. Could I wield enough of it to contest a bullet?

It was dangerous, going this deep, I knew that, but the asshole was still drawing closer until the gun was pressed into my temple.

"Get out of the way," he snarled.

But then I heard her breath behind me, the faintest sound that I wouldn't catch without heightened senses. *"It's not loaded."*

A rumbling sound rose up my throat as those words sunk in, half growl, half purr.

I'd told Angel I wouldn't get blood on my hands... and I shouldn't. I really *really* shouldn't.

I'd made myself a slave to my instincts to get closer to what I wanted. Sometimes, though, they led me further away. That was the way life worked.

And really... this fucker was asking for it.

I nudged her from behind me.

She shouldn't see this next part.

"Run, Havoc."

Havoc

I fled Viper's room, terror pushing me onward.

I heard a blood-curdling scream behind me. It was strangled and awful and every hair on my body stood on end.

I needed a way out.

Eli was in my mind, a ball of energy. I was trying to shut the connection down, but with my heat putting me on edge, and trying to navigate a way out of this huge mansion, it was almost impossible.

I ended up in another hallway like the last. The walls of velvety wallpaper and expensive paintings taunted me.

My mates were coming. I had to get to them.

Another spike of heat blitzed through my body, and I crashed to my knees, clutching my stomach.

No.

I had to make it to them.

Keep it together. I tried to level my breathing and shove away the terror. It would push me into heat faster.

The world faded for a moment, and I swallowed a scream of pain. I knew this was the cost of pushing my heat back so many times. I rode it out, thinking of my pack.

Bane. Kai. Angel. Caspian.

They were coming for me.

I reached into my bra and tugged out the folded paper. Not the one Eli had given me. My photo. The one I took everywhere. The one that I'd told myself as I was getting ready today, that I wouldn't need to carry with me after the night was over. For I would have their bites instead.

Instead, Eli's bite throbbed, still open on my neck. I stared at them.

If they came... Might they get hurt? Lain had been carrying a gun.

The four men in the picture blurred in my vision.

I needed them to come for me, and yet I was terrified they would.

Slowly, the world steadied, the patterns along the carpet swimming into sight. The best thing I could do for them was to get out of this place, reach them before Eli could—I jumped as I saw shiny, leather shoes before me. I was inhaling the scent of sage.

I tried to scramble away but Eli's grip was on my arm. "You *ran*?" he demanded. My breath caught as he dragged me to my feet.

"I told you, Havoc," he spat in my ear, then he ripped the photo from my grip. "All you have to do is behave and everything goes smoothly."

I tried to grab it back, and to my surprise he let me have it.

"Rip it up."

The command was violent as it slammed into me. My fingers almost moved before I realised. I let out a breath of rage and shook my head. My chest heaved as I stared at the photos for strength.

Pain prickled across my skin. It rose and rose like the tide, and tears streamed down my face as I stared at them.

Bane.

Kai.

Angel.

Caspian.

I wouldn't let them go.

"Rip. It. Up." Eli's voice was furious.

A groan of pain rose in my throat as my legs gave out, but Eli was pinning me to the wall.

"They can't save you, Havoc."

"Bane can," I hissed, tears flooding my cheeks as the pain ripped through me like fire.

But he *could* save me. It was exactly the kind of thing rogues were feared for. The institute had put those laws in place, including the one that protected packs an omega chose after they rejected a princess bond. Bane could burn right through that law.

"Rip it up." The third command was too much, the pain turning the world white.

My fingers moved, my resolve cracking at last against the thundering waterfall of agony.

No.

He wouldn't make me do this.

I held on, my head pressed against the wooden panels behind me as I let out a wail of agony.

Eli snatched the paper from my weak grip and ripped it up himself. The pain stuttered out as I choked on my sob. I grabbed his wrist, but my muscles were weak. With each tear I felt my heart wither until there were nothing but little pieces of it tumbling to the floor at our feet.

Silence rang in my ears as a desperate whisper slipped from my mouth. "Bane *will* save me."

He would come.

He would come and take me from this nightmare. They all would. They had to, because I couldn't do it.

I couldn't survive this.

They had shown me something more, and I could never become again, what I had been to Logan.

Eli snorted. "No. He can't, because he's not actually a rogue."

"What...?" Those words snapped me from my daze.

"Logan gave him rogue alpha blood that day."

"Why—? *How* d-do you know?" I asked.

"I took his laptop during my little visit. I dug up all his dirt. By the looks of it, he wanted to see if it pushed Bane into claiming his aura, and if he'd be more powerful for it. It might well have, but the... *side effects* were bad enough that Logan was too nervous to try it again on himself."

I stared at him in horror, bile rising up my throat. "It... was a bluff?" I asked.

"It was. And it worked. So if they do turn up here they won't be able to touch me. I almost hope they do. I want Angel to get a look at what he threw away when he stopped me biting you. But you never know, he might be auraless already."

I was still processing what he said as Eli tugged the dressing gown from around me. Then he froze, his grip on me tightening as his scent became smothering. "You're in heat."

A sob caught in my throat as I shook my head. "I'm not."

I wasn't.

I was close, but I wasn't in it yet. Eli was ignoring me, hauling me down the hallway. "Viper wants a bite first? He better get on with it."

"No." I fought him.

"Enough!" Eli snarled. "Cooperate with me, Havoc." His command gripped my mind, urging my feet to step on their own accord. Still haunted by the pain I'd just felt, I didn't fight it.

It was something else too that crushed my resolve. *Was what Eli said about Bane true?* If my mates were coming, they couldn't save me.

We were back at Viper's door and Eli was shoving it open. That was good—right? Viper was good, but... He'd told me to run. Right now, I couldn't remember why—

Eli let out a hiss. *"What the fuck?"*

That was when the scent hit me. It was bitter apple—Lain's scent, that horrible red-haired alpha. But it was quickly curdling in the air to something foul. I'd experienced that before.

I struggled from beneath Logan's weight, his blood seeping into my clothes, wetting my skin, marking me in a way I thought I'd never be free of. Whisky and chocolate hung in the air, but it was turning foul and bitter with every second that passed until I felt as though I was going to throw up.

Beside the couches and tabletop with half-finished boxes of noodles, was a body.

It was mangled, unrecognisable.

A low sob rose in my chest.

"Where's Viper?" Eli demanded, turning to me as if I would know.

I couldn't take my eyes off the body.

Eli took a step forward. "He has a gun—? The *idiot*... It's good, actually. If this was self-defence...?"

Mats of dark red hair were sticky with blood, skin was sliced as if from blades. A jaw hung askew, bones were visible—I gagged, and with that reaction came another wave of heat pain.

I didn't know how I got there, but I was suddenly in Eli's arms. He was carrying me across the room. The twisted scent was fainter.

"No..." I groaned. Something soft was beneath me. A bed, or a couch. I didn't know. Eli's hand brushed my cheek. "No." My voice was firm, even if the world was still spinning, pain stabbing my stomach.

"You know, Havoc." His voice was different. Strained. "We don't *have* to consolidate a dark bond like a princess bond, but I want to."

"No." It was all I could manage, as my instincts began to scream otherwise, demanding I drag him toward me, demanding I free it of this agony.

"I can make the pain go away," Eli murmured in my ear. "I'll take you to my room and Viper can wait his turn." His chocolate brown eyes swam into view. He was above me, his pupils were blown, something unhinged in his expression, but he didn't move. "But I won't do it without a word from you."

"I don't... want you."

"You will."

"Never..." Tears were hot against my cheeks. He brushed it away, and the touch was like static, demanding more.

Fight it.

Fucking fight it.

"Get your hands off her."

My heart soared for a moment. That was *Bane's* growl cutting across the space. But then reality hit, and everything Eli had said about Bane came back. He wasn't a rogue.

Above me, Eli froze. Then he sat up, tugging me against his chest as he sat at the edge of the bed, peering around at the others.

It was all of them. Their scent tangled in the air, between the mint and mist, and souring apple, and Eli's sickening sage scent.

Cinders, leather, roses and cinnamon.

They were through the doors, crossing toward us. Bane was first, his eyes burning with fury, a gun in his hand. Auras burst into the room, Eli's included.

They'd come for me.

They'd really come.

At the sight of them, I fought to break from Eli's grasp.

"Stay." Eli didn't bother holding me tighter. The pain from the bond collided from my heat pain, and I curled up, shaking. "You fucking idiots."

I forced myself straight, opening my mouth to warn them, but Bane was already nearing. He stopped at the bedpost, feet away, expression twisted as he tried and failed to lift the gun.

"You want me dead, Bane?" Eli asked.

The clench of Bane's jaw, the murder in his eyes, it was answer enough.

Eli snorted. "You can't touch me. None of you can."

"Bane!" Angel's voice was a warning.

"He's not a rogue, you fools."

"Logan—" Angel began.

"Logan gave him a rogue alphas blood to see what would happen. You were adopted by his dad's pack, right?" Eli looked to Bane. "He never liked that, did he? Wanted all the spotlight to himself, and you got in the way."

Bane stared at us both, dumbstruck.

Eli let out a low chuckle. "I've never seen an alpha upset to find he's *not* a rogue."

FORTY-SIX

Kai

Logan gave Bane rogue *alpha* blood?

A spark of hope hit me at those words.

It had been the strangest thing Logan had ever done. I had been twelve, and Logan had given me something—I don't remember what. In return he'd asked for my blood.

Could it be...? Was I... A rogue?

I threw myself against the claws strangling my mind, the ones trying to hold me back from Eli. It was possible I had lived this long and never known. The magical laws upon alphas *tried* to contain rogues, too, and some never made the discovery until late in life.

The first time a rogue broke that magical leash was devastating. It cleaved alphas apart, scattering their aura before stitching it back together. It was agony.

But I'd suffered worse. I'd do that for Havoc. I'd do it a thousand times.

I strained against the chains holding me from Eli, ripping at them with every ounce of my strength. A growl sounded in my chest.

She was feet away, in *his* arms. Still wearing that wine red dress from the ball, and the bite on her neck... My aura flared as I saw the blood—the darkness creeping along her skin, marking the foul bond.

I'd thought, once, I'd do that to her.

I would never forgive myself for that.

Her scent was smothering, her heat so clearly near. And she'd been crying, her eyes ringed red. She was shaking as she clutched Eli, as if her body was about to give out.

What had he done to her?

Again, I threw myself against the chains in my mind. My aura flared once more. I would kill him. I had to. I'd kill him *for* her, so she would know what we'd do to keep her safe.

"I'd call the cops and watch you all sent to prison." Eli was speaking again, eyes darting between us. "But I think it might be more fun this way."

Still. Nothing. Gave.

She needed this from me—from us. I didn't care if it shattered me. She had shattered the day she'd killed Logan, she had been strong enough to free herself, strong enough to find us. Now we had to be strong enough to free her.

Havoc was staring at me now. There was something sad in her eyes, as if she had given up.

"Please. Let them go," she whispered.

"No," Angel growled. "We aren't leaving without you."

I tried again, desperate, now.

And then the truth hit me... I remembered my father. Every alpha had an omega parent—mine had been my father. He died when I was four, but I could picture him, even now. He hadn't had a golden ring to his eyes like Havoc. Even with no colour, his eyes had been as dark as Caspian's.

I wasn't a rogue.

Was it possible Logan had asked for blood from *other* alphas, too?

I heard the click in my periphery.

I glanced over in time to see Caspian lifting his gun. He pointed it straight at Eli. His hand was shaking, his jaw clenched, the muscles along his neck taut.

Eli laughed. "You can't do it, you *fucking* idiot."

Caspian's face was white as a sheet as he took a step forward.

Eli looked delighted, not even flinching as Caspian pressed the trembling gun to Eli's temple.

"Let her go." Caspian's voice was guttural.

Eli stood, dragging Havoc with him. Caspian's eyes fell to her for a moment, and when they looked back to Eli, there was blood-lust in them like I'd never seen before.

"You really want to give me a good reason to kill you, mutt?" Eli asked.

"No." Havoc's grip on his arm was white knuckled. "You *can't*." Her voice shook, but then she let out a gasp of pain. She buckled in Eli's arms, her eyes squeezed shut, a low sound coming from her chest.

There was nothing but her at that moment. I was smothered by her scent of rainfall and firewood and my mate in agony.

"She's in heat." Eli's voice was a taunt. "Is that what you came for—to get a look? Don't you think she's had enough Mandela pack cucks watching as I—?"

BANG!

Caspian

The world splintered apart as I pulled the trigger.

Blood sprayed across the bed and Elliot crumpled. I barely saw it.

417

With the bang of the gun, my aura shattered, dragging my essence into a million tiny pieces. The room, my brothers, for a moment they were gone, but—No. Not her. I forced the world back together, despite scorching agony. I realized I was crying out with pain as my knees hit the floor, gun slipping from my grip.

She was there. Blood sticky upon her face as she scrambled from limp arms.

He was dead.

She was free.

Her eyes were wide and terrified as they found mine.

But... Havoc... Was free.

It was all I needed to know before I let this agony swallow me whole.

Havoc

"Gold pack just means you are what nature intended Havoc. But the world doesn't want you to have that freedom and survive in one piece."

I could feel him. Caspian was like me. As free as he was shattered.

Heat was burning me alive.

The disorientation of Eli's death threatened—another bond, ripped away—but I ignored it as I forced Caspian's face into focus. My mate. His eyes were squeezed shut and I could hear the wounded sounds of pain in his chest.

I didn't want him to feel pain like I had. Right now, he was fragmenting, pieces of him falling away, creating wounds that would never heal.

A protective growl rose in my chest, and I was drawing myself against him. Despite my own pain, from my heat, from the dark bond, I knew *his* touch didn't hurt anymore. Instinct gripped me and I sunk my teeth into his neck.

A bond flared. Not a pack bond—not like Eli's, or Logan's, but it *was* a claim. A promise. Protection.

Our auras collided and mine reacted instantly, roots digging deep down as it also grew upward, branches reaching out and latching onto those pieces so close to falling away.

Caspian gasped, his embrace crushing me as his chest heaved.

FORTY-SEVEN

Angel

I didn't fully understand what had happened. All I knew was that Eli was dead and Caspian had done it.

Now he was slumped against the wall, bowed over Havoc as she held onto him.

Kai had rushed to their sides first, reaching for both of them, fear in his eyes, but she *growled* at him. Like, proper growled. So now he was kneeling at her side like a lost puppy.

Much too slow, the truth dawned on me.

Caspian was the rogue. Not Bane. I had no idea how. We all knew he'd never known his omega father; it went assumed his mother would have *told* him if his dad was gold pack. Still, those were questions for later.

"We..." I had to clear my throat. "We have to go."

There were two dead bodies in this room. I didn't know what the fuck we were going to do. Kai would know better than me. Cass was best, but... He looked better already. His chest was rising and falling slower than before, and his eyes were open, though they were staring blankly. Havoc was holding her forehead to his, trembling fingers pressed to his pale cheeks. There was blood smeared across her face. It touched her lips, stuck her hair to her skin, and dripped down her neck, blending into the red dress she'd worn to the ball.

Something about the sight of it sent a shiver up my spine, and for a moment, I couldn't believe there had been a time I hadn't seen who she was.

Our omega.

And she was more than we ever deserved.

She had acted first, reaching for Caspian the moment he'd crumpled—her own pain, the horror of this place she'd entered to protect Bane—inconsequential before her instinct to get to him.

"*Can* we move him?" Bane asked, seeming finally to come to himself as he glanced to me.

I cleared my throat. "We don't have a—"

"Oh good, you dealt with Kingsman." Viper's voice had me spinning around. He was standing in the door, a glass bottle in hand. He wore a black mask sewn with huge white fangs across the front. "Excellent. Two bodies are easier to explain than one. And in the same room."

"Did you do that?" I asked, waving at the other body. It was... Well, it was horrific.

"I lost my temper."

"You said you wouldn't get involved—"

Viper waved a hand. "Too late now. If dad gets wind of *that* body, he'll know it's me. Don't know anyone to get rid of it that won't rat to him anyway—so, obviously, only one thing for it."

He sounded much too cheery, but there was a sharp edge to his tone, as if he was one shade from cracking.

"And that would be?" I asked.

"*The headlines!*" Viper chuckled. "Daddy Oxford's spoiled brat drops molotovs in every room after being forced to join a pack he didn't want. And..." He shrugged. "If there were two alpha corpses that looked like an omega feud—no one would know. He'll be smothering the investigation for my *fragile* reputation."

"Where's the molotovs?" Kai finally looked back from Havoc and Cass.

Viper grinned, lifting the bottle in his hand. I realised there was a piece of fabric sticking out of it.

"I'm *long* overdue for a tantrum, anyway. But if I were you, I'd get going. Security cameras have been off for an hour, they'll reset in fifteen or so. Hoping the fireworks will be up and running by then."

Havoc

"How is he?"

That was Angel's voice.

I'd had to let go of Caspian while Bane helped him to the truck. I nearly lost it and launched myself from Kai's grip the moment he was in the back seat.

Every moment was a war with my heat, but using my own aura to hold Caspian together, it was keeping the burning, stabbing pain of my heat down somehow.

I had seen the concern of the others, though.

We were back in the apartment now. Caspian was conscious, sitting on the couch, but he looked... Well, he looked like a shell of himself.

His aura was no longer splintering. I could feel that.

"He's... better."

"Good," Angel murmured. "Here." He pressed a little pink tablet into my palm.

"What is it?"

"He needs to rest. So do you."

"But... I'm going into heat." The pain earlier, it had been so bad. I'd delayed it too many times.

"This won't suppress it like last time, but it will put you out and give your body a chance to heal. Dampen your hormones too, so there's no stress—"

"For how long?"

"You'll burn through it in a couple of hours," Angel said. "I just got off the phone with a doctor, he said you'll do more damage engaging in heat while you're still recovering."

"And Caspian?"

"I got one for him too. You can rest together. Are you able to let him go for a few minutes? Let Bane help him to his room?"

"I..." I frowned. I didn't want to. But he was better than before.

"I'll... be okay, dove." Caspian's grip on me was weak, but he squeezed my arm. "You need to get cleaned up." He lifted his hand to my cheek and found my eyes at last. "His scent... his blood is on you. You shouldn't have to..." But he closed his eyes, flinching for a moment as if something had struck him.

I knew what it was. It had been like that for me the day I killed Logan, each time I thought of the gunshot.

Caspian had broken the same way I had. "Please," he said quietly. "Let them take care of you. I'll be waiting."

I nodded, though it went against every instinct to let him go. Bane was hauling him to his feet.

Kai was at my side in a moment with a glass of water. "The drug will hit in fifteen or so."

"Can you help me?" I asked. I was still shaky, from the heat pain, from the dark bond. Kai nodded, and I sank against him. His arms came around me and then he was picking me up.

I was back in the bathroom of the nest.

It didn't feel real. I was here, with them.

Eli was gone.

Logan was gone.

Forever.

I could hear the bath running as I peeled my clothes off. The pill was doing its job and my scent was fading.

Kai held me as he sunk down into the tub, still wearing his joggers. The water was perfect and soothing. I tensed as the bite from Eli touched the water, but it didn't hurt.

"It scarred the moment he died," Kai murmured. "It's over, Havoc."

I just buried my face into the crook of his neck and held on as he washed the blood away with a soft sponge.

Then he set me on the bathroom counter and dried me off with a towel. Next, he bundled me up in a silken nightgown and did a poor job of patting my hair down, but it was enough to give me a smile.

"Where are we going?" I asked, as he carried me out of the nest.

"We need the room while you sleep."

"Okay..." But my mind was fuzzy now, the drug like cotton balls in my brain.

"You won't leave me?" I asked.

"One of us will be here. I'll leave you with Cass until I get out of these wet clothes."

I nodded.

That was good.

He settled me onto sheets that smelled like rose and cranberry. I fumbled for Caspian, knowing he was near. My bite was on his neck.

My fingers found his, and I laced them together, letting his aura tangle with mine once more.

Was he sleeping? I hoped so.

When Kai returned, he held me tight, and I finally drifted into dreams.

FORTY-EIGHT

Havoc

I woke to a dull ache in my stomach. My eyes blinked open in a dark room, and I groaned, trying to sit up.

"Hey. Hey, pet. I've got you."

Bane...

"I... I need..."

The scent of leather and applewood sent another tremor through me.

"I'm here."

"I know. I need..." Fuck. "I need..."

"What?"

Was he fucking joking right now?

Bane

She was the most beautiful woman I'd ever seen. She was also vulnerable and wounded. And asleep.

I needed to be careful about where my thoughts were racing, even as she clutched me.

Kai would have no such hang-ups. But Kai was currently rushing about the house in an absolute mania. If he didn't think I'd seen him scent marking the pillows from my room, he had another thing coming. Cheeky fucking bastard.

The olive skin of her leg seemed to glow in the low light of Caspian's room as she straddled a pillow. Her hand tugged from my grip, instead winding around my arm. She hugged me closer.

I wanted to be closer. But I also wanted to make sure she was in her right mind first. Well. Awake, and then in her right mind.

I hadn't saved her.

I'd sworn I would, and then I wasn't enough.

Her groan startled me.

"Hey. Hey, pet. I've got you."

Quit with the nicknames. You don't deserve it.

She let out another low sound that set me on edge. "I... I need..."

"I'm here."

"I know. I need..." Her breath caught. "I need..."

"What?"

Her perfume was tangling in the air, trying to wipe all rational thought from my mind. A low, angry growl rumbled in her throat. It made me panic. Should I get the others? Would Kai or Angel know?

"What is it?"

Her breathing sped up as she reached for me. I held her by the waist, tilting her head toward me. "Havoc. Tell me."

The whine in her chest sent hot lava through my veins.

"You." She was breathless. "I need you."

"I... But... The heat. You need to be sure—"

"Sure?" Her voice cracked. "I *am* sure."

"Okay." Right.

Her grip was vice-like on me. "Why are you still wearing... things?"

"I don't... What if you—?"

"*I love you*. Didn't I tell you that when I *was* in my right mind?" Her voice was choked.

"But then I—"

"*Bane!*" Her voice was almost a shriek, her perfume hit the room like a smog. Her fingers were like claws on my arms.

Shit.

Okay. I was tearing my shirt off, tugging her closer.

Her scent filled the space. There was nothing else but rainfall and firewood.

If she ever left, I'd have to take up camping in autumn, so I didn't go crazy.

I was trying to undo my belt, but she was on me, running desperate kisses up my neck, smothering her scent all over my skin. The silken dressing gown had parted, revealing—fuck.

My hindbrain took over. I think my belt snapped beneath my grip as I lifted her with my other hand, turning her on the blankets and pressing my lips to hers. I managed to get my jeans off, somehow.

Every one of her desperate moans was like little lightning bolts.

I was crushing her into pillows with kisses. Her fingers curled viciously into my hair.

"Fuck. *ME!*" She was wet with slick.

A growl rumbled in my chest.

The sound she made when I slid into her. It was low and wild. Leaning back, I watched as I pressed in. The black silk tumbled about her, revealing perfect firm breasts that momentarily stole my attention. Her tanned body clenched around me, and she just looked too small. I had to go slow, so I didn't lose it, but the way she pulled at my hair, it was as if she wanted me to.

Havoc

I saw stars.

The good kind. In my heat haze, I hadn't remembered how absolutely huge Bane was.

The low noise I made didn't sound like me. I could see his silver eyes burning, even in the dim room. He looked half wild.

He had come to save me. I remembered that moment when I'd looked up and seen him, gun in hand, all those safeguards he kept up, finally all gone for the beast beneath.

My beast.

He would have killed Eli for me.

That thought spiralled me. I wanted that man here now, under the sheets. The air around us shifted with my hormones. Bane's expression flickered, and I watched as the last of his self-control slipped away.

At. Fucking. Last.

His fingers were bruising on my waist as he held me down. I wrapped my legs around him, needing him closer as he set a ruthless pace. I'd been put out for countless heats and had two pushed back.

Bane was everything my body had been waiting for.

It didn't take long before an orgasm rolled through me, burning through the first wave of heat. I clenched around him with a gasp, and he lifted me up against him as I sent him over the edge after me.

There would be more to come, I knew that. But *this* meant something. This was the first time I'd faced my heat head on. The first time I'd had someone to do it with me. Someone I trusted.

I sagged in his arms, holding on tight, more at peace that I had ever been.

My heat still roiled, but it was like distant thunderclouds. I could have a moment here with Bane.

"We... Should have... gone to another room." Bane sounded

suddenly sheepish. I looked up and followed his gaze over to the other figure on the bed.

Caspian. This was *his* bed, after all. Roses and cranberries lingered in the air. He was out like a light, though.

I giggled, tugging Bane closer once more.

We fell into the next round with ease. My heat was like a tide of hormones, and that first orgasm hadn't even burned away the first layer.

"Knot," I begged, the fourth time I was nearing my orgasm. I could feel the swelling at the base of his shaft and my body ached for it.

He was too far gone, I could see it. He wouldn't deny me.

But he did hesitate, looking down at me with fierce eyes. "Let me bond you."

I froze, staring at him.

"I don't want another second on this earth where someone else could take you away. Take the princess bond."

Could he do that? Could he offer the princess bond again? Confused thoughts tangled with the heat haze in my mind. I'd rejected these men... which meant they couldn't interfere with my future packs. Now, I was packless, though.

And I wanted it.

Whether it was truly possible, or if the lingering offer they'd made at the ball simply still had enough potency, I didn't know. The bond opened between us the same as it had on the stage with Angel. I choked a sob through my smile and nodded. Tears leaked down my cheeks.

"Yes. A thousand times yes."

My back arched as his knot pressed into me and I let out a moan as I stretched around him. It took a moment for my body to adjust. Goosebumps lit across my skin as he settled in, all of my senses turned up to ten.

I took a moment, my chest heaving. "Do... you want to bite me?" I asked, at last.

"Not until you're ready."

I swallowed. Eli's bite, Logan's bite. They were both scars on my neck. Faded. Useless. Dead.

This would be different.

I nodded.

"Where?" he asked.

Since I'd woken, the world had been a blur of light and stars and sensation, but very few coherent thoughts. Right now, the weight of what he was offering crashed into me. My eyes brimmed with tears as I reached up, pressing my fingers to where Logan's bite had been. "Get..." I had to take a breath. "Get rid of it."

It would be embarrassing to cry right now. In the middle of sex. *Heat* sex—no less.

But Bane was drawing me up against him until I was pressed against his chest, looking up into his silver eyes. Every slight shift of him inside me was bliss. He pressed a kiss to my forehead and then shifted down my cheek to my neck. I held onto him tighter as his teeth grazed where Logan's old scar was.

He was enough.

He had seen me when no one else had. He was the only one who could rid me of that scar.

Bane held me tight against him as his teeth broke the tainted skin of my neck. The bond between us lit up.

At the same time, I felt something shatter. A dark, crusted shell of hatred and cruelty I'd been holding onto, it crumbled to dust under Bane's bite.

"It's okay to cry, Havoc," he murmured and then kissed me.

It wasn't grief I was feeling as tears spilled from my eyes, though.

I lifted myself to face him and took his cheeks between my hands. This was something I'd never had. Not truly.

This was love.

FORTY-NINE

Kai

Everything had to be perfect. Absolutely completely fucking perfect. I had no idea what the hell this was going to look like once Havoc woke up.

Our first heat. It felt a bit like Christmas. Actually, while I did love Christmas with our pack, it never made me nervous. *Sex* had never had me nervous either.

Some packs without omegas had rut problems, but our pack never had. Me and Angel had each other. Bane was... Well, I wasn't sure what Bane did to keep himself sane. Logan had engaged with omegas in clubs like Gavin's. Cass visited local bars if he wanted to hook up with a beta—before Havoc, of course. He said it was to keep it simple, but I'd always thought it was something else.

Sex between alphas and omegas was... intense, and that wasn't always what we needed. Omegas had a way of making everything more intimate. I don't think Cass wanted to risk forming any sort of bond—even be it chemical, with an omega until we found a mate. There was always the risk of bites, too, during heat. It was rare for bonds like that to form unplanned, but it was always a risk when perfume was involved.

"Sit down. There's not a single piece of stuffed fabric left in this whole house." Angel was lounging on the couch as I straightened one of the towers of pillows around the bed. Her mighty nest. Screw Angel. It had to be perfect.

The door banged open, and I spun.

Holy crap. Rainfall and firewood crashed into the room and my hindbrain wiped everything else away.

Havoc was in Bane's arms, legs tangled around his waist. He leaned against the door for a moment as she drew him into a kiss. "Why did we stop?" she whined, nipping his ear.

"I need backup."

She swivelled in his arms, as if she hadn't really been paying attention. I had already reached the two of them. Her blown pupils found me, and she wet her lips. I let out a low growl and reached for her. She scrambled from Bane's arms and fell into mine, that black silken dressing gown loose.

Bane's hormones were all over her.

"Wait. You already... How long? You didn't call us."

"No time." Bane sounded smug. "Was there, pet?"

I didn't get a chance to reply because Havoc was trying to climb me like a tree, clearly not at all interested in our conversation. Their voices vanished as Havoc's fingers wove into my hair, her eyes simmering with irritation.

I had her over my shoulder with a yelp and carried her to the huge pack bed. I dropped her down onto it and she finally paused, her eyes finding my last few hours of labour. The bed was surrounded by every blanket, couch cushion, and dressing gown in the house.

It was a nest like no other, and there was a beam on her face as she examined it.

She turned and burrowed in, a small pile collapsing on top of her. I heard a squeal of delight, and then out floated a demand so bratty it made me proud.

"I need dick."

Angel fucking beat me there, diving after her and untangling her from the blankets and pillows as he drew her against him. He looked ready to devour her whole, kissing her neck and breasts and stomach.

I sunk down onto the bed next to them, unsure if I'd ever been so hard. It was mesmerising, watching Angel hold her like that.

I don't know how or when his clothes came off, but suddenly she was pinned beneath him and he was tugging her legs apart.

I tilted my head, hand gripping my own shaft as I watched him slide into her, heat building in my veins, absolutely captivated. She let out a low moan, fingers biting blankets, her back arching. Angel was feral, her wrists between his grip as he began to pound into her. Her legs tangled about his waist, drawing him closer as they tumbled off a cliff together.

And that was when I saw it.

In the very last moment, as she shattered beneath him and he drew her against his chest, he looked at me.

My breath caught.

For the first time in my life, I saw Angel completely. The warm brown of his skin, the way his freckles were slightly richer and brighter, the stunning colour of his eyes flecked with different shades of green.

A growl rose in my throat, something wild and delighted and then I'd moved, fingers winding through her hair. She was the missing piece.

I dragged her into a kiss, and when I released her, there was a breathless smile on her lips.

Havoc

This was what heat should be like. My mind was all over the place. I hadn't felt pain since the moment I'd fallen into Bane's arms—and onto his dick. My brain was filthy right now.

"Where's Bane?" I asked. Kai had just broken away from kissing Angel, and his eyes were hungry as they slid up my body.

My nest was everything, the space filled with every one of their scents. All of my mates.

"Catching his breath and getting food," Angel chuckled.

"But I want—" My whine cut off as Angel took my chin in his hand, grip firm.

"We're going to take good care of you until he's back."

I nodded, unable to take my eyes from him, more wetness pooling between my thighs. I'd thought, so many rounds in, some of this buzz in my brain would be settling, but it wasn't. It was getting worse. Hormones were slicking off me in droves and I watched them start to lose themselves to it, too.

I needed them.

My touch slid to Kai's cheek. "I want you both." Their knots, too. I'd taken Bane's, and it had been amazing. Warmth slid through my veins at the thought.

Angel hadn't let go of my chin. "Let me see you ride him real good, and maybe."

Next thing Kai moved beneath me, shifting my body until my knees were on either side of his shoulders. Angel kept my chin steady. I had to grip his wrists to keep my balance as Kai's grip sunk into my hips.

What was he—? But then Kai dragged my centre down onto his mouth.

I let out a low sound deep in my chest as his tongue piercing found my clit, and my fingers shifted, instead biting into Angel's chest. Angel didn't let me go, drinking in every inch of my face as I panted with soaring pleasure.

Kai's finger entered me, and I saw stars. My whole body buckled under the sensation, but Angel still held me up as I panted. Kai added a finger and began pumping in and out, each stroke getting a moan from me as another climax built.

"Eyes on me, princess, I want to see the moment you shatter."

Kai's grip clamped down, drawing me against him with more force as he added a third finger. I gasped, my climax slamming into me as I drenched Kai with my juices. Angel leaned forward, pressing his lips to mine, driving his tongue into my mouth as Kai's tongue sent me into wave after wave of my orgasm.

I sagged against Angel as Kai ducked from under me. I turned, my head spinning.

Kai leaned against one of the walls of the nests, already tugging off his clothes. At the sight of his cock, I tried to reach for him, but Angel snagged me around the waist. "I want a view of everything."

I was heady by this point. Kai was hard, and right now he was holding the base of his shaft, eyes fixed on me. I moaned with need, trying to process what Angel had said. His hands were slipping along my shoulder, tugging down the dressing gown. Right. Clothes.

I didn't want anything between me and them.

Finally, I was crawling to Kai, slinking over his tattooed chest, hands running up the rough skin of his scars as I mounted him.

Kai was staring up at me with something strange in his gaze. "I... love you."

The words caught me off guard. For a flash, there were so many giant feelings warring in my heart. I realised, for the first time, that right now I felt... confident.

I was more vulnerable than I'd ever been around them, and they still wanted me. Logan had been wrong about everything. They wanted me just as much as I wanted them.

"I love you too, Kai," I whispered. That perfect, pointed-canine smile spread on his face, and then I felt Angel's hands on my waist. "And Angel." I turned to look up into forest green eyes. My knights.

The ones that had come.

"And Bane and Caspian. I love all of you." My heart felt like it was bursting with that truth.

Angel's lips pressed to my neck. "I've been falling in love with you for a while now," Angel murmured. "You turned us upside-down since the moment you arrived. You believed in us, even when we didn't deserve it. You stayed with Kai when I was gone, you gave up everything to protect Bane. You held Caspian together and you healed my aura. You're our missing piece, Havoc, and I want to be enough to deserve you."

"Your aura?" I whispered.

His aura burst into the room, stronger than I'd felt. It was just as strong as Kai's, only with it came a wave of sweet cinnamon. "It was back the moment Bane bit you. You're pack, Havoc."

Every scar Logan had left with me was swept away like dust in a windstorm. And it wasn't just my hormones. It was the fervour in their eyes they couldn't hide. Their passion.

A possessive little growl escaped my throat. I needed them both.

Right now.

Angel's touch was running up my chest, squeezing my breasts as he held me upright. I was soaked, slick dripping down my thighs as I slipped over Kai. He was long enough that a whine broke from my chest as he entered. Kai's lips parted as we connected for the first time, but Angel held me tight, slowing my pace so I couldn't sink down on him completely.

Another growl slipped from me as he held me just above Kai's swelling knot. I wanted to feel it before it was too big to ride without locking me in.

Angel laughed, nipping my ears, and then he drew back. I

caught myself on Kai's chest, moaning with pleasure as I took him all in.

"Fuck." Kai drew me up so he could drive his tongue into my mouth as I clenched over him. "Taste yourself on me, sunset," he growled. His grip found my waist, and he rocked into me. I moaned, needing more. I kissed him deeper, starting a steady rhythm, lightning in my veins with every stroke.

That pleasure built once more, and I wondered if it would ever be sated. My heat was a rising wave, and nothing seemed to be enough to burn it away. I quickened my pace, desperate moans rising in my chest as I rode him. His knot had swelled completely now, and I wanted it so badly, but I knew this would stop the moment I did.

He was so beautiful, mismatched pupils wide, and his messy white hair askew and damp with my juices. He gazed at me hungrily, his hand squeezing my breast as he groaned at the way I felt over him. Then I felt Angel's touch again at my back. I arched, Angel's scent of cinnamon tangling again with Kai's maple.

"Do you want us both?" Angel's growl vibrated in my ear. I moaned, only able to nod. I felt his touch brush along my thighs that were wet with slick. I bowed over Kai, nails digging in as Angel's finger trailed upward. Kai sat up, holding me against him as I sunk onto him but for his swollen knot.

"Relax, princess." Angel's other hand held my waist, and his touch was soothing as he gently pressed a finger against my other entrance. I took a breath as he pushed in, and Kai's finger massaged that spot on my neck that had me melting. I loosed a breath as Angel worked in and out. Another kind of pleasure built, and I shifted, suddenly wanting more.

Angel's breath was against my ear as he drew me back against his chest. I was trapped between maple and cinnamon. "You like that, princess?"

"Yes," I whispered, and it was a desperate plea.

Angel added a finger, but I shook my head. I needed more. My heat wracked body was ready for it. Ready for both of them.

"Patience." I could hear the humour in Angel's voice. He held his fingers within me as Kai leaned back against the pillows. I groaned as Kai lifted his hips and thrust into me. Angel's grip closed again on my chin, trapping me against his chest as Kai began to fuck me with long, slow strokes.

I moaned, my climax building again.

Kai growled, and I felt the moment he came, hot seed filling me. I seized with my own orgasm, sinking over him, letting out a whine at the stretch as I took his knot. My body clenched and his fingers became bruising on my thighs as he shuddered.

I was panting, my skin sticky with sweat.

He shifted, and I gasped. Every slight adjustment of his knot was like a shot of static in my veins, another flicker of the orgasm that wasn't over. He grinned, adjusting again, pressing deeper into me. I buckled, barely holding myself up on his chest, seeing stars once more.

But then Angel's fingers slipped from me, his other hand pinning me down by my hip. I tried to shift again, to feel some of that bliss, but Angel didn't let me move. Kai's grip joined him, and I glared.

"Only one way you get to ride his knot, little omega," Angel growled in my ear.

Kai looked delighted as he watched me. Then I felt Angel against my back entrance.

"Eyes on him," Angel murmured.

My eyelids fluttered the first moment Angel pressed in, my nails digging into Kai's chest. The burning sensation changed quickly to something else as he shifted deeper. He was wet with my slick. I let out a guttural sound as he drew out.

"Doing alright, sunset?" Kai asked.

I nodded. I needed more.

With every one of Angel's thrusts, Kai's knot shifted inside me, and another shot of lightning hit my veins. I whined with a crescendo of pleasure like I'd never felt before until I was nothing but trembling liquid between them.

FIFTY

Angel

Stepping back into the nest was like walking into a wall of hormones and her earthy omega scent. I inhaled a storm of rainfall and campfire, enough that it was almost possible to glean traces of a fall breeze with damp leaves and petrichor in the air.

I didn't know if it was light or dark outside. I think we were at the twenty-four-hour mark and Havoc was finally worn out. The wildest part was over.

She was far from out of heat, but it was safe for us to take it slower now. We'd burned through the most vicious of her hormones which would leave her writhing in agony.

Kai was passed out on the bed, his arm draped over the side—fair play, since he'd done the longest of the relay stretches. I'd never thought I'd see Kai out-fucked.

Havoc was curled up in Bane's arms on the couch in an oversized nightgown—we'd lost the silk black one somewhere in the nest. She plucked this one from the jumbles of blankets and pillows. I noted it smelled like roses and cranberries.

She was missing Caspian.

There had been a few moments—especially in the last hour

right before the first wave crested, when she'd barely been present. She'd begged for him.

"Is he alright?" she asked as I sat down on the other side, setting the tray of food down.

"Sleeping still. Not restless at all." Caspian looked well; he'd wake up soon.

Actually, he *had* to.

I was starting to realise why heat helpers were preferable in groups of four or more. Every muscle in my body was sore, despite using the huge bathtub for part of it. I wouldn't complain —every time I was near her it was like I was riding a high. Everything about this experience was thrilling.

The problem was, no matter how brilliant it felt, my body had limitations—even with my full aura back. Limitations Havoc didn't seem to be feeling at all.

"Is it okay to leave him alone?" she asked. She sounded worried.

"I don't think being in a room full of hormones will give him a restful sleep. He's out of the woods. When he wakes, he can join us." What had happened to Caspian was traumatic, but it wouldn't kill him, and Havoc seemed to have diffused the worst of it.

I tugged her from Bane's arms so he could get at his food. He looked dazed. Pleased, but dazed.

There was a buzz in my veins as she settled in beside me, something child-like and giddy. My life had—for a long time— been responsibility after responsibility, and putting the others first. I had to, so I didn't have to face the looming shadows, threatening to steal everything away.

But Havoc was safe, and my aura was back. For a moment, it burst across the room again before I could catch it. Heat crept up my neck as Bane shot me a sideways glance, fighting a smile. Havoc loosed the slightest purr, hugging me closer. I didn't know if there was enough room in my chest for the gratitude I was feeling right now. It had been a looming pain for so long, one I'd shoved away over and over for the sake of the others. And now, because of her, that weight was gone.

"The bite doing okay?" I asked as Bane grabbed his sandwich. It was his bite on her neck. He'd already checked it a dozen times. Bane nodded, and Havoc had a smile on her lips.

Good. Even with just Bane's bite, she was ours. She was safe.

She stood and slid onto my lap, looking up at me with those golden doe eyes. It didn't matter how tired I was, every brush on her skin on mine was welcome.

"Tell me if there's anything else you need, princess."

She shook her head. "Everything is... perfect."

Those words hung in the air, something about the way she'd said them sent a chill down my spine. And for a moment I saw a flicker of fear cross her face.

It might have been more than just her words; Bane's bond on her neck tied her to us, made her pack. Perhaps I'd felt that fear slip through.

How close...

How close had we come to losing her? How close—and then this heat would have been so very different?

I shut my eyes.

The alpha in me wasn't great at handling those sorts of possibilities. I couldn't imagine what that thought must be like for her, how she could trust when we'd been so close to failing her.

"You'll... bite in too?" she asked.

I tucked a tangle of chestnut hair behind her ear. "Of course we will."

She nodded, sliding back to my side, resting her head against me. I held her close as I clung to that promise, able to use it to anchor me. With that bond the world would know she was ours.

We could have done it weeks ago—even the very day we'd met

her, but we'd been blind. If we had, she would have been safe. I didn't blame Bane for not waiting.

She was... Home. That was the only way to describe how it felt. She was our omega. Before, we had been broken. With her, we would have a chance to heal.

"We'll be there for you, always," I murmured, but when I looked down, she was asleep.

Caspian

I woke alone and disoriented.

The room was dark, and it was night out on the deck. I sat blearily, a dark shadow over my mind as I tried to remember what was going on.

Something was wrong.

I'd... *Shit.*

Havoc.

I couldn't tell what was real and what was nightmare. I ripped my blankets off and tore out into the hallway. It was silent as I crossed it to her room.

I ripped the door open and stepped into a stone wall of rainfall and firewood and sex.

Sex with *Havoc.*

Heat.

This was heat, and my brain was melting away at the thought of it. I was crossing toward her when I caught sight of her, and it was enough to draw me up.

She was in her bed, which was coned in by walls of pillows, blankets and cushions. My brothers were there.

She was trapped between Angel and Bane, her eyes closed peacefully as she slept. Her hair was a mess, tangles drifting passed her long eyelashes. Her cheeks were rosy, her perfect lips parted just slightly as her chest rose and fell gently. Her hand draped over Angel's stomach where her fingers were outstretched toward Kai. He was slumped at the foot of her bed, face on his arm, drool pooling on the sheet below him.

My pounding heart settled. It was enough to elbow back my hindbrain, which was good because I realised I smelled like blood and sweat.

She was sleeping.

She was safe.

I owed her at least a shower—even if I made it quick.

In the scorching water however, I had time to process what had happened. My mind flashed to the gun I'd held. To Eli. To the moment my aura had splintered.

I let out a groan and my knees hit the shower floor, my eyes squeezed tight shut as I clutched my head.

Eventually, I forced myself back to my feet. My mind raced. It had been white hot agony after that moment. All the way until...

I blinked.

Havoc... I stepped quickly from the shower and stared at my reflection, tilting my head up. Along the black tattoos on my neck I saw the scabbed wound.

I traced it with my fingers, even that touch soothing my soul. My aura, which felt jumpy and erratic—as if it might just burst free at any moment, calmed.

She'd bitten me. Havoc had protected me.

When I got back to the nest, my jaw was still clenched with that realisation, my eyes burning.

It was the hormones in the air—obviously. But when I got to the bed, I hauled Angel back a few feet across the massive bed and slipped in beside her. Whatever. He'd had a turn—and Bane was way too big to move.

I drew her close to my chest, inhaling her perfume like it was a drug. A smile quirked on my lips as I heard the low rumble of a purr in her chest. I didn't even mind when Angel shuffled back, sleepily winding his arms around my stomach as if I was her.

Havoc

I woke to the scent of cranberries, roses and leather. Against my back was the low vibration of an alpha's purr. I blinked to see Bane's beautiful, sleeping face before me. Dark stubble shadowed his jaw, adding to the devastating rugged look he had going on.

But... I turned, wondering if I was conjuring up that scent from my dreams.

Caspian was there, beetle black eyes holding mine.

"Morning, dove," he murmured. I fumbled for his face, drawing myself up, ignoring, for a moment the heat that had built in my body while I slept.

"You're okay?" I asked.

"You're here, Havoc. I'm perfect," he murmured, pressing a kiss to my lips. "You seem much too with it for heat," he said as he drew away.

"First wave passed."

"How long was I out?"

"I don't know, a day, maybe?" I said.

His face fell, but I wasn't having any of that. Neither was the rising tide of warmth in my stomach. "You're here now."

He dragged me closer, pupils dilating as my arousal at seeing him seeped into the air.

"Yes—but wait."

"What?" His brows furrowed with concern.

There was something I needed to tell him. I couldn't tell all the others and not him. Not when it had been him... "You... came for me." He hadn't just come. He'd shattered for me. For my freedom.

"Of course I came—"

"No. In the truck, the night I blew up Gavin's. I said you wouldn't have." My voice was low so I didn't wake the others.

He stilled.

"I was wrong," I whispered.

"No. You had every right not to trust me, Havoc. It was on me to fix that."

"You did..." I swallowed. He *had* fixed it. "I love you," I breathed.

He stared at me, dark brows knotting, a shadow crossing his face for a moment as if he couldn't understand what he'd heard. His nose scrunched up and his eyes darted away from me. "I need you to know the full truth before you say that." His voice was thick.

"What do you mean?"

"The day I dealt with Gavin, I got security footage from the building."

My blood chilled.

"I should have told you." He went on. "I'm sorry. I... saw a few of them—before, when I was still... angry." He swallowed. "Wish I hadn't. The rest were handled by Angel's legal team."

My heart was pounding in my chest. "I don't... understand."

"You protected me—Halley, *from* him. Before you ever knew me, you believed in me." He was shaking. "And then you met me, and I... hated you for *him*, when he didn't deserve it."

I stared at him, my heart in my throat as I processed it all.

"I don't know if I deserve to say how much I love you, Havoc. You're more than I ever dreamed of, and I was so fucked up I couldn't see it. I don't know what I can ever do to make up for that."

"You already did."

Caspian had given up everything. He'd shattered in body,

mind, aura and soul. More than that, he had given up Logan. For me or for himself, it didn't matter.

I knew that pain. The day I'd killed Logan, *that* part—letting go of what I wished he was—had broken me as much as pulling the trigger. When Logan told me he wanted me at last, I could have said yes. But I'd looked into his eyes and seen a monster.

Saying no to him—it had been agony because it had meant I'd given a monster *everything*. I had chased him and begged him and handed over my dignity a thousand times over.

Logan banked on pride and fear, and the tangles of knots we tied for ourselves.

There had been a part of me, that day, that wanted to give him what he asked for, because then I would never have to face the truth.

The truth of what he was. But more than that, the truth of what he'd turned me into.

And Caspian had been beneath Logan for years.

"I love you," I said again. "And you're stronger than he ever imagined."

Caspian stared at me with a clenched jaw, as if he didn't know what to make of me. So I kissed him, and thankfully, he found himself enough to kiss me back. I drew away, smiling.

"Okay, but... You did kind of hint at it, so... I still want to hear you say it."

"The day you put a bullet in his brain," Caspian murmured. "You saved us all."

I snorted and finally a slight smile quirked on his lips. "Is that *love* in Caspian language?"

"I do love you, Havoc. And I've been waiting for you for so, so long."

A broad smile spread across my face, but it fell away at a spike of heat. My eyes were wide as my nails dug into Caspian's flesh, my hormones hitting the air again.

Caspian grinned, canines flashing. Then he was above me, pulling me carefully from Bane's arms until he was caging me in. "Quiet now, I want our little omega all to myself."

Bane

I woke to a sharp pain. My eyes found her nails on my arm first, biting down. I frowned before I oriented myself.

Heat.

Shit, had she had a spike without waking us?

I sat up, reaching for her, and then drew up at what I saw, my cock instantly rock solid.

Holy fuck.

Caspian was pinning Havoc to the bed, his hand pressed over her mouth as he fucked her. Her olive skin was bare, glowing in the dim light of the room. Her legs were tangled around his waist, her breasts rising and falling from her heaving breaths.

"You woke him." Caspian's voice was a low growl.

Havoc moaned as he drew out of her halfway and stopped. It was impossible not to notice how good that looked, her tight little body half impaled on his cock. She tried to shake her head, her eyes darting between me and Cass.

He lifted his hand from her mouth.

"Not on purpose," she hissed.

"Too fucking bad." He drew out of her completely.

For a moment, she lay there, chest heaving as she glared at him, then she slid her gaze to me. I saw her breathing hitch just slightly as that gold-ringed gaze dropped down to the tent in my loose pyjama bottoms. Then she was moving for me, fire in her eyes as I reached for her.

"I don't think so." Cass was dragging her away, flipping her on her front. He grabbed her hair and pressed her face first into the blankets. Then, he brutally drove into her from behind.

My jaw dropped as lava seeped through my core.

The sound she made was purely animalistic. There was no way it hadn't woken the others.

Next thing, Cass was dragging her against his chest, his hand around her neck. "Do you want him too?"

She nodded desperately.

"Ask nicely." Caspian drew back before pressing into her again. She let out a little whimper, her fingers buried into the muscles on his arm.

"Fuck." That groan was Angel's. I glanced over to see him staring at Havoc, eyes full of desire. Next thing, Kai was clambering over, his eyes mischievous as he took in the scene.

"Please," she whined. "I want you all."

Havoc

"Come here, dove," Caspian guided me down onto his cock.

I was dripping with slick already as I straddled him in the nest. He drove into me a few times, leaving me panting before I felt Bane's grip on my chin.

I looked up at him as Caspian continued to thrust. I could feel Kai at my back, and then Angel was at my side, his hands winding up my stomach until he reached my breasts.

Caspian drove upward, just as Angel twisted my nipples. I moaned. Then Bane's huge length was right there, and I was reaching for it.

"I want to see you gagging like last time," Caspian murmured.

A thrill lit in my chest at those words, and I took Bane's tip in my mouth. I could feel my wetness pooling around Cass as he fucked me, heat streaking through my body. I tried to focus on

Bane, my eyes searching up his massive muscular chest until I was swallowed by his silver gaze. It was burning with lust as I pressed my lips further over his length.

But it wasn't enough, not with them all here. My whole body was still shaking with need.

I felt Kai behind me and something between a growl and a purr rose in my chest. He used my own slick as lube before he pressed into me slowly.

I was heady with the rush of it.

Caspian and Kai found a rhythm, and Bane was pressing himself deeper into my throat. Angel's lips were at my neck. "Look at you, princess," he breathed in my ear. My fingers fumbled for him, and he directed my hand to his face so I could feel him drawing right up to my chest. He took my nipple between his teeth and bit down. My pleasure spiked, goosebumps erupting across my skin.

Kai's grip on my waist tightened and Caspian slammed into me. My first orgasm hit as I felt Angel's teeth break the skin on my breast, marking me. His bond flared to life as ecstasy hit.

My eyes rolled back, Bane swimming in my vision for a second. The feeling of connection swallowed me, and it was only these men holding me up as my muscles gave out. They weren't done, and I didn't want them to stop. Angel drew away.

I heard Caspian's grunts, and I knew he was close, just as Bane tilted his head back, still thrusting into the back of my throat.

I stretched over Caspian's knot as he came, and a second wave of an orgasm hit. Bane slammed his cock forward, unloading hot seed down my throat.

When Bane drew away, I caught myself on Caspian's chest. Sweat beaded his forehead as he gazed at me with those intense, beetle black eyes. I rocked back on his knot, and it was ecstasy. Caspian shuddered.

Behind me, Kai let out a low groan. He dragged me against him, but he wasn't finished. I found the strength to turn to him.

He was stunning, shaggy white hair bright in the dim room, that crimson eye lighting up.

Angel was behind him. "Don't you dare stop fucking her while you take me."

Kai bit his lip, a low growl rolling from his chest as he shifted forward, his knot pressed against me.

Angel's fingers closed in my hair, dragging me against Kai, arching my neck back. Caspian twisted my nipples roughly, but my whine was cut off by Bane pressing his tongue past my lips. Kai drove forward, grip biting down on my arms and dragging them back, stretching me further over his every thrust as he rocked me over Caspian's knot. I trembled, whimpers breaking from me with every movement.

I was completely overwhelmed, forced into an arch as I took them, the cacophony of sensation rising to meet my heat like a cresting wave.

I was dizzy with pleasure, each movement sending me over the edge again and again. I was gasping and trembling by the time Kai came, unsure of how many times I'd shattered.

"Bite me." It was all I could manage. I took Caspian's hand and placed it on my neck where I wanted his bite. Over Eli's, just like Bane had covered Logans.

Caspian drew up in an instant, pressing his teeth to my neck just as Kai drew my hair out of the way and did the same. I gasped as the bonds flared to life, the pain of the bites tangling with the orgasm I was still riding.

As I sagged between them, catching my breath, a contented hum rose in my chest.

All of my mates had marked me. With them, I was safe, I trusted that now. And they loved me just as much as I loved them.

FIFTY-ONE

Angel

Havoc's heat finally broke on the fifth day.

That was yesterday, and right now we were recovering.

Our life was in a fun state of chaos. There had been a fall out when Havoc had *accidentally* let slip that Kai's nests—while absolutely adored—were not up to scratch. Which... Well *obviously*. Kai was an alpha—she was the omega.

Consequently, she'd spent the next hour hiding beneath piles of said nest, while Bane tried to coax her out with Sweetcrisp bars, and Kai sulked on the couch, swearing he was fine. But he had turned on the Grand Prix to full blast.

So now Caspian was leading the charge—with perhaps a little too much glee—in tearing down Logan's room to design the perfect nest for Havoc's tastes. I couldn't wait to see what *that* looked like.

And while they all did that, I waited for an email.

A *very* important email.

I was mindlessly scrolling through Hound's Weekly to catch up on the scandal, and make sure all of Viper's promises about keeping us out of the news had been met.

The headlines I read as I scrolled were about as defamatory as one might imagine they'd be. *'Daughter of Gold Pack Terrorist Sparks 300 Alpha Brawl', 'Mandela Killer Centre of Riot at Winter Ball',* or *'Gold Pack Omega: Havoc Saint, Living up to Her Name.'*

I rolled my eyes and set my phone down. The TV in the corner was playing the news on a low buzz, and I glanced up to it as I heard Havoc's name.

I recognised celebrity omega, Romeo Knight. Right now, he was speaking to the cameras. "She's a force to be reckoned with. We're used to leaving a trail of broken hearts in our wake, but she's got broken hearts *and* broken skulls on her resume—" He cut off with a grin as the alpha on his flank nudged him. "Mark me. Havoc Saint has only just begun. We have a new diva on our hands. If she's watching this—*Saint,* darling, my PR team is open to your call anytime."

I snorted. What would Romeo Knight think if he found out Havoc Saint didn't even have a phone? Well. I'd bought her one, but she'd left it in my room untouched.

Still anxious about the email that was overdue, I switched to the Beta-Watch channel. That was where the true damage would be seen. Sure enough, it was exactly as expected. *"... Half a million in damages, once more sending insurance costs for alpha-omega events skyrocketing... lucky no regular citi—betas citizens were harmed... Begs the question on everyone's mind: is the danger pay for events with this level of proximity enough?"*

Channels like this were always vying for ways to attack alphas and omegas, but I was looking for something in particular. One notoriously feisty reporter, Tanya Rice, was mid rant. *"... Just as bad as Ruin Winters—only, guess Saint had the guts to actually choose gold pack..."* I watched for a little longer, heart settling as I saw nothing I was on the lookout for, until... *"We all saw Kingsman whisking her away. Then the Oxford mansion burns down and suddenly, she's back in the Mandela Pack's arms? No one else thinks that's suspicious?"*

I turned the remote in my hands absently. If Pablo O'Reily's conspiracies were the worst of the attention Viper's mansion fire garnered, we were in good shape.

Havoc had spoken to the police briefly this morning, flanked by a dozen of my firm's best lawyers. Viper had already called to tell me the story he was spinning, and Havoc's account was brief.

There was a fire. She had run. Her recently heartbroken pack was nearby, and she'd taken them back. That was where we needed it to settle.

Everyone would *know*, and no one would be able to prove it. Still... all the more reason to keep Havoc away from the press. She didn't need any of it.

The door to the office opened, and I glanced back to see Bane. He took a seat next to me.

"We need to chat pack lead."

"Right." I had known that was coming.

"We all think it should be you." Bane said it like it was so obvious.

"Actually, I was wondering, after everything..." I said. "If you changed your mind?"

Bane's eyebrows rose. "No."

"Years..." I said. "And we never realised what you were going through. How can I—?"

"Angel." Bane shifted in his chair, eyes narrowed. "I hid from you. No better than lying, and after what I did—"

"It wasn't your fault."

I knew he'd want to talk about this more. The secret he'd held all of these years—that he was responsible for my parents' deaths... I think it haunted him more than me.

I clenched my jaw. I'd given this enough thought.

Bane had been taken in by the Mandela pack and raised like

Logan's brother. But he'd never had a home, not really. He was always treated as... other. It was one of those uncomfortable truths that got swept under the rug. I'd never felt it was my place to say anything, even after he had become my pack brother.

That part was on me. Bane's place among us, it had been shaped by Logan from the start.

"You told me you're alright, but it's not really good enough," Bane said.

"I'm even more alright than I was before. You didn't go rogue. It was just another thing that Logan fucked up."

"It's not that simple," he growled.

"At the end of the day, I trust you Bane. It *is* that simple."

It was at that moment, that my laptop pinged a notification, and an email popped up. I scrambled for it, clicking it open, my eyes scanning the text before me.

"What?" Bane asked, as a broad grin spread on my face.

I'd... Well, it was exactly what I'd hoped for, but still, seeing it confirmed... A delighted laugh slipped from my lips as Bane took the laptop, reading what I just had.

"No fucking way... You did this?" Bane asked.

Bane leaned back, eyes still fixed on me. "That. Absolute. Fool."

Havoc

"What the omega wants, the omega gets." Kai clutched me to his chest defensively. "If she wants an entire wall made up of candy bars, then who are we to say—?"

He cut off as Caspian's pen nailed him in the forehead.

"I was joking," I snorted, nudging Kai. Though, on the other hand... "But like... Would it be possible—theoretically, I mean?"

"I think Peter might just fire *me* at this point," Caspian

groaned. Peter, I knew, was the very enthusiastic interior designer who had been on and off on the phone with Caspian all morning, trying to accommodate ridiculous requests.

"How much is this costing?" I asked.

"Don't worry about it," Caspian straightened, waving me away just as the door to my room burst open.

Angel was there, a dazed looking Bane at his back.

"Havoc!" Angel was crossing the room toward me, something wild in his eyes.

"What?" I straightened in Kai's lap, worried for a moment. "Is something wrong?"

"The hell is going on?" Caspian straightened, looking concerned, but Angel almost bowled us over as he took the couch on our side.

"Okay..." He straightened, eyes still glistening, a beam on his face. "It's good news. I just—"

"Back it up a little," Bane chuckled, taking an armchair. "Explain from the beginning."

"There are a few things I need to catch you up on. I would have told you before, but I wanted to be sure that everything would go through."

"All of *what* would go through?"

"What you did to Logan has been ruled self-defence."

"What?"

"Your record is clear. There were..." He glanced to Caspian briefly. "Tapes from Gavin's that were reviewed by a legal team."

I nodded. I knew that already, though Angel wasn't aware of that. "And they... said it wasn't my fault?" I asked, my heart in my throat.

"Yes. Well, I didn't push it any further. The court dropped charges the moment Logan's dad got wind of what might be on the tapes. I didn't want you involved if it wasn't necessary."

"Further than what?" I asked.

Angel cleared his throat. "You know how when we went out that day to organise all your stuff, passport and everything, I got them to examine the bite from Logan?"

I nodded, not at all sure where this was going.

"Right. That's what I'm really here about. They identified it as a princess bond from him. It's all documented. I've been dealing with his dad's legal team. There was a bit of a fight over his will. Most of his stuff should have defaulted to us, but his will handed a load of stuff back to his dad's pack, instead."

"Okay?" I was still confused.

"He made his will after forming a pack, so it holds. But it was before he bit you."

"Fuck... Wait...?" Cass leaned back in his seat, his eyes wide.

Kai tensed behind me. "What does it mean?"

"Legally, princess bonds hold the same weight as marriage."

I wasn't keeping up. "But he never—?"

"What happened *after* he bit you isn't their business. The bite is proof. He gave it."

"No way..." Kai sounded dumbstruck. "So she—"

"Got *everything*," Angel said. "The two vacation homes, the boat down at Stanford harbour, Havoc." Angel fumbled with his phone for a moment, "*This* is your bank account."

He showed me a number on the screen I couldn't compute. I was pretty quick at math, but Jeremy's burgers weren't an efficient unit of measurement for the number of zeros staring back at me.

"I don't... understand..." I whispered. "That's... mine?"

"You're rich, princess."

"With Logan's money?" I asked through shock. "But what... am I supposed to do with it all?"

Kai squeezed me tight. "If you could have anything in the world, sunset, what would it be?"

Angel

"I have to admit, I didn't see this coming." Cass's voice was strained. He stood at my side in a busy parking lot. I was still scrambling to pick my jaw off the floor.

She'd only told Kai what she wanted, and he'd directed Caspian to the parking lot of a supermarket.

"Anything you want, from the *whole* shop. It's on me!" she'd screeched before bolting toward the shopping carts.

"She knows she could probably buy the entire chain, right?" Caspian asked.

Right now, Havoc was violently manhandling a shopping cart before Bane reached her and inserted a coin.

"I'm going to go with... no." I blew out a breath, catching Caspian's eyes with a grin. "We should probably go after her, before she clears the store of anything sweet."

Kai was helping Havoc into the cart, then he ripped it from Bane's grip. A middle-aged employee at the door raised a hand as if to stop them, but then withdrew with an eye roll—perhaps sensing the ridiculous auras in the air.

Kai charged the doors, while Havoc gripped the front of the shopping cart like a kid on her first roller coaster, shrieking with delight.

"*I'll* provide the candy bars for the wall myself, thank you very much!"

EPILOGUE

Angel

The unknown number lit on my phone screen, and there was only one person it could be. I answered instantly.

"Hey Angel."

"Viper?"

He didn't sound like he had in the mansion. His voice was a low croak, something strained in it.

Everyone in the living room paused, but Havoc was on her feet in a moment, crossing the room, her hand outstretched.

I gave her the phone. "Viper?" she asked.

"Havoc." Even from here, I could hear the way his voice softened.

"I never got to thank you."

"Don't mention it, little omega. Nice call on the gun. How'd you do that?"

"Loaded chamber indicator," she said. "Can't see the red if it's loaded."

"Good to know. Not really a gun man myself."

"Are you okay?" Havoc's brows furrowed, as if she could hear the difference in Viper too.

"Better than ever." He chuckled, but there was something off about it, then he sounded like he was stifling a cough. "Don't worry about me. You got back to them."

"Thanks to you."

"What's...?" There was a long moment of silence. "What's it feel like?"

Havoc sank down on the arm of the couch, her eyes darting to mine for a moment, her brows furrowed.

"It's... Like all the world makes sense when it didn't before." She swallowed, still not taking her eyes from me. "I can breathe again."

"Good... Good. I'm glad. I have to speak to Angel. I'm going to need to call in that favour."

Havoc handed the phone to me. "Whatever you need, it's yours," I said.

"Angel..." There was a pause. "I haven't got anyone left. Dad watches everything I do. I need to know you'll keep it quiet."

"I understand."

"You don't. You don't know what he's got on me. Burning down his house to get out of a pack bond is one thing, but if he thinks I'm coming for..." He hesitated, and I could hear the fear in his voice. Viper Oxford was not the kind of man who allowed others to hear his fear. "You don't understand what it could cost me. I have to know you won't tell, no matter what price is offered."

"Viper. Hear me when I say there isn't a price in this world worth more than what you did."

There was another brief silence. "Kai Ekon, in your pack. He's a hacker, right?"

"Best you can find."

"Good. We start there."

THE END

THANK YOU!

> But I want more of Havoc :(

r/AmItheAsshole

Am I the asshole for telling my alpha I threw his suits off the balcony for banning me from waffles?

TLDR: I Have four boyfriends, and none of them will get me waffles.

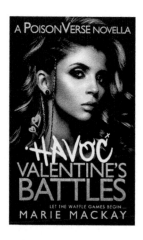

> There's MORE HAVOC! For FREE happily ever after waffle battle novella by signing up to my newsletter at MarieMackay.com

> Is Viper getting a story?

> Ugh. Yes. Forget Me Knot is Viper's story! Our now

THE POISONVERSE

Havoc Killed Her Alpha - *Marie Mackay*
Forget Me Knot - *Marie Mackay*
Pack of Lies - *Olivia Lewin*
Ruined Alphas - *Amy Nova*
Lonely Alpha - *Olivia Lewin*
Sweetheart - *Marie Mackay*
And more to come...

POISONVERSE SHORTS

His Gold Pack Omega - *Miyo Hunter*
Something Knotty, Something Blue - *Lilith K.Duat*

Go to PoisonVerseBooks.com for more. Find happily ever after
novellas and pack collision bonus content!

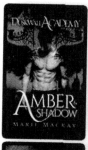

Need some shifter romance? Read The Dusk Wall Academy series next.

Amber and Shadow is the first book in an enemies to lovers, paranormal—*Hold up.* Stop.

I'm not even sorry. Cut the blurb, I'm venting.

Sylas.

You. Absolute. Prat.

You remember what we sacrificed to get to this godforsaken academy, right? All for you, I might add. And while I downed that potion to qualify—the one with a *fifty* percent chance of killing me—what were you doing?

Oh, that's right. Opening your bleeding heart to a random woman and accidentally binding her to your magic. (You know—that minorly important thing your 'condition' requires for survival?)

And *that*—that's not even the kicker, is it?

You should be popular with the ladies, you have that whole

'strongest-vamp-in-academy-history' thing going, right? But congratulations, you found the one exception, because Briar Bishop *hates* you.

To add to everything, she's untrained (also, insane). Come the trial, demons are going to eat her alive, and she'll take your magic with her—magic she's now burning through, it seems, just to spite you.

And who'll end up fixing this mess?

Right.

Me.

Where did I put my matches? I need a bloody smoke.

ahem. Download NOW for a **Witcher** meets **Zodiac Academy** four book romance. Broody vampires, and **shifters**. *Enemies to lovers.* **Monsters** and *magic*. Check. Check. Check. All the good stuff. Go buy it. Or Axel will find you. And he's in a bad mood.

Author's Note: This is a slow burn (2nd book explicit spice) adult romance. It contains dark themes, adult language, intimidation, violence, and triggering situations detailed in front of the book. For mature readers.

Printed in Great Britain
by Amazon